Arthur W. Bahr

Simon & Schuster

CERTIFIABLY INSANE

SIMON & SCHUSTER

Rockefeller Center

1230 Avenue of the Americas

New York, NY 10020

SIMON & SCHUSTER and colophon are registered trademarks

of Simon & Schuster Inc.

Manufactured in the United States of America

10 9 8 7 6 5 4 3 2 1

Library of Congress Cataloging-in-Publication Data

Bahr, Arthur W.

  Certifiably insane / Arthur W. Bahr.

    p. cm.

    I. Title.

    PS3552.A358C47 1999

    813'.54—dc21   98-43660

      CIP

ISBN 0-684-80232-5

The author is grateful for permission to reprint excerpts from:

*"My Girl." Words and Music by William "Smokey" Robinson and Ronald White © 1964
(Renewed 1992), 1972, 1973, 1977 Jobete Music Co., Inc. All Rights Controlled and Ad-
ministered by EMI April Music Inc. All Rights Reserved   International Copyright Secured
Used by Permission*

For A.

Publisher's Note: While revising this novel for his editor, Arthur Bahr died suddenly of a heart condition. His widow, Aniko, completed the work.

J a n i c e peeled each grape carefully and held the shiny naked bodies up to the light. She popped them one by one into her mouth, chewed like a marionette, and spit the seeds on the rug. She was bathed in blood. It plastered her hair to her skull, streaked the delicate blond fur on her arms, and coagulated in her eyelashes. She smelled like freshly polished copper.

When the last grape had been plucked, she peered at the bare stem up close and giggled. Then she dropped it on the blood-soaked rug and stared into deep space, eyes betraying nothing.

March had been the pits for Janice. She'd lost her job. It was a man's world and they'd proved it to her in spades. Sean, her infant son, had developed fluid in his lungs. Janice had to care for him even though her maternity leave was officially up. She was sure they'd understand. She was wrong. They let her go.

Dennis had become increasingly agitated as her pregnancy progressed, she later told the doctors. He was a cop first and a husband second, meaning he knew more about hurting than caressing. He knew how to inflict pain and avoid bruises, restricting himself to kidney shots.

But all that was over now. She embraced the silence. The voices that populated her universe had finally quieted. No more crying. No more bitching. Blessed silence.

Soon police officers swarmed through the apartment, snapping pictures and blowing black dust on the furniture. The forensics wore transparent latex gloves that reminded Janice of hospitals.

She would have resented any voice interrupting her silence, but the fact that they were cops' voices really rankled her. So she sat in her calming lotus position, munching the last crushed bunch of grapes that she had squirreled away in the pocket of her work shirt. She spit the remaining seeds into her lap.

One of the officers, a rookie patrolman, asked her a question, but she just smiled. She looked like the young cop's childhood fantasy of hell. And she seemed unaware of what he had encountered in the war zone of her home.

She didn't seem to know that her husband lay dead on the couch and her infant son lay dead in his crib while she sat and munched and stared and spit.

She was out of it, the patrolman reported. "Totally fucking gone" was his precise phrase.

It had been a bad month. But all that was over now.

one

HOMEBODIES

L a t e   March is nasty and incorrigible in New York. The weather sucks, hacking up its final gobs of winter phlegm. If you're not an obsessed hoops fan it's a good time to commit suicide.

I don't do suicide anymore. It got too heavy. I'm an expert in the psychological autopsy of the suicide victim. Nothing a good cop couldn't do if he had the time to investigate every suicide as if it were a murder, which of course it is.

My private practice had become a haze of self-destruction: slicing, starving, drugging, drowning, shooting, and immolation. I was so good at putting together the puzzle after the fact that people started thinking I could save their hellbent loved ones *before* they did themselves in.

They were wrong. I couldn't do that, so I quit.

I gave up suicide and turned to crime—rape and incest sometimes, but mostly murder. People killing someone other than themselves was, for me, a breath of fresh air.

What I do in late March to ward off the gloom is watch endless contests among hormonally imbalanced young men trying to put a ball in a hole. The symbolism has never been lost on me. I just ignore it.

In the early morning while the dribbling giants sleep, I sit in the window seat, my bubble on the world. There I indulge my chocolate habit with Swiss bittersweet and pour my soul out to my best friend, Tupelo Honey.

She is, strictly speaking, a dog, but Tupelo is really a cultured pearl, my shrink and my companion, and the only known surviving heir of Sara Smile, the Mother of all golden retrievers. I was into golden retrievers before they signed on to endorse the American Dream, when they were just dogs.

Tupelo is medium height, has a distinguished gait, and wears a tight-fitting body stocking covered in amber fleece. She's easy to look at.

I'm a bit more of a challenge. Tall and gangly as a kid, I grew up the same. My hair has grown unhassled since the sixties and remains mostly brown. At my temples it's growing white, a curious blend of venerable and scuzzy. My beard, the same beard I've hidden behind for over twenty-five years, has gone for the most part to salt.

One morning after a particularly rigorous triple-header, I sat in my bubble and Tupelo sat on her ratty throw rug slightly behind me, just out of sight. I don't know where she picked that one up, because I never used a couch, not even in the days when I still acted like a real shrink.

"I don't know where to start," I said to Tupelo, but it didn't matter. She got up, shook herself from head to toe, and walked to the door. Either she was bored or someone was coming and Tupelo heard it before I did, as usual.

I watched from my bubble, hoping it wouldn't be work, hoping I wouldn't suddenly have to act like a forensic consultant, hoping I wouldn't have to get up at all. Tupelo's insistent pointing told me I was sunk.

I answered the door before it asked me anything. I stepped outside and the cold drizzle sprayed my face, pebbling my granny glasses, rendering me sightless. But by then the sound was unmistakable. It was the K-mobile. It wasn't work. It was Kate.

I returned to my perch and cleared away the colorful squares of silver foil that still carried a faint aroma of chocolate. It would take some time for Kate to make it to the door, but I had learned early on that offering help was an insult to her integrity.

Kate had designed her K-mobile and supervised every facet of its production like her life depended on it, which, in part, it did. It had once been a Nissan Pathfinder, but was now much more. The driver's seat swiveled one hundred eighty degrees, coming to rest facing a platform that supported her wheelchair. She deftly swung herself into the chair and activated a remote control similar to the super model used by the average couch potato. Only Kate's didn't turn on her VCR. It opened the rear doors, turned her chair around to face the street, and gently lowered the platform. Once outside, with the same remote, she then raised the platform and locked the doors.

The chair was no ordinary model, either. She could handle it manually if she chose, or kick in her motor, borrowed, I think, from a Harley 950. If she popped it just right, she could do a wheelie.

Kate preferred to propel herself without mechanical help. She had been an accomplished wheelchair marathoner for many years and although she no longer raced, she worked out regularly and stayed in shape. It was important to her to be physically powerful.

She waved to me in the window seat and I could hear her whir up the ramp, in low, to my door. Low was best for rain.

"Are you sufficiently fed up with March yet?" she asked as she rolled in to love up Tupelo and accept a gentle lick on her cheek. She was wrapped in an elegant crimson cape with a hood that she wore against the rain.

"No," I said, "but I've missed you." I bent down and laid a bear hug on her and was squeezing the last bit of air out of her lungs when she groaned. I released her. I'm not violent, just demonstrative.

I stood looking down at her as she struggled to release herself from her cape. "Do you have time for some tea?" she asked in her small voice, the one reserved for intimates. The public only heard the big voice. Everything in its place. Kate was grounded better than anyone I knew.

"Sure, make yourself comfortable. I'll put the kettle on." Kate had given me the kettle.

She moved into the "head shop," my pet name for the consulting room, smiling at the lettering on the door as always. It stated that Simon Rose, M.D., Ph.D., Forensic Consultant, could be consulted therein. It said so on glass intentionally pebbled, a page stolen from Raymond Chandler, the most obvious manifestation of my professional ambivalence. Kate thought it was a roar.

"You still can't decide what you want to be when you grow up!" she yelled down the hall to the kitchen.

"No, but I feel I'm on the verge of a breakthrough!" I yelled back. I heard her laughing.

I served the tea on a Japanese lacquered tray that had also been a gift from Kate. One of the ways she ensured her comfort in my home was to give me everything she liked and to trust that I would have the good sense to use it. Kate was a master manipulator, essential for her profession, and

I was clay in her hands. I had known her for fifteen years and had loved her for the better part of that time.

As always, Kate preferred to sit by the fire. She squared herself in front of the antique Morris chair, flipped into it, folded the wheelchair and stowed it on the floor beside her. She was a transfer expert. She could flip in and out of the chair effortlessly. She passed me her cape with a one-handed dismissal that said "Get it out of my face." I draped it over the bentwood coat rack and sat in a leather sling chair, right next to her, one of my favorite spots on the planet.

"Thanks, Simon," she said as she wrapped her chilled fingers around a cup of fresh chamomile.

In general, Kate's clothes wore her and she wore all of her forty-eight years on her face. She had on funky old wool slacks and a bulky cableknit sweater that she probably made herself.

I countered with a vintage Lovin' Spoonful T-shirt, rough-hewn cotton drawstring pants big enough for friends, and Birkenstocks. We sat in front of the fire, two relics of another time, basking in the glow.

She was lovely as always, fine features, thin angular face, and ivory skin. Her straight brown hair was cut short and simple, no nonsense. It lived behind her ears. She was vain, but not about her surface. She couldn't care less about fashion, and even in court, her playground, no one ever commented on her gray-on-gray ensembles. She even made them forget the chair.

The name Katherine Newhouse shone with the best and the brightest in a profession overpopulated by mediocrity. She was a criminal lawyer and her speciality was women in deep shit.

Kate defended women who killed their pimps, women who liquidated their rapists, women who squashed their oppressors, whether they were husbands, lovers, or fathers. She would work on any provocative, challenging case without regard for money. She had more than enough. She was a force, a fact that she appreciated, cultivated, and worked hard not to abuse.

She stirred her tea gently, watching the swelling flowers and stems swirl around the cup, breathing in the sweet essence of the chamomile. She set it on the coffee table until it calmed. Only then was she ready for real conversation.

"Have you seen the news in the last couple of weeks?"

She knew better. It was March.

"Uh-uh," I said, shaking my head. "Pure hoops, not even a bulletin." Just the way I liked it. I hoped she wouldn't ruin it by telling me anything of substance. The slightly devilish look in her eye told me she had a surprise.

"Have you heard anything about Jensen yet?"

"Who?"

"Jensen. First name Janice."

"No, should I have?"

"Maybe." She appeared to think it through and decided against continuing. "No, first things first," she said, picking up her tea. She considered it, tasted it, and smiled at me, like a fox.

I saw it coming. I knew that look. It meant she'd found another woman for me.

"No. No way in the fucking world. Forget it." I only resort to profanity when I'm speaking.

"Simon." She exhaled the breath of infinite patience, a virtue she did not possess. "How long has it been now?"

"You know perfectly well how long it's been. Probably to the day." Prickly. I get that way when my scar tissue is disturbed.

"And that's why I claim the right to talk to you about it, straight, without your getting defensive on me. It's me, right?"

"Yes, it's you." I sighed, knowing I would hear her out. "But no blind dates, understand?"

"Okay, I'll skip the part where I tell you that your widowerhood has become your identity, your armor against the world, your all-purpose defense mechanism. All that goes without saying.

"I knew you'd go the hard way if you could find it and I never doubted your ability to find it. But you're forty-five years old. I thought that by now, if you weren't willing to drop it, you would've at least learned to use it. Widowerhood is a gold mine. Women love it. Right up there with paraplegics for conquest value. And I should know. I've seduced more men with this damn chair than with my lush and alluring body.

"For some reason you must explain to me someday, men assume I'm uninterested in sex. It never occurs to them that I might like it as much as they do. As if legs were the only erogenous zone. Have they missed something? Am I dead because I can't tap my feet? When they finally get the idea, it's an unbearable turn-on. They can't help themselves. I know it and I use it, unashamedly. But you use your most enticing quality as a chastity belt. It's ass backwards and such a waste."

I could have told her that I fully appreciated the perks of widower-hood, I simply hadn't learned to enjoy them.

I could have told her that I had long since given up defining myself by whether or not I was with a woman. Single women have the same prob-lem. No one imagines that they could actually choose to be alone.

I could have told her I loved her.

I could have told her to shut up.

Instead, I sat silently watching the fire, smelling the burning cedar, trying to imagine Kate walking.

"I'm worried for you, Simon. I'm afraid that if you don't break out of it now, you never will. You don't let anyone in."

"I let you in."

"I know, but I'm different. I'm no threat."

"And Debby?"

"She's different, too, and you know it. You always pull this on me. And you know what I mean."

"I know what you mean and I have one thing to say. No date. Forget it. Don't even give me her name."

"I won't give you her name."

"Thank you. How's Sidney?" I inquired. Sidney was Kate's latest, as she put it, "squeeze." He was wealthy, which made them even, and he was an adventure that had lasted longer than most, almost a year. I didn't like him, but I never liked any of her beaux.

Kate had a talent for choosing the wrong guy. While capable and often dominant in the cerebral sphere, she was a miserable failure at romance. She chose victim after victim, loser after loser, promise after promise, in a vain attempt to find connectedness. She usually got the shaft.

"He's gone." She cracked it off like it didn't hurt but her face said dif-ferent. "I think I tired him out."

The part of Kate's face that most intrigued me was her upper lip. It curled curiously when she got emotional—angry, upset, sad, excited—I never knew exactly what emotion triggered the curl, but it was always worth watching. "Are you unhappy or relieved?"

"I'm hovering around Acute Situational Depression, nothing a little frenetic work and another pot of tea won't cure." With that, her upper lip relaxed again. She was resilient, tempered. "Will you take care of the tea?"

I took the pot to the kitchen. Kate was difficult to comfort and comfort was not what she'd come for. She didn't want to moan about Sidney's departure. Nor had she come to beat the long-dead horses that are my love life.

I could try the analytic power tool, the open-ended question. Or I could cajole it out of her with silence. Silence makes most people so uncomfortable, they begin to blather. Shrinks are trained to handle silence. Real people aren't. But Kate wasn't real people, either, so I was running out of ideas.

I brought the fresh tea and set it down. Kate fussed with it and at her leisure announced, "I've got a special case. I want you to work with me."

Kate and I did not work together. It had come up many times since our first and only courtroom encounter. But each time, we decided not to compromise our specialness to each other by submitting it to the almost unbearable strain of a murder trial. We always chose instead to play, acting as each other's oasis.

Surprised and intrigued, I asked, "Why now?"

"Because this one's different and so are you. You're a hot commodity since the prediction thing. The *Mother Jones* feature hasn't exactly hurt your credibility."

"Bullshit," I snapped. "That was almost a year ago and you know how many people read *Mother Jones*. Sixty, that's how many. Religiously."

"And the rest of the country watches Peter Jennings, religiously, every night. What did he call you? 'Private dick of the mysteries of the mind.' I love that one. And your prediction was positively flashy."

That pissed me off.

"I've already told you, I didn't exactly predict anything. I was mad and I ran off at the mouth. I didn't see the damn camera. And ABC wasn't even covering the trial. They aired it after the fact because it was August and they were out of beached-whale stories."

"But you were right, weren't you? That was the whole point of the story: Shrink predicts felon will rape within thirty days of his release. Felon is released from hospital after successful insanity defense and brief but effective treatment. Felon then obliges shrink. Thirty days exactly. That's what Peter said, and he wouldn't lie."

"It wasn't like that. I was furious so I talked to the reporter outside the courthouse. This asshole rapes three women and says the devil made him do it. He does his act for the jury. Schizophrenic, paranoid type. Does his six-month cure and walks. The only rapist I've ever seen who was legally insane raped his mother. And it wasn't this guy. So I opened my mouth. That's how it happened."

"How did you know when the perp would rape again? Magic?"

"No, a time-tested analytic maxim: 'Once a scumbag, always a scumbag.' Freud, 1933, I think."

"Be that as it may, this case is perfect for our first collaboration. It suits you. Hear me out. All I want you to do is a competency."

Kate told me what March had been like for Janice Jensen. Apparently, she was responsible for the bloodbath in her home. There would be no bushy-haired stranger, just a woman and her demons.

"She's probably fucked," I said. Insanity as a viable defense has taken a beating since John Hinckley shot President Reagan, claiming an irresistible impulse to impress the actress of his fantasies. The jury bought it then but the public didn't. These days it's even harder to sell.

Kate nodded.

"Is she legally insane?" I asked her. She had been down this road often enough to know.

"I don't know. That's why I want you to see her." The devil popped back into her eye. I saw it.

"Are you going to tell me?" I asked.

"What?"

"Whatever you're holding back. It's me, remember?"

"Yes, it's you. And that's precisely why I want you. Janice Jensen wants you, too. She asked for you."

"She asked for me?"

"She wants you."

Chapter Two

I l e f t Kate sipping her tea and took Tupelo for a walk.

We walk together twice a day, in the morning and in the dead of night. The level of denial necessary to pull this off without packing an Uzi is staggering. To make matters worse, I prefer to leave the gentility of my Gramercy Park neighborhood and revisit my roots farther downtown.

We travel unarmed and untethered in flagrant violation of the laws of survival, not to mention leash and scoop. In a city where paranoia is a survival skill, not a pathology, I walk unhindered by concern about who might be following me. I've been mugged three times, but I haven't wasted any time worrying about it.

I was agitated and Tupelo could smell it. "What's bothering you?" she asked.

"Women," I said honestly, picking up the direction I'd been heading when Kate came to call. Women are a central part of my life, in theory. In reality, I am a confirmed widower, unwilling to get close enough to a woman to care if I lose her.

"Get specific." Tupelo is impatient with resistance.

"Kate."

"Go on." She bobbed her head in encouragement.

"I wish she'd stop meddling in my love life."

"You don't have a love life." Tupelo can be brutal when necessary.

"In my hypothetical love life, then. I would prefer to handle it myself. I want her to give it up."

"She wants you to give it up, too." A point for the golden.

"I want her out of my love life completely."

I swear she raised an eyebrow. "Did you tell her?"

"She knows."

"You didn't answer the question." Brutal.

"I told her no more dates. You were there. I'll find my own women."

"Prove it."

"How?"

"Ask one out."

"I will."

"When?"

"Soon."

"Go back to women. What's bothering you?"

"Kate."

"What about Kate?"

"She mucks around in my love life."

"You ran that already. It didn't fly. What else about Kate?"

I sensed that Tupelo had a direction in mind so I went with it. "Frankly, I dread the thought of working with her. I swore I would never share a courtroom with her again. In my life."

"So it isn't only your love life after all."

"No."

Tupelo smiled, as she always does when I finally get on the right track.

Kate and I met in a courtroom.

I was a forensic psychiatrist for the State of New York, green as sinsemilla, grinding out fifty opinions a week on competency to stand trial, processing a dozen or so obvious no-go's on criminal responsibility, and providing care and treatment for the forgotten hordes already found Not Guilty by Reason of Insanity. Care and treatment consisted of filling out prescription pads and advising the inmates to prepare handmade writs of habeas corpus that would do them no good. It was grim and miserable work for all concerned.

The rookies get to evaluate competency to stand trial. The veterans determine criminal responsibility, the cornerstone of the insanity defense. This is the heart of forensic psychiatry, the power and the glory.

The psychiatric experts hold forth, under oath, about the unknowable.

At the time of the alleged offense did the defendant know the difference between right and wrong? How the hell could anyone ever know that about anyone else? But we get paid to know and so we do. Could the defendant have resisted the impulse to slice up his father? Expert or no, nobody can truly answer that question.

But the responsibility is awesome, or at least it feels that way, because hanging in the balance is a life. In capital murder cases, the difference between Not Guilty by Reason of Insanity and Guilty as Charged is life and death. The forensic expert's testimony can mean twenty to life or a stint as brief as six months in the state hospital.

The length of the hospital stay depends on the docs. When they can safely predict that the patient is no longer dangerous to himself or others, another impossible task, that patient walks. You can do six months' soft time for murder. And the docs make mistakes.

Criminal responsibility is high-stakes guesswork in a business with no margin for error. Mistakes mean blood on the tracks.

Which is why they give the rookies the competencies. It's gorilla work and errors are correctable. A tenth-grader could perform a competency examination.

The issue at stake isn't life and death, just whether or not the defendant can aid in his defense in a "rational and reasonable manner." It takes the examiner or the tenth-grader approximately three minutes to determine competency to stand trial.

"What are you charged with?" "Rippin' off a 7-Eleven." "What happened?" "Nothin', man. I wasn't even there." "What happens now?" "I get a trial, and the Man sends me to Dannemora." He understands the scene, he's competent to stand trial.

Occasionally you find a defendant who's in such deep left field that he has no idea what they say he did, what a lawyer is, or why the dude in the high chair is wearing a black clown suit. He is remanded to an appropriate state house of pain to await his enlightenment. The truly incompetent stay that way and never see trial. They populate the back wards.

In the midst of my rookie season as a forensic psychiatrist, I encountered, briefly and quite by chance, Katherine Newhouse. It turned out to be a memorable learning experience.

Before she became a star, Kate ground it out like the rest of us. She was representing a woman accused of boosting an expensive pearl necklace from the jewelry section of a large department store. Shoplifting is easy to prove. Either you'd paid for it or you hadn't before you left the store. Kate's client hadn't.

I got the competency because my number came up. I spent twenty-two minutes with the woman, during which time she explained that the pearls went well with her beige outfit, that Daddy had cut off her allowance so she couldn't actually buy them, and that she had a hotshot young defense attorney who was going to take care of it for her. I found her both competent to stand trial and deserving of one.

I was surprised to be subpoenaed. In straightforward cases like this one, my written report was usually stipulated to by the attorneys, accepted without comment. Katherine Newhouse didn't stipulate. She cross-examined.

Deep-fried might be a better choice of words. She asked me if I was aware of certain intimate details about her client, some of which I might not have known if I had psychoanalyzed her for three years. What form of birth control did she use? Might she be gay? Had she ever had an abortion? Was her grandmother mentally ill? Had she experienced any unusual trauma during toilet training? None of it was relevant to the defendant's competency to stand trial. But the cumulative power of the young forensic expert answering "I don't know" to a hundred and fifty questions left such considerable doubt about my competency to offer testimony that the judge ordered another evaluation.

It was humiliating and enlightening. I learned about trial preparation, advocacy, the inherent limitations of working for a state bureaucracy, and the charismatic presence of Katherine Newhouse.

Outside of the courtroom, while I waited impatiently for an elevator, Katherine Newhouse pulled up next to me. I had plenty to say to her but I couldn't think of any of it.

"Have a cup of coffee with me, Doctor. I won't bite. I promise." Her voice was soft and enveloping, the small voice, not threatening as it had been in the courtroom. "I promise I won't jump on your bones. Really. You've nothing to lose."

"You already extracted your pound of flesh, Counselor." I clawed the air with imaginary talons.

"Let me make it up to you. Coffee?"

"Coffee will never do it," I answered, already taken by her. "Dinner might be a start."

She took me to one of her favorite uptown spots, the kind that specialize in salads, pasta, and mineral water. At least there were no ferns. The owner was an ex-client who obviously owed her and he doted on us shamelessly, preparing our meal himself. None of it was on the menu and all of it, from the antipasto through the puttanesca to the espresso, was exquisite.

We talked about the law business and the forensic business and slowly edged into more personal terrain. By the end of dinner I felt like we had always known each other, perhaps were siblings. She would have been the big sister, although by only three years in real time. In wisdom and solidity she seemed much older.

She shared my sense that we had been friends forever. She called it finding each other. It happens.

Since then we'd spent at least two evenings a week together, and made countless phone calls back and forth, staying close, soul mates from the day we met.

But she had never asked me to collaborate with her on a case. For over fifteen years we had shared intimacies and discussed cases without names, but never had the line been crossed until this gray March morning.

And that's what was bothering me. Knowing Kate, I was sure she had a very good reason for breaking with tradition. Whatever it was, she hadn't told me.

"She's playing with me," I finally announced, after thinking about it for twenty-two blocks. "That's what I don't like. She isn't being straight with me."

Tupelo walked along, tail up, head straight, without saying anything, which is how I knew I was right. Now all I had to do was figure out Kate's game.

She had said this was different, "a special case." Special how? The defendant had asked for me. Why? If she knew me by reputation, she thought I was an expert on rape. Would that turn out to be the surprise element in the Jensen case? The devil in Kate's eye said no.

"The case suits you," she had said.

What was it that suited me about a woman who had made four new holes in her husband's head with his own service revolver? I don't have a husband. What was it that suited me about a woman who, after dispatching her husband, perforated her infant son with a knife intended for scaling fish? I don't have a son and I don't like fish.

"She wants you," Kate had said. I didn't even want to touch that one.

Tupelo and I turned toward home. The walk had brought me no

peace, but at least I knew what was bothering me. I had to get this competency over with just to find out what Kate was up to. I wished I hadn't agreed to it without a complete confession on her part. But I had, so the solution was to act, end the discomfort before it got out of hand.

It was still relatively early morning. The sidewalks were getting congested, so I headed for my bubble and the illusion of safe haven. I turned down Sixteenth Street, where I live, and walked past my house.

I do that often. I don't like my house, perhaps because it's not really mine. It belongs to Ladislav Fritsch, my ex-analyst. In an unusual moment of candor, years after my therapy, he confessed.

"Analysis is the most boring profession on earth," he had said. "You listen for a few years and act like you care. Throw in a few fancy interpretations once in a while to keep it interesting. Most people's lives are unbearably boring, which is why they come to you in the first place. They're in love with the idea of themselves and want to share it all with a paid hostage. At a hundred bucks a throw you make out like a bandit. I hate it. You, at least, get into the action," he told me. "I am, as they say, out of here." His Viennese accent made the last three words comical.

With that, he joined the Peace Corps and went off to Ecuador to teach the natives how to suffer with America's help. He was last seen chatting up a goat on a high Andean peak.

Ladislav left me an entire grand old brownstone. I live in the ground-floor apartment. The head shop overlooks scenic East Sixteenth Street, as does my front bedroom across the hall. There are three additional bedrooms off the hallway that leads back to the kitchen. I'm most comfortable in the kitchen. The rest of it feels like someone else's house.

When I finally found my door, I was greeted by the smell of fresh-brewed coffee, scrambled eggs, and bacon, which I wouldn't eat but Debby would. She was an unashamed carnivore and she looked it. Twenty years old, she could appear anywhere from twelve to thirty, depending on how she felt, which was now rarely good, but rarely terrible, either. She was plain looking, had shoulder-length straight brown hair and brown eyes, and was slightly overweight, with a face like mashed potatoes. She was, I guess, a late bloomer, but the wonder is that she bloomed at all.

I washed my hands and sat down at the kitchen table. Debby enjoyed making me breakfast when our schedules permitted, a kind of offering. She didn't dress for the occasion, appearing in a ragged bathrobe that covered her from neck to floor. She poured our coffee and served the eggs, with home-fried potatoes she had made especially for me. She ate the bacon.

"You missed Kate," I said.

"No, I didn't. She just left. We had breakfast number one together." She colored a little, embarrassed. Though unhappy with her extra weight, she'd done nothing about it other than eat double breakfasts and endless quantities of junk food.

Debby was generally depressed and had discovered the value of body fat as protection from unwanted invasions. She spent hours in front of her deluxe cable TV soaking up as many old films as they could unearth. She planned her days around her flicks except for the few hours she spent as a part-time student at Hunter College.

"What'd Kate have to say?" I asked, making conversation. Debby seemed more distracted than usual, more inward. She would talk to me. That's one of the things we did together, talk.

"She told me I should get my own place. The usual. She says I should be on my own and stop sponging off you."

"You are not sponging off anybody." I was defensive about Debby, and if you asked Kate, overprotective and overindulgent. I figured that anyone who had her youth as savagely interrupted as she did deserved a break, a little more time of belated childhood, time to heal the wounds and find her place in the world. Kate, for her own reasons, saw it differently, and as usual, she wasn't shy about expressing herself.

"Anything else?" I asked.

"Yeah, she said she hired you."

"Is that all?"

"No, she told me about the case. Anyway, I knew already. It's all over the news. Dead cop. Dead baby. Nice work."

Maybe that explained the sadness in her face. Dead cop. Dead baby. That would do it.

"It doesn't matter. She didn't make me feel bad. I already felt like shit." She looked it. "Do you have time, Sigmund?"

"Sure."

"Get your pad. It's time to write stuff down."

We cleared the table and went to the head shop. When Debby wanted to talk her body always began the conversation. She sat in the Morris chair, pulled her knees up to her chest, and became smaller. She had been feeling progressively better, which is why we weren't having many sessions anymore.

"I had another dream," she said, addressing her knees.

"Great!" I knew my enthusiasm wasn't shared. I love dreams, other people's dreams. Probably wouldn't be working without them. Dreams provide psychotherapists with rare, unhindered views of the unconscious. But they're tricky and demand respect. Under scrutiny, they demonstrate an uncanny ability to change.

Debby's dreams changed only in degree of horror. If I had dreams like hers I wouldn't want to talk about them either.

I settled in, hoping it hadn't been a bad one. "Do you want to tell it to me? It always makes you feel better."

She glared at me. "No lies."

"I'm sorry. It *almost* always makes you feel better. Sometimes it sends you into the pits. You want to tell me?"

"No." Telling it was like seeing it. Why would anyone in their right mind want to do that?

"*Will* you tell me about it?"

Debby dreamed in series, some terrible, some worse, now occasionally some innocuous. The fear in her eyes was not innocuous. It had been a bad one.

"The explosion one. That's all. The flashes, the shattering sounds, and . . ." She shut her eyes, pressing her fists into the sockets. "And the flesh."

"I'm sorry, Debra." I had recently begun using her full first name, an experiment. She seemed to like it. Her adult name, not the kid in the explosion dream.

"Can't you do anything about it?" she said. "Isn't there a drug or something that makes you forget? How about a lobotomy?" She stabbed an imaginary knife into her prefrontal lobes. Her lips quivered, but she didn't cry. Never let the floodgates open.

At times like this, in the face of real pain, psychotherapy is totally impotent, which is why I'd resigned.

"How about a hug? They always help and that's no shit." I opened my arms and she filled them. We stood together, clutching, neither of us able to cry, but finding some comfort in the warmth.

On the whole, not very Freudian. But Debby was not my patient. She was my daughter.

Chapter Three

My only child came to me fully formed, sixteen years' worth. I regret that I missed her early years, but it couldn't be helped. Debby had other parents at the time. So there was empty space where the memories should have been. But from the moment we found each other, we'd woven our own tapestry.

The scene had an eerie Alice-in-Wonderland quality, the girl, small and vulnerable, the bench, high and mighty. But it was just another courtroom, not very regal at all. The creature on the stand was not the accused, yet she looked like she was about to be burned at the stake. Her face was puffy, like that of a child who had cried too much. At the same time she seemed old and bloated by too much experience.

And in her eyes I recognized myself.

I've heard many parents describe the feeling of pride and well-being they experience looking into their children's eyes and seeing themselves there. I had always considered it primary narcissism. Until I saw it.

And the moment I saw it, I knew.

"Ms. Hinson, please tell the court what you saw on the evening of July 19 past."

Debby quivered in the witness chair, prompting Judge Bonner, a kind, blue-haired woman, to offer a glass of water, which was haltingly accepted. She needed both hands to get the glass to her lips.

The trial was low-key, no press, not even a jury. No one wanted a jury. In the case of the State of New York versus Warren Hinson, the questions were medical-legal and difficult to sift. Judges are more sensible in these matters, or so goes the common wisdom.

"You may take all the time you need, dear. It's all right," Judge Bonner comforted. But of course nothing was all right. The young woman in the hot seat had been virtually orphaned by the firestorm, grandparents and a baby sister dead, and she was about to see her beloved father sent to some cuckoo's nest, and with her help.

Debby's mother was unavailable. She had taken leave of the family years earlier when Warren turned strange. She would return every so often and live with them for a while, but eventually she'd get fed up again and hit the road. She had last left the family following the birth of baby Lisa and could not be located at the time of Warren's trial. If she read about it, she chose to steer clear. If she cared about losing a daughter, she didn't tell Debby. She was unavailable.

Debby, at fifteen, had to juggle caring for the house, the baby, and her father, as well as school. She understood her father and loved him, and they both lavished attention on Lisa. It was a functional family with a dysfunctional member until it finally and irrevocably came apart.

"Uh," Debby coughed, looking vaguely in the direction of the Assistant District Attorney, "where do I start?"

"Start when you first noticed something out of the ordinary, if you will."

Debby glanced at her father sitting at the defense table. Warren smiled, nodded, and mouthed, "It's all right." Debby dropped her head, composed herself, and told us what she had seen.

"I was in the living room, watching television. Dad was out on the porch 'cause it was so hot. He couldn't stand the heat. He'd been kinda quiet at dinner, even quieter than usual. It was the heat. My grandmother and grandfather were staying with us 'cause Dad had been feeling bad for a while. They went to bed early and I had just put Lisa down. She's the baby. Was the baby, I mean."

She sobbed, shook it off, and I would have sworn in that moment she considered bolting the courtroom. Instead, she took a deep breath, held it, exhaled slowly, and continued.

"I heard slapping, like someone swatting mosquitoes, only harder and faster. Like frantic, if you know what I mean. I went out to see what was going on. Dad was on the ground, thrashing around, slapping himself. I got scared. I wanted to stop him, but I didn't know how. He's so big." Debby contracted.

"When he saw me standing there, he stopped flailing around. He brushed himself off and stood up. He never once took his eyes off of me. He just stared at me. It was an incredible look. He stared through me, past me. I said, 'Daddy, are you okay?' but he didn't answer. I don't think he heard me. He picked up his green sack and pulled the screen door open, and he went right by me, upstairs.

"He was in the jungle. I knew it. He'd told me about it. I knew I should get Lisa. I knew he was going to do something. But I froze halfway up the stairs. I couldn't make myself run all the way up. I was scared."

She stopped, clutching the glass, and gulped some water down like it would stop her from vomiting. I could sense the guilt course through her, all too familiar to me. She thought there was something she should have done but she couldn't figure out what it was.

"It was fast, you know, real fast. Maybe ten seconds in all before the explosion. I saw him running down the hall carrying Lisa by her feet. She was naked 'cause I let her sleep that way when it's so hot. She was like a rag doll in his hand. He tossed her in the guest room where my grandparents were sleeping, rolled something on the floor, and came diving down the stairs. He sort of hugged me as we fell. He landed on top of me halfway out the door. He was covering me, I knew it, protecting me. Then the house exploded."

She winced, as she did now when she relived it in her dreams. "I somehow scrambled out from under him. He rolled on his back, breathing real hard. His eyes were wild. I ran through the doorway toward the stairs but there weren't any. I couldn't get upstairs. I saw chunks of furniture all over the place, scraps of cloth, and an arm, the baby's arm." Debby bit her lip without mercy. "And I must have passed out."

The prosecutor did not ask for more details.

Warren's lawyer would have preferred to let her testimony stand, but he felt obliged to act like a defense attorney.

"Do you love your father, Ms. Hinson?"

"Yes, of course."

"What do you want to happen to him?"

"I want him to get help."

"And what do you want for yourself?"

"I could use a little help, too." That was the clincher. I was ready.

"Are you afraid of your father?"

"No. I'm afraid *for* him."

"No further questions."

Then the experts poured forth, myself included. We all agreed on the schizophrenia part, with meaningless skirmishes over the type, paranoid or undifferentiated, but it was academic. Warren's fate was sealed.

And with it, so was Debby's and mine.

Warren Hinson was a six-foot-six, two-hundred-and-eighty-pound casualty. He had served his country in a long-ago and best-forgotten war, one tour of duty as a grunt, plus six years as a POW.

Post-traumatic Stress Disorder hadn't been discovered yet, but Warren knew all about it. He couldn't eat right or sleep well or work at a decent job. For years he managed to load trucks by day and spend his evenings with his daughter, watching cable TV until he dropped.

He plugged along until the incidents started. He'd forget where he was. He would find himself crouched by his window or belly down in the kitchen, and he got frightened. The VA docs said these were flashbacks and would diminish in time with a little medication. They didn't.

But they changed. They involved more and more of his life until his real life seemed like the flashback. Debby worried and called the VA. The docs told her to make sure he took his pills. They told her there was nothing to worry about.

They were wrong. One hot summer night, he rolled a grenade into his parents' bedroom. In Astoria, Queens, Long Island, New York. In the world. The count: three dead, one survivor. Warren went into a deep catatonic funk and stayed there.

I was called to evaluate him for criminal responsibility a couple of months after he "secured" his family home. He refused to do me the favor of being a monster. He was a man, proud, confused, troubled. He spoke honestly and openly about his shame and his pain. I liked him.

"It's not like I got mixed up and felt like I was there. I was there. And I could *be* there any fucking minute. I thought it was all in the past. It had been years since I'd been there. I read a book and saw a couple of Chuck Norris flicks, figuring I could handle it. And just like that"—he snapped his fingers—"I was there again, no memories, I was there. If it happened now as we speak, I could tear your fucking throat out, Rose, without thinking. It could happen."

Warren wasn't threatening me. He was much too scared of himself. He knew, only too well, that for him there were two realities and he could slip from one to the other without warning. He did not possess multiple personalities. It was the same Warren, but the venue changed and everything else with it, especially the rules, and he damned well better change with them or he was dead.

"I told them, Rose, I fucking told them." He meant the docs at the VA hospital. "I fucking said it, 'I am a land mine!' They didn't give a shit. I went off."

He trembled, tensing his muscles to control himself. Trembling turned to sobbing and we sat together, helpless. I wanted to give him something, something to salve the wounds, but my science has yet to invent such a balm.

During our last session I asked Warren the perfunctory legal questions.

"At the time you killed your parents and the baby, did you know the difference between right and wrong?" As if there's an obvious boundary.

"Yes," he said, "my mission was to destroy the inhabitants of that dwelling. I did it. I knew the difference between right and wrong. We all did."

"Could you have controlled your impulse to do what you did?" A truly ridiculous question. How would anyone know?

"Of course I could have, if I wanted to die. There ain't no friends in those villages."

"There's one thing that doesn't wash, Warren," I said, checking out the inconsistency that could spell a fake. The forensic expert's worst nightmare is the malingerer, the individual who feigns mental illness. "Your mission failed. You didn't kill all the inhabitants of the dwelling. You protected your other daughter and left her alive. Why?"

"I always chose one survivor in each village, one I would save. I wasn't a killing machine, not even then."

Finally, the elbow test, the common man's approach to judging impulse control. "If there had been a policeman at your side, touching your elbow, would you have acted as you did?"

"I was the policeman."

The legal definitions turned on their ear. He knew right from wrong, but from another time. He was in control of himself, but in another place. Since he was here and now, not there and then, he was a murderer. And if you believed Warren, then he was also legally insane.

I believed Warren. I was sure that he should be cared for, not punished.

My involvement might have ended there.

At stake at Warren Hinson's trial was not his freedom. It was only a question of where he would be incarcerated, once again a prisoner of war.

He would spend the rest of his life either out at Island Hospital or in a state prison somewhere up north. In neither case was there much chance of imminent release. But the verdict mattered very much to Debra Lee Hinson. She had known for years how sick her father was and she didn't think he should be treated like a criminal.

Debby's face tightened as the judge was about to announce her findings. She disintegrated into tears when Warren was found Not Guilty by Reason of Insanity.

I wanted to hold her, to reassure her that he would be all right, but I knew better. It would have been a lie. Lacking adequate care and treatment, he would in all probability get progressively worse and one day just stop breathing.

Debby was accompanied by a caseworker from Social Services, a woman who expressed compassion by touching three fingertips to her charge's right forearm. I shook the social worker's hand cordially, as if to confide that I understood her burden. Debby hid her face in her hands and didn't look up.

"Ms. Hinson? Debby? Please, talk to me for a moment." She would recognize me. I had testified in Warren's defense just two days earlier.

She raised her red, puffy face and I checked her eyes up close. She reciprocated the soul check. She was the one.

"Will you wait for me?" I asked her. "I need to talk to your father."

"Yes, I know," she said.

I took off in the direction of the lockup, hoping that they hadn't yet transported Warren. The bailiff stopped me. The judge wanted to see me in chambers.

Judge Bonner's chambers were reminiscent of a civil service office, furnished with a bulky nondescript wooden desk and two serviceable armchairs. No grandeur whatsoever. The bailiff stood by the door. Her Honor, out of uniform, appeared smaller and less powerful. In one of the armchairs sat Warren, perhaps thirty pounds heavier than when I had examined him. He looked enormous and sloppy in the manner of heavily medicated schizophrenics. His wrists were handcuffed to a chain wrapped around his waist and trailing down to the shackles binding his ankles.

"I'm glad they found you, Dr. Rose. Mr. Hinson would like to speak with you, if you have no objection," the judge said.

"No objection, Your Honor," I said. She smiled and ushered herself and the bailiff out of chambers, leaving me with what was left of Warren Hinson.

"Hello, Doc," he slushed. It seemed as if he wanted to sound more enthusiastic but the drugs controlled his emotions, all of them. "Sit down, Rose. I can't hardly shake your hand. It's good to see you again."

We managed both the handshake and an awkward, one-sided, clanging hug. He looked puffy, which was part psychoactive drugs, part character. His face resembled his daughter's, made of the same mashed potatoes.

I took the chair opposite him. He slouched forward, as if he wanted to tell me a secret. He would probably have had his huge hands on my shoulders or knees, but the chains prevented the contact.

"I need a favor, man," he said, his voice clear for the moment, the dreaminess gone. "And it's a big one. Where I come from you take care of your own problems, especially family problems. I got one I can't solve. How does a man ask another man . . . ?" He left the question in the air.

He sobbed and, like Debby, tried to hide his head in his hands. He wasn't weeping for himself, but for the daughter he'd saved, the one he'd left alive. And alone.

"You know why I'm asking you, other than I got no choice?"

"No."

"Because you didn't shit me. You told me how it was gonna go. No shit." He seemed to wander off into the past, or perhaps the future. He wet his dry, cracked lips.

I helped him out. "What happens to Debby?"

He shook his head and slurred, "I don't know. They can't find my wife, so Debby's in foster care. That's no place for her." He wept again.

"No, it isn't," I agreed. "Would you consider letting me take care of her? I'm alone. I have the space. I think it might be good for both of us."

He spread his shackled arms as wide as the chains permitted. He enveloped my hands in his and trembled as he cried. He didn't say a word. He nodded, rocked, and wailed like a giant mutant child.

When I reached Debby she was no longer crying so her caseworker was no longer comforting her. The woman was sitting like a stone, searching for something to focus on. I told her she was needed in chambers. She stood and left.

Debby spoke first. "Did he ask you?" She was shrinking into herself. "Yes, he did."

"What do you think?" she asked, curled up now like a steamed shrimp. "I think we ought to do it."

A smile formed on her face only to lose out to worry. "Look, I won't be any trouble, but I ain't perfect. I *am* a teenager," she informed me, as though I hadn't figured that out yet.

"I'm not perfect, either. I'm just older. Shall we do it?"

She nodded in agreement but I still saw the fear in her eyes.

"Don't worry. We'll figure it out together. I've never done this before, either. But we picked each other. That should help."

"Why are you doing this?" she asked.

"I'm alone, too. I think we can help each other." I believed it. Debby looked skeptical.

I turned out to be right. We did help each other. We also proved over and over again that neither of us was perfect. We learned that teenagers are a pain in the butt as a rule and so are middle-aged parents. But we managed to share the road together, the father, a survivor of suicide, and the daughter, a survivor of criminal insanity.

I c o u l d n ' t get near Janice Jensen. She was booked solid. There were four psychiatric evaluations on her schedule and I would just have to stand in line. Which meant that even if she hadn't been psychotic at the time she liquidated her family, she would undoubtedly be that way after being poked, pricked, and mauled by four forensic sharks. It also meant that Kate was hedging her bets. Each side customarily employed two experts in such cases. Who hired the extra one?

I settled into my cocoon in front of the TV. Debby derived nourishment from ancient films but in March she gave control of the action over to me. She taped whatever movies she couldn't bear to miss and watched them while the tall guys fed.

Debby had seemed unsettled to me, not exactly agitated, not quite depressed, but somehow apprehensive. It certainly could have been the dream. She wouldn't have bothered to mention it if it hadn't hurt and frightened her. She didn't cry wolf and she rarely cried tears. She was a fighter and sometimes she got knocked down.

Just after tip-off of the Memphis State–Clemson game, the phone rang. This wasn't a problem. If the call was for me, Debby would dutifully lie to the caller, saying that her father couldn't come to the phone, when the truth was that he wouldn't. If it was for her, she'd spend two or three hours jawing with a friend. She didn't go out much but she had an active phone life.

It turned out to be a problem. Debby appeared at the door, glanced in at the game, and said, "It's for you."

"So what?" I said, mildly annoyed. If it wasn't an emergency, and Debby was acting far too casual for that, why the hell was she telling me? "Who is it?"

"Jemma Marin."

"I don't know any Jemma Marin."

"That's right. But I do. Or rather, I know about her."

"What're you talking about?" I had just missed a monster slam that sent the crowd into a frenzy.

"Kate told me about her and I thought you should take the call."

It was a conspiracy. Kate must have given out my number after I refused to cooperate.

I glared at Debby, who became suddenly fascinated by the cakes of a Clemson forward.

"I'll take the call on the condition that you leave me in peace and don't say anything."

She put her fingers to her lips like a nun and backed out of the room. I pressed the mute button on the remote and picked up the phone.

"Dr. Rose, my name is Jemma Marin. You don't know me and I don't want to sound foolish, but I thought I would enjoy meeting you. I'm a reporter for the *Post*. I covered the Gromsky hearing. I thought you were worth pursuing, so I called the American Psychiatric Association and got your number."

So Kate hadn't given her my number. Maybe she was someone else.

"What were you doing at the Gromsky hearing? Nobody was there, not even Gromsky."

Gromsky was a twenty-eight-year-old mildly retarded, mildly strange young man, whose hobby was peeking in bedroom windows. His delight in life was interrupting coitus whenever possible. His father was my bagel pusher and he asked me to make an appearance, so I did. Gromsky was obviously competent. He knew he had been naughty, but someone had to swear to it just the same. So I'd left basketball heaven, put on a tie, and spoken in psychological tongues for ten minutes.

"I'm a reporter, a working stiff. I arranged for the paper to send me so I could check you out. Katherine Newhouse speaks highly of you. Would you like to have dinner with me tonight?"

She wasn't someone else; she was Kate's blind date.

I had long ago stopped accepting blind dates, after a spate of inevitable failures. Kate was right about widowerhood. It affects women, sometimes in bizarre ways. And I'm no garden-variety widower. I came by my status through suicide, an enticingly double-edged sword. Poor man, how he must have suffered. I wonder what he did to drive her to it?

The majority treated me like I was Tupelo. They petted me, fed me, and became after-dinner laps for my tired head. Some got aggressive about their mission, which was to make me forget HER. The real crusaders hoped to replace HER. They usually went home early. And then there were the legions of lonely, wounded women who wanted to be with someone as abused by life as they were.

Almost all of them wished to sleep with me, and not because I'm irresistible. Because they liked fucking with death.

It got pretty sad.

This date would be blind in one eye only. Jemma had seen me, but I didn't know her from Eve. And she had called me, which didn't happen often. I was, quite frankly, intrigued, which made matters easier for me.

I found her refreshing, direct and unapologetic, a woman who knew what she wanted and wasn't afraid to go after it. Or she was afraid and gutsy. Either way, she was to be avoided at all cost.

"I'm sorry," I lied. "I have to work tonight. Maybe some other time. Thank you for calling." I hung up. Multiple lies and my daughter was lurking in the doorway.

"You forgot to say 'Have a nice day,'" Debby said, and she stalked off, disgusted.

Debby's lurking pissed me off. I thought we had an understanding. I'd made my needs clear and she had indicated, if not sworn, that she was willing to respect them. Instead, she eavesdropped on my phone call and then had the poor taste to make a snide comment about what she had heard.

That wasn't like her. Something had to be bothering her. This wasn't the way we dealt with each other.

When Debby and I hammered out the agreement that would govern our life together we were four years younger and painfully naïve. But we recognized that we had a unique opportunity to negotiate the rules of behavior and power in our relationship before becoming family. We took the task seriously. We were building our foundation.

We brainstormed about rules: Who owned which household tasks? Who got to stay out until what hour? Who got control of the remote? We found ourselves swimming in details, missing the point.

The point was respect.

"What do you need?" I asked her.

"I need truth. No lies."

"No lies?" It sounded like something to shoot for. "Let's give it a try."

"And what do you need?" she asked.

"Privacy. I need closed doors to be inviolable."

"No sweat. Me, too. What else?" she asked.

"I don't know, but I know there'll be more. I'm going to have to learn the parent business as we go along. I need us to keep talking. Lots of shit will come up."

"Like what?"

"Like someone someday will insinuate that things are going on between us."

Debby turned purple.

"Hey, it happens. It's just not going to happen with us."

She nodded. She understood.

"I think we can handle most anything if we keep talking."

"Do you have the right to shrink me?" Debby asked.

"If you mean by that, do I have the right to care for you in my way, the answer is yes, but there's a proviso, a fail-safe mechanism. Any time you don't want to talk about something, all you have to do is raise your hand. The moment you do that, I will stop, midsentence if necessary. And I won't resent you for it. You have the option not to talk if that's what you need."

"Do I get to talk to you about your life, as in ask questions, or is that out of bounds?"

"You can ask about anything. I'll raise my hand if I don't want to deal with it. Fair?"

"Fair. I have a question."

"Go ahead."

"How did you become a widower?"

"Same way everyone else does. My wife died." I knew the answer was wise-ass, but I get like that under duress.

"I meant *how* did she die?" Debby said.

"I know what you meant and I'll answer you." If I were a real analyst, here's where I would have sucked on my pipe. "I don't know."

"What do you mean, you don't know? Didn't they do autopsies in those days?"

"They did, often on drugged-out hippies. Sometimes they identified the fatal substance, sometimes not. In her case, not. It goes down as a suicide, without a known chemical agent.

"Look, Debby, I'll try to answer your real questions. I came home one night and found her dead. Had I gotten home earlier, I believe she would have lived. I was too late. That's all there is to it. It's something I've come to accept. Not her death. The not knowing."

"What do you *think* happened?"

I raised my hand. "Debby, I think one of the reasons we chose each other is that we have something in common. We've both lost family to senseless violence and we have to live with it. Trust me. There's hope."

"Maybe," she said, hard at work on an already badly chewed nail. "I hope so."

We were still working on it.

The real challenge was to keep talking. It was easier to take refuge in hoops or late movies than to talk when it hurt.

I knocked on her door. I would tell her how I felt. It was part of our deal.

"Come in," she said, hiding under her comforter.

"That wasn't particularly cool. You listened in and made a crack. That phone call was my business, not yours."

"I know it was an asshole thing to do. I'm sorry. I'm nervous."

"I noticed. What is it?"

"I got a date. Tonight. That's why I wanted you to go out. So I wouldn't have to feel guilty about leaving you alone."

"I like being alone." Especially in March. But a date for Debby was not an unremarkable event. She had averaged one date a year for four years, which is misleading because she went out with one guy twice in the same year.

"Is it okay with you?"

"You don't have to ask me. You're free to do as you choose. You got condoms?"

"We're going out for a pizza. Pepperoni doesn't get you pregnant and AIDS isn't transmittable through casual conversational contact. Jesus, Simon, what do you think? We're gonna ball at Pizza Hut?"

"Sorry, girl. I thought I should bring it up. I've been a shrink a lot longer than I've been a parent. How did you meet him, if I may ask?"

"Of course you may ask. You can ask anything," she reminded me. "I just don't have to answer," she added coyly.

But she did answer. In a flood, one long sentence. She like met him at the public library where she was like looking some stuff up for me, but not really in the library, like more like outside the library, on the steps, where she like stopped to tie her shoes and then she was like tucking her papers into her satchel and he like asked if he could help which of course wasn't necessary, but which meant that he was like interested in something else and he's a student at City and he's like real nice, but not that good looking, but he is smart, being that he wants to go to law school if he can scrounge the money and his name's like Bobby.

"Sounds cool," I said, happy for her and disappointed that she didn't want to stay home with me for the rest of her life.

"Cool is not what he is. He verges on totally awesome."

Debby was unrelenting in her attempts to launch me into the nineties. All I had to do to be totally modern, an egregious thought, was to substitute "awesome" where I thought "cool" belonged. I couldn't bring myself to do it.

"Cool," I said defiantly. "What time do you expect to be home?"

"Deep down, you like playing father," she said. "I'll be home at a decent hour."

"Good enough." I didn't quite believe myself.

"I'm outta here," she said, and proved it.

I settled back in with the game. It was nearly over, having continued without me while I dealt with Jemma Marin and Debby. There would be more if I could stand the commentator's patter. I lost patience with the postgame rehash and channel-surfed. I was nervous about Debby. I accidentally settled for a moment on the local news. That was my mistake.

A newly retooled talking head said something about Janice Jensen.

The actual film couldn't have lasted more than six seconds. The voice-over mentioned an arraignment, but that was of no consequence. It was the six seconds of film.

The action was typical videocam, two beefy officers flanking the defendant, who is being ushered to transport only a few yards away. The defendant is attempting to hide behind the beef and she's covering the vulnerable side of her face with a hand. For some reason one of the deputies lowers her hand, perhaps trying to help her into the car, and for a split second there's a shot of her profile.

I caught blondish hair pulled back in a simple ponytail and the whisper of a cheek. And she was gone.

The initial sensation was decidedly genital. Something like when the elevator settles on the eighty-sixth floor and for a moment there's nothing supporting you and someone is gently but firmly pulling your testicles up into your throat. The feeling gradually eases as your scrotum agrees to continue hosting your balls. Mine had yet to agree.

"I know her," I said to myself, but the talking head had moved on to other matters, leaving me with a glimpse of a cheek and a memory that refused to focus. I needed some chocolate.

Anyone can be a chocolate freak; the syndrome is only too common. But a connoisseur has standards and knows there's an appropriate chocolate for every occasion. Now my finely tuned instincts told me it had to be something juvenile. I rummaged around in the kitchen and came up with Oreos. That seemed right. I downed six, convinced that they would jog my memory, but illumination didn't happen. Instead, I fell asleep. I even had a dream.

I rarely dream and do everything possible to suppress the exceptions. This one broke through my fortifications. It was a curious dream, no action, a still-life of two nearly ripe peaches in a basket, barely touching.

Debby's key clicked in the front door and woke me. She looked worse than before. She slumped down next to me, not bothering to take off her pea jacket. ESPN was showing a downhill slalom championship that I switched off.

"Shit," she said, and pounded her thighs with her fists. "I can't stand it. I can't stand myself. I blew it."

"What?"

"He wanted to sleep with me. I wanted to sleep with him, so I said no and here I am. Shit."

I searched for something fatherly to say, something to comfort or console her, but I was too sleepy to come up with anything.

"How was the game?" she asked. "Better than an evening with a beautiful woman, I hope."

"How do you know she's beautiful?"

She looked at me sadly, picked herself up, kissed me good night, and said, "I'm going to call Assholes Anonymous and see if they have any openings."

"Find out if they have a family plan," I called after her.

I tried once more, in vain, to focus on Janice Jensen. Debby reappeared breathlessly.

"Oh, Simon. I'm sorry. I forgot to tell you. Gabe called while you were out with Tupelo. He'll be in town and he wants to come by tomorrow. I should have written it down but I forgot. I'm sorry. Good night."

"Did he say anything else, like what he's doing here?"

"No, he just said he wanted to see us. Are you glad?"

"Sure, why not. Good night."

Gabriel Rose, my father and Debby's doting grandfather, lived in Michigan, hated to travel, and had never visited me in my home in his life.

I slept fitfully, but with no further dream invasions.

By the time I got up it was almost eleven and my father was already in the head shop. Fortunately, Debby was all over him and they could surely entertain each other while I showered and tried for a quick wake-up.

But first I went in to kiss him on the cheek as I had done every time I'd greeted him since I was a boy. "There's no shame in kissing your father," he would always say, unnecessarily, because I never felt any.

Debby was assailing him with old-flick trivia, mostly who directed and starred in what. He loved it, the kind of pursuit he thrived on the older he got. She was on *Beach Red*, an obscure antiwar film. Gabe faked consternation in order to highlight his triumph. "Directed by and starring Cornel Wilde, I believe. Rip Torn in a supporting role."

"Damn," she said. "I thought I had you. Okay, try this one. Name the actress who is attached to *Claire's Knee* . . ."

I stole off to the shower.

My father wasn't much for small talk. He had an attorney's mind and bearing, and a tendency to be brusque, which he cultivated. He was an imposing man, heavy, bald, and bearded. The effect worked. When Gabe Rose held forth, whether you were a juror, a client, or his son, you paid attention.

He looked tired and drawn, sitting across from me in the head shop. In six years, he hadn't completely recovered from my mother's death. Flying had never entirely agreed with him, and reaching into his seventies alone had improved neither his stamina nor his tolerance for high-tech wonders like the airplane.

He asked Debby to leave us alone, and surprised me by inquiring about Tommy.

"How's your brother? Just answer fine or not fine and don't tell him I asked."

"I always tell him when you ask," I said. "He's fine."

He grunted. Tommy was not actually a subject of discussion, at least not since he found himself on the wrong side of the law on a B. and E. and possession of a listed substance. The substance was heroin. Tommy had done some time, taken care of his drug problem, and was doing well, a journeyman musician destined to float from one average rock band to another, making a living. My father never forgave him his weakness.

None of which meant squat to me. I had hung with Tommy since childhood. He was my little brother and my main man. Simple.

"Simon, I have a problem."

"I'll bite. What is it?"

"You tell me."

I hated this game. Gabe held psychiatry in about as much esteem as he did phrenology. He was challenging me. Show me your stuff.

"Okay." If he needed it, I'd play. "It's a favor. You hate asking for favors and this one you need from your son, an extra burden. You can't quite bring yourself to ask, but you will. You didn't come all this way for the pleasure of hearing me psych out your motives." I paused. "How'd I do?"

"You have redeemed my faith in your medical education, costly as it was." He smiled. I always suspected he liked me, but couldn't bring himself to admit it.

"Ask," I suggested.

"I've just been to see an old friend. His kid is in trouble and it's right up your alley. She's not a kid, really. She's your age. And her father is a client as well as a friend. I want you to see her."

"That shouldn't be much of a problem. That's what I do." But something was missing. My father had come a long way.

"There's a slight catch. You know my client and probably remember his daughter. He was your English teacher your senior year in high school."

It didn't take long to scan my high school files. "That would be Donahue. I didn't know he was your client."

He shrugged. "There are probably seven or eight things you don't know about me yet."

"And you want me to see her, is that all?"

"Yes, she's in serious trouble and, as you said, it's what you do. I want her to get the best and that's you, though you'll never hear me say so in front of witnesses."

"I certainly remember Donahue's daughter. Janice was—" My heart and my voice both came to an abrupt halt.

It couldn't be.

"Her name is Jensen now."

It was.

Chapter Five

I w a t c h e d Janice Jensen, but I saw nothing.

I was waiting in the observation cubicle on the dark side of the one-way mirror. I loathe sitting alone in the examination room while the detainees are brought to me. Suddenly, it's not clear who is the prisoner. And I'm never quite sure someone isn't on the other side of that mirror doing exactly what I was doing now. Observing. Watching as the unwitting subject does all those nervous little dances we do while waiting for the doctor. Private business.

People reveal themselves in their anxiety, but that's not why I was there to observe her. I needed to see her before she saw me.

But Janice knew about the mirror and situated herself in such a way as to offer little more than a down-turned profile. I'd seen her better on the news footage. All she gave me now was a blondish ponytail and a slender, ringless, slightly freckled hand covering her face. I witnessed that pose for twenty minutes and never got a peek.

In frustration I knocked on the window. Not cool and not professional, a failure to control an impulse. But it worked. I startled her and she betrayed herself, facing me for a split second before resuming her pose. But the split second was enough.

My testicles took another elevator ride. My head turned into an echo chamber and my spirit floated away. I was having an out-of-time experience. Unless of course this was her daughter, and for a moment the notion comforted me.

It had to be her daughter. The face was identical, but that happens with daughters. I did the appropriate calculations and they worked out. I headed straight for the examination room, sure now that any further delay would unhinge me more than her.

She now had her back to the door, finally facing the one-way mirror she had avoided for the past twenty minutes. Her perfume hit me before I got to my side of the table. It was Shalimar, I think, but the name didn't matter. It was *hers* and before I could corroborate it with the face again I was transported back to a time when Canoe met Shalimar on old throw pillows that smelled of dope. I remembered joking that if we ever got down to stems and seeds we could always smoke the pillows.

But it couldn't be. Maybe I was hallucinating. If only I could make out crow's-feet, or cellulite, or some other sign of the aging process.

"Oh, Simon, it's you." There was disappointment in her voice. "They told me I had a special visit. I thought it was Will."

Only then did she smile, a hint of crinkling at the corners of her eyes, the only perceivable change in that face.

"I'm glad to see you," she said, recovering. "I really am." She stood and extended her hands across the table, inviting mine. I took them and they felt familiar.

I shook my head in disbelief. "Janice Donahue."

"You've been watching me, haven't you?" She indicated the mirror. "Yes."

"I'm glad. It makes me feel safe"—she hugged herself inadvertently—"to know that you're watching over me again." She tried to smile but this time her face melted into tears. I let her cry. She probably needed it.

As for me, I could have used a stiff slap in the face to stop the flutterings of cellular memory.

Up close, her hair was the color of pale tangerine, somewhere between red and blond. It was baby fine and she wore it pulled back in that familiar ponytail, not much longer than mine. Her face was narrow and her features were small, but attractive. Her nose turned up a bit, as if she had had a nose job. Her round blue eyes didn't dominate her face. Her lips did that, petite like the rest of her, but full and lush.

She had not gained a pound; her figure remained firm and supple. She looked like she could still break into a rousing cheer. She could be quite beautiful in a teenybop sort of way, but when she felt worried or pensive she bordered on plain. The same Janice.

Her body exuded a youthful, vibrant sexuality. None of it was lost. Her bedroom lips still invited tasting.

She was wearing a Scottish-plaid skirt with a big brass safety pin looking like it was holding her together. A sky blue sweater clung to her just as its predecessors had done a few decades earlier. Not even her breasts had changed. They were pert and cheerful. A gold panda pin perched above her left nipple, which, along with its twin, was conspicuously pointing up at me through the soft wool.

Janice had neglected to age. Her face was unmarred, save for a few smile lines. She was a near-perfect replica of her younger self. She looked tired, like on a Monday, after a hard weekend of drinking and partying. The only thing missing was the letter sweater.

While I had gone on, graduated from adolescence, and established myself as an adult after a fashion, Janice hadn't changed a bit, literally. She wasn't a grown-up version of the beautiful teenager I had known. She was the same beautiful teenager.

And it made her feel safe that I was watching over her again. It made *me* feel strange.

I didn't want to consider, at the moment, what that could mean, so I fixed on an old standby. The First Word Test.

A former professor of mine, Herbert Simms, had spent the waning years of his career investigating the hypothesis that the first words a patient uttered were the most significant ones. Simms meant this literally, and as a result all of the analytic trainees were obliged to note verbatim the manner in which the patient greeted the new therapist. He then built elaborate, publishable theories based on whether the subject had opened with "Hello" or "Hiya," or was audacious enough to say "How ya doin'."

Simms would have loved this one. "Oh, Simon, it's you. They told me I had a special visit. I thought it was Will." She put me right in my place.

My memory cells, only recently awakened, positively fibrillated now. The sensible course was to get on with business. I would sort through the muddle later.

"Janice, this isn't an ordinary chat between two old friends. I was asked to do an evaluation of your competency to stand trial. I may be called upon to write a report or even testify. You need to know that none of this is privileged communication. Anything we talk about may come up in court. Do you understand?" I had read her her psychological rights.

She nodded, squirming in her seat, drying her eyes.

"I thought you were here to help me," she said. "I asked for you. I thought we were friends, at least." Friends? A quarter of a century had passed since I last saw her. She sounded like Debby, only younger.

"We were, and I'm here to help if I can. I just thought you should know."

She yawned, studied her nails for a moment, and began talking, exactly like she was having an ordinary chat with an old friend.

"So, Simon, you certainly have changed. If I hadn't known you were coming I would never have recognized you. You're so much . . . older." Most of my contemporaries were.

"But you're not. You haven't changed at all. You look like you did twenty-seven years ago. It's amazing." How did she do it?

"Thank you," she said shyly. "Do you see much of the old crowd? Have you seen Will?" Will again. She wanted him, not me, but what else was new?

"Will?" I asked.

"Hardin, silly, the Passing Machine."

I wasn't asking who. I knew who Will was. I wanted to know why he was on her mind. "You were expecting him to come. You were surprised it was me."

"I'm always sort of waiting for Will. People don't stay married forever." She shook her head once, definitively. "No, I know he won't come. I just think sometimes it's possible. It could happen. Anything can happen." Spoken like a true believer. "Have you seen him? Lately, I mean?"

I shook my head. I hadn't seen him lately. "No, I don't go home much. The only one I still see from high school is my brother, Tommy. You wouldn't have known him. He was a druggie and three years younger than us."

"No, I don't know any of the freshmen."

If she had forgotten the freshmen, that was apparently all she had forgotten. Her recall was total and alive, as if her past were her present. I had spent four years in the school; she, only one. But she was an encyclopedia of ancient gossip, of names and events recounted with eerie precision. I listened in awe to this woman frozen in another time.

"That was a good year for me," she explained. "There weren't many."

Maybe this was her way of warming up. It was easier to reminisce about a happy past than to face the future that was facing Janice. But someone had to bring it up.

"Janice, do you understand why you're here?"

"Of course I do. The police brought me here. I've been in lots of these places. And I assure you I am oriented to time, place, and person," which she proved by declaring, "April second, New York City, and Janice Jensen." She even added the exact time, to the minute. She had done half my job for me.

"You know the procedure, don't you?"

"Oh, yes, I've been here before."

"Maybe," I said, thinking how to broach the subject of the night in question, "but you've never had legal troubles before, have you?"

"No, silly," she said with a touch of embarrassment.

I wished she'd stop calling me silly. I'm not silly. I never was. "And you understand that you do now?"

"So they tell me."

"Do you know that you've been charged with certain crimes?"

She nodded, engrossed in her hanky.

"Can you tell me what they are?"

"Just murder, I think. Are there other charges?"

I shook my head, thinking that two counts of First Degree Murder were enough.

"Can you tell me what happened the night they brought you here?" The issue was really whether she could tell her attorney, not me, but I'd come to hear the story and pass minor judgment. And I was interested in her.

"Why is everyone harping on that night? If I did something bad, then punish me. Ground me for a year, but stop hounding me."

Ground me for a year?

She began to rock, rhythmically. I couldn't hear the tune.

"Can you tell me what happened that night?" I asked again. She was visibly angry, but at what or whom was unclear. If I persisted it would probably end up being me.

"Okay, I'll tell you. Someone killed Dennis. And I'm glad. I'm sorry, but it's true. He should be dead. He deserved it, the way he treated me."

And out of the haze came that moment of clarity. What she saw brought tears again. Her hands covered her face, but the tears just dripped through her fingers. When she stopped, she was calmer and sadder. Her mascara had streaked down her cheeks. She wiped her face carefully and methodically with the overworked hanky.

"Tell me about it," I encouraged. The issue wasn't yet solved. She had said, "Someone killed Dennis." She didn't have to admit actually doing anything, not yet. If she went for insanity, she would eventually have to describe her every action at the time, but for competency she only had to be able to aid in her defense.

"Oh, Simon, I'm competent, really. Don't worry." Who was worried? "I can tell you about it. I just don't want to."

She fiddled with her panda pin. My eyes followed her hand briefly.

"I'm embarrassed," she said, and she looked it. "Look, I've already told Ms. Newhouse the whole story. If you decide to take me on for the CR, I'll tell you all of it. I promise." CR is shorthand for criminal responsibility. She knew the jargon. Kate had educated her well, which, of course, was her job.

But Janice was playing with me. Teasing. Withholding.

"The son of a bitch deserved killing, I'll tell you that. We've talked about it for years."

"Who's talked about it for years, you and Dennis?" Odd.

"No, my mother and I. She thought I should have stopped him years ago." Very, very odd.

"Stopped him from what?"

"Stopped him from hurting me. Mom said I shouldn't take it. I shouldn't allow myself to be so subservient, the perfect cop's wife. The Kewpie Doll. She thinks I'm weak, but she's wrong. He's not going to hurt me anymore."

"How did he hurt you?"

"He hit me. He had other women. He wasn't like Will at all. Will was kind and sweet. Mother has always said that I should have stayed with Will. Or you. I would've been a whole lot better off."

I didn't miss her allusion to us, but I kept on task. "Janice, can you tell me what happened to your son?"

"What?" she shrieked. "Mother told me he's all right. Is something wrong with Sean?" She was momentarily frantic until she hugged herself back under control. "No, Mother would have told me." Not likely.

I wished someone had informed me that she didn't know about her son.

"How often do you see her? Your mother, I mean."

"All the time." She rocked again, picking up where she had left off.

"Janice, do you ever hear voices, the kind that you hear when nobody's there?" Basic and hard to ask. If the patient is psychotic, who can say what's real? She would know.

"Yes, all the time. I hear Mother when she's not here. I always hear Mother."

"How long has that been going on?"

"A long time. You can read all about it, if it interests you. Ms. Newhouse told me to give you this release. You're supposed to sign for my records at the nurses' station." She handed it to me like it smelled. "You should love it. It's loaded with Conduct Disorders, Anxiety Disorders, all the way up to Schizophrenia, Undifferentiated Type. Mixed nuts. It's all yours."

I had what I needed and more, except for the cold shower. I got up to leave before someone fell into reminiscence again. "I'll see you soon. Take care of yourself."

She stopped me. "Simon, do you remember?"

"Of course I remember."

"Did you really like me then?"

"Yes, Janice, I really liked you."

She nodded as if to say, "I thought so," and the interview was over.

Janice was competent to stand trial, but she was not ready to plead insanity. To do that, she would have to acknowledge committing the crimes. As it was, she had left her options open, a lesson I remembered learning from her years earlier.

I remembered another salient fact. Janice's mother, Margery Donahue, had died the year before Janice and I met.

And that wasn't the worst of it. I had a problem, an ethical dilemma. I wanted to take her case but I never worked with people I knew personally, even in passing. And this was worse, much worse.

I had once been hopelessly, mindlessly, in love with the defendant.

Chapter Six

It was the year I discovered pot, my father had his heart attack, Tommy "borrowed" his first car, and I possessed Janice Donahue, only to lose her.

Nixon was in the White House, it was pre-Watergate, and the Beatles were history. The pain of Kent State was still there, but it was beginning to fade from the collective unconscious, along with the energy of the peace movement. The sight of dead students, murdered by homegrown soldiers, had changed our world.

And so had the dope. I discovered marijuana on the University of Michigan campus where I would soon, if I survived my senior year in high school, begin the rest of my life: college. Although I had always lived in Ann Arbor, I left behind the townies' mentality to seek enlightenment in the very nest of the student movement. The campus that had spawned the SDS seemed a good place to begin the search.

There were teach-ins, sit-ins, be-ins, and smoke-ins of every persuasion. I hung out with a group of psych majors who were into experimenting, mostly with mind expanders. They didn't want so much to change America as to change their own states of consciousness and talk about it ad nauseam. Being a high school senior in the hallowed halls of academia was ego-building. I got off on it.

I was tolerating my senior year like a canker sore, spending as much time as I could away from home, and staying as stoned as possible while still being able to function. Then my father had a heart attack.

He had earned it. He ate too much, smoked too much, worked sixteen-hour days at his law practice, worried constantly, and, in general, defined the type-A personality. He collapsed during the preliminary hearing of a divorce.

As a result, he was confined to the house for the better part of the winter, grousing and carping, making everyone as miserable as he was. He wasn't cruel. He just wanted company.

I kept out of his way, knowing full well that if he discovered me smoking a joint in the john, it would add nothing positive to the already stressed family atmosphere. Of course he discovered me anyway, but not in the john. I was working on a history paper and left a roach in the ashtray, where he spotted it because he still smoked too much and the ashtray was his first stop in any room.

"Simon, I thought you had more sense than this." He held up the roach.

I could have told him that I didn't inhale, but no one would buy that, not even back then. "It's just pot. It's not even a drug. It's a plant."

"And heroin is a flower. Don't play wise-ass with me. It's an illegal substance and I will not have it under my roof. Go out there," he said, pointing to the street, "if you need your fix." No one is ever really a modern parent, not in their own time anyway.

We didn't pursue it, but the tension built between us. Then Tommy helped me out. He took someone else's car for a spin, literally. He was brought up on juvenile charges and my father had to deal with the shame of having his own child pulled into the web of the legal system, his system. Tommy got off with a strong warning, but my father didn't get over it. One of his sons had become a drug addict and the other a common thief.

We stayed out of his way. Tommy did whatever freshman hoods did and I kept going over to the U. to expand my horizons and become politically aware.

For the time being I was missing the part of the scene that most intrigued me. I was personally committed to sexual freedom but I'd fallen in with a group of conscientious objectors to the sexual revolution. No free love, just endless sessions of free association and flying rhetoric. So I listened and learned about the military-industrial complex and how it was giving us all a royal screwing. I did smoke a joint once while naked at a be-in, but that turned out to be more shriveling than sexy.

It began with a single kiss, a moment suspended in time. This particular kiss was preceded by some elaborate nocturnal fantasies and at least two spectacular wet dreams. And it probably would have stayed a fantasy had it not been for a host of circumstances, chief among them the combination of youth, lust, and the aftermath of the sixties.

Every man at some point in his life experiences a kiss that awakens the beast like no other, the kiss that goes right to the sexual center and defines "turned on" for the rest of his days. Mine came from the lips of Janice Donahue.

Ann Arbor High School, Sweetheart Dance, Valentine's Day of our senior year. I had a convenience date with Bev Reilly, a quiet, studious type with frizzy, flaming red hair that she found embarrassing. She would have preferred a simpler shade of brown, to blend in better with her classmates. I thought that if Bev had let her flag fly she would have been beautiful, but she insisted on braids and plainness.

Bev and I had spent most of senior year together, talking endlessly about politics and sex. She was Catholic, straight, and had even considered entering the convent. She suffered from a permanent crush on Will Hardin, our All-Everything sandy-haired idol of a quarterback.

I was agnostic, a budding hippie, and was content for the moment with my active Janice Donahue fantasy life. I smoked joints and suffered while Bev drank beer and suffered. Bev threw up more than she would have liked, so she gave up the beer.

Since neither of us had a real date, we went to the Sweetheart Dance to watch the ones who did. Janice would be there with Will. They were an item long before Janice moved to Ann Arbor, when she still lived in the boonies out at Workman's Lake. She would be gorgeous and so would he. Will's thing was being athletic and physically attractive, but he was also genuinely kind and, unfortunately, not dumb, just not school smart. Janice's thing was being bright, cheery, and the biggest turn-on since Tuesday Weld. She wasn't elected Homecoming Queen, but she was out only on a technicality; she'd come to AAHS as a senior, which prevented her from competing. It didn't prevent her from being class valedictorian, a position she deserved. She never saw a B.

Math was not my forte but the equation was clear enough. Will had

Janice. I wanted her. Will was stronger, better looking, and nicer than me. I was smarter. Next case.

I was marginally acknowledged by all the cliques at Ann Arbor High. The brains, mostly sprouting hippies, tolerated me because I was into weird shit like meditation, vegetarianism, and ESP. I also smoked dope, which made me kin. The jocks respected me for my size but I was uncompetitive, which they couldn't understand or forgive. The hard-cores, heavy druggies and bikers, left me alone because if they hadn't, Tommy would have killed them.

I remained ultimately unaffiliated, free or excluded, depending on who was looking, which pretty much ruined my chances as far as Janice Donahue was concerned.

I actually liked Will, and he respected me. We had our separate domains, his physical, mine intellectual, and we had worked out an amiable power-sharing arrangement. He was president of the class, and I got the student council. We occasionally shared the dais at school events and we talked, usually through whatever ceremony we were officiating.

Will appreciated his assets and liabilities. He couldn't understand why he should bother to think himself around a problem when he could just put his head down and bull his way through it. This was no dumb jock. This was a smart jock.

He understood the value of his body. I understood the value of my mind and the rude reality that it wasn't much use to me until I could show it off in college. At the moment, the hunk was winning, but we both knew that that was about to change.

Will also knew my secret. I had the hots for his girl. He could have guessed, because probably eighty-five percent of the male population of Ann Arbor High, including the principal, had the hots for Janice. The combination of innocence and sexual innuendo moved the beast in most of us.

I had made my pale attempts to get next to her. We had spoken twice at student council meetings. She laughed heartily once when I proposed allowing marijuana on school grounds. Only on Fridays.

Having captured her attention, however briefly, and having nothing on God's earth to lose, I'd invited Janice to sit with me on the lawn during lunch. She accepted and we spent some time chatting, but lightning failed to strike her. I was captivated and used all of my conversational prowess to keep her interested. We might have become "good friends," but even that didn't happen because Janice arranged to have her lunch period changed to coincide with Will's.

Everybody at the Sweetheart Dance was drunk except Bev and me. We arrived late, after driving around the block long enough for me to get well stoned. It worked. The school colors took on new brilliance. Bev went off in search of anything chocolate for me, being a kind soul, but leaving me on the periphery as usual. I was wondering if I could psychically attract a plastic spoon from the table across the gym into my hand. I'd seen Uri Geller do it with silverware on "Ed Sullivan." Plastic should be a breeze.

Janice Donahue placed herself in my line of sight, breaking the force field between me and the spoon.

"What're you doing, Simon?" she asked groggily. She smelled like beer mixed with roses.

"I'm trying to move spoons. Telekinetically."

"Any luck?"

"Not so far." I put on a determined expression to let her know I wasn't beat.

She touched my cheeks and pulled my face down to hers. She kissed me. Her lips were warm and wet and sent a surge of blast-furnace heat to my soul. Before she let go of my face, I felt my erection and worried that she could, too. I pulled my hips back. She followed with hers, rhythmically grinding herself into me. I almost came.

"Keep trying," she said. "You'll get it." I wondered if she meant the spoon or the kiss.

And I had my moment. I should have left it at that, but I was young.

Janice made the next move. She insisted that they double with Bev and me. Bev was intensely uncomfortable being around Will and feeling so deficient compared to Janice. I talked the balls off the proverbial brass monkey, leaving Will in the proverbial dust. Janice found ways to rub up against me enough to make me aware of the firmness of her small breasts and their unavailability to me. Will didn't mind. He liked me, thought I was funny, and he understood the nature of power, which he explained to me simply and without malice.

"She loves your mind, Simon," he said without envy. "But she loves my dick." He shrugged. I shrugged. Truth is truth.

And karma is karma.

I became obsessed with her, or at least with her body. I ached to have her. I fantasized her dressing and undressing, something she did in my mind at least thirty times a day.

I didn't exactly imagine making love to her. She seemed too pure for anything so common. And I was too young, inexperienced and insecure, so I kept it simple, Janice's splendid body unencumbered by clothes.

The safest fantasies are those that cannot be ruined by reality. That's probably why I'd picked Janice. She was unapproachable, unattainable, and spoken for. There was no danger that my fantasies would become reality. She'd stay with Will Hardin forever and I would stay horny and high.

Except that my fantasy object, who was supposed to stay innocent, if naked, came to call.

She was dressed, but otherwise just as I had imagined her.

I was doing my lounge act on the front porch with a beer, a book, and a bong, enjoying the first days of my freedom. It was just after graduation, steamy summer already. I was wearing my uniform of cutoffs, tie-dyed T-shirt, and an orange bandanna to keep the sweat out of my eyes, should I exert myself enough to produce any.

I was cool, a lazy summer ahead before starting college, and I had my own private space, a tool shed I had turned into my pad. My father, who insisted on calling me a dope fiend all year, had given me the shed so I could have some privacy and he could be free of my nasty habits.

Janice drove up in a car without a top and hopped out. She was wearing cutoffs, too, but hers were cut off much higher than mine, along with a sunny yellow T-shirt, a wide-brimmed panama hat, and platform heels. She was a walking sunflower.

"Simon, hi!" She waved enthusiastically.

Fortunately, I was stoned, or I would have stood mute before my live fantasy. As it was, I felt chatty.

"Janice, how's it hangin'?" As far as I could see, it was all hangin' just fine.

"Pretty cool. You busy?"

"Not really." I flashed *The Prophet* long enough for Kahlil's face to mellow her out.

"I need somebody to talk to. I thought if you weren't busy . . . ?"

My reputation was well established. I had become the seniors' official, albeit amateur, shrink. Got a problem? Consult Simon, everybody's friend, nobody's lover. Even then, I gave good ear.

"Sure. Come to my office." And I took her around the back, past my mother's geraniums, to my tin-roofed shack. It was done in postmodern tool: picks, rakes, shovels, and all manner of lawn-care products. I had strewn psychedelic pillows around my bed and the floor, which was covered in carpet remnants. I kept a desk chair for my visitors. I sat on the bed, my head propped against a coiled length of garden hose.

"Music?" I asked, the gracious host.

"Sure, got any Carpenters?"

"Not in my house." I put on Santana's "Abraxis." I lit a Camel filter. She extracted a True Green from a leather case that held her lighter as well. We smoked together for a few moments. I raised an eyebrow as if to say, "So? Talk."

"Look, I'm going away to college in a couple of months and frankly, I'm scared to death. I've been with Will so long I feel like I'll be a cheerleader all my life. I can't handle it. It's time to move on. I have no idea what to expect and I'm scared, is all." She seemed uncomfortable admitting a weakness. "What's it like? What are the college students like?"

I told her about the people I hung out with and the kinds of things we did. She was fascinated. Her eyes danced around my face as I described the dope, the talk, the togetherness we shared. She asked about what they wore, what they read and what they saw at the movies. She took mental notes.

"It's just that I've been a robot all my life," she said. "We've moved every couple of years since I was a baby. I've always had to learn to fit in and I'm gonna have to do it again. It's not easy and it's not real. I'm sick of it."

"So what do you want?"

"I want to stop following everyone else's rules. I hate it. I've been a fake so long, I don't think I know who I am."

"How does Will feel about this?" Never let relevance interfere with self-interest.

"He's got nothing to do with it. We broke up. He's going on to college football and Jesus, of all things. I'm done with that shit. It's time for me to cut loose."

"You want to smoke a joint?"

"I've never smoked pot before."

"There's always a first time," I said, stretching across the bed to reach my stash under the mattress. I rolled a beautiful slim little number, fired it up, and handed it to her.

"What do I do?"

"You hold it in as long as you can. Don't cough or you won't get high." I did a demonstration toke and held it forever.

She reached for it, looked it over, and took a delicate little puff.

"It'll take you a week to get high at that rate. Take more and hold it." I was beginning to like being her teacher.

She took a better hit the second time and better yet the third.

"How will I know when I'm high?" she asked.

I explained it all to her, the colors, the sounds, the munchies, the laughter.

"It's not working," she said.

"Yes, it is. Give it time." I put on the new James Taylor album. It had "You've Got a Friend" on it, the precise message I wanted to convey. "Close your eyes. You're safe."

She closed her eyes and got into the music. "Open them again." I spoke very softly, like a TM instructor. She took the suggestion.

"Wow! Far out! Holy shit!" She spun her head around.

"It's working," I said. We sat and listened to the music.

"Got anything to eat?"

I tossed her a package of Oreos and she ripped into them like the last dessert. She suddenly stood up and kicked off her platform shoes.

"I'm done with those, too. I'm short," she affirmed. She seemed to be getting the idea.

"Far out. You're just the right height."

"You know, I wish women could get drafted."

"Why?"

"So I could have a draft card."

I didn't have one yet and couldn't think of any reason to want one. "You *want* a draft card?"

"So I could burn it."

"You've got a bra, don't you?"

And right before my amazed and delighted eyes, Janice performed the magical act of removing her bra without taking off her shirt. She shook herself loose, got up and found the charcoal lighter. She asked if she could borrow the hibachi I used as an ashtray, threw the bra in it, doused it with the starter fluid, and set it aflame.

She was definitely getting the idea.

Janice visited the next day and the next and almost every day for the next two months. It could not be said that we were going together because we never went anywhere. We hung out in my shed smoking dope, listening to music, and talking about a world that awaited us, literally, just outside. We could have gone over to the U. and enjoyed some of the freedom we talked about, but Janice was reluctant. She wanted the future there and then, in the shed.

She took to the dope. It suited her hunger for new thoughts, new feelings. She soaked up the ideas of Kahlil Gibran, Germaine Greer, and me. Which, of course, was the point. I was furiously seducing her with my mind, amazing her with the length and breadth of my limited knowledge of many subjects. It was working. She was falling in love with my mind while my body waited on the sidelines.

Then Janice called it into the game.

One languid afternoon, both of us well fried on sun and cannabis, Janice asked, "Do you think we could be naked together? I know how to use my body to get guys, that's not the problem. I don't know how to accept my body as a part of me, a part I don't have to hide. I feel safe with you. I don't want to have sex. I want us to be together without covering up. What do you think?"

What could I say? Unabashed, unashamed freedom had been my idea. I stripped off my clothes like I did it all the time, which I did, but not in front of my fantasy object. Janice followed me and we sat in the buff listening to Hot Tuna. I was so cool about it, I was sure my penis would be, too. But, alas, the naked ape got an erection.

"Don't worry," she said reassuringly, "I've seen them before. I've even had them inside of me. I've just never loved one."

I would have offered mine, but it was feeling small and insignificant. It eventually realized that gratification was not on the horizon and mellowed out.

I barely saw my family that summer. Most days, Janice and I waited until everyone was gone so we could have the house to ourselves, and then we would cook, eat, and watch TV, all in the nude. If Janice felt free and breezy, I felt frustrated by my own philosophy. My eyes feasted and the rest of me suffered the famine.

When my parents were around, Janice turned into a polite, wholesome charm machine. They liked her and counseled me to be kind to her. She had lost her mother and was hurting. Janice never mentioned it.

As the summer progressed and Janice metamorphosed into the consummate flower child, I realized that I'd gotten exactly what I'd dreamed about, Janice Donahue getting dressed and undressed repeatedly before my very eyes. There must have been a lesson there but I failed to see it.

For her final exam in "The World According to Rose," Janice decided to take her show on the road. We were going out together.

She picked Ann Arbor's annual Blues and Jazz Festival, a three-day event held in a field adjacent to town. It was attended mostly by university types, not the high school crowd.

We spent the first two days smoking, dancing, and grooving to the likes of Junior Walker and Buddy Guy. We kept our clothes on. Janice talked to everyone who would talk to her, trying out her newly raised consciousness.

On the third night, the finale of the festival, she produced two small squares of blotter paper with a picture of a diabolical hippie on each one. Mr. Magic, LSD. I was not enamored of psychedelics, but I was of Janice. We each dropped a hit. She danced and sang wildly while I gritted my teeth and nearly froze to death in the eighty-degree heat.

On the way out, a column of young hippies began chanting one of the day's mantras, "Show us your tits! Show us your tits!" The departing crowd mostly ignored them. Janice tore off her shirt and performed a cartwheel that ended in a topless split. The crowd roared. She kissed me on the mouth and said, "Thank you, Simon. In my own special way, I will always love you." She put her shirt on to the growing boos of the crowd. "That's all, folks," she said. Janice had graduated, with honors.

We got back to my shed about three A.M. I was exhausted by the chemicals. I barely made it to the bed before collapsing. Janice was ready to take on the world. I seemed to be losing to the sheets. But I couldn't sleep. I was too wired.

She sat beside me on the bed. I was sweating. She wiped my forehead with a bandanna and started unbuttoning my shirt, cooling my chest with the wet cloth.

"You know, we've never made love."

I knew.

As she unbuttoned, she explained. "If we make love, things will change between us. It means we're together, really together. Maybe forever. I don't make love with just anyone, you know. It has to mean something. Can you handle it?" she asked, stroking my chest and beginning to unzip my jeans.

"I can handle it." It was everything I thought I wanted.

"You don't look it," she observed doubtfully. "Will seems to get stronger the more stuff he does. You look wasted."

She undressed me this time as I undressed her. My body felt miserable from the acid and hers looked like a dream come true. She stroked me, kissed me, and maneuvered herself on top of me. I came the moment I entered her, either a premature ejaculation or the result of two months of foreplay.

"Don't worry, there'll be other times," she said.

She left around dawn. I was in the twilight zone, but I managed to hear her say, "See you later, I love you."

She left a note. It said that she had been tied down too long with Will, that she thought it a bad time to get involved. She reiterated that in her own way she would always love me. "But," she said, "in matters of the heart, I know better than you." Her best course, she concluded, was to leave her options open.

She didn't come around the next day, or the next. I reached her father three days later. He told me that Janice had gone off to school early.

Chapter Seven

I s h o o k myself out of the memory. Sloshing through the past wouldn't help. Seeing the present clearly was my task. I took Tupelo for our evening trot.

"Let's go, girl. I need to think."

Tupelo shook herself out of sleep. "Ready." Tupelo is always ready. "You think. I'll watch for trouble."

I had a fair amount of data to process. Janice had let me see only what she wanted. She was in control. But I had surprised her.

"Oh, it's you" cannot be misinterpreted as enthusiasm. I was the tuna-noodle casserole showing up at a gourmet spread. She'd been nurturing her own fantasies. Her special visit, probably a long-frozen dream of rescue by Will Hardin, had not materialized. I had. But Will Hardin would be a key player in our unfolding drama, if Herbert Simms was worth his salt.

Then what was my role?

She'd answered that, too. "I thought you were here to help. I asked for you." That's who I was, helper, caretaker, and perhaps salvation in the real world where fantasies are stripped of their mythical power. Will was not a forensic consultant. I was, and that's what she needed. Sloppy seconds.

And just to prove that adults are nothing more than the sum of their developmental parts—infant, child, adolescent—I felt the slightest twinge of rejection.

Janice's last words to me were perhaps the most telling of all, although

I didn't know yet what they were telling me. "Do you remember?"

As if I could ever forget. Was she playing coy? It wouldn't be out of character. She was the right psychological age for it.

"Did you like me then?" Not truly an issue unless your reality tended to float. I had made it amply clear how I felt about her.

The underlying question was probably, What will you think of me now? Now that I am a murderess. Will anyone love me again?

And her appearance had stunned me.

Everybody ages. I am not beyond wonder when I notice new flecks of white in my beard. But they are there, even if I don't feel them. And I can see them for what they are, merit badges for survival. Janice had remained, physically and mentally, a teenager. She looked flawless, as though the passing years had not touched her. But they were there, those years, and it was my job to find them.

And her dead mother visited her every day. I wanted to know what she had to say. Janice had seemed lucid enough, not psychotic while I was with her. But that is the nature of psychosis. It ebbs and flows, appears and disappears.

There was indeed a great deal to consider. For example, if she did exterminate her family, why? Even crazy people have motives.

"You got any ideas?" I asked Tupelo.

"I haven't even met her. How would I know? Introduce us if you want an opinion."

"Not likely," I said and went back to ruminating.

Suddenly, I felt a pain shoot through my lower back as something pressed into my right kidney, setting it on fire. A steel shaft? As I remembered it, this was how muggings began. I was apparently going for number four. Tupelo was blithely unaware and trouble was supposed to be her business.

Stale cigarette breath wafted toward my nose as he whispered in my ear. "Your wallet, nice and easy, or your guts are all over the street."

I stopped dead.

"Which is it, muthafucka?"

"I think this time I'll take the guts all over the street, thank you," I said, as if I were reading a menu. "I like this wallet, it's real leather."

The kinky-haired maniac, my little brother, sprang from behind me, moon face beaming, arms spread ready for his bear hug. I hadn't seen him in three days.

"You scared the shit out of me," I told him, only half amused. This wasn't the first time.

"Don't gimme that." He squinted up at me. "You knew it was me."

Tommy scared people. It wasn't his fault. He just looked different, short, stocky, muscles like bricks, and that magnificent head. His face was round and wide, framed by an outrageous afro, but it was the eyes that got you. They were slits that made him appear either half asleep or extremely sinister. He was generally just stoned, but he'd looked that way when we were kids and he wasn't stoned.

"Hey, bro, what's up? No, let me guess. Jensen. Am I right?"

"How the fuck did you know? And how did you find me?" I had no idea where I was, how could he?

"Easy. I followed you from your house so I could listen to you think. And about Jensen, see if you can follow me on this. Girl practically next door, damsel in deep shit, having murdered husband and kid. And if I'm not mistaken, you had a thing for her in high school. Too tempting to pass up. That's how I did it."

"You should be the shrink." I didn't bother telling him our father had asked me to help. He upset Tommy, too.

"I know. Is she crazy, Simon? That's what it's all about, right?"

"I don't know what it's about yet. It's not clear if she did anything, much less if she was crackers at the time."

"It's clear," he said, lighting up a Salem from a crunched-up pack.

"What's clear?"

"She did 'em both."

"What?"

"Are you deaf?" He pronounced it *deef*. "I said, 'She did 'em both.'"

"How do you know?"

He frowned at me. "Gideon."

"What does Gideon have to do with this?" I was missing an obvious synapse.

"You're not smart today, Simon. I hope you're at least intuitive." He pronounced all four syllables. "Gideon is a detective, NYPD Homicide, you will recall, and Jensen's husband was heat. Reason enough to know what's going on, wouldn't you say?"

"Yes, I would."

"So what do you think of her? Is she a goner?"

"Do you remember her?" I asked.

"Are you kidding? I'm almost gonna forget her. She—"

"Wait!" I shouted. "Don't tell me! I don't want to know what you think before I know what I think." Why further contaminate an already pol-luted environment? "Let's talk later."

"Afraid I'll get her pegged before you do?" He jabbed my ribs with his elbow.

"Yes. It's my turn to get one right."

"In any case, Sherlock"—he said *Shoylock*—"you're gonna need me on this one and you're in luck, 'cause I just happen to be available." Tommy was always available, except when he had a gig. We'd worked together for years. He could go places I couldn't go and do things I couldn't do.

"What do I need your help for? I talk with people all the time without your help."

"You'll need me," he said, too sure of himself.

"Why?"

He raised a pinky to count. "Can you fight?"

"No."

The ring finger rose. "Can you handle a firearm, like in can you shoot anything other than the breeze?"

"No."

"Then I'll leave the psychodiagnosis to you, and you leave the cover-ing of your pretty little behind to me, like always."

"I don't think that'll be necessary this time."

"You never think it'll be necessary." I do have a tendency to minimize danger. "You forget that it's never simple, Simon." He loved to say that. "It's murder.

"Wanna smoke a joint?" he asked as we walked. Tommy never gave up. I hadn't touched pot in over twenty years but he was still hopeful.

"No, Tommy," I answered patiently.

"Your place then. Besides, I haven't seen my niece in almost a week. I'll bet she needs hassling."

Tommy and Debby got along like brother and sister, not uncle and niece. Tommy was more like fourteen than forty when he was playing. He has-sled her about staying home all the time and watching the tube. She has-sled him about his clothes, his face, and anything else she could hurl at him. They insulted each other constantly, verbal wrestling with no ill in-tent. He even got her to leave the house with him. Tommy could be very therapeutic.

"What's happenin', Debs? You look ravishing, as usual," he said. She had on patched jeans and a frayed brown turtleneck, no shoes.

"Off my case, melon face."

He laid a cruncher on Debby, pinning her arms to her sides and lifting her off the floor. She reciprocated, complete with picking him up.

"Hey, no shit, Debs, you look good. What's the matter?"

"Simon, where did you find this useless sack of fertilizer?" She generally cursed like a sailor, but since Tommy was such a guttermouth, she affected gentility.

"He held me up," I said. "At fingerpoint."

"What's the matter, couldn't get your shiv out of your boot, Quick Draw?"

"Shiv?" Tommy said. "What the fuck's a shiv?" He didn't watch as many late-night movies as she did.

"It's a knife, usually carried by sleazeballs like you for the purpose of shivving," she explained.

"Sleazeball?" His tone rose an octave. "Sleazeball? You really know how to hurt, Debs." Tommy looked wounded and he was good at it. She went for it.

"I'm sorry. I was just messin' around."

"Make it up to me," he said.

"What's he got in mind?" she asked me.

I shrugged. I almost never knew what Tommy had in mind until after he'd done it. Even then, I often wasn't too sure.

"Smoke a joint with me, Debs," he said.

The playfulness drained from Debby's face. She nearly cried. Drug use was an untouchable. She had never experimented with drugs. She was phobic about it. Warren had been doing pot nonstop just before he finally lost it. She tolerated Tommy's smoking but it was not a topic of discussion.

And Tommy was not trying to lead her down the pathways of sin. He figured since she lived in the world and went to college with other young people, she would eventually get bummed enough to try something. He figured if he couldn't stop it, he could at least be around to help out, if needed.

"You wanna hear what I think?" Tommy asked.

"No," she said. "That's the last thing I want to hear."

"I think," he said, "it's easier for you to blame dope and yourself for what happened than to really look at it. One"—up went the pinky—"your father did it. He's a person, all by himself. Two"—ring finger—"it was some combination of your father and the war. If you gotta blame something, blame the war, and if you gotta blame someone, blame your father. You want to think it was you and the dope. You're wrong on both counts and you're a chickenshit for copping to a lie."

She punched him in the arm. He dragged himself to the kitchen, overplaying his agony.

We could hear him slamming around in the cupboards, which meant he was making a snack. I kept some desiccated lunch meat and toppings around the house for such occasions.

"Don't blame him on me," I said. "He's not my fault."

"It's not your fault that he's right, either."

"I guess not. He's right about something else. You do look good. Are you in love?" I was kidding, but only partially.

Debby turned beet red and got nervous. She regressed to age thirteen in seconds. "I'm going out with Bobby again. It doesn't mean I'm in love."

"What does it mean then?" This was date number two, which followed date number one, which, as I recalled, had ended when Debby refused to sleep with him.

"I don't know yet," she answered.

"Cool," I said. "Can we talk seriously about the condoms this time?" Debby was aware and sensible about sex, in theory. We had talked endlessly about AIDS and birth control as well as the emotional dangers of indiscriminate sex. As far as I knew, she hadn't engaged in any sex to speak of yet, but Bobby sounded promising or threatening, depending on which one of us you were.

Tommy happened to be sitting down with some disgusting sandwich made of pig by-products just as I said "condoms." He jumped up like there was a tack on his seat.

"Father-daughter stuff. I'm outta here. Let me know when you've figured out Janice Donahue. I'm interested." Him, too.

He split, leaving a fragrant wake of mayonnaise, ketchup, and mustard in the air.

Debby's color returned to normal and she regained her poise. She showed me three multicolored condom packages. "I have no intentions of getting knocked up. I'll be home early. You won't even have time to worry."

I was already worried, and not just about Debby. Janice Donahue lurked in the background, casting a discomfiting shadow. But I could deal with Debby, so I did.

Behind the blush of new love, I had seen her growing more upset for days. It could have been the dreams. It could have been the boyfriend. It could have been anything. Rejecting the direct approach, I went for a rainbow three-pointer from midcourt and accidentally scored.

"What were you doing that day at the library?" She had met Bobby there. My best guess about her agitation was that some combination of love and sex was at the core. I thought I could get her talking about Bobby.

"I do take courses, you know. They give assignments and everything." She was turning petulant on me.

"You said you were looking something up for me." I was fishing.

"I did that, too. Background, you know. I checked on Janice Jensen. Like always." Debby had on occasion done research for me. You gotta know how it's playin' in Peoria, she would say, and she'd check the press coverage. But I hadn't asked her for help on Janice Jensen.

"What did you find?"

"The usual. You know, strictly crime beat, gory pictures, not even a fancy cop funeral. He wasn't killed in the line of duty." She sounded disappointed.

"Anything else?"

"I looked up the baby." She stared at the floor. We were approaching the source. "Not many mothers kill their children, you know."

"More than you'd think," I said. "What were you looking for?" I was pushing and risked losing her for the moment, but there was something in it.

"The baby's sign. I wanted to know his birth date because I wanted to know his sign. Is that so strange?" Her voice came from a person who felt strange.

"What sign was Lisa?" I asked, wondering where it would go. The lion's share of Debby's guilt centered on her baby sister, some fantasy that she could have somehow, some way, saved her.

"You know, for a shrink, your timing is sometimes lousy. I gotta get dressed." She was about to cry.

"It's three-thirty in the afternoon and you gotta get dressed to go out tonight. Okay, go get dressed, but answer me. What sign was your sister?"

"Aquarius," she said, beginning for the first time to sob, quietly. "And she wasn't my sister."

"What?"

"She was my kid." She raised her right hand, ending the discussion.

Chapter Eight

D e b b y didn't come home that night. She stayed out and I stayed up. It made me anxious that she was out in the world, unprotected by me.

In the morning I was determined to find company for my misery, so I headed for Kate. I had decided for the moment to keep Debby's revelation to myself. Kate could have her say some other time. I had plenty of other business with her.

"Calm down," Tupelo said as we walked. "You're no good to yourself when you get like this."

I bared some tooth at her but transference doesn't move her, only truth.

By the time I reached Kate, what had begun as low-grade anger flowered into full-blown rage, probably a testosterone buzz. Kate was meddling more than usual, involving herself with pockets of my life I reserve for myself. She was trespassing.

She'd been advocating Debby's independence for more than a year. She'd been fixing me up forever. But not telling me about Janice, holding back what I surely had the right to know, was wrong, and by the time I got to her place I had reached maximum pissed.

I scowled at the doorman, Carmelo, whom I liked. Tupelo stopped to say hello. I summoned the penthouse elevator, barked at Tupelo, and waited impatiently for the near-silent whoosh of the doors parting to reveal the third most secure apartment entry in New York, custom-designed by Tommy to be unbreachable, even by himself.

I owned the necessary keys and cards to gain admittance, but at Kate's request I never used them when she was home. Until this day when, propelled by righteous indignation, I entered her penthouse unannounced.

I knew where to find her. It was Sunday. She would be in the center of her enormous sectional, facing the free-standing fireplace, surrounded by the *Times* and *Washington Post*. I stormed right into the living room but was stopped dead in my tracks.

She was pointing a 9mm semiautomatic pistol at my heart. She lowered it and tucked it in the pillows behind her. Unpleased, I could tell.

She scratched Tupelo at her leisure and finally addressed me. "Sit down. I hate it when you loom over me. You used your key. I'm home. When I'm home I always appreciate it when you use the doorbell."

Kate was protective of her space, maybe because she had to manage it differently than the ambulatory. And I had broken one of her rules. The piece aimed at my center made her point eloquently.

I sat, my legs rubbery. "May I?" I said, indicating the far end of the couch.

"Certainly," she said, clearly irritated. "But state your agenda."

"You're messing with my life, my women, but worst of all, you're messing with my head."

"I so enjoy it when you rant, especially on Sunday mornings. It's one of your charms, Rose, knowing exactly the wrong times to vent. I thought analysts prided themselves on timing. Yours is poor. Sometimes," she amended. "Now, please, do enumerate the problems you have with me."

She only called me Rose when she was pissed off. But I wasn't about to be deterred. I had my own anger and had nurtured it for sixty-odd city blocks.

"One"—I raised my little finger—"I would appreciate it if you would stop telling my daughter to move out on me. Two, I told you no more fix-ups and you sleazed around me. You told Jemma Marin to call me. Three, Janice Jensen. No way you should have let me stumble into a competency exam without warning me that I was about to face my past. No way. Unprofessional." The unkindest cut of all.

Kate took a deep breath and let it out slowly. "As our very own Debby would counsel at a time like this, chill out, Rose. Have a cookie. It'll do you good."

The coffee table, a cross-section of a tree trunk, was littered with the usual debris, coffeepot, cups, and a heaping plate of Kate's inedible leaden oat cakes. Cooking was not her forte, as she was the first to admit, but for some unknown reason she thought her oatmeal cookies were an exception to the rule. They weren't. Their presence in abundance suggested she'd been waiting for someone, probably me. I dropped in on Sundays.

I reluctantly put one of the gnarled brown things to my mouth, bit off a small chunk, and began chewing it into submission. It didn't do me any good nutritionally, but it did exhaust my jaw and make me feel twenty pounds heavier. I calmed down despite myself. After the battle with the oat cake, when Kate sensed the immediate threat of unpleasantness had passed, she picked up the conversation.

"I will answer your charges, in order. Hear me out on each one before you respond. In other words, shut up and listen."

I acquiesced, sure I could do it. Besides, I needed to work out the oat gluten stuck to my teeth before I could speak.

"First"—no fingers for emphasis—"you know full well what I think about you and your daughter. She is a woman now and she has to be allowed the freedom to grow without you watching out for her. It's time to let her go."

"I am not—"

"You're forgetting the shutting up and listening part."

"Good point," I said. Tupelo agreed.

Kate continued. "I know how you feel about it. You can't bear that Debby's past remains a mystery to you. You think that if you listen long enough and ask the right questions you'll figure out what you never saw. Eventually, in your fantasy, you'll know everything as if you'd been there and then you'll be her real father. It won't work and you know it."

I didn't need another reminder of how much I didn't know. "No way in the world—"

"I'm not done and you will hear me out." She raised her voice just enough to stop my interruption. "You might not be as mad if you listen, which is probably why you don't want to. Don't worry, you'll get your chance.

"I know you think she needs a break, a deferment from life's demands for a while because she's been hurt. So you give her everything. You're there for her whenever she needs you and many times when she doesn't. You're not doing her any favors by holding on to her. But you already know how I feel about it, and you even know why."

Kate's journey to independence had been a traumatic passage. The daughter of an alcoholic father, she'd been subject to his unpredictable violence until at the correct age of twenty-two she got married to get out of the house. She soon discovered that she had simply traded one abuser for another. Harry was a cokehead, and he grew more and more cruel with Kate as the years went by. Kate had gone nowhere.

One night on their way home from a party Harry was coked out and driving like he knew what he was doing. He had lost control of their car and slammed into a retaining wall. He was unharmed. Kate would not walk again.

When Harry left shortly after the accident, perhaps out of guilt or, more likely, out of hot pants for his secretary with whom he immediately took up residence, the world shook its finger at his selfishness and callous behavior. Only Kate knew the truth. She was free. Men would no longer dominate her life.

Her passion for the law came later as a result of her liberation, which is how she referred to her confinement to a wheelchair. Kate would brook no perception of tragedy in her life. "We all pay a price for freedom," she had said, and she meant it without a trace of self-pity.

Kate lived her feminism as few others did, and that's why she had no patience with Debby remaining dependent on me, even though that was how Debby and I wanted it.

"And as much as you would prefer to stay angry with me and as much as I enjoy it when you are, I'm going to ruin it for you. I owe you an apology and I'm offering it. I have no right to insinuate myself into your family affairs. It was wrong and I'm sorry."

"Shit," I said, deflated. "I hate it when you do that. It leaves me with nothing." I'd never been able to stay angry at Kate anyway.

"Have another cookie."

I did because had I not, I would surely have told her Debby's secret. I munched valiantly for a few minutes, to no avail.

"Remember Debby's little sister, the one blown up by her father's grenade? It was her daughter, not her sister." I would have sworn someone else said it.

Kate sighed and reached over to pat my hand.

"You're not surprised?" I asked.

"No, I'm not surprised. It explains a lot."

"Not to me." Debby's motherhood was a shock. It posed more questions than it answered. "I don't get it."

"Give yourself a break. Life does not imitate psychoanalysis. It takes its own time. You're not supposed to know how you feel about it yet. Debby will help."

I nodded. She was right, of course. I had never mastered real patience, although I talked a good game.

"To charge number two, sleazing around the no-fix-up rule, I plead not guilty. I did not tell Jemma Marin to call you. Yes, I have spoken of you in her presence, but I don't remember any gag rule to the contrary. She acted on her own. Don't blame me. And don't blame me if she's persistent, because she is. She's also beautiful, bright, and your kind of woman, but I will desist before I really make myself guilty of sleazing. Am I exonerated?"

"On Jemma Marin, yes. But you have one more charge to answer."

"Yes, I do, and I believe the charge was unprofessionalism, a heinous crime. If you're willing to bargain it down to irresistible impulse to play, I'll plead." She smiled playfully.

"No way you should have hung me out to dry like that. I had a right to know what I was walking in on. Not cool."

"It was her idea, although I'm not offering that as an excuse. She thought it would be fun. Was it?"

"I wouldn't have chosen that word."

"Tell me about it. I'm dying to hear." Even Kate, the ever mature, was turning into a teenager. Janice had that effect on people.

"Well, she's obviously a very troubled lady. But I have several problems with the case, not the least of which is prior knowledge."

"Carnal knowledge," Kate corrected.

"What did she tell you?"

"All in good time. What other problems do you have with the case?"

"There's one so obvious I thought you would've seen it. Given my prior knowledge, regardless of any alleged intimacies, a good prosecutor could have me for lunch. Why risk it? Why not just use Darling? It would be cleaner.

"And besides the small matter of a compromised expert witness, there remains the matter of legal culpability. She told me nothing. I'm not even sure I can certify her competent on the son. She didn't seem to know he was dead."

"She knows and competency isn't a problem. She's competent."

She handed me a document, a report to the proper authorities, evaluating Janice Donahue Jensen's competency to stand trial on two counts of murder, degree not yet stated. It started in the usual manner, describing Janice as a "bright, attractive, forty-five-year-old Caucasian female appearing younger than her stated age. She was oriented to time, place, and person, and made good contact with the examiner . . ." The report ended by finding her legally and psychologically fit to be tried. It was signed by Brice Darling, M.D.

"So you already got Darling?" I asked. "You wanted two competencies?" One was usually sufficient.

"Yes. He does the CR at the same time. No waste, no extra charge. Can you work with him?"

"He's a whore."

"I know what you think of him. I asked if you could work with him."

Brice Darling was the slime mold of my profession, the hired gun. For the right price he would make the necessary determination and put on a brilliant, flamboyant performance in court. He got results and he got very rich. His handlebar mustache and his reputation for not taking shit from anyone in the courtroom were his trademarks. He and the news media were having a continuous affair. Brice Darling, one-man circus.

"I can work with him," I said. "I just prefer better company." We had shared the stage once before and we weren't friends. "Then you've decided to plead her insane."

"I have. The evidence is inconsistent with any other theory."

"I haven't seen any evidence."

"If you agree to do the CR you can have everything I have. It's very little, but it's all here." She waved a file.

"You've already got Dr. Flash, what do you need me for?"

"You know it's customary for the defense to present two experts. Listen, Simon. We're talking about a trial here. High drama, all choreographed by me. I know Darling can be . . ."—she paused, searching for the word—"abrasive, shall we say, but he gets the job done. For those who respond negatively to his sleaze factor, we have you: solid, sincere, earnest, verging on sweet. And you knew her when. Together, who wouldn't believe you?"

"Kate, I had no idea you could be so cold." I was honestly astonished by her.

"And I had no idea you could be so naïve. I do my job, Simon, and it should be no surprise to you that I do it well. You call the fact of your prior knowledge a risk. It's not a risk. It's perfect. The jury will listen to you. Not only are you an expert in the field, you are an expert on the defendant. It's drama at its best. It's certainly not a problem for me."

"It is for me," I countered. "Prior knowledge doesn't necessarily help in a case like this. I'm not sure I can render you a clean psychological opinion."

"Then render me a dirty one."

"I won't do that. If I can't give you unpolluted testimony, I won't give you any."

"That, I believe, is strictly your business. If your psychological house is not in order, and you can't evaluate her without prejudice, you'll decide not to become officially involved. Then you can help me on the side. I can't imagine that you're not interested."

"I'm interested. I'm just not sure it's for any of the right reasons."

If I was going to take on Janice Jensen I'd better have my shit together. I could render a clean evaluation only if I didn't need anything from her. If I did, I had no business on the case.

I remembered my adolescence clearly and without prejudice. I remembered it for what it was, the worst time of my life. A gangly, uncoordinated bag of conflicting hormones doesn't have an easy time. Janice Donahue had provided some exciting moments in an otherwise painful passage. Could I see her clearly despite my hormone-blurred past?

Kate interrupted my thoughts, knowing they could continue unabated for hours. "I need you to declare yourself. There's a show to be put on here. If you're in, we're set. We have Darling for fire and brimstone. He's point. We have you for warmth and light. Counterpoint. If you're out, tell me and I'll find another counterpoint."

"I've never seen this side of you."

"That's why I've never wanted us to work together. I was afraid you wouldn't like what you saw. I'm still afraid, but I'm willing to go through with it because it'll work so well. It will change things between us for the duration, but we won't lose anything. I have faith in our ability to handle it."

"I'm sure we can handle it."

"If your report is soft, I just won't use you. Here are the police reports and her admission physical. Not much, but enough to give you the idea. Do the criminal responsibility and we'll talk after."

"Tell me something, though. Do you like Janice?"

"I'd like to reserve judgment."

Kate always reserved judgment. I was formulating my next question when she turned the tables on me.

"Do *you* like her?" she asked foxily. "You used to. That much I know."

"What else do you know that I might be able to use?" I had dodged her question.

"I know that she wanted to marry you once upon a time. She told me. She said you went off to college and forgot her. She, on the other hand, did not forget you."

"That's news to me."

"Listen, Simon, my only real interest for the moment is to mount the best defense I can for her. Will you agree to evaluate her?"

"Yes."

I can taste bad judgment. It has a slightly musty flavor. My mouth tasted like rat shit.

It was a relatively peaceful Sunday in Manhattan, not one drive-by shooting the entire walk home. Tupelo investigated hydrants in silence while I went on freethink. It worked because by the time I reached home I didn't remember one single thought. I felt lighter without my anger at Kate.

It was three and Debby wasn't there. As far as I could tell, she hadn't been home yet. She would come and meanwhile I could browse through Kate's file on Janice. Kate was right; it wasn't much.

A handwritten note briefly outlined the content of their first interview.

Janice had, in fact, acknowledged the killings. At times she seemed blocked, unable to remember the events of the night in question. She apparently alternated between clear, detailed recall and periods of amnesia. She couldn't face what she'd done to her son.

The notes were sketchy, clearly not those Kate took in the interview itself. It was an abstract and one that divulged nothing, other than that Janice had spoken openly to her. I knew little more than I did before.

The initial police reports shed a little more light but fell short of completely illuminating the scene.

There was no evidence in the Jensen apartment of forced entry. In fact, there was no evidence that anyone other than the three principals was present at the time of the murders. Dennis, Janice's husband, was killed first, a fact ascertained from preliminary blood spatter studies. Janice had both Sean's and Dennis's blood on her clothes. The baby's appeared layered on top of her husband's. Dennis was covered in only his own blood, while Sean showed traces of Dennis's, supporting the hypothesis that Dennis had been murdered first. Janice's prints were on Dennis's service revolver, along with his own. The fish knife used on Sean yielded only Janice's prints.

Dennis had been shot while asleep on the sofa. The first bullet killed him; the other three were superfluous. Sean had been stabbed in his crib as he slept on his back. Again, the first wound was fatal, but he had been stabbed twelve additional times. Both were dead only a few minutes when the first officers answered the call, a 911 from a neighbor who'd heard the shots. The time was 11:52 P.M. Dennis had been killed shortly after getting home. His car was still warm when the officers arrived.

The rest of the police report was an attempt by a young beat cop to describe the bizarre behaviors that led him to diagnose Janice as "totally fucking gone." She hardly acknowledged his presence and when she did, she only repeated what he had said. He knew that this was called echolalia. She rocked, hummed to herself, and occasionally giggled. She was deeply involved in a one-sided conversation with an unknown participant, when she wasn't staring into space or giggling. He correctly labeled it hallucination.

Upon admission to the psychiatric wing of Bellevue under heavy police guard, she was found by the resident on duty to be "an attractive, apparently healthy Caucasian female." She was most definitely not oriented to time, place, or person. She was a drooling, quivering mass engaged in a violent argument with an unseen companion. She wailed. She cursed. She cried. But she never once responded to the doctor. It was like he wasn't there.

"Totally fucking gone," the cop's diagnosis, seemed right on the money.

The shrink's supposition, that Janice was otherwise healthy, was confirmed by the physical exam and blood and urine studies. Aside from a fair amount of psychoactive chemicals in her blood, she was indeed healthy. She showed no external bruises.

Janice was uncooperative, making the doctor's job nearly impossible. She would not allow the vaginal swabbing, thrashing violently when he tried to approach her. He gave up.

And that was all Kate had written. Except for the pictures, the ones the prosecution would pass to the jury, which would make most of them groan and some of them cry. The pictures that would help the defense as much as the prosecution because of their wrenching testimony to insane fury unleashed.

Dennis appeared sprawled on his back on the couch. He didn't have enough of a head left to identify him as a human being, just a body with a bloody stump at the top. Sean was nailed to his crib by a curved fish knife that penetrated his center. He looked like a bleeding note pinned to a bulletin board.

All preliminary, pending further reports. Insanity appeared to be the way to go. I closed the file so I wouldn't vomit on its contents.

For hours I sat in the window seat, staring out vacantly, my brain awash with images of my daughter cradling her daughter and the photo of Janice's son caught forever with a stake through his heart.

At around dinnertime the door clicked, responding to a key, bringing me back from the twilight zone. It was Tommy.

"What did you do to her?" he asked as he floated into the room. "And where's the bottle?"

"In the fridge. What did I do to whom?"

He brought in a bottle of Egri Bikaver, Hungarian red, poured himself a glass, held it up to the light, and quaffed it down. "Jensen," he said. "You saw her a mere . . . what?" He checked his watch. "Thirty-six hours ago?"

I nodded. "So what?"

"So she tried to kill herself tonight, that's what. Nice work."

The wraps were on for a while. Janice was on suicide watch, which meant they would check her breathing every ten minutes. If it stopped and they missed it, someone's underparts would be in a sling. It had already been embarrassing, but at least she was alive.

I take suicide seriously. I've worked on both sides of the fence, in suicide prevention, crisis phone calls and the like, and I have suffered the consequences of prevention failed.

To the suicide-line worker, the repeat attempters are a major irritation. Their cries for help sound like an infant's calls for attention. The repeaters usually get brushed aside in favor of someone in immediate trouble.

Worse than these suicide failures are the onetime success stories, the hope castrators. They call or come in, describe the pitiful emptiness of their lives, and buy the farm.

Somewhere in the middle rest the accidents, the substance abusers who don't intend to die. They simply like to get stoned, numbed out temporarily to whatever pain they can't tolerate. They die by miscalculation or desperation, sometimes both. I was widowed by such an accidental suicide, a fatal mistake.

I needed to know more about Janice's attempt. I called Kate for details. Janice was in for a nice rest after her shot at the big sleep. She'd popped an unknown amount of Valium, enough to knock her into next week, but not into the next world. I asked Kate if she knew where Janice got the pills. Kate didn't share my curiosity.

"That's your bailiwick, not mine. Why does it matter?"

I had no idea what Janice's intent had been. "I want to know what she was trying to say. And to whom."

"How the devil would I know what she was saying? You're the doctor."

"Look, there are a couple of obvious possibilities. They were her own private stash or somebody brought them to her. If they were her own, why did she have them along? I hear they have plenty of downers right there in the hospital and they're not reluctant to use them. What did she want?"

"Ask her," she said.

"Thanks, you're a big help."

I was getting nowhere with Kate. It was clearly time to stop ignoring the odious ream of yellowing papers that was Janice's documented psychiatric history. The pure volume of it was impressive. Over the years she had been to dozens of therapists of all varieties. She saw most of them for only a few sessions. She had done some long-term therapeutic work as a college student and once as a married adult, but her staying power was questionable.

The files did demonstrate a certain chronological integrity. Janice's early diagnoses were consistent, if soft. Acute Adolescent Reactions, what today would be called Conduct Disorders, peppered her evaluations. The category roughly describes teenagers who give their parents a hard time. I've never known anyone who didn't suffer some sort of Acute Adolescent Reaction, even if it wasn't identified. All part of growing up.

Janice had bouts with Nocturnal Enuresis, bedwetting, and briefly, after her mother's death, there was a series of Major Depressive Episodes. In college she traded these up for Anorexia Nervosa and Bulimia. She was a psychological innovator, well ahead of her time. Anorexia didn't get popular until Karen Carpenter.

During her early married life, fresh out of college, she smoothed out into the general category of neurosis, with a heavy emphasis on Histrionic Personality Disorders, part of the flock that keeps most suburban shrinks in their Beemers.

In roughly the past five years Janice had entered the big leagues with Chronic Schizophrenia. She had been hospitalized for short periods and stabilized, which meant that they gave her enough antipsychotic medication to down out New Jersey. And she had made five suicide gestures prior to this one, always Valium. She was a repeater.

I rechecked our senior year in high school and the year before that to get a better feel for the aftermath of her mother's death. She'd taken it hard, requiring maintenance doses of Elavil and Mellaril to keep her hovering above chronic depression. Janice had earned her first psychotic label as soon as her mother's voice returned from the grave.

What didn't make sense was my memory. If she was so disturbed when I knew her, how come I hadn't noticed it? I wasn't a psychiatrist yet, to be sure, but I wasn't blind, either. Janice Donahue had been an active, sociable, successful, undepressed young woman. If she was suffering, she was accomplished at hiding it. Or was I seeing only what I wanted, needed to see? Could my memory have been so clouded?

If I was confused, Janice wasn't. She had called it. Mixed nuts.

I would have to organize them, separate the cashews from the almonds, if I was going to testify. Mixed nuts wouldn't do.

Debby attempted a surreptitious entry at about eight. I was relieved by the sound of her key in the door, glad that she was home where she belonged. She seemed less than thrilled.

She kissed me on the cheek without letting me see her face. "I gotta take a shower."

I nodded. I know about showers. There are lots of good reasons to take them other than to remove postcoital goo. Maybe she was sweaty from her jog home, except that Debby didn't jog.

"Are you gonna yell?"

"About what?" I wasn't playing dumb. I didn't know what she thought I'd be mad about.

"Because I stayed out all night?"

"No." Whether I liked it or not, it was her right.

"Because I lied about Lisa?"

"No, but I would like to talk." It hadn't occurred to me that the lie itself was an issue. And it was Debby's issue. From our beginning she had insisted on truth.

"I'll be right back." She rushed off to the shower and was back in a record six minutes, looking wasted but cleaner.

"Simon, I'm sorry I dropped that bomb last night and walked out. Not cool and I know it." She assumed one of her "Let's talk" positions, a third-trimester fetal curl. "I guess that's the only way I could deal with telling you. You're not pissed?"

"No. I'm glad you told me. It explains a lot."

"Like what?"

"Like why you're having such a hard time with the guilt." I recognized the process. "And the dreams," I continued. "I see why you suffer with those dreams. Mothers are supposed to have supernatural powers over their children. Powers of life and death. You were supposed to save Lisa and you didn't." I knew the feeling well.

"And so you live with some nasty, abusive, self-hating guilt over what you imagine you could have done, despite the fact that you couldn't have done anything." I, myself, could have gotten home on time.

"But Debra, Lisa's place in your life didn't begin and end with her death. It feels that way now, but it won't always. You helped create and nurture her. She lived. Try to remember her life." After twenty years I was sometimes able to remember my lady as a living being who shared the road with me for a while. Mostly I remembered her death and how it destroyed me. I'd never solved that part of the grief process and so I was stuck there. It was unfair to both of us, robbing me of my memories and her of her integrity.

Debby's tears flowed freely now, and I was glad she allowed herself some relief. I'm not good at that part either.

I wanted to know stuff, my nature. "Tell me about the father. Were you in love with him?"

"Shit, no. It was a grope, Simon. At a drive-in, no less, in Jersey." She was embarrassed.

Having dispatched the fatherly duties, I went on to the shrink material. "What was it like to be a mother? What was Lisa like?"

"It was great. I loved it. I even loved being pregnant. Something good was coming out of me. The minute she popped out, and that's how it was, no pain, no screaming, she just popped out, I felt . . . good with myself." She paused, remembering.

"And none of the bad shit I read about came down. I didn't get bummed out. I didn't hate taking care of her. I loved it. I was a good mother, Simon, and she was a great kid."

"I'm glad. I think the good memories will make it easier in the long run. Hold on to them. They'll save you when it feels like nothing can." I said it nicely. I just couldn't do it.

She talked for two hours about herself and Lisa. About how Lisa was bright and full of it and how she crawled all over the house and about her first comical attempts to walk. Debby laughed and told stories and she was alive, vibrating. For a time she forgot how it ended.

As she ran out of steam and the rush of memories slowed, she asked me, "Will you throw me out if I fuck up?" What did she have in mind?

"No. I want you to stay. But if there are any more lies outstanding I wish you would clear them up now."

She looked doubtful, confused. "There aren't any more," she declared, less than convincingly. Much less. I decided not to pursue it for now.

"How was your date?"

"We drank wine and talked at his place. I like him, Simon, and I'm going to see him again. A lot, I hope. But don't worry. I still love you."

"I'm not worried. Can I meet him?" I pictured the scene where the father checks out the boyfriend.

"No."

"No? Are you kidding? Why not?"

"I want to keep him to myself. That's why not."

I would not challenge her. It didn't seem right. She went off to sleep and I sat in the window seat thinking about women in general and mothers in particular.

I couldn't get near Janice again. I couldn't get near her mother, either. That left her father.

Edward Donahue was not difficult to find, but then he wasn't hiding. Kate's secretary gave me his address. The Mohawk was sensible and correct, a family hotel that offered a rarity in New York, weekly rates. It wasn't the Pierre but it wasn't a crack house, either. It's what retired teachers have to look forward to, serviceable and next door to the Algonquin, which they can't afford.

I didn't call ahead. I didn't want to give Mr. Donahue a chance to study the files that retired teachers keep in their heads on former students.

When he was teaching me Shakespeare, he'd had a round body, three distinct balls stuck to each other by connective tissue, evoking roly-poly snowman images. Donahue was a decent-enough guy, mild, not one to humiliate kids. But he did have a certain institutional power, which he enjoyed exercising. He supervised and graded the senior theses, and a failing grade meant no graduation. For those of us in Honors English, a fake-leather-bound copy of our manuscript remained in the school library, and shame on our heads for eternity if we got less than a B.

I liked Donahue. I did my thesis on the Oedipal themes in *Hamlet*. Donahue enjoyed it, being a psychology buff. We had spent hours discussing it, and I got my A and fake leather binding.

A quarter century and three heart attacks had rearranged the snowman. The top snowball had become long and gaunt. His eyes receded significantly behind his glasses. Snowball number two had melted into number three so that he had poor Yorick's head on Dom DeLuise's body.

He wasn't glad to see me.

"Dr. Rose." He shook my hand and didn't invite me in. He used to call me Simon. "I have been instructed by counsel not to speak to anyone before the trial. I'm sorry, but I won't do anything to hurt my daughter." Who said you would?

"May I ask who gave that instruction? I work for Janice's counsel."

"I know, but Ms. Newhouse herself told me. And she didn't mention any exceptions. So I must . . ." He never finished the sentence but he managed to get the door closed in my face. I forgot the boot-in-the-door trick.

I was examining my nose for tip damage when the door opened again.

"I can't do this," he said, head down, ashamed. "I cannot treat an ex-student and friend in this abominable fashion even if she told me to. Come in, Simon. It's good to see you, considering the circumstances."

He led us to the sitting area, done in early understuffed hotel.

"It's not like inviting you into my home. Were you ever in my home?"

"Yes, a couple of times to talk about my thesis." He apparently didn't remember that Janice and I had had a brief fling.

"I'm sorry," he said. "Things haven't been normal lately and I'm feeling a little under it. It was nice of your father to offer his help. Or rather, yours. I'm desperate, Simon. I don't think I can stand to lose Jan, too."

I sympathized. The only remaining member of his family, and his jewel as I recalled, was about to be consigned to one hell or another.

"Mr. Donahue, it stands to reason that I can do a better job for Janice if you fill in some of the history that she can't give me." I had no reason to believe she couldn't provide what I needed. I wanted to hear his version.

"Well, if it's just history I can't see how that will hurt anything. That's all public information anyway. Go ahead, Simon. Maybe I can be of some use. I've been doing nothing but sitting and waiting."

Trying not to make a liar of myself, I kept the questions light and un-threatening. I asked about his wife's pregnancy: normal; Janice's birth: unremarkable; and her early months of life: all roses. Almost.

"Margery did drink some during her pregnancy, come to think of it, but that was before we knew it could harm the fetus." He hadn't just come to think of it. There was a whisper of blame in his voice.

"Did your wife drink heavily?"

"I don't know if I should be talking about this," he mumbled into his cardigan. "She drank, yes. Mostly in binges, but she was not an alcoholic in any sense of the word." He got nervous.

"Were you happy together? Did you have a good marriage?"

He lit up, a Christmas tree of memories. As he talked I could smell the turkey basting itself in the oven. And he didn't stop with Margery. Janice had never made him anything but proud. Their relationship was a mas-terpiece of father-daughter bonding. Good, warm American memories, and too many of them for my taste.

I interrupted, pure self-preservation. "How did your wife die? She was quite young." I thought I got it by him.

"Why would you ask about that?" His face hardened.

I didn't get it by him. He responded like a cornered animal sensing danger, wary and watchful.

"History, Mr. Donahue. It didn't appear in Janice's records and I'd rather not upset her right now." A lie, but believable.

"Of course. I'm sorry. It would be better if you heard it from me."

He described in coroner's detail the cause of his wife's demise, a cere-bral hemorrhage brought on by a fall, probably alcohol-induced. The fall had resulted in the meeting of her skull with the marble base of a favorite reading lamp. Donahue didn't mention the alcohol part. That was my idea.

He continued with a survivor's account meant for public consumption, the kind of recitation that ossifies through the years. All of it might have been true, or none of it: Janice couldn't take the stress; she had always been fragile and dependent on Margery; they'd been inseparable, real pals; her death was too much for Janice; she fell apart.

Donahue was hitting his stride when he abruptly stopped, as if he'd just noticed I was there. "I'm talking too much. I'm a tired old man and I think I've said more than I should. It's been very stressful, as I'm sure you can appreciate. I must ask you to leave, Simon. I apologize. I never should have . . ."

He got up to show me the door. I slipped in one more.

"Did you find Margery's body, Mr. Donahue, or was it Janice?"

It was one over the line.

"Why in the goddamn world would you ask such a thing? You have thoroughly abused my goodwill and I must insist that you leave." The words were civil enough, but the snarl and the intense, burning stare were fierce. Mr. Donahue had a nasty streak.

"Mr. Donahue, the event was enormously traumatic for Janice. If she happened to be the one who found her—"

I got my nose clear this time before he slammed the door.

In my line of work, no means yes, yes means no, and a door in the face is a slam-dunk.

Chapter Ten

J a n i c e and I spent eighteen hours together over a two-week period after the suicide watch was lifted. Spacing the sessions gives me time to think and plan, as each encounter has its own unique personality.

Had I come across Janice during my tenure as a state forensic drudge, I would have had none of the luxuries I enjoy as a private forensic consultant. I might have managed an hour for her evaluation because there would have been a father killer, a mother raper, and six other assorted felonious loonies waiting to be seen on the same day. But as a consultant I had all the time I wanted and could even test her if I thought it prudent.

Janice looked sparkling, showing no ill effects from her suicide gesture. Someone was dressing her up in a slightly more adult fashion. She resembled a secretary in a prestigious law firm, except for the bobby socks and penny loafers. Half girl, half woman.

She was relaxed and eager, as if she had long anticipated these talks and the time had finally come. Occasionally, she became irritable and touchy when we got too close to her mother, but she quickly dominated her unruly emotions.

We started off with history.

People paint their childhood experiences in either pink or black, all petunias or pure hell. Many pretend to have forgotten that they were ever children. Some really have.

Janice's memories of the first twelve years of her life were sparse. Occasional warm fuzzies dotted her childhood desert, but the time was essentially spent in training for real life, the onset of puberty. The family moved around a lot, necessitating adjustments to new schools. Janice saw the changes as empowering. "It made me tough," she said.

Her mother dominated the landscape, a kind, gentle, helping soul who tended toward overcontrol. "She never let me out of her sight," which Janice took as a challenge. She was forever playing hide-and-seek in department stores, the game ending when a furious Margery Donahue heard herself paged over the public address system between the sale in lingerie and the closeout in home furnishings.

"I was kinda mischievous," Janice confided with a slight grin.

Her mischief gradually matured from disappearing games to a fascination with the wonders of flame.

"Did you just play with matches or did you actually set fires?" I asked.

"Small fires," she admitted.

No wonder Margery never wanted to let Janice out of her sight.

The Early Memories Test is a sneaky little instrument devised to evoke either a real or fantasied incident. I remember one woman who recounted in detail her journey down the birth canal and a man whose earliest memory was the previous evening. That's why I like the instrument, lots of variety. The single most striking image from Janice's formative years surfaced in response to the EMT.

"I was standing in the doorway of my parents' room. Mom was asleep propped up on pillows. Her book was open and lay face down across her chest. She had on a black silk mask covering her eyes, so the light wouldn't wake her. She even put in ear plugs so my fuffling wouldn't bother her. That's what she called it, the noise I made, 'fuffling.' I remember wishing she would wake up. I needed her, I don't remember for what. Maybe I just wanted her to be with me."

"How old were you at the time?"

"Four or five. I had Teddy with me. I carried him around like a baby 'til she took him away from me when I started first grade. She said it was time I grew up."

Puberty proved more fertile ground. In Janice's mind her real life began at age thirteen.

"I was so excited to be in junior high and finally grown up," she said. "I was popular, I mean, the boys liked me. They said I was pretty and they fought over me, stuff like that. Juvenile.

"And it just got better and better. I went steady twice in freshman year. Did you know that?"

"No, I didn't." I hadn't met her yet.

"Yes, and three times in sophomore year, and finally, in junior year, I met Will out at the lake and we got pinned. That's the year Mom died." She paused, gathering herself. "I took it hard. She was very important to me. I think she *was* me."

"What do you mean?"

"We're very complicated, my mother and me. She was very strict, you know what I mean? She picked all my clothes so I would look as pretty as I could. 'If you look pretty, you feel pretty,' she used to say. And she planned my meals so I wouldn't get fat. She said, 'A fat girl is an unhappy girl.' She gave me lessons in etiquette and she taught me how to talk to boys. I was shy. And everything she did, she did so that I would have a happy life and never be lonely. She was my best friend."

It sounded like Margery had been a typical stage mother, her goal in life to perfect her offspring so she'd be more salable. Most children of stage mothers deeply resent the manipulation. The message is that you're not good enough. "Did you ever get angry at her?" I asked.

"Are you kidding? I told you she was my best friend."

"Best friends get mad at each other."

"No. It would have been like getting mad at myself. I was part me and part her. Sometimes I was the mother and she was the daughter. Like when she was sick and I had to take care of her."

"Was that when she'd been drinking?"

Janice pierced me with a murderous glare. Right between the eyes.

"I'm trying to explain it to you. You're not listening. We were like one person. When she died I felt like half of me was gone. I started going to hospitals. You read all that, didn't you?"

"Yes, but according to the records you started going to hospitals *before* your mother died."

"Oh, yeah, I did, but it wasn't 'cause I was sick. I was wild. I was into a lot of drinking and running around. My mother was worried but I wasn't sick, not yet. That all started after Mom died."

"How were things for you senior year, the year we knew each other?"

"I was in bad shape, totally depressed. They put me on a lot of meds, antidepressants and stuff to turn off the voices. But you wouldn't know because I decided not to show it. If I was going to be popular in my new school I couldn't be depressed. So I didn't show it and I kept Will. We were together almost the whole year. You remember that at least, don't you?"

"Yes, I remember that."

"You were next. You said you remembered."

"I do."

"You really helped me, do you know that?"

"How?"

"I was hurt real bad after Will. I really needed help, for my confidence, you know. And you were great. You were my anchor. I needed to stop acting so crazy. I don't think I would have made it without you. I have a lot to thank you for." So I had been her pillow.

"You're welcome."

"How did you get the Valium in here?" I motioned vaguely at the hospital's vastness. "Don't they search you? They did examine you, didn't they?"

"I don't remember. But it didn't matter. I put them in my . . ." She pointed to what she couldn't say.

"You smuggled Valium in here in your vagina?"

"That's it. I hate that word. It's so clinical."

"Why did you smuggle in the Valium?"

"I didn't know how bad things would get. Sometimes I can see real clear and then I hate myself." The ring of truth.

"Did you think you were going to die? Did you want to?"

"Yes. This time I was sure I took enough of that stuff. I was real surprised when I woke up." The first out-and-out lie she had told me.

"Why did you want to die?"

"Wouldn't you, if you were me?"

"You never mention your father," I pointed out one day.

"Oh, he was part of it all right. It's just that he wasn't as strong as my mother. He's kind of wimpy. We don't really respect him. He isn't a bad guy. He was real nice to me after Mom died, real nice. But it didn't make him strong. He sort of faded out."

"Did it make you strong?"

"Everything that happens to me makes me stronger. Mom says so and I believe it. I really do. I have to."

We cruised through her college years at Bennington, more social and academic successes, more short-term hospitalizations, and more trips on Club Meds. And then came Dennis Jensen, a night student at the University of Vermont and an ex-marine, hence war hero to Janice.

Dennis swept her off her feet. He wore his uniform often when they were together. She thought it was sexy. He dropped out of college but traded up for a new uniform, this time NYPD blue, and still sexy. They got married and life took a turn.

"It's no fun being a cop's wife, no fun at all. Especially NYPD. It's the worst, which is why Dennis wanted it." She wrinkled her nose.

"I could write a book about it. You sit home a lot, while he's out all hours doing stuff. When he did come home he was always pissed off and frustrated and he always took it out on me. He hit me, not just once, either. And hard." She rocked back and forth as she spoke.

"It was horrible. I was always bored. I worked at this and that, but he had all the thrills, if you can call them that. He was a desk jockey most of the time. Do you know that in all those years he never fired his gun on patrol? Not once. Oh, sure, he practiced at the range and won some trophies, but he never used it in real life."

Janice did.

"I don't think I ever enjoyed myself. And to top it off he got me pregnant. By force. He fucking raped me one night before I could get my diaphragm in. I didn't want kids. We'd managed to avoid it for years. We had no family life. Why bring a child into it at our age?

"That's when Mom got real mad at me. I think she didn't want me to have a kid. Or maybe she was just mad that I got myself raped. Or maybe she was jealous, I don't know. But she yelled at me the whole time I was pregnant. She called me stupid. She told me I should have known better, and . . ." She was rocking again, faster this time.

"She was at me constantly. Do this. Do that. Nothing I did was good enough. She wouldn't let me out of her sight. She didn't use to be like that." I thought she was exactly like that.

"How was she when you first started hearing her?" I wanted to know more about this voice that permeated her life.

"Oh, at the beginning it was just like when she was alive. She was helpful. She gave me advice and solved my problems.

"Did you know I started hearing her when she was still alive, but in another room? I'd have long talks with her, usually about boys. I was so embarrassed one day when I realized she wasn't there, I almost died." She covered her face with splayed fingers.

"Where was she?"

"Sleeping, in their bedroom."

"Was she sleeping because she'd been drinking?" It was worth a second try, so I tried it.

"She was just sleeping." Janice stopped and refused to start again that day.

"How did your mother change when you got pregnant?" Something significant is going on when the quality of the hallucinations changes from benevolent to malevolent, and it's not a good prognostic sign.

"She got so critical. And nasty. She turned into a shrew. And then I had to do what she said."

"Why?"

"'Cause if I didn't she'd get mad and yell at me all the time, day and night. I hate it when she yells at me."

"Do you always do what she tells you?"

"I do now. I have to. Once I disobeyed her, but that was ten years ago." She blushed.

"Will you tell me about it?"

"Well, I can't tell you all of it. It was about sex."

I figured I could handle it, so I nodded for her to continue.

"I did something she told me never to do. It was with Dennis, so don't be thinking anything funky. But she specifically told me not to do it and I did it anyway." She licked her lips.

"And what happened?"

"She called me whore and cunt and she wouldn't stop screaming at me."

"For how long?"

"Seven years."

Chapter Eleven

I w a s pretty sure I had exhausted all the available conscious avenues. More questions would not yield new insights. A Rorschach would. I asked Janice if she minded looking at some inkblots with me.

"Don't you have the one I did for Dr. Krueger? It was my best one."

I hadn't seen any Rorschach protocol among her records. "Your best one?"

"Well, I don't mean best. I mean most creative. Usually I just see blots. That time I saw all kinds of stuff. I've taken it lots of times. It's fun."

I wanted corroboration, and the Rorschach opens up otherwise closed doors. If she was hiding anything I'd find it. We agreed that I would return with my bag of tricks.

I rarely use psychological tests because most of them are bullshit. Projective testing, the exception, is too costly and time-consuming. An entire battery can take six to eight hours to administer. And the time to interpret the results is incalculable. It's a vestigial art, priced out of the market. But I still love the work.

The Rorschach is the psychological laser that, in the hands of a skilled examiner, achieves true penetration. It is revealing, insidious, and effective if you want an X-ray of somebody's psychic innards. I was aware that Janice was a veteran, but that didn't matter. People change, what they see changes, and what they see reveals who they are. Simple.

And the Rorschach is unfakable. It cannot be deceived. It sees right through your defenses.

Ten white cardboard rectangles hold ten images, erroneously referred to as inkblots. They are not. They are complicated designs done mainly in shades of gray, but there is color in five of the cards. And they are not folded-over mirror images of themselves. While the shapes are clearly divided into two sides, they are not symmetrical. The possibilities are infinite, and no two protocols are ever the same. It's an adventure.

And it's relatively easy to administer. Subjects are tested one at a time. My job as examiner is to observe and record; the interpretation comes later. The subject sits on my left and I hand over a card. I then ask, "What do you see? Describe it for me." Most people find two or three images of interest in each card, thirty or so responses for the whole set. Next, I check each response to verify that I am seeing the teddy bears where the subject saw them. Additions, revisions, and new details pop up during the location run. I also record these.

For me, it's like listening to the secret music of the soul. It is undeniably intimate, permitting entry into the subject's most private and guarded places. The responses form a psychological collage that is so powerful and accurate, it is positively frightening. Kate called it magic.

"I hope we're going to start with the blots. They're my favorite. I see tons of stuff."

"Yes, we are," I said, removing the cards from their box. I flipped through them to be sure they were in order.

Janice grabbed the cards from my hands. She leafed through them one at a time, selecting the one she wanted to respond to.

I interrupted her browsing. "Janice, I prefer to administer the test in the standard sequence. It makes it easier for me."

"Oh, loosen up, Simon. That's what you tried to teach me once. Let's go crazy. I'll do them all, but in a different order."

She was taking control of the testing in a way I'd never encountered before. She would choose the cards, Hermann Rorschach's order be damned. Live a little.

I'd had peculiar experiences with the Rorschach in my day. Several subjects refused to say anything at all. A teenager once threw a card out the nearest window. A very upset psychotic even tried to eat one of the cards. But never had anyone taken them all from me and perused them, like a *Vogue* magazine, to choose her favorites. Always an adventure.

"Okay, Janice. We'll try it your way." There was no point in making this a battle of wills. Her maneuver was duly noted and put away for subsequent consideration.

She chose card ten, the last card, the wildest card of all. It displays some twenty distinct colorful shapes, interconnected, depending on how you see it, but everything depends on how you see it.

"This is the one I was looking for. It's loaded." She neatly stacked the other nine cards face down to her left, out of my reach. "Let's see. The blue thing in the middle is a brassiere. You can see the nipples sort of sticking out here." She pointed to the nipples. "These two big pink things are babies, sucking on the bra, which I think symbolizes the mother. This gray thing here is biting the mother's back. If the blue thing is a bra, that would make the green wormy thing her vagina." She had conquered her shyness and now could say the word. "And that's an orange wishbone, just hanging out there in space. The two things standing on the babies' heads are beetles trying to get unstuck from the babies. These blue blobs are amoebas. The orange things over here are blood stains, but they don't have anything to do with the rest of the picture. The yellow parts over here . . ."

And so she went, responding to every detail, sometimes combining them into little stories, using a small part of the image. "These are green worms. No, they're caterpillars. They'll probably grow up to be beautiful butterflies if this blue thing doesn't eat them. I think the blue things are going to win." Finally, she made the whole card into an entire underwater world, filled with tropical fish and manta rays. When she stopped I had an impressive thirty-seven responses.

But she wasn't finished.

She took the card, rotated it clockwise ninety degrees, and started again. The "bra" turned into "blue tears," the "pink babies" turned into "melting strawberry ice cream," the "gray thing biting the mother's back" turned into "an old wrinkled tadpole." Every detail became something else. Every emotion, every nuance, altered to fit a new scheme. What was she doing?

She slowed down, and I thought we had a prayer of seeing another card. Instead, she rotated it another ninety degrees, now upside down in relation to its original position, and started again, all new, all different. When she finally finished with the only card she had yet responded to, I had eighty-three responses. An hour and a half had passed.

She continued that way with each card she picked. She saw mothers, babies, little creatures eating bigger creatures, blood, body fluids, an occasional penis, usually unattached. And vaginas everywhere, either grabbing, holding, or eating, eighteen of them, a personal record for me.

Each time she rotated a card to a new position, everything changed. Happy turned to sad, afraid to enraged, alive to dead. Janice saw countless neonates of various species, most of them ingested by something related to them. On card three, where two red blobs hang from a connected blood-red cord, she saw "fetuses, in utero," and she proceeded to show me in excruciating detail how the two were different, both females, but different. One of them "wouldn't make it." Card four, nicknamed the father card because it is dark gray and menacing, made her laugh. She said it was "melted rubber, probably old galoshes being recycled into something useful."

She was indefatigable, renewing her energy at will. She never tired of hearing herself free-associate. The volume of her responses was overwhelming, as was the amount of blood and gore, dominance and sadism, violence and pain, that populated her fantasies. By the time she finished all ten cards, it was seven hours later, and she had produced four hundred and sixty-three responses. My previous record had been a meager one hundred twenty in four hours, but that subject had suffered from cerebral palsy.

Before leaving I tested some limits, probing sensitive areas to see how deep the lesions went. I asked if, all in all, she had come from a loving family, and she painted Christmas trees rivaling her father's. I reminded her of her mother's drinking problem and she shut down with an audible hiss. I asked how she felt when she found her mother's body and she almost ran out of the room.

I had had enough.

But Janice wasn't done yet.

"Simon, you know, I have faith. It's all going to work out for the best."

"I hope so." I wasn't sure what the best would be.

"You know why?"

"Why?"

"Because you're back with me." She squeezed my arm as though she were admiring a well-developed bicep. I don't have one. "You're my anchor again."

"Janice, please tell me what happened the day Dennis and Sean died. Tell me about the whole day, anything you can remember." The official inquiry began.

She straightened up in her chair and smoothed her skirt, ready to recite the lesson.

"Where should I start, in the morning when I got up?"

I nodded.

"Okay." A big chest-heaving sigh. "I slept real late, maybe eleven. Dennis was on days so he fed Sean and changed him in the morning so I could sleep. He left him in the crib. Sean was getting better. His lungs were almost clear, only a gurgle left. He could amuse himself in there for hours." She laughed, an uncomfortable combination of gaiety and shame. She didn't want to appear a negligent mother.

"I didn't always have my mornings for lolling around in bed. I had a job." She stopped.

I bit. "Tell me about it."

"I worked for the city, in a shelter for the homeless. Oh, Simon, it was so sad, all those people living in the streets, never taking a bath. It was horrible." She wrinkled her nose, and I couldn't tell if it was their pitiful state or their odor that disgusted her.

"I was good at it, social work. I'm empathic, if you know what I mean. So they talked to me and I could help them get jobs, find places to live, like that." She turned grim. "I really like helping people. But they fired me because Sean got sick, and that sucks." She seemed to toy with the idea of a full-blown fit, but decided to control herself. She bit her lower lip.

She had maneuvered us away from the day in question, which I took as permission to roam.

"Did you breast-feed the baby?" I asked.

She clamped her hands to her chest. "God, no." A shiver. "I couldn't handle it. No way." Enough said.

"Go on with the day," I chided gently.

"So I got up and took a bath. Since I'm unemployed . . ." She let out a minor-league growl. "It doesn't matter when I get up. I love to bathe in the morning. It's my one luxury. Then I did the wash. There's tons of it. We can't afford a diaper service so I do it all, but I don't mind because I get to carry Sean around with me. I've got one of those baby carriers that lets you have him right up against you in the front." She cuddled an imaginary baby to her breast and rocked slightly. She looked serene, unaware of her ambivalent feelings about her breasts and mothering.

"So we did the laundry and then we watched the soaps. I know they're stupid, but I like them anyway. They're more like real life than mine." Sadness, regret, maybe a touch of depression.

"Then I took a little nap with Sean and got up to cook. For once, Dennis was coming home for dinner. He promised, so I fixed his favorite, spaghetti and meatballs with fresh mushrooms, not from the can.

"Then I put Sean to sleep and put on a dress that Dennis loves. It's got buttons down the front . . . never mind, it turns him on." She blushed slightly. "And I waited."

She began to rock.

"And I waited and waited. He'd promised. Then I got mad. Damn him! I took off the dress and threw it on the floor. I put on my grubbies. I'd been getting sloppier lately. It usually means I'm prodromal." Psychotic states are often preceded by a period of slow slippage from health to craziness. Most of the world wouldn't know what to call it, but Janice was a veteran.

"That's when Mom started in on me. She hates it when I mistreat my good clothes. 'Pick it up, bitch. Can't you do anything right? You've become a total loss. And it's all because of him. Why don't you leave him? Show some guts, for Christ's sake. Throw him out! Get him out of your life!'"

She rocked more quickly, agitated.

"She wouldn't stop. 'Do something, bitch! Make him disappear!'"

Janice's face blanked out, a death mask. The rest would not be fun.

"Dennis came home around eleven. He'd been with another woman, I knew. I can smell it, lilacs and jism.

"And he got pissed off 'cause the spaghetti sauce was burned and the house was a mess. He slapped me around good."

Tears welled up, anger or sadness, hard to tell.

"Where did he hit you?"

"All around here." She indicated her midsection, kidneys and thighs. "He doesn't like to leave marks. He thinks I'm pretty.

"And then he went to sleep on the couch. He wasn't even hungry, probably ate before he came home." She said it like it was something dirty.

"Mom started up again. 'Do something for yourself for once in your life. Make him disappear!'" She shuddered.

"Mom got more and more upset. She used bad language, which wasn't like her, usually. 'Listen to me, bitch! It's easy and it won't hurt. Go on! Do it!'" Janice looked me straight in the eyes as only crazy people can.

"And I did it."

"How?"

"Do I have to?" she asked timidly. "Of course I do." She smoothed herself again. "I took his revolver and followed Mom's orders. She got very specific. I did what she told me.

"I cocked the thing and put it right in his ear, the one facing the coffee table. Mom said, 'Do it! Pull the trigger!' He woke up for a second but I squeezed the trigger just like he taught me. Never pull, always squeeze. He jumped a little, but Mom was right. It didn't hurt. Then I turned his head. It was all gooey, but I did it anyway. I put the barrel in his other ear and did it again. He didn't feel it.

"I couldn't look at him. His eyes were all bulgy and he was staring at me, like a dead trout. I couldn't handle it.

"Mom said, 'Put his eyes out. He can't see you anyway.' So I did, one shot in each eye, and he didn't stare at me anymore. That's it. I went to the kitchen to wash my hands. There was lots of blood. Then I went back to the living room and ate all the grapes I bought just for him. I didn't have to share them or anything." She stopped, the unpleasantness now behind her.

"Aren't you leaving something out?"

"You mean Sean, don't you?"

That's what I meant.

"I don't remember. I'm not sure, I'm really not. They said someone used the fish knife, for God's sake. It couldn't have been me. I don't remember much after I went to the kitchen."

"Could you have gotten the scaling knife?"

"I suppose I could've," she said, resigned. "There wasn't anybody else there, so they tell me. I know I went to check Sean. I always check him. Maybe I did do it."

"What do you think?" I thought she knew.

"It must have been me. I can't believe it." She cried real tears.

"What happened next, after you ate the grapes?"

"The cops came. I thought they were coming to pick Dennis up for something. They took me instead."

■

"At the time you shot him, Janice, did you realize that what you were do-ing was wrong?"

"I did what I had to do. I did what Mom told me. I made him disap-pear. It didn't even hurt."

"Isn't killing wrong?" Maybe keeping it abstract would yield a higher moral judgment.

"Sometimes, sure. But not always. He deserved it. Mother said so."

"Why didn't you stop yourself?"

"Mom would've killed me."

No elbow test today. I would not ask her what she would have done if there had been a policeman present. Dennis was a cop.

"Simon, I don't know. Either I did it or she did it or we did it. I wasn't myself. She was."

"Look, you want the truth? I'm not sorry he's dead. I'm only sorry I did it. It should have been one of his junkie friends on the street. He deserved to die in the street. And I deserve to die in the hospital. And not for Den-nis. For Sean.

"But don't worry, Simon. I won't try to kill myself again. I deserve to die, but not that way. It's too easy."

Yo u don't look so good," I said to Debby. She could be vibrant and lustrous one minute, washed out and featureless the next, if her mood took a dip. Her face was pale and pasty.

"I'm surprised you noticed. You've been drooped over your legal pad looking like Tupelo when she gets yelled at."

"Tupelo never gets yelled at," I said, but the admonition was duly noted. I was missing something.

I had been working on the Jensen report. I'm careful, almost meticulous, about my reports, one of my weaknesses as well as one of my strengths. The reports are public record, and I hate making an ass of myself in public. I'd rather do that in private.

I had been mentally masturbating the report, brooding over it, sweating it. The words were stuck in my fingers, doing a superb imitation of hysterical paralysis.

Debby floated in and out of my personal field, but for days I had been too involved with Janice to notice much of anything. Now that I did, I got worried. I put the legal pad down.

"Are you sick?" I asked, genuinely, if belatedly, concerned.

"No, I just got a lot on my mind." She let it dangle.

"Like what?"

"Like Bobby and what we're into, relationship stuff."

"You're not telling me anything." I was being impatient.

"I don't know . . ." She ended up mumbling into her armpit.

I should have listened, but I was overwhelmed by an attack of parenting. I got suspicious and accusatory, a helpful combination.

"Are you doing drugs?" My evidence was flimsy; she looked tired. But I was willing, nonetheless, to set aside good sense and open my mouth.

I expected righteous indignation and I got a confession instead.

"We've been doin' some lines and a few joints, but mostly wine. I guess we've been overdoing it."

"Debra, that's not like you at all." Sure it was, she just finished telling me. Parents aren't necessarily intelligent.

"It's just that Bobby likes to get high and he likes it better if I join him. I kind of like it." She shook her head. "No, I don't."

"But you do like him."

"I don't think that covers it. I think I'm in love and it scares the shit out of me." I could get into that.

"And what about him? Is he in love?"

"I think so. That's what worries me." I could get into that, too. "Among other things."

I returned to the drugs. "Debra, being in love doesn't mean you give up making choices. Maybe you can find a way to be with him without sharing the drugs." Nancy Reagan couldn't have said it better.

"Look who's talking. My father, the ex-pot-smoking aging hippie chocolate addict."

Ouch. I suspected my own habits would get thrown in my face someday. Debby knew that I had had a long and lovely relationship with marijuana, but that wasn't the point. Debby's relationship with drugs was the point.

"I'm not saying that you should become a chocolate addict. I'm not even offering an alternative. I'm leaving that to you. I am suggesting that sometimes drug use is a bad idea. Like when you're not at full strength or you're stressed out. You can end up in tunnels that always lead to your most vulnerable spots. You can get lost in those tunnels and then you're screwed. It's happened to me."

"When?"

"After my lady died."

She thought that over. "What did you do?"

"I flushed my stash down the toilet and haven't smoked since."

She thought that over, too, and softened. "I'm sorry I called you names. Not very adult. You're not really aging anyway, more like lovably mature. I'll work it out. And thanks. I'll let you write."

She left me to my labors. Her easy acquiescence could only mean one thing. I had missed another point.

Kate called to tell me that the trial date was set for the coming week. She needed my report for a meeting of the defense team the following day.

But the words were stuck.

It shouldn't have been a close call. I didn't know why I was having such a hard time.

On one level, the only one I needed to be operating on, Janice clearly met the criteria to be adjudicated Not Guilty by Reason of Insanity. Given the police report of her behavior when they arrived, her own account of the events, and her formidable psychiatric history, it would not be a difficult position to defend. She was out to lunch when the police got there, had been in and out for years, and she was not in control of herself at the time of the murders. Legally, she had it nailed.

Janice wasn't a legal problem for me. It was much more personal. I wasn't seeing her clearly.

I went over it again.

Her earliest memory revealed a lonely child shut out by her mother. Mom, propped up in bed with a book covering her chest, the nurturance center, and with her eyes and ears, her receptors, either screened or stuffed to insure isolation. Margery Donahue was hermetically sealed to her daughter.

It was no coincidence then that the wounds Janice inflicted on her husband and child were directed at the very same areas, Dennis's eyes and ears and Sean's chest. Janice was speaking to us through her actions, striking back at an overinvolved yet unavailable mother, someone who was always there and never there. She was trying to solve some deeply ingrained psychological puzzle with her violence. And if her demons were not satisfied, more violence could be expected.

Janice and her mother were, as she said, a complicated pair, taken separately or together. Together they were also deadly.

By all rights Janice should have been furious with the controlling, manipulative tyrant who, alive or dead, hounded her. Why did she cling to the illusion that Margery was her best friend? Perhaps she was too frightened of her mother's power to be angry at her. But of course she was angry anyway, and what she did to Dennis and Sean was the result of a spec-tacular displacement.

I was sure the Rorschach protocol held the key to Janice's evaluation, but I didn't get enough time to do it justice. One should approach it as a blind outsider, but in this case I was neither blind nor outside. It had taken me days to wade through the data and I was drowning.

In Janice's inner world one had to overcome unfathomable odds in or-der to simply survive, a good reason to pay attention to detail, something Janice did without fail. Control was her issue and manipulation was the preferred method.

She controlled the test situation from the outset, appropriating my very tools and using them in her own way. She also controlled me, keep-ing me glued to her, writing down her every utterance for almost eight hours, a narcissist's dream. And Janice was nothing if not narcissistic. Af-ter four-hundred-plus responses, it was obvious that the person she loved best in the world was herself.

If control was the goal and manipulation the method, then sex was the vehicle. Her eighteen vaginas chewed, swallowed, smiled, and cried, crea-tures with lives of their own. Sex for Janice was a weapon, the modality of her conquests. She manipulated with her sexuality as if her life depended on it. Maybe it did.

Naturally, sex was never too far removed from violence. The only ref-erence to tenderness in her protocol, elephants kissing on card two, was immediately followed by blood spurting from an open wound, a bleeding vagina. Intimacy for Janice was like a knife through the heart.

She squashed lives as easily as a boot dispatches a cockroach. Her pro-tocol was so awash in violence that it was impossible for me to decipher the nuances in so short a time.

Given her recent history, the amount of death and destruction in her head was not surprising. But the way she processed information was. I was extremely disturbed by her habit of turning the cards ninety degrees and beginning anew. A true Darwinist, Janice created a world in which everything was in constant evolution, changing from one state to another, one being to another. Pink babies became strawberry ice cream, bras be-came tears. All with the turn of a card. Janice simply changed her world to suit her whims.

She didn't want what the rest of us want, but it was because she didn't get what the rest of us got. Children need a sense of security. Janice had never felt safe. Children need to know they're loved. Janice had been deprived when it counted. She didn't know what she felt other than damaged.

Life would have been easier for me if she would just sit still. If she would either remain a sad, degenerating schizophrenic or settle on an evil sociopathic monster, I could have handled it. But she was like liquid searching for a container. And I was unable to pin her down.

Besides the outline of a very fragile psyche, I couldn't tell what I was seeing. Was this psychosis or prime sociopathy? I longed for more time, to meditate properly on the Rorschach.

And how did the murders come down?

There's Dennis, asleep on the couch, exhausted from his day's work near the action while Janice waits at home, bored stiff, for her dose of attention. When he fails to provide her fix, the rage is unleashed.

The baby boy, a product of a real or imagined rape, is an intolerable weight on Janice's fractured psyche. Infants make demands. Janice doesn't have anything to give, being too needy herself. She eliminates the object in need, eliminating at the same time the competition for the small amount of attention going around. There will be no more demands on her body. No more caressing, no more pawing.

Janice doesn't seem to know what her breasts are for, is obsessed with vaginas, and blushes at the thought of oral sex.

That's not how I remembered her at all.

The most formidable obstacle to producing a fleshed-out psychological IdentiKit of Janice Donahue Jensen was my memory. I had known her at another time, in a different world.

When a picture doesn't come clear it's either because the subject doesn't make sense, a psychological impossibility, or because the eyes of the beholder are clouded. Static in the receiver. Static that leads to errors of perception and judgment.

In the trade it's called ambivalence. In English it's called mixed feelings.

I felt power over her and I liked it. Here was the most popular girl in the class, the unreachable star that I had once reached and then lost. And she had hurt me in the only way possible at that age. Deeply.

And now I had the power. I could help send her to prison for a long time or I could help her find temporary shelter in a hospital from which she would emerge, probably unscathed. Will Hardin couldn't hold a candle to me now.

Unclean. Unfinished business. And whether my ambivalence stemmed from an ancient need to possess her or from some current reality made little difference.

The cloud would not lift.

Kate commanded the meeting from the head of the conference table, with a law clerk at her side taking notes. That left Brice Darling and me eyeing each other across the table. Not a face I wanted to face.

When we had been served our coffee by a youthful male secretary, Kate raised her hand as if calling to order a much larger gathering.

"We're here to discuss strategy. Or rather, we're here for me to lay out the strategy and see where you fit in." She glanced at both of us. Even though no words had been spoken, it was clear from the ionic buzz in the room that Rose and Darling were not in harmony.

His Brooks Brothers suit hung like pearls on a pig's neck. His dark hair was parted in the middle and greased back. The tips of his handlebar mustache were greased, too. A well-dressed can of Spam.

He probably didn't care for my Grateful Dead T-shirt either.

"Strategy is hardly the word for it, actually," Kate continued, after removing her glasses and rubbing her eyes. "You gentlemen are essentially the whole case. I want you to compare notes and see if we are of one mind."

Neither of us volunteered anything, so Kate facilitated. "I dislike surprises. Dr. Darling's report is clear and strong. Paranoid Schiz, NGRI. Are you shakable, Brice?"

He grinned like a rodent and shook his head.

I watched Kate writing something down so I wouldn't have to waste eye contact on Darling.

Kate turned to me. "Dr. Rose." The last time she called me Dr. Rose she'd humiliated me in a courtroom. "I have not as yet received your report, so I must ask you if you concur."

"I do." I had spent time thinking about how to say this. "But I will not be writing a report to that effect, not to the court, at least. And I won't be able to offer testimony.

"I've had reservations from the beginning about my participation in this case. I knew Mrs. Jensen a long time ago. Our relationship, for a time, could not have been called casual. We were involved. This fact has made it impossible for me to provide you with an untarnished opinion regarding Mrs. Jensen. So I'm out."

"This is rather sudden," she lied for Darling's benefit. The show had begun. "Do you possess any information that bears on the case?"

"I regret any inconvenience I may have caused you. I'm not hiding anything. I don't believe that my relationship with Mrs. Jensen relates in any way to your case, nor should it. It was a long time ago. But the fact of my previous knowledge of the defendant simply means that I must withdraw. I'm compromised."

Darling chuckled, undoubtedly to irritate me. He was about to formulate an appropriately tasteless crack, but clamped his teeth together before letting it loose. It could have been denture lock.

Kate didn't find any of this amusing. She had to recast the show. "I'm sorry that you will be unable to work with us, Dr. Rose. Fortunately, I have an expert in reserve who will render us a usable opinion regarding Mrs. Jensen's criminal responsibility. If you will excuse us, we have a trial to prepare for." I was suddenly not sorry to be out of the script.

No one spoke. I was expected to make a gracious exit. Kate had turned to her notes. Darling, who had yet to say a word, offered his hand. I shook it and went to the bathroom to wash up.

Chapter Thirteen

Th e trial answered the question "What if they gave a war and nobody came?" It was orderly, noncombative, and positively polite. It lacked even a trace of color until Janice added a splash of her own.

The spectacle was staged in a musty, airless courtroom. The gallery was all but nonexistent. Debby, Tommy, and I sat to the right of the aisle. Ed Donahue shared the other side with a woman typing furiously on a laptop, three apparently unrelated men, probably reporters, and two elderly women who were munching sandwiches wrapped discreetly in their hankies. The senior citizens were the courtroom groupies, regulars attracted to any trial involving death or dismemberment. They got bored early by the procedural nature of the Jensen trial and left to seek a more massive murder somewhere down the hall. They missed all the fun.

Janice sat at the defense table next to Kate like a frozen Barbie doll. She shot a peek our way, drumming her fingers in the air by way of greeting. Kate admonished her and she turned back, as if she had been caught passing notes in class.

Jury selection proceeded mechanically with neither side using any of its challenges. The consensus was that a reasonably educated middle-of-the-road jury suited everyone's needs. The issues were medical and arcane; the testimony would be almost exclusively expert. Seven women and five men, African-American, white, and Hispanic, were seated along with two alternates. The attorneys were satisfied.

Janice made eye contact with each juror, lingering on the men. She wore a tailored suit and had her hair pulled back off her face, open and sincere. She didn't wave to the jurors, but instead let her eyes do the talking. She was flirting with them.

During the prosecutor's presentation she amused herself with a pad and pencil, provided for writing notes to counsel. She never wrote anything, but she tapped the pencil on the paper continuously, giving the proceedings a peculiar arrhythmic heartbeat.

Patrick Flannigan, Assistant D.A., the lamb sent to this particular slaughter, was in an unenviable position. There is no glory in convicting a clearly disturbed, attractive white middle-class woman of a brutal double murder. He was, however, expected to put up a good show of fervor on behalf of the state. But Flannigan left his fervor home.

The investigating officers testified about the mayhem they had encountered at the Jensen home. On cross-examination a low-key Katherine Newhouse elicited a description of Janice's condition when they found her. One for her side.

An assistant medical examiner explained to the jury how the two deceased got that way. Kate led him to admit that three of the four shots fired into Dennis's head were redundant. The first was sufficient. Same for Sean's stab wounds. The first introduction of the fish knife killed him. The dozen or so additional stabbings were gratuitous. Flannigan then passed around the photos that had made me queasy. Soon, everyone was queasy. Each juror grimaced in his or her own way and two of the women cried. So far, the prosecution was doing Kate's job.

The rest of Flannigan's case turned out to be Clair DeWitt, Janice's supervisor at the shelter where she used to counsel the homeless. Mrs. DeWitt, an overweight matron in her late fifties, acted like she would rather be anywhere else. She testified that at the agency's Fourth of July barbecue, eight months before the murders, Janice had commented that Dennis carried a ten-thousand-dollar life insurance policy, double indemnity if he was killed in the line of duty. Janice had also referred to his pension.

She further testified that Janice complained constantly about her life with Dennis, the "lack of thrills." Janice was, however, an exemplary caseworker, she said, possessing a special ability to bond with the more agitated clients, the ones who found it irritating to be homeless and unnecessary to be overly grateful for a cot and a bowl of soup. Janice was especially gifted at calming them down.

On cross, Kate asked Mrs. DeWitt about the context in which the comments about insurance and pensions had been made.

"Her actual words were," said Clair DeWitt, an unhostile but uncomfortable witness for the prosecution, "'If you put the damn policy together with that excuse for a pension, it's not worth a fiddler's fuck.'" Janice laughed, embarrassed, hiding her face in her hands. The jury chuckled along with her.

Kate sensed the woman's discomfort and posed only one last question. "How would you describe Mrs. Jensen as a person?" Ordinarily, an open-ended question like that would be too risky. But Kate wasn't a gambler.

Mrs. DeWitt thought for a moment. "I would call her strange."

Kate didn't ask for clarification, but instead allowed the words to hang in the air like unclaimed flatulence.

Flannigan, seeing no advantage in further scrutiny, rested his case and his weary bones.

What followed was the battle of the experts. Kate's entire case was psychiatric, consisting of Albert Stein, an academic neophyte in the world of forensic testimony, and Brice Darling, the veteran. Both testified that, at the time of the murders, Janice was mentally ill, unaware of the nature of the crime she was committing and oblivious to the meaning of right and wrong. In short, she met the legal requirements for being adjudicated Not Guilty by Reason of Insanity.

Customarily, it is the defense attorney's job to explore with the experts the basis for their opinions, which gives them a chance to expound. Kate didn't do it. She left the jury with only the conclusion.

Judge Detweiler, probably responding to the monotony, called for a recess, hoping that lunch and a splash of Aqua Velva would resuscitate him and the moribund jury.

We stood as the jury and His Honor retired from the chamber. A female deputy approached Janice to escort her to the lockup. Janice spoke a few hushed words to the deputy, walked to the handrail, and beckoned me with her index finger. I approached the business end of the courtroom, glad that the polished wood gate would prevent a hug. Janice took both my hands in hers.

"How did you get permission to talk to me?" I asked. Normally, defendants were briskly escorted out of court, no visits.

"I told her you were my therapist."

I looked at the deputy, who nodded like she understood.

"I'm so happy you came. It makes me feel cared for. Thank you, Simon."

"This must be hard for you," I said, a stock phrase murmured at funerals and murder trials.

"Oh, yes, it's the hardest thing I've ever been through." She looked fresh as a daisy. "I feel like I'm going to pieces." She squeezed my hands and surrendered to the waiting deputy.

The woman who had been typing waited until Janice was safely escorted out before coming over. I thought she wanted to interview me.

"Dr. Rose, I'm Jemma Marin." She offered her hand. She was lovely in that soft, unflashy way that I can't seem to resist. Deep auburn hair brushed off her face, a pleasant glow emanating from her dark, semitic complexion. Small and slender, she wore a nondescript tan pantsuit with a spectacular earth-toned shawl draped over her shoulders. No makeup. Kate was right when she said she was my kind of woman. "I expected to see you on the stand today."

"It didn't work out," I said, more coldly than I intended. I was not prepared for a social encounter, which Jemma quickly sensed.

"Well," she said, stuffing things into her purse. "It's been nice meeting you." No it hadn't. "I'll just see if I can find a seat for the second half."

Lunch must have been tough on Janice. Her hair was no longer submitting to her barrette. Wisps of it floated around her face. She blew them away with irritation. The suit still looked crisp, but the woman had clearly wilted. For once, Janice looked her age.

She no longer tapped a cadence with her pencil. She rolled it around through her fingers like Captain Queeg worrying his marbles. She fussed with the strap of the purse hanging on the back of Kate's chair. She was a flurry of random fidgeting. Kate ignored her and consulted her notes.

Maybe it hadn't been lunch. Maybe what unnerved Janice was the prospect of hearing the prosecution's experts. So far, no one had offered any evidence contrary to her version of the truth. She knew that their next task was to explain to the court why she was *not* legally insane.

Dr. Chen, a pleasant Korean psychiatrist who did not have full command of the English language, pegged her as a Schizotypal Personality Disorder, a nonpsychotic category exempted from the legal definition of insanity. He added a side of Brief Reactive Psychosis. He was vulnerable.

Kate: "Doctor, how long have you been practicing psychiatry in the United States? That is, when did you become Board-certified?"

Dr. Chen: "After three months."

Kate: "Could your diagnosis be validly stated as a Psychotic Disorder with Schizotypal Features?"

Dr. Chen: "Yes, it is the same thing, I believe."

So much for Dr. Chen. Nothing damaging to Janice's case, and there was only one more expert to go. But she was a bundle of nerves. She fiddled with Kate's purse. She fiddled with her hair and her pencil. And she began to rock.

Dr. Benito Falconi, a somber Continental gentleman, spoke as if this were his first trip to Manhattan, having been a lifelong prisoner of Brooklyn. But he liked to talk, and Flannigan gave him his chance.

Falconi roamed through Janice's life, sharing tidbits of personal information about her. He explored her childhood, adolescence, and adulthood in turn, as if she weren't in the room. Each anecdote supported his theory of the crime. Janice was a Histrionic Personality who had most likely lost her temper and along with it, her better judgment. It was a crime of passion, not insanity.

"The key to understanding Mrs. Jensen is to understand her relationship with her mother," he explained. "Margery Donahue was a difficult, ill-tempered woman, very much involved in her daughter's life, controlling it, you might say, in the way that many alcoholic mothers do. Mrs. Donahue had been an alcoholic throughout Mrs. Jensen's childhood . . ."

And that's as far as the good doctor got.

Janice stood.

"If Your Honor please," she said, like she was the lawyer. She slid past Kate, who tried to grab her sleeve but failed, and faced the bench. "He has no right to talk about my mother like that. He can say whatever he wants about me, but I don't think he can talk about my mother like that." She was furiously rolling the pencil around in her hand, emanating a high-voltage agitation that charged the air in the room.

Judge Detweiler, temporarily stunned by this behavior in his courtroom, looked toward a bailiff who wasn't paying attention. He finally said, "Mrs. Jensen, please take your seat. You will be given ample opportunity to speak in your own defense."

Janice looked over her shoulder directly at me, as if she had an urgent question. She turned back to the bench.

And she shouted. "He cannot talk about my mother like that!" The din put everyone back on their heels. The bailiff woke up but not soon enough.

In a dash and thrust that took no longer than a couple of seconds, Janice bolted toward the witness chair, rounded the protective railing, and slammed her knee between Falconi's legs, causing his hands to immediately clutch his throbbing genitals. Then she raised the pencil and plunged it into Falconi's right eye. Blood spurted, painting her hand red. The pencil stayed there.

Janice retreated and fell to her knees in front of the jury as Falconi wailed, trying to dislodge the pencil. The bailiff, now fully awake, called into the hall for assistance.

Janice shrieked, "Help me someone! Daddy, help me! Simon, help me!" She held out her bloody hands in supplication.

Ed Donahue was stuck to his seat in horror. So I went. I reached her about the same time as the deputies. She pawed at my ankles, smearing blood on my pants. "Help me, Simon!" They took her away and someone ministered to Dr. Falconi, who had paid an eye for his testimony.

Kate rolled up to me. "I think that about wraps it up," she said.

And so it did. There were motions for a mistrial, denied, discussions in chambers, final arguments, and eventually, Judge Detweiler managed to charge the jury. It was no surprise when, a few days after Janice's blinding outburst, with only an hour and a half of deliberation, the jury, out of earshot of the defendant, who was being held in separate quarters, returned a verdict of Not Guilty by Reason of Insanity in the case of *the State of New York v. Janice Donahue Jensen*. She was remanded to the custody of the New York State Department of Mental Health for observation and treatment for a period of no less than six months, after which she would be reevaluated.

It was not clear whether Lady Justice had been served, raped, or murdered.

two

CRIMINAL RESPONSIBILITY

Th e   trial finished my unfinished business with her, or so I believed. I didn't completely understand what I'd seen and I willfully
blocked out the gruesome images. I rubbed my eyes a lot, grateful there
were two. When I suffered flashbacks I always saw Falconi dislodge the
pencil and slump down semi-conscious in the witness chair, my futile attempt to revise reality because, in fact, the pencil stayed there and Falconi
simply howled endlessly.

And then there were Janice's blood-soaked hands grasping at my ankles. "Help me, Simon!" I sent the pants to be dry-cleaned, but since I'd
failed to send my psyche along, I still couldn't wear them. I threw the
pants out and decided to forget Janice and everything she stood for. I had
other responsibilities, like work and family.

My work took a decidedly sexual turn. Shortly after Janice's trial I was
hired by a drifting runaway with no money and no home who had been
date-raped by a very proper fraternity type. She suspected that with her
history they would never prosecute, much less convict him. She figured
she at least had the right to tell her story. I was up against a fairly strin-
gent code of silence among the "brothers," but I had it beat. I located several women who'd been at the party who didn't feel bound by the
brothers' code. It could have happened to any one of them. It looked like
there would be a trial.

I was also engaged by a hotshot Wall Street CEO whose daughter was
crying incest. He wanted some psychiatric evidence of her obvious delu-

sional state, something he could use to "help" her, to send her for a long vacation in a private rose garden somewhere. I charged him an exorbitant fee. When I met his daughter and heard her version of events, I handed over the money. She used it to begin civil and criminal actions against her father.

Debby was working on her new relationship. Hunter College was on break, and she took the summer off to be with Bobby and think about the rest of her life, which sounded like a decent plan to me.

She seemed somehow strengthened, sure of herself and questioning herself at the same time. No father could ask for more, nor could a therapist, for that matter. I did wish she would allow me to meet her boyfriend, but she staunchly refused. I didn't see any reason to hide him. Debby did. "You'll meet him when the time is right," and she raised her hand, preventing further discourse on the matter. In general we were getting along nicely, more like friends than family, at least the families I knew.

So I had no trouble losing myself in work, relegating Janice to a dark corner of the vast root cellar that is my unconscious. Then, as summer surrendered uneventfully to fall, I got a letter from her.

Hi Simon,
How come you've never come to visit me? It's been five months and I miss you. It was so much fun doing all those interviews and tests with you. Those talks opened doors in me that had stayed shut too long. I feel like I'm finally facing my demons and it's all thanks to you. I have to struggle but I *am* winning, slowly but surely.

I have a nice young doctor to talk to in here. Of course he's not you but he cares about me too. He says the road to recovery is not always smooth. He's helped me to understand that there are bound to be ups and downs. I'm riding it out though, learning something new every day and on my way.

One of these days I'll get up the courage to call you. In the meantime, it helps just to know you're back in my life again. I think about you all the time you know. That's what really keeps me going. Thanks for everything you're doing for me. Thank you for being you.

See you soon, I hope. Love ya,
Jan

It was all wrong.
It made me nauseated. And tight, like a guitar tuned by an amateur. I

took the letter to the person who deserved like no one else to share my discomfort. After all, she had started it.

I found Kate having lunch by herself in the conference room. She was chewing absentmindedly while absorbed in a legal pad.

"You want company?" I asked.

She finished the page she was reading before looking up with a smile. "As a matter of fact I've been searching for an excuse to take a break. Have lunch with me. Be my excuse."

"My pleasure." I bent down and kissed her, no air kisses between us, solid smackers planted firmly on each cheek. There was nothing even vaguely French in the gesture. One cheek only whetted my appetite for the other. Kate wiped the mayonnaise from her lips before reciprocating.

She had on a silky lavender blouse with frilly cuffs and a collar to match, opened at the throat. Her linen skirt was a slightly stronger tone of lavender. Her face seemed calm and untroubled, and her hair had been brushed, not stuffed, behind her ears.

"You look nice," I said.

"Are you surprised? I try to look nice all the time."

"No. I like the blouse. It reveals just the right amount of collarbone." I followed the line from her neck to the junction of blouse, button, and skin. Kate did not play cleavage games, which didn't mean she wasn't sexy.

"Are you teasing? I hate being teased about my clothes."

"I'm not teasing. I said you look nice because I thought you looked particularly nice today. If you think that means you usually look like shit, then you don't know how to take a compliment."

I peered at her lunch to see if there was any way I could share it. She generally ate sliced-animal sandwiches, which left me out. I couldn't tell through the special sauce, but chances were slim that it would turn out to be tofu. "What's in the sandwich?"

"I asked for a club so I think it's got turkey and bacon. Which would you like?"

Kate resembled Tommy in her eating habits. She ate to fill her stomach, without regard to grease or sludge content. I, on the other hand, being a firm believer in the you-are-what-you-eat school of nutrition, had decided years back never to consume anything that had a mother. But Kate cared nothing about the lineage of her food.

"You've got enough fat in that sandwich for a month. You ought to watch what you eat." We vegetarians tend toward self-righteousness.

She spread her arms wide open. She was lean and muscled, with fatty deposits only where they belonged. "Do you see one ounce of unnecessary flesh on this body?"

"Good point."

"You want me to send Peter out for some roasted fiber from the healthy store?" Peter was her law clerk.

"No, don't bother. I'll just watch you."

"That's what I was afraid of." She punched something on her phone console and asked Peter to run over to the Chapati House. "What do you want?"

"You paying?"

"Sure."

"Then make it the barbecued veggies, deluxe platter."

Kate wrinkled her nose but asked Peter anyway. In ten minutes we were both happily munching. We chatted about politics, the elections mostly, no conflict of views, safe ground. I don't like to upset people while they eat, especially me. But once we finished it was time to replace the serene calm on Kate's face with a seriously curled lip. I went for it.

"I got a note from Janice."

"I did, too."

"Mine's strange. I don't like it." I handed the letter to her.

She read it carefully. "What's wrong with it?"

"It's inappropriate. What's she thanking me for? I haven't done anything. And I'm really what keeps her going? What the hell is that?"

"You're the shrink. It doesn't seem strange at all to me. She wrote me almost the same message. Things are going well for her. Why shouldn't she write and tell us? And the flirting shouldn't surprise you. She likes you. Surely you've figured that out by now."

"No. There's something more to it." I shook my head, perhaps a bit too vehemently. "It's not as benign as you're making it out to be. It's sort of . . ." I searched for the right word but could only come up with "crazy."

"Another shocker. Simon, the woman is nothing if she isn't crazy. The judge knew it, the jury knew it, and now even Falconi knows it. She's certifiably insane. I can't imagine why a little inappropriate behavior from her should throw you. What did you expect from her, normal?"

"I didn't expect anything at all," I said.

"Well, you should have and probably would have if you were dealing with your feelings. Do you realize that except for a few misplaced pencil jokes you haven't mentioned her since we got the verdict? That's not like you. Normally you would have dissected every moment of that trial. But you haven't said one word about her in months. You know what I think? I think the problem is you, not Janice."

"How so?"

"Look, Janice is a sad case. Her mother was alcoholic and abusive. You know what that can do to people. Why is it a mystery that a pathological mother-daughter relationship might be schizophrenogenic? It's crazy-making. I know."

"Kate, you're missing the point."

"What point might that be?"

"The point is that she's trying to reestablish a relationship with me." I rubbed my beard with one hand. "Shit. I don't know."

"Well, I do because I've seen you like this before. You only get like this when you haven't done your homework. Listen, you decided to withdraw from her defense because you couldn't render me 'clean' testimony. Well, in my opinion, you still can't. If I were you, I'd go home, make a cup of tea, and get my act together. Now go. I've got work to do and you're making me nervous with your fidgeting."

"I'm not fidgeting. I don't fidget." I got up, gathered my leftovers and threw them in the trash. I didn't want to leave Kate's work area messy. "I'll take you to dinner tonight. How about Vietnamese?"

"I'm busy. I have a date."

"A new squeeze? Who's the lucky guy?"

"Never mind that sarcastic tone. You take care of your own problems. Leave mine alone." Her lip was relaxed, not even a hint of a curl. And she loved Vietnamese.

I kissed her good-bye and left her and her arteries alone to deal with the fresh pound of cholesterol.

Feelings don't bother me. I have them all the time. It's confusion I can't tolerate. Psychic untidiness is a cardinal sin for a shrink who is limited by his vows to mild ambivalence. It was confusion that I noticed when I allowed myself to notice anything at all.

Kate was right about one thing at least. I'd been avoiding the issues long enough. I needed to consult with my family.

Debby, for example. Being the kind of father I am, I should already have explored the whole experience with her. Surely she, too, had feelings about what we had seen. One, she had sat in that witness chair herself. Two, Janice had killed her child and Debby felt as if she had done the same.

But instead of exploration I'd chosen silence, a selfish choice if you didn't live in a bubble. I wasn't being any help to my daughter.

I pulled her into the window seat and showed her the letter.

"God, that's totally creepy. Makes my skin crawl."

"Mine, too. You willing to discuss the trial with me at this late date?"

"Sure," she said enthusiastically. She clearly wanted to talk, but I hadn't been listening.

She moved down next to Tupelo and petted her absentmindedly. Tupe didn't care as long as she kept petting. "The whole scene was fucking bizarre. I was just glad I didn't have to be up there on the stand. Once was enough. For a lifetime.

"It's just that Janice reminded me so much of my father, the way he was that night. She was like out of it, gone, not really there, watching it all from some distant point inside her head. I watched her and saw Daddy. The look in her eyes right before she nailed the shrink, I've seen it before. Daddy had it." She shivered slightly, and the tremor passed through me.

"I can see her space out and shoot her husband, pop, pop, pop, pop." Debby pantomimed the moves she imagined Janice made. "The problem is that I can see her take the knife and stab her son, too." She didn't pantomime the infanticide.

How come she could see Janice killing her son and I couldn't? How come she recognized something in Janice's behavior and I, the supposed expert, was unsure?

My vision was murky. I wasn't exactly depressed, but a kindred mood dulled my senses. And I missed the point of what Debby was saying, a signal passing unnoticed. She never talked about her father.

I called Tommy and invited him over for bagels and a consultation. I knew I could count on him to come. He never turned down free food.

Tommy got comfortable in the head shop and opened a bottle of California burgundy to share with Debby. She and I fixed tofu and sprouts on onion bagels, Tommy piled Polish sausage with Dijon mustard on a pumpernickel, and Tupelo graciously awaited the inevitable handouts.

Tommy always finished eating first. He fired up a joint and read Janice's note. He didn't like it, I could tell, because he forgot to toke on the jay and ended up having to relight it. "So now you finally want to hear my Janice stories. Good, 'cause I got a whole shitload of them."

"It's about time," Debby piped, eager for what I hadn't given her.

Tommy passed the joint my way and I waved it off. "Simon, my brother, this is serious. I'm holding in my hand the best sinsemilla this side of Oahu and I believe you're saying no. I think you better talk it out, get it off your chest, if you catch my drift. Come on, tell us, how was it for you?"

Debby cackled.

"How was what?"

"The trial, did they get it right?"

"Probably. Janice is a very disturbed woman."

Tommy sat back, a smug know-it-all smile blooming on his moon face. "Just don't bet the farm on it, Sigmund. You'd hate spending your retirement in the South Bronx. You got the bitch all wrong." Tommy didn't call all women bitch. He reserved the term for a special sort of woman.

He offered the joint to Debby, who also declined, took a couple more tokes, and gave us his evaluation of Janice's character.

"Janice Donahue is a nasty piece of work, is what she is, always was. She used to steal shit just to prove she could do it. Most of it she took from friends. Clothes, records, knickknacks, shit like that disappeared after Janice spent the night. Everyone knew it but who the hell was going to do anything about it? Her pappy was a teacher and her mommy had just died. So nobody said anything, and she just kept rippin' off her friends.

"She drank like a fish and fucked like a bunny and it was all for number one, herself. That's the part I couldn't stand about her. She didn't give a shit about anyone else. If she wanted something she just took it, a regular collector. And you know what she ripped off more than anything else? You don't, so I'll tell you. Guys. She collected guys like other teenagers collect zits. Sorry, Debs."

"I'm not a teenager and I don't have zits."

"Anyway, she wasn't real selective about the guy as long as he was going with someone else. Then she'd go after him with sex, booze, whatever it took. She didn't care who she hurt. I think she liked watching the chicks she ripped off. She dug the power. Her all-American boyfriend either didn't know or didn't care."

"How come you know all this," I said, "and I went to the same school, the same parties, and I never knew any of it?" Not to mention that Janice and I had been intimate.

"Not to mention that you slept with her," Tommy said. Debby choked on her wine. I hadn't shared that morsel with her. "Just goes to prove one sad fact, big brother. You weren't always the penetrating, heavily profound–type guy you are today. You started out just like the rest of us, young and stupid."

"Is there more?" Debby prodded.

"Lots more. She had a used-rubber collection."

"Oh, gross," Debby said.

"I don't know what the fuck she did with those. Maybe she labeled them and put 'em in her scrapbook."

"Are you making this up?" I said.

"Don't insult my integrity. She was your altogether not nice chick. I never knew what you saw in her. You spent a whole summer with her."

"Something like that." I was almost going to touch it.

"Let me tell you one story. I don't know why I remember it. I take that back. I do know why I remember it. It made me sick, is why.

"It was some fucking dance or other. I'd bought her some booze. Our relationship was strictly business. I got her shit she couldn't steal through her normal channels. She gave me my cut. Nothin' fancy. Business. This night she's already piss drunk, but she wants more and she comes to me. I tell her to meet me outside in half an hour.

"She meets me all right, offers me a hit off her brand-new bottle of Jim Beam. I accept. Next thing, she grabs my face and kisses me on the mouth, all tongue. She's grinding into me like she hasn't seen a man in years." He turned to Debby. "This gets worse. Maybe you should miss this part."

"Are you kidding me? Who'd miss this part?"

"Okay, it's up to you. Anyway, I get a hard-on and she starts to rub it. 'Fuck you want?' I ask her, 'cause I ain't her kind of people. She meets me in parking lots and school johns. 'I don't have any bread,' she says, which is bad news for me 'cause I fronted the cash.

"So right there in the middle of the fucking parking lot, she gets down on her knees, unzips my fuckin' fly, and starts lickin' me. 'Your car or mine?' she asks, real cute. She's gonna go down on me for a fuckin' fifth of Jim Beam."

"Did you go?" I asked, voyeurism conquering good taste.

"You fuckin' kiddin' me, man?"

It made me wonder what Janice had wanted with me that summer. I hadn't been going with anyone. I hadn't bought her any booze. We didn't use a condom. And, as far as I could remember, she'd never stolen from me. All the rakes were still there when she left for college. So what had I been to Janice?

She had, of course, told me. I was her anchor. An anchor steadies the ship. It also pulls you in one direction, down. Into the muck . . .

The more I went over it in my head, the more my confusion grew. Kate thought Janice was a sad case, Tommy thought she was sociopathic, Debby thought she was crazy. And I still didn't know what I thought.

"Fuck it," I said. "She's in the bin for a nice long stay. I'll file the letter, just in case. There's no reason to pursue this any further now."

"Let's hope you're right, Sigmund."

Tommy's words reverberated in the silence of the head shop.

Do you want some help with this?" Tupelo asked.

Her concern was well-founded. I'd been walking around for days in a gray cloud that refused to lift.

"With what?"

"Janice."

"No thanks."

"Denial's not going to work."

"I said no thanks."

"She bothers you, Simon. You don't have to be a golden to see it. She turns you on."

"Who turns me on?"

"Janice. That's who we're talking about, isn't it?"

"No, that's who *you're* talking about."

"Well, you ought to join me if you know what's good for you."

"Tupelo, down!" I said with authority, reminding the dog which one of us was the dog.

She settled herself on the rug, mildly chastened. "It doesn't make it any less true," she said, and she nuzzled her nose into her butt. "I'll hold the rest until you've recovered your personality."

"What rest?" I barked, but Tupelo was already napping.

The family consultation hadn't solved my confusion. After a week of dedicated window-sitting and mental meandering, clarity still escaped me, and for the moment all I had to go on were my painful memories.

The thought of Janice led me straight into the miasma of chronic adolescence. I could see clearly the disconnected hormonal blur that was me
as a kid. I didn't care for what I saw—frustration, yearning, disappointment, deprivation—the usual menu for most teens. Not one decent feeling in the bunch.

Who in his right mind would dive headlong into that sewer of emotions?
Being an adult, fully grown and more psychoanalyzed than most, why
would I take such a leap? I wouldn't. Not this boy. Not unless I was pushed.

I didn't have to wait too long. Debby, had she been there, would have
saved me from the next intrusion, but these days she was hardly ever
there. Bobby saw more of her than I did. I was alone and had to deal with
the phone myself.

I hate the telephone and resort to it only when I'm desperate. I could
have severed the cord completely by putting some lie or other on the answering machine, but sometimes I wanted to hear Debby's voice. And
sometimes the cursed thing just rang and I answered it.

That's how it happened. It rang. I answered it.

"Hi, Simon. Look, I only got five minutes. Would you do me a favor?"

And that's what I hate about the phone. Once you pick it up, put it to
your ear, and utter a hello, you are its prisoner, hostage to whoever might
be holding the other end.

"What can I do for you, Janice?" See, if it hadn't been for the telephone and I'd had some time to consider, I never would have asked that.
Far too open-ended.

Wasting none of her three hundred seconds, she got right down to
cases. "My hearing's coming up soon. I'm so nervous." She stretched out
the "so" for effect. "I thought maybe you'd make an appearance," she
said. "For me." I'd have bet she was chewing her nails waiting for my answer. I had the power again.

She was inviting me to the court-mandated six-month reevaluation of
her mental condition. The rules would be different this time. The issue
was no longer criminal culpability. That had been decided by the jury.
She had none. The issue now was civil commitment.

The docs would huddle in closed session somewhere on the grounds
of the hospital. They were not concerned with impulse control or notions

of right and wrong. Only two questions would be considered. Is she mentally ill and is she a present danger to herself or others? If the answers were no and no, Janice was free.

She was asking me to help her get out. If I would say no for her twice she could walk. I indeed had the power and I knew just what to do with it.

"Janice, I'm sorry, but I can't do that for you. I couldn't appear at the trial and I can't appear for you now."

"Why not?" She whined like a kid who's been told she can't go hang out at the mall.

"Because I can't. I can't testify for you, against you, or about you. It wouldn't be ethical. I can't do it. Janice, you and I were acquainted a long time ago. That's the problem."

"What a funny word. Acquainted? Is that what you call it?"

"You know what I mean. Maybe involved would have been a better word."

"A much better word. Much better." Having settled that, Janice put it as succinctly as she could. "Are you telling me that because we were lovers you can't help me?" Her voice rose half an octave.

"Yes, Janice, that's exactly what I'm telling you."

"Good," she said, docile again, without a trace of spite. "It's not a problem."

"What's not a problem?"

"That you can't come to the hearing. At least it's for a good reason. If I really needed you, you'd come. I know you."

What do you mean? I thought, but I had the good sense for once to say nothing, a challenge for me.

"You don't have to say anything. Listen, time's up. I gotta go. I *will* see you. I know. 'Bye," and she was gone, clicked off, zapped.

Had Ladislav been around I probably would have called him for a fifty-thousand-mile check, a few sessions to smooth out the blips on my screen. But Ladislav was high in the Andes and Tupelo wasn't talking to me.

Whether I liked it or not, I would have to act.

If I couldn't sort it out with my shrink, I'd share the worry with the one person who *had* to worry about Janice—her shrink. This was no saintly impulse to rescue her, just a profound desire to pass the buck. As far away from me as possible.

Entering the forensic unit at Pelham State Hospital didn't require a strip search, at least not every time. But you did have to empty your pockets and submit to a patting down.

It was remarkably small for a state hospital and I'd been there before, too many times. So I knew most of the docs, some of the clinicians, and all of the orderlies and clerical staff. Doris, who was shaped like a grapefruit with a head, had power at Pelham and she knew it. She was nominally the switchboard operator but she controlled the keyboard that controlled the little switches that clicked open the traps.

The system was simple and terrifying. At critical junctures throughout the institution the traps were set. A trap was nothing more than a claustrophobic square room formed by the walls of the corridor and two facing doors, like an elevator with bars. It worked like a lock in a canal. You walked in and the door automatically shut behind you. All occupants had to remain in the trap with both doors shut while Doris decided if everything was kosher, at which time she told the computer to pull the switch that opened the second door, freeing you to pass into the next wing.

The actual time spent in each trap was short, maybe five or six seconds, unless Doris felt like playing with you or if she was chatting. Then you waited until she saw fit to press the magic key. Thirty seconds in a trap were sufficient for your life to pass before your eyes several times. It made me wonder what thirty years would feel like.

"Any weapons?" Doris asked me. She laughed because she thought of me as a vegetarian hippie who stuck flowers into gun barrels.

I gave her my keys with the rape whistle attached.

She laughed again and actually gave me a little chuck on the chin. Rumor had it that Doris was thirty-three years old and had never been kissed, not even by her mother; three hundred pounds of unrequited love who thought sexual harassment should be a part of everyone's diet, like a little spice.

"How 'bout a quick one when you're done?" She winked.

"A quickie couldn't possibly to justice to all of you, Doris. Offer me two weeks on the Riviera and maybe we can talk."

"Yes!" she cried and made the appropriate pumping motion with her right arm. Then she told me where to go and whom to see. The doc's name was Justin Katz and I didn't know him.

"What's he like? Any good?"

"Young," Doris said, shaking her head slowly. "Young."

His office had been a utility closet and hadn't lost any of its charm.

There were no windows, and an overwhelming mustiness hung about chest-high. It had the spacious ambiance of a library carrel.

Dr. Katz invited me to take the other chair and offered a handshake as soft as butter. He was maybe twenty-five. Tall and slender with short-cropped hair, he gave the overall impression of a pencil with a dark eraser. If my estimate of his age was close, he was just a couple of years this side of complete geekdom. He wore a tie that was too thin and too short and served only to emphasize the extreme length of his bony torso. He would have been better looking if he could have been.

"How can I help you, Dr. Rose?" he asked pleasantly. He seemed eager to please. Mostly he seemed just plain eager.

There are two kinds of shrinks when it comes to privilege and confidentiality, the hard-asses like myself who won't say a word about a client without a court order, and the soft ones who are willing to be coaxed. The latter usually begin with a weak statement of their position and invite you to find the loophole. Usually a simple manipulation will do: "I understand the delicacy of your position, but given your constraints, what can you tell me?" Then they tell you everything.

"I've come to consult with you about Mrs. Jensen."

"I'll do what I can." What, no coaxing?

"Don't you need a release?" I asked, foolishly, because if he didn't think he needed one, why the hell was I bringing it up?

"She signed one for you the first week she was here. She says you'll be treating her when she gets out. You're one of the three people on her visitors' list."

I wanted to ask who the other two were and I wanted to shout "No fucking way!" to the notion of my treating Janice. Better to hear what he had to say than for him to hear what I had to say.

"How's she doing?" I tried to match his level of earnest.

"She's coming along, she really is. The auditory hallucinations are coming under control, but I don't know whether that's the meds or the therapy. She is capable of quite serious insight and she's bright. I think I can work well with her." He said the last like I might tell him he couldn't.

"How do you see her?" It's the PC way to ask, How crazy is she?

"I think she's clearly paranoid schiz, with perhaps an underlying character disorder, histrionic type. She slips in and out just like everyone else here, but when she's in she can do some good work. She's the only one

I've got who'll even talk to me." The Maytag repairman syndrome, only here everything was broke and nobody knew how to fix it.

"Is she committable?"

"I think so, but I don't do commitments yet. I'm only the treating clinician. I won't testify at the hearing."

"Who will?"

"Belton and Underwood. Do you know them?"

I nodded. I knew them and I knew how they operated. They pushed paper and the bodies with them, more responsive to the bed count than they were to the condition of the patient. At least they were honest.

"Tell me about the voice." Her mother's voice had been the cornerstone of Janice's insanity defense. It varied in intensity and brutality; its level of punitiveness would be a good indicator of her progress.

"Her mother seems to be receding as the other voices become stronger."

Other voices? When I interviewed her only one voice had hounded Janice. If the cast had grown, that was significant, although not exactly hopeful.

"Other voices?" I asked.

"She didn't tell you?" He seemed genuinely surprised. "Dr. Rose, the other primary voice in Mrs. Jensen's head is yours."

A prickly current climbed up the back of my neck. "And what do I say to her?" I asked, betraying nothing.

"You soothe her. You encourage her. You are her voice of reason, in direct contrast to her punitive mother. She sees you as her salvation."

I nodded slowly, buying time to think, stroking my beard in standard psychoanalytic fashion.

"Occasionally she hallucinates one more person, but he doesn't appear unbidden in her head the way you do. She has to call him. Her high school boyfriend."

I nodded again. "Any others?"

"Not yet, but you never know with Mrs. Jensen. Things change. She's like liquid, but I'm sure you know what I mean."

I recognized the diagnosis.

"Are you going to treat her if she's released?" he asked, as if for him that was the whole point.

"No, and I've never given her the slightest indication that I would. It's out of the question."

"Well, her delusions are firmly entrenched. And you are at present her major delusional object."

I thanked the young doc for his help and encouraged him in his work with Janice. He seemed to like her and he surely got something from working with her. But he was visibly saddened by our talk. Maybe he had hopes that I would take over for him on the outside. Maybe he liked my company better than his alternatives. Or maybe he was just a depressed shrink.

"Can I ask you a favor?" I said as I was leaving. "Can we keep our talk just between us? I'd rather she didn't know I came."

"If you think it best, I can promise you that Mrs. Jensen will hear nothing from me about your visit."

I thanked him again and would have left but he had a question of his own.

"Dr. Rose, does it get any better?"

Then I understood the sadness in his eyes. It was the same sadness that had driven me from his job and could eventually drive me from the field, hopefully with enough of me left to function in a kinder and gentler world.

"No." I left Justin Katz to his demons, but took my own with me.

What did Janice need from me? Did she want to consult with me? Did she want to crawl in my lap and hold on? Did she want to replicate the teacher-student roles we once played in a converted shed? How had she latched on to me as her salvation? Where did she get the idea that I would treat her?

Where do paranoid schizophrenics get any of their ideas? I wondered on the way to the elevators and the traps that lay ahead.

I almost had it made. I was retrieving my keys from Doris, who had lost interest in me in favor of a veritable hunk of a deputy who was emptying his service revolver for her. I couldn't top that so I chucked her on the chin, helped myself to her visitors' Rolodex, replaced it, and headed for the door.

Several offices and conference rooms occupied the open, lightly guarded peripheral areas of the hospital. Visitors had reasonable freedom here while they were waiting to be admitted. I was struck by an incongruous sound emanating from an arched doorway in one of these public courtyards, a sound that I had never before heard in the halls of a state mental facility. Children's laughter.

I went to investigate. Was this the new trend in class trips—a visit to the local farm? It didn't seem right. Curiosity didn't do me any good either.

Scrumbling around the corner, ushering three little urchins toward the same archway, came Janice. She actually stumbled into me and I had to catch her to stop her from falling.

She had on a simple A-line dress covered by a thin blue smock that identified her as a trusty, one of the well-behaved inmates who had earned a measure of special privileges. She could have been a primary school art teacher.

She looked up at me, brushing herself off like she'd spilled something. She smoothed back her hair. "Oh, Simon, it's you," she said happily. Too happily. No disappointment this time. She was thrilled to see me.

I was speechless, so I nodded and smiled.

"I'm so surprised. I never expected to run into you here. Don't look so shocked. I'm a trusty. I help out with the kids while their parents are visiting. It's good for me. I feel useful." She nudged the children through the arch into a small auditorium but she hung back.

"It must be nice for you," I said, regaining my voice but not my verbal skills. The irony of her responsibilities was not lost on me.

"Of course it is, silly. It gets me off the ward. You wanna know depressing, try the ward. It's driving me crazy." She laughed, belatedly catching her own joke.

She had called me silly again. Maybe I'm sillier than I think. "Let's walk a minute," she said. She took my arm, plastering her breast against my monocep, and led me down a quiet, little-used hallway.

"You did come to see me, didn't you?"

Before I could answer she responded for me.

"You can't help yourself. It's an irresistible impulse." She set my arm free but caught my fingertips in both hands and started swinging our arms like kids in a circle game. She let them drop when it was no fun anymore.

She was looking at me hungrily. If Doris had undressed me with her eyes, Janice already had me between the sheets. Time to split.

But not without a question, always one damned question. That's my irresistible impulse.

"Janice, why did you tell Dr. Katz that I'd be your therapist?"

She dropped her face, shielding it with both hands, caught. "Because I'm hoping you will be."

"Janice, that's not possible. I cannot under any circumstances treat you. I—"

"Yes you can! And you will." She got that lean-and-hungry look on her face again. "You're gonna treat me real good," she said, affecting an African-American dialect. "Real good," she concluded as she took her abrupt leave, shaking her butt emphatically down the hall toward the auditorium and the children in her care.

Chapter Sixteen

De b b y was changing. She was belatedly acting the quintessential teenager, lazy, combative, sultry, and a general pain in the ass. I figured she deserved a break. Life hadn't given her many. She figured she had the right to vanish for two days without so much as a call. She was twenty and, according to our rules of behavior, she could come and go as she wished. She even had the right to be inconsiderate, which she was exercising. Everyone's an asshole sometimes.

When she finally reappeared she looked like shit and greeted me with a perfunctory hug. She was a mess, like she had been partying for days. I sensed the aftertaste of drug use, but with no proof I chose this time to shut my mouth. She got right to her own agenda.

"Is it all right with you if Bobby and I sleep here in my room? We do sleep together, you know," she added petulantly.

"I assumed so, but you've never told me."

"Now I've told you. Answer my question."

"Well," I stalled, "I haven't given it much thought, but I know there's something about it I don't like. I'm not sure I want to sanction your current lifestyle under my roof." The phrase stuck in my throat. I was a bona fide parent now. I had pulled the under-my-roof routine.

"That's fucking hypocritical," my daughter pointed out.

"True. Let me think about it. I might want to meet him first." That one stuck in my throat, too.

"That sucks."

"It might. At least give me a little time to get used to the idea," I said, the best I could do at the moment.

"I'll just stay there then."

"Your choice."

"That sucks," she repeated. She shot me an emphatic bird, which was a first, and she disappeared again.

My love of all things chocolate gets played out on three levels. When my soul is at peace I'm a gourmet. I pick and choose, savoring each mouthful with true delight. When something upsets me I have been known to overindulge, so much so that Kate once called me a glutton after watching me inhale a half pound of chocolate-covered raisins during a particularly difficult trial. And rarely, in states of extreme anxiety, I behave like a complete junkie.

Debby split and I nestled into the window seat. I went through three giant Dove Bars in ten minutes, so I knew my psychic equilibrium was significantly off. A quick mental inventory produced two items. The talk with my daughter had left me feeling inadequate as a father, but it was the hospital visit that churned relentlessly in my thoughts. I turned it over and over again, without resolution, until fatigue overcame me. Or maybe it was the Dove Bars. I fell asleep and had another dream.

Tommy and I are kids. I'm thirteen years old, on the cusp of hormonal manhood, but more child than man. We're wearing white coats, dressed up as doctors. We order double-dip cones at the Baskin-Robbins. Tommy is licking along contentedly on his. I'm having difficulty holding on to both scoops. I'm running around balancing the cone like a broomstick on the tip of my index finger. Finally, the ice cream goes tumbling to the ground. I try to replace it scoop by scoop into the cone. I'd be perfectly satisfied to eat the dirty ice cream, but I'm still unable to balance the slippery mess. It falls again. Tommy is laughing his ass off and I'm getting more and more agitated, but for the life of me I can't get the ice cream back onto the cone. Tommy just laughs and laughs and my agitation grows into high-speed anxiety.

I awoke bent and partially mutilated. Debby hadn't called. I'd slept in my bubble, hard as it was, instead of the waterbed. And I'd had a dream that just seemed all wrong. First of all, the cone in the dream was topped with shiny sprinkles. I never took sprinkles on my cones. And when

Tommy and I were kids, we never went to the Baskin-Robbins. In those days we were strictly Dairy Queen freaks.

"Something's off," I said to myself. "Why am I anxious about an ice cream cone?" Anxiety always carries a message, the subconscious offering information essential for survival.

Truth was, I'd been uneasy for weeks, ever since Janice's letter arrived, and our encounter in the hospital had only made the discomfort more acute. I couldn't turn off the nervous energy buzzing the back of my neck. Kate's suggestion that I get my act together rang true, but psychic residue alone didn't account for the danger signals flashing on inside my head.

I'd deliberately put Janice out of my mind, half believing, half hoping that she'd be safely tucked away in the hospital for an indefinite stay. Now her future was not so certain and I sensed trouble just around the bend.

When you've worked intimately with violent crimes and the people who commit them, you develop a finely tuned sixth sense for danger. You have to. Your life depends on it.

I got my combat training on a four-year tour of duty in a psychiatric hospital. I lived in close quarters with violence. Someday I would like to understand what karmic impulse pushed me to show up there voluntarily every day and allow myself to be locked up with those folks—people generally held by the society at large to be the scum of the earth.

It was a sixteen-man ward in the maximum-security complex of the hospital. It housed the NGRI's, Janice's male counterparts who had "won" their insanity defenses and were being treated for various legal categories of mental illness. A few of them were genuinely crazy. All of them were genuinely violent.

Besides the tunnel-like room with its double row of beds, the ward boasted a nine-by-nine TV room outfitted with comfy metal folding chairs, a surprisingly decent Ping-Pong table set up where two corridors met, and a paved courtyard barely sufficient for a half court where, weather permitting, the men could shoot some hoops. The total usable area was less than the space in an average suburban house intended for a couple and their two point two kids. Close quarters.

In addition to the court-ordered evaluations, which I did in the administrative wing, I was expected to spend at least fifty percent of my time on the ward, providing therapy, supervising medication, and in general keeping my finger on the psychic pulse of the inmates.

The room where I saw patients for therapy was slightly more cramped and several shades less cheerful than Justin Katz's cubicle. The interior decorator had furnished it with two gray vinyl-upholstered metal arm-chairs weighing about fifty pounds each, and a bare hundred-watt bulb overhead. There were no windows, unless you counted the peephole in the steel-reinforced door.

The procedure for the therapy sessions was truly charming. I'd enter and sit down first to wait there while the guard escorted the inmate into my presence, after which he'd lock the door and stand just outside until the end of the hour. It warmed my heart to know he was there, ever atten-tive to my needs, while he and his partner watched the remaining fifteen bodies floating on the ward.

One inmate, a two-hundred-eighty-five-pound genuine wacko, had been nicknamed Tuna Can Charlie by his ward mates for the unusual form of his sexual organ. Charlie actually liked me and we'd developed a friendly working relationship in spite of his propensity for unpredictable outbursts.

Halfway through one session, Charlie stood and lifted his armchair over his head like it was made of Styrofoam. He threatened to kill me if I didn't authorize a conjugal visit from his prostitute girlfriend. I would have offered him my sister, had I had one, if he'd just put the damned chair down, nice and easy. I called to the guard but he must have been terribly busy for the moment. Charlie finally calmed down when I dis-tracted him with the promise of a full pack of Marlboro's, flip-top box, of course.

A newly arrived inmate didn't fare quite so well as I had. The trouble started as soon as word got around that he was in for child molesting. Prison hospitals have rigid hierarchies, and pedophiles are the bottom of the scummy heap. The most gruesome murderers felt superior to these meek, twisted abusers because even in this pitiful subculture, children were still seen as innocents and in need of protection. No one thought that a pedophile deserved one more shot at another kid, so by unspoken consensus they usually found a way to make sure the creep never got out on the street again.

This particular wimp was helped over the great divide when Tuna

Can Charlie repeated the weight-lifting trick. This time he used the industrial-sized mop wringer, which instead of landing gently on the linoleum floor fell swiftly and firmly on the new arrival's balding head.

Every last man on the ward, including the two guards, swore he was occupied at the time and so was unable to offer information about the murder. I learned the truth several months later and decided not to pursue the matter because Charlie was so crazy and so violent that there was no chance he'd get out anyway. His commitment had long ago become a matter of routine every time he came up for reevaluation.

And Charlie was just one of several expert instructors who dutifully nurtured the young Dr. Rose's sixth sense and ensured his continued survival on the ward. Those years left their mark. Since then, whenever I smelled danger, I respected the warning, as well I should.

Kate didn't see things my way. "What's your problem really, Simon?"

We were seated on her sectional facing the fire, sipping coffee, Kate's incredible brew that could melt spoons. She did it on purpose. She drank mud and I drank it with her, secretly happy that she hadn't made cookies. We were discussing the theoretical question of Janice's committability.

"I think Janice is dangerous. That's my problem," I stated. "In the seventies we used to call it a gut feeling."

"Yes, but this is the nineties and we don't do gut feelings anymore. And certainly not in court. If you want to discuss recommitment seriously, get specific," she said in her lawyerly tone. "To whom is she a danger, self or others?"

"Definitely others."

"Any evidence?"

"Sure, she killed her husband and child. Is that dangerous enough for you?"

"Legally it doesn't wash. You can't predict her future dangerousness based only on her previous acts."

"You can't predict dangerousness based on anything, Kate. This isn't news to you." In trial I always began my testimony with the disclaimer that given the present state of the psychiatric art, dangerousness cannot be predicted with any degree of confidence. Then, because the court so orders, I make the prediction. I base it solely on past behavior because I have no better predictor at hand. I know it's not fair.

"We can't just leave it at that," she said. "The law says she must be restrained if she's dangerous and we have to prove that she's dangerous as a result of mental illness. So, is she mentally ill? Does she meet that criteria?"

"I don't know. I've already told you that."

"Simon, look at the evidence. She cold-bloodedly murdered her husband, which is admittedly no big deal, happens ten times a day. But the baby, Simon, he was an infant diddling in his crib. A dozen redundant wounds. You don't think that's mental illness? She is in constant conversation with her mother who's been dead since she was a kid. And she stabs a pencil into an expert witness's eye. If that isn't schizophrenia or some other illness, what is it? I'm no psychiatrist, but the package is pretty convincing. It seems to me that at the time of the crimes and probably at trial, she had to be crazy."

"Okay, you're convinced. She's a paranoid schizophrenic and a dangerous one. She meets all the criteria. They'll never let her out. Next case. Why are we even discussing it?"

"I brought it up because I was notified this morning that she's being released a week from today."

Adrenaline flooded my veins. Janice free. Free to do what? And what did that mean for me? Sparks shot up and down my spine. A Kirlian photograph taken at that moment would surely have captured my flaming red aura. I flashed to Charlie lifting the armchair in the air but I quickly squelched the image. No need to overreact.

I realized I wasn't at all surprised. I'd known as soon as I heard the docs' names that they would let her out, and preferably sooner than later. Patients' correspondence was routinely read by hospital staff and Janice's letters showed signs of optimistic self-reflection, my own gut feelings notwithstanding. Her behavior on the ward had to be exemplary or they wouldn't have given her trusty status. The single fact that she was engaged in ongoing talk therapy with Justin Katz would have been sufficient to ensure her release. Anybody in good-enough shape to talk coherently belonged somewhere else. That's how the docs had to think. And in some ways they were right. Compared to the rest of the hospital population, Janice was a gem.

"Let's assume for a moment that the system worked," Kate said, "that she was legally insane at the time of the crimes and that she's come out of it somewhat. They've got her on meds and when she looks good, she looks real good. In fact, she looks good enough to release. And maybe she is.

"I think the woman deserves a chance and you don't want to give it to her. And what's your evidence that she's a danger? You don't have any, not now. You have a feeling. When I look at her I see a sad, needy, very sick woman. You see danger. Why?"

"For the moment, I can't articulate my reasons any better."

"You know what I think?" she asked rhetorically. "I think it's counter-transference."

I glanced at the blow, absolutely unprepared for such a comment from my best friend. It was a return volley. I had accused her early on of unprofessionalism with regard to Janice.

Transference is the patient's way of displacing feelings for significant figures in her life onto the analyst. If she mistrusted her mother, she'll mistrust the shrink; if she was seductive with her father, she'll be seductive with her shrink. Transference is therapeutic because it can be explored in the light of day, today, in the context of the therapy.

Countertransference, on the other hand, is the complementary condition suffered by the analyst when he or she, for example, becomes angry in response to the patient's lack of trust, or gets turned on by the seductive behavior. The analyst is expected to maintain emotional equilibrium in the therapeutic relationship. Countertransference is a no-no. If it can't be successfully dealt with, the analyst should withdraw from the case, tainted by an imperfect psyche. Every therapist suffers from it sometime, because we aren't machines. But we are supposed to keep it under control. Kate was suggesting that I had not yet dominated my countertransference.

She poured herself three more fingers of coffee and was fiddling with it, waiting to see if I was going to blow up before or after she had her say. If I blew up before, I would only prove her point, so I held my peace.

"First, once upon a time, she turned you on. Big time. I think she still does."

"You been talking to Tupelo?"

She ignored my interruption. "Second, I think your problem with her is the very fact that you once misjudged her so completely. You were infatuated with her then, and now you find out from Tommy that she wasn't the unsullied flower you thought she was. He tells you she was promiscuous and vengeful. And it kills you that you could have been so wrong about somebody, anybody, even that long ago. So you're stuck with a useless, largely fabricated memory of an innocent Janice that makes you unable to see her clearly now. I think she makes you anxious because she touches something unresolved in *you*, and that's the obstacle to seeing her clearly. Does that sound right?"

"Yes, it does. Undeniable. But it still doesn't explain away my perception of danger."

"No, and we're going to have to wait and see on that. Let me go on, though, because I've wanted to say this to you for a long time, before Janice Jensen returned to your life. Now I think it's absolutely required, so I'm going to say it. Please remember that it's because I care for you that I'm telling you this.

"Janice is only a minor disturbance but she's making you focus on profound issues in your soul. Simon, you've had a problem with women ever since I've known you. Now before you attack, answer this. How long is the longest sustained intimate relationship you've had with a woman other than me?"

I started counting my fingers, in months, not years.

"And leaving Zora out for the moment, before she destroyed your life as you knew it, how long a relationship did you ever sustain?"

I didn't bother counting fingers because they would have represented days this time. And hearing Kate say Zora's name brought a burning coal up in my throat that I was almost unable to gulp back. There were tears right on the horizon.

"Just look at the most recent example, my friend Jemma. We both know she's your type and yet you've done nothing to respond to her obvious interest in you. My point is this. You like to attribute your armor to the tragedy of Zora's death. You won't get involved because if you did, you would risk feeling the loss again. And that, understandably, you couldn't deal with. But what if you saw the truth? Your issues with women didn't start with Zora, they started long before. You would probably say in the crib. Being a layperson, I can say only what I see, a lonely adolescent heart beating inside your chest. And I see a capable, successful, mature man who has never dealt with that hurting, yearning boy. You have no compassion for your younger self. But you'd better find some. Didn't you ever do that part in your decades-long analysis?"

"No. We never got out of the crib."

"Well, you're out now and you have some decisions to make about your life. You're a beautiful man and you have so much to give, but you're not available. You've got to decide if you ever want to have a real relationship, or stay stuck somewhere in your defenses. If you choose the latter, you can expect to find yourself moving to California, chasing young ice cream cones down the Sunset Strip. I can't see it."

Ice cream cones? She not only talks to my dog, she free-associates to my dreams?

"And Janice has shown up in your life right now for a reason. Maybe it's time for you to deal with your unfinished business. Not with her, she's just a catalyst. With yourself. And maybe, just maybe, you won't sleaze around it this time. Janice has her own business with you and I think she's going to force you to finish yours. Try to see it as an opportunity."

Kate was my person, and in a way we belonged to each other. We had certainly proven over the years that we could continuously care about one another. Her words stung me because they came from the heart.

"You know me far too well," I said.

"I know you just well enough." She had been staring at the fire as she spoke, not at me. I took the same refuge. Now she turned to me, took my face in her hands, and kissed me on each cheek, not like a greeting but more like punctuation, maybe a period. "You'll work it out. I know you. You have to. Now please take your beloved self home because I'm expecting a visitor."

"The same one who made you miss that great Vietnamese dinner?"

"No, this is entirely different."

"You're being very mysterious. Who is it this time?"

"You'll know soon enough."

K a t e ' s comments were doing laps in my head. Normally she and I agreed on the basics no matter what the issue, but she was seeing Janice so differently, I felt shaken. I didn't know if I should trust my instincts or my most beloved friend.

I was about to get new data.

Debby had come home for a change, I knew by the crashing and churning of the ancient washing machine. She only stopped in now when she ran out of clean clothes. I squatted on the kitchen floor elbow-deep in the fridge, removing last month's leftovers, making Tupelo so happy she forgave me for refusing to explore my adolescence with her. I think it was the gray Tilsit that finally brought her around. I found two undistinguishable items covered with moss that I relegated directly to the sink. The disposal clanged as if it were grinding up my flatware along with the mysterious green paste. The noise was already destroying my sense of reality when yet another sound penetrated my consciousness.

Someday an ambitious clinical psych major must do an analysis of the relationship between personality traits and the number of times a subject presses the doorbell when seeking an audience with the analyst. I would hypothesize a direct correlation between aggressiveness and the frequency of bell ringing. I shut off the switch over the sink and my brain registered the front-door chimes merrily repeating their melodic sequence, nonstop, no mercy for the indwellers. It didn't require too much effort to guess my visitor's identity before opening the door.

Despite my correct guess, I was unprepared for the monstrous impact on my nervous system when my eyes actually took her in. Heat flooded my groin and spread up my belly as if I'd been catapulted back in time.

Janice stood framed in the doorway with the late afternoon sunlight behind her, a stunning vision no matter who was looking. Defying the October chill, she'd come coatless and hatless. Her soft fair hair hung shoulder-length, freshly washed and shimmering. There wasn't a trace of makeup on her face and no need for it either; she was flushed with excitement. She wore tight black jeans that disappeared into black leather boots and a thick, soft turtleneck sweater, also black, that made me want to reach out and touch her. She was a study in how to be provocative by covering everything.

I forced my temperature down below the boiling point, but I had to admit it—I was unnerved. She looked great sealed in black.

I made a mental note of my reaction and plunged into the challenge of the moment. I greeted her with the most distancing handshake I could manage, and I have long arms. I was just showing her into the head shop when Debby came sauntering down the hall. We hadn't talked since she gave me the finger and left without further comment. This was an encounter I would have prevented had I seen it coming.

"Oh, excuse me, I'm just passing through." She brushed past us, making significant eye contact with Janice. She grabbed her umbrella off the stand near the front door and ducked back into her room.

"And who might that be?" Janice asked, eyes open just wide enough to be noticeable without being overtly insulting.

"That's my daughter. She must be getting ready to go out."

"Your daughter," she mused, drumming her fingers over her lips. "You weren't married long enough to have a daughter, although she looks the right age." Janice gained the first advantage. She was telling me that she had been looking into my past and knew about my wife.

I led her to the armchair facing my desk and invited her to sit, but my demeanor lacked warmth. I felt wary and resentful of her. She accepted my offer of tea so I escaped to the kitchen and made two cups of Earl Grey, suddenly needing the caffeine buzz to fortify me.

She was waiting impatiently, drumming her fingers on the edge of my desk. Her fingers were always drumming something. I set the tea down and took a seat opposite her, vaguely glancing at the fire. I hadn't wanted to invite her to the sitting area that took up the other half of the head shop. I had plans but I needed to give her a chance first to reveal hers.

She took a deep breath before she spoke. "Well, I'm finally free."

"Yes, I can see that. It must be a relief." Neutral enough so far.

"It hasn't quite sunk in yet, but I'm already feeling better. The only problem is that I've been staying with Daddy in that dumpy old hotel of his and it's not working out at all. I'm too old to be living with my daddy." She looked at me meaningfully but the significance of her words escaped me. Perhaps she expected me to offer her a room in my house?

I decided to treat the visit as an informal consultation and shifted into my best counseling mode. "What other options do you have?"

"I could look for a new apartment, maybe a little studio somewhere, now that I'm a single girl." A quick glance into my soul, again fraught with meaning. "Or maybe I should take a trip. I have a little money that Dennis and I kept in an investment account. We didn't touch it for years and the broker says it's actually quite a healthy portfolio now. I could even use it to put down on a condo if that's what I decide to do. What do you think? What would you do?"

"Whatever your heart says."

"My heart? That's not very psychological."

"No, but it seems to work for most of the important decisions in life. So, what does your heart say?"

"Two things, to be honest. First it says, 'Hit the road, girl, you've been locked up for months.' That's appealing. I'm not sure I want to tell you the second thing right now."

I was being barraged with deep, searching looks. One more and I would be forced to put on shades in spite of the twilight hour. Refusing to swallow the bait, I changed the subject. I had my own agenda to cover.

"Janice, I didn't know you had an identical twin. What happened to her?" I was mildly interested, because a dead twin has been known to cause psychological imbalance, but that wasn't why I brought it up. I threw it in for dazzle, to show her that I had a few tricks myself.

"How in the world did you know that?" She was impressed.

I knew from the red blobs on card three but I wasn't about to explain. "So what happened to her?" I asked again.

"She died at birth, strangled on the cord."

"She would have been younger than you, by a few minutes at least."

"That's spooky, Simon. How could you tell?"

I shrugged again, deliberately leaving her spooked, and went for the throat. "What happened to your mother, Janice? How did she die?"

The effects of the dazzling were evident on her face. If he knows about my dead twin, he probably knows about Mom, too. Janice's veneer cracked for the first time. She thought about it, considered lying, but under the weight of my magical powers she wavered.

"Why do you ask?"

"I'm interested."

"Why, Simon?" Suspicious and titillated, an irresistible combination.

"I knew you a long time ago." I paused and studied her face. "You've come back into my life and I don't know what that means. You're my personal psychological mystery." I was totally convincing because I wasn't lying.

She looked pleased, sad, engaged, and wary all at once. What would she decide to do?

"Well, you might as well hear it from me. If you're interested in me you'll find out anyway. You know what a small town Workman's Lake is. There were rumors. The neighbors had heard my parents fighting. When my mother died, people started suggesting that my father actually killed her. Can you imagine that? You know him. He's a total dishrag. I think it's positively ridiculous. My father had never even hit her. He was too afraid of her. She was drunk as usual and she fell, I guess. My father had nothing to do with it. It was small-town gossip. That was it. We left because of the talk. That's how we ended up in Ann Arbor."

"How can you be certain that your mother fell? Are you sure he wasn't involved?"

She mulled it over as if it had never occurred to her. She shook her head. "No, she fell all by herself. Daddy would never have hurt her. He loved her too much. We both did."

"Where were you when she died?"

"I was out with Will."

"Did you find her?"

She swallowed hard. "Yes."

"Where was your father?"

"I don't know." She was now drumming both feet and all ten fingers. Touchy but under control.

It was not time to push. It was almost time to end the visit and digest the contents. I had gotten much more than I could have reasonably hoped for. I backed off.

"Janice, that's a pretty heavy load to carry all your life. What are you go-ing to do about therapy now that you're not seeing Dr. Katz anymore?"

"Actually, I *am* seeing him. There's an outpatient transition program at the hospital and he encouraged me to continue with him. I think he kinda likes me. I've already gone twice since I got out. I wanted you, you know, for therapy, but maybe life has something different in store for us." She looked down at her lap this time, sparing me the penetrating visual in-spection. I waited quietly for the last round. I'd won this one hands down.

Janice got up, walked to the fireplace, and struck a dramatic pose that would have challenged Vivien Leigh on the Tara set. She leaned sideways with her elbow on the mantelpiece and one leg crossed in front of the other, her foot balanced coquettishly on the tip of her boot. Scarlett O'Hara ready for the ride. I was tempted to applaud.

She let her eyes peruse the head shop. "This is quite an elegant place you've got here. It's not at all how I pictured your home. I expected it to be more informal, kinda like a hippie pad, with lots of cushions all around and a fancy hookah in the middle. You know, like that old garden shed, only maybe a little bigger."

"Janice, that was a long time ago. I'm older now. I work here. This is my office."

"You must have a spot where you just hang out though, don't you?"

"Yes, but it's private."

Disappointment and anger flashed across her face but she instantly subdued both. "Well, maybe someday you'll show me that, too."

Silence hung in the room and she showed signs of discomfort again. She came back to her chair by the desk and took the first sip of her tea. "I guess I'll take the trip then. I was thinking of one of those Amtrak spe-cials, you know, maybe a couple of weeks, maybe a stop in Ann Arbor to revisit my old hunting grounds."

"Sounds good. Be sure to let Justin Katz know. He'll be concerned if you don't show up." Relief was almost at hand. She was gathering herself to go.

"I'll do that. Listen, it's really good seeing you but I'd better go now. I'll be in touch though, you can count on that." Nothing I would have liked more. We both stood up and I let her precede me to the hallway.

As I was seeing Janice to the door, Debby emerged from her room once again, clad in her beat-up parka, army surplus backpack slung over her shoulder, obviously on her way out.

"Debby," Janice chirped, "which way are you going?"

"Downtown."

"Good. Let's share a cab." Ed's hotel was uptown.

Gooseflesh rose on my back. Earlier, she had seemed surprised that I had a daughter. Now, though I hadn't mentioned it, she called Debby by name. How did she know it? What was the game? What the fuck was going on?

Debby looked at me and then at Janice, unsure of the next move. "Okay, let's go," she said.

Janice headed out the front door. Debby lagged behind a moment. "Don't worry, Simon, it's just a cab ride. It's all right."

If once is an accident, twice is a conspiracy. Obviously, each one for her own reasons wanted a taste of the other.

Debby's last words echoed in my head. " . . . just a cab ride. It's all right." It wasn't all right with me.

So much for the relief part.

To m m y breezed in at lunchtime and found me at the kitchen table. With the fridge clean and ready, I had prepared a week's worth of vegetarian lasagna and this was only day three, so there was plenty.

"Man," he said between mouthfuls, "I don't know how you eat this shit without the hamburger. It don't taste like nothin'."

"I like it this way. You can smell the herbs. It's more subtle."

"No accountin' for tastes."

"Nothing wrong with yours. I notice you're on your third plateful."

"Good point. I was hungry." He flashed me that irresistible grin by way of gratitude.

He had finished three helpings while I was still enjoying number one. He ate like when he was eleven, in and out between day camp and Little League, driving our mother crazy. He washed up, unlike when he was eleven, and used the kitchen towel to dry himself.

"I hear your old honey is on the loose," he said. "Have you heard from her yet?"

"As a matter of fact, she came by the other day."

"An impromptu visit, no doubt." He winked at me, a gesture almost no one would have discerned in those slit eyes of his. But I knew his face better than anyone else on the planet.

"Not impromptu, no. Definitely premeditated, with malicious intent. She was dressed to the teeth and dropped hints left and right about our supposed future together. Made me ill."

"Are you gonna see her again?"

"Probably."

"Are you nuts, or what?"

"Never felt more sane in my life."

"Then what is it? You still want to get in her pants?"

"You have such little faith in me, Tommy. I promise you, I harbor no prurient motives whatsoever. What are you looking at me like that for? Okay, yes, she's still attractive. But I am not going to act on that. I have a feeling it's in my best interest to keep tabs on her. She can't be ignored. She reminds me too much of those characters I lived with in the hospital. She's dangerous."

"You know something I don't?" He shifted into working gear at the mention of danger.

"I know she's the one who found her mama's fresh corpse. That's bound to have left scars. And it seems meek old Ed Donahue wasn't so meek back then. There was talk at the time that Margery's death was not exactly accidental. I'm not saying he killed her, but it wouldn't surprise me if she died somehow as a result of a drunken conjugal brawl. It would be nice to know."

"Man, what a family. No wonder Janice was such a mess in high school. How'd you get all that out of her?"

"I wowed her with Rorschach magic."

"I'm duly impressed. So what's she up to now, other than seducing you?"

"Seducing Debby. She took her downtown from here even though she was going up."

"Slimy bitch. Maybe she's trying to get to the father by way of the daughter."

"Maybe. Anyway, I didn't encourage her so she decided to take a train ride cross-country. Wants to breathe in her freedom. I don't think I'll hear from her for a while."

"Boy, you be wrong if you think that. Don't kid yourself. This broad is not good at hiding out."

"Do you think I should be doing something?"

"Nah, she'll come back as soon as she needs you." Tommy was right. Janice would not be good at keeping a low profile. She was an exhibitionist and primary narcissist. She would turn up. "And when she does, do me a favor, watch your ass or hire me to do it for you. I'm cheap."

"I'll do that, little brother, worry not."

"I'm serious, Simon. If she shows up here again, I want to know about it."

"I'll keep you abreast."

"No, you can have 'em both."

"Cute."

He sipped the last of his beer and scrunched up his forehead as if working out a puzzle. "Where is your daughter anyway? I didn't see her the last two times I was here."

"That's not a simple question."

"Shit, save the psycho-sermon. Just tell me."

"We had a fight, she got pissed at me, cursed me out and split. She's holed up with her boyfriend, trying to put her life together. Sometimes she even attends classes. End of story."

"What did she get pissed at?"

"She wanted to sleep here with her boyfriend. I told her I wanted to meet him first. She lost it."

"I don't blame her. That sucks. Why does he have to pass your inspection before he earns the right to sleep with her here? He's her boyfriend, not yours. Seems to me you're a better shrink than a father."

"Easy for you to say. You don't have any kids."

"But I *have* been married three times. You've hardly been married at all. Anyway, if I did have a kid I hope I'd be less hypocritical. You don't have to repeat every mistake our parents made. You could at least invent some new ones."

He left me nursing my cold lasagna.

Tommy's point hit home. My daughter's distress demanded attention. Janice would be away so I put my concerns about her on the back burner and turned my thoughts to Debby.

She was in turmoil and she wouldn't share anything but the resentment. She and Janice cabbing off together made me uncomfortable, but there was something else. She had never shown me such direct, untainted rage. She wouldn't have acted out if she wasn't upset.

There hadn't been any time to talk. All I knew was that she wanted permission to be intimate with her boyfriend in her own room. Not an outrageous request, but my response hadn't been outrageous either. I told her I had to think about it. I hadn't said no.

I dialed Kate's number because I needed to talk to someone and I was too lazy to walk the sixty-plus blocks for real contact. Tupelo pointed out that the exercise would do both of us good. I kept punching numbers and she sighed in mild disdain.

Like Tommy, Kate had never been a parent, which is perhaps why she had such keen vision when it came to children. Her ego was not on the line so she could see clearly.

"Talk to me about my daughter. She's incredibly pissed at me and I don't know why."

"I'll do you one better. I've been talking to her for two days. She's here. And she's not pissed at you anymore."

"Why the hell is she staying with you? She lives here."

"Don't get sensitive on us. She's here because she needed to talk to a woman."

"Oh," I said. That made sense. Women need to talk to each other and both Kate and Debby were women. I could deal with that. In fact, there wasn't a person on earth I would rather have had Debby talking to.

"And don't worry," Kate said, "I'm not trying to convince her to leave you."

"Thank you. I appreciate that."

"I'll bet you do."

"Well, enjoy yourselves then. I feel better knowing that you're talking with her. She's in good hands. The best."

"Thanks for the vote of confidence."

"Tell her one thing for me. Her father has the patience of a sinner."

"She knows. And she'll go home as soon as we're done." I heard Debby's voice in the background. "She says, 'Chill out.' She's almost ready to talk."

Sure enough, Debby showed up three hours later, notably less upset. I silently thanked Kate. I reminded myself of the need to be compassionate. I had carried around vast oceans of anger at my parents. Only recently had they shrunk to manageable pools, and I was a lot older.

"Debra, talk to me. I have no problem with you being mad at me, but you bitched me out, and you've never done that before. You have business with me?"

"No, not with you."

"With whom then, your boyfriend?"

"No."

"Are you going to tell me?"

"I went to see my father a few weeks ago. It's been years."

That explained the lost look in her eyes and probably the anger, too. Warren was being held, and allegedly treated, at Island State Hospital, a psychiatric facility for the criminally insane on Long Island. I had been there so I knew what Debby had seen. None of it was agreeable, especially if someone you loved had to live there.

Debby rarely mentioned her father but she did send him an occasional letter. He wrote to her regularly, long dirges about current wars, crimes, and politics. Television was the only stimulus in the hospital, aside from the drugs and ambient insanity.

She had shared his letters with me because they upset her. He seemed to be losing ground. But he never once suggested that she visit. And she'd never expressed any desire to see him, although I should have expected it to come up eventually.

"How was he?"

"Awful, real bad." She shook her head gravely and fought tears. "Simon, he's nothing like himself. I lived with him for sixteen years. I know him. But I don't know the person I saw there. It wasn't my father I saw. I don't know what I saw . . . he was like out of it, but not completely. He knew me and was happy I came. Simon, he's so fat I could hardly find his face in the folds. Daddy's never been fat. He wouldn't tolerate fat.

"He smiled at me and sat there like he was dreaming. When I asked him something it was like waking him up. If I asked him a second time he'd answer, but just yes or no. He could hardly make sentences, Simon. It was so sad. He's like a baby.

"He moved like he was underwater. He's like drunk, half dead. It's terrible. Is he gonna stay like that?"

"Probably. What you saw is mostly the drugs. They make him like that." Warren was in a permanent Haldol dream, under control, shuffling his way up and down long hallways, lost and searching. I'd seen it all too often. In such places treatment consists of chemical restraints, massive doses of antipsychotic medication, and a talk with a clinician every couple of weeks. Not many move on from there. It's a dead end.

"Why do they do that, drug him up? It's not human."

"To keep him calm. It stops the hallucinations and keeps him under control so he doesn't lose it and kill someone again."

"So in order to prevent him from losing it they make him into a zombie. He was like out of *The Night of the Living Dead*."

"I know. The only thing I can say is that its predecessor was shock treatment." And possibly its successor as well. Electroshock therapy is once again on the rise.

Debby shook her head in disgust, angry at them, at him, at me, but mostly at herself for being unable to prevent any of it.

"Will you go again?"

"No." She brushed away her tears. "When it was time for me to leave he was crying. He said, 'Don't come back, Debby. I love you. Don't come back.'" Her voice broke and for a couple of minutes she couldn't continue. I waited. "I love him, Simon, and I won't shame him again. I made him feel worse. No, I won't do that again."

"Can I help?"

"Yeah, hug me and tell me you won't throw me out."

I did both. I wondered why she thought I'd throw her out. She heaved against my chest and I held her tight so she wouldn't fly apart.

When she quieted I asked her, "Why did you go now? He's been there a long time."

"I've been thinking about it ever since she got out." I didn't need to ask who "she" referred to. "I figured if she could get herself cured in six months maybe there was hope for Dad. But I didn't see any."

"Is that why you hung around to see her, why you took the ride downtown with her?" I was still pissed that she had chosen to act out around Janice, but it was beginning to make sense. Debby was experimenting with differential diagnosis.

"I had to see what she was like."

"And?"

"She was like a regular person. She was very nice and she really seemed interested in me. She asked a lot of questions."

"What questions?"

"About us, how we got related and all that. And about me. Do I have a boyfriend? What it's like to live with you, stuff like that."

"Did you tell her anything?" What did I think, she'd refuse to answer?

"Don't get paranoid. I didn't tell her anything personal. I know better than that. We just talked."

My anxiety level rose unabated. "Did she say anything interesting, anything significant?" I wasn't sure what I meant.

"No, but there is one thing you ought to know. She's got the hots for you."

"Yeah, I know. I'm a man. How could you tell?"

"I'm a woman. Trust me on this."

"I trust you."

"Watch your ass." That was twice in one day. My loved ones were forming a derrière guard.

"I will." I gave a backward glance, a check, and Debby laughed.

"Simon, seriously, how can those two people both be schizophrenic? They don't have anything in common. Daddy's gone. She isn't. Someone got it wrong."

"Wouldn't be the first time."

Ja n i c e must not have needed me. She was far away. I felt it in the gradual opening of my throat, which had remained constricted since she and Debby walked out my door together.

She didn't call and life continued, each day the breathing becoming a little easier. Debby was splitting her time between my house and Bobby's. She hadn't solved the problem of the rest of her life, but she was in the process. I asked her to bring Bobby by whenever she was ready, but that moment hadn't arrived yet. Her anger at me passed and we were, once again, watching late-night movies together, when she was around.

One afternoon I took a spin through the Guggenheim in search of the perfect woman. I found her on a canvas about halfway down the spiral. She reminded me of Kate's friend Jemma, and a whisper of longing passed through my chest.

I came home to the sound of laughter coming from Debby's bedroom. The door was open and she was talking and laughing with Kate. I'd seen the K-mobile parked down the block so the only surprise was the presence in the room of another woman, a skinny specimen who looked to be in her early thirties. The thought immediately crossed my mind that Kate and Debby were conspiring again to fix me up. I entered with appropriate caution, emotional armor in place.

Kate never smoked dope, but the other two were having a high old time, the pungent smoke filling the room. Debby took the last toke on a nearly invisible roach and introduced me to their friend.

"This is Roberta Kelly. She's helping me figure out my life. She's my counselor, really."

Roberta extended her hand and took hold of mine. It was a friendly grasp. "Nice to meet you, Simon. Debby has talked a lot about you and now Kate, too."

I was in no danger. She wasn't my type. She was blond with limp straight hair and a painfully thin body. She wore bulky clothing to make herself appear more substantial, but to no avail. Her clothes contained more air than flesh. Her features were all sharp points, but her eyes, gray and kind, shone out in a warm appealing way. I decided to play along for the time being.

"Are you getting anywhere?" I asked Debby.

"I'm pretty stoned."

I had to laugh, she reminded me so much of myself at her age. "It doesn't take a swami to see that. I mean figuring out your life. You seem to have two excellent advisers here."

"As a matter of fact, yes. I could transfer to City College next spring. I could get my degree in five or six years if I work. Bobbi did it that way and she can help me. She works at a law firm and thinks I could get a job as a researcher."

Bobbi.

Bobbi could help her get a job.

Bobbi, Debby's counselor and friend.

The light dawned. Their ease with each other was evident and familial. They belonged to each other.

I was secretly amused at my self-centeredness and the automatic assumptions I had made. New woman in the house. Must be for me. For the moment I was speechless.

Debby cleared her throat and shot Kate a conspiratorial glance. Kate passed the look on to Bobbi and asked her, "Shall we tell him?"

"I think he already knows." Bobbi was no slouch.

I shook her hand again. "Now it really is nice to meet you," I said. "I've heard a lot about you, too, and much of it wasn't true. Debra, no lies was your idea. Why did you go back on it? Didn't you think I could handle it?"

"It's not that. I thought if you knew, you'd want to send me to therapy or something. I was afraid you wouldn't approve so I went over to discuss it with Kate."

I looked at Kate for confirmation. "That was the day you sent me home early?"

"Yes. She didn't want you to be there when she arrived, couldn't deal with you yet. Needed female company who wasn't Bobbi."

"I thought you might throw me out," Debby went on. "Kate said no way, but I was still scared. I was just afraid you'd say I fucked up."

For a moment I suffered an ache in my heart, remorse for whatever it was in me that had failed her so. I recovered quickly, realizing this was just life living itself out. The reluctance to talk to me had its roots in her own fears and in the general homophobia of our time. I didn't have to blame myself for all of society's ills. My words finally came, crystal clear.

"Debra, loving women is not fucking up."

Bobbi broke into spontaneous applause and Kate joined her with a chorus of "Hear! Hear!" Debby stood and hugged me hard. I guess I passed the test, and I hadn't even known there would be one.

"This calls for a celebration. Wait right here, don't anybody move." I hurried down the hall to my room, on a quest for gourmet chocolate.

Davey-H, my longtime college roommate, had gone straight from med school to the Amazon rain forest on a grant to study tropical fevers. He fell in love and married a Black Orpheus beauty and eventually settled in Rio. Well aware of my addiction, Davey-H still made it a point every Christmas to send me, along with the card and a family portrait, a box of fine chocolates. Recently, his Brazilian Garrotos had gained first place on my list of favorites. This year's latest was an exquisite confection of milk chocolate and hazelnut cream. I still had seven left of the box of twenty.

I offered them to the ladies and we communed in heavenly silence, savoring the moment as well as Davey-H's wonderful gift. Then we moved into the kitchen, where for the next three hours we collaborated on a sumptuous curried-rice-and-tofu dinner followed by homemade apple pie. It was a true celebration. We pigged out shamelessly.

Kate sat regally at the head of the table and beamed her approval at us, satisfied that we'd all lived up to her highest expectations. Debby seemed comfortable with herself and Bobbi and me. The two of them were very nice together, none of the sarcasm and subtle putting down so common between lovers.

"How long have you known?" I asked Debby.

"Ever since my body changed, basically, I just couldn't deal with it. You know, too young. So I got pregnant instead, from my first and only sex with a man. Sort of. Anyway, I knew I didn't like it. He was about as gentle as a buffalo, hands like bricks. He didn't know the first thing about women, nor did he care. As long as he got off he was happy."

Kate nodded, eyes off in the distance. A nuance of curl played on her upper lip. "I remember those," she said. "From last month." There was laughter, ironic, but from our hearts. "Some of them never grow beyond that stage. I wonder sometimes why I still bother. Never mind, of course I know why," and she smiled and let us catch the glint in her eye. For a split second I could see her as a sixteen-year-old girl. She focused her gaze on Debby, serious again. "But you went ahead and dated other boys, didn't you?"

"Yes. I think at some level I must've known all along but I wasn't ready to admit it to myself yet. I began to fantasize about the gentle ones with the sweet, feminine faces. Pretty soon, and it was a small step, I started thinking about women's bodies. And I still wasn't a hundred percent sure.

"Until one day after gym class I got turned on. In the showers. I was glad I wasn't a man, at least it didn't show. Then I knew for sure. I just hadn't ever fallen in love before I met Bobbi. Now, I'm not only sure, I'm happy about it. I'm also scared. I was afraid that if you knew, you wouldn't want me to live with you anymore."

"That's why you kept asking me if I'd let you stay."

"Yeah."

"You can stay. And you're lucky."

"Why?"

"Because you're sure of at least one thing in your life. You're in love."

"Really," Kate said. "That's more than either of us can say, and we're supposed to be the mature ones around here."

"Then you don't have any problem with us?" Bobbi asked. "I was more worried about our age difference. I was afraid you might think I had seduced her. I'd hate being seen as a corrupter."

"No, I don't have any problem with it," I said. "My mother was eight years older than my father. Tommy and I learned early not to hold age prejudices. Or any others, for that matter. She trained us well, used to sit us kids down and say, 'Now repeat this: True love does not know age, color, or gender.' Her ideas were way ahead of her time."

"Now there was a remarkable woman," Kate said. "No wonder you turned out so lovable, Simon. Good mother, good man. I'm glad I met her and got to talk with her a few times before she died." She turned to

Bobbi. "She'd have approved this new match thoroughly. Wouldn't have cared if you'd seduced her granddaughter."

"Actually, I think it was the other way around," Debby said. "I seduced her." She did a Groucho Marx eyebrow trick, emphasizing her culpability. Bobbi cracked up and we were all laughing again, a very unlikely family.

Over coffee Debby asked if Janice had shown up yet.

"No. She's vanished and I hope it's for good."

"I don't blame you," Bobbi said. "She gave me the willies."

"You know her?" The internal alarm rang. There was no obvious connection.

"Yes," Debby answered for her. "The time we shared a cab. She invited herself in. It was nothing."

"Nothing?" I repeated, certain that nothing meant something. I turned to Bobbi. "What gave you the willies?"

"I don't know exactly. It wasn't anything she said or did, it was more *how* she said and did it. I don't know. She was stilted, sort of wooden, trying too hard to be nice. She made me uncomfortable."

"She didn't stay long," Debby offered.

"Long enough," Bobbi said.

"You got news?" I asked, but I knew the answer by the grin in Tommy's eyes.

"Tell me yours first, if any. Mine can wait a little while."

I told him Bobbi was Roberta and let him draw his own conclusions. He thought for a while, looking puzzled, and I gave him a clue. "Your niece is gay."

"Thank you. I would never have come up with that word. Shit. I was wondering how it got by me." He scratched his head, both hands, every follicle. "It's no surprise," he concluded. "So, big brother, you been lookin' for Janice by any chance?"

"No. As a matter of fact, I've been basking in her absence. I told you I wouldn't be hearing from her. She obviously doesn't need anything from me."

"Yes she does."

I raised my eyebrows.

"Remember show'n'tell in school?"

I nodded.

"Okay," he said with a mischievous smile, "I'll show. You tell. Go to the window."

I went. Adults get to play learning games, too.

"Look straight ahead."

I did as I was told.

"Now move your head slowly about forty-five degrees to the right. Slow, now, what do you see?"

"I see a big truck unloading stuff. I see some chairs and rugs piled on the sidewalk and there's a giant teddy bear. Are you telling me . . . ?"

Impossible. Unthinkable.

"I told you she'd be back when she needed you. She's back now."

I got the shivers. I popped a triangle of white Toblerone and gulped it down, minimal anxiety control. "It can't be." I had had patients who followed me around, but this was completely out of hand. Transference run amok.

"Please note this down in your book of life." Tommy loved to gloat. "You are not, contrary to your own opinion, the only intuitive one in the family. I did tell you so." True. He had.

It was dizzying. I felt like Sundance in that heart-stopping instant when Butch grabbed him by the arm to take an unforgettable screaming leap into the rapids below. "Let's go out there and just throw her damn things right back into the truck. What do you say?"

"Christ, Tommy, all the bloody brownstones in Manhattan and she has to set up quarters across the street from me. Why didn't she just ask to rent one of my bedrooms? We could be housemates."

"I'm sure the thought crossed her mind. Look at the bright side, at least it'll be easy for you to watch her."

"And for her to watch me." I could barely squeeze the words out. My throat had clamped shut like a rusty valve. It should never have relaxed in the first place.

My window seat is magical. I believe that if I bury myself in a book or my own thoughts, no one can see me. I know it's delusional but it gives me a private space, as long as I believe in magic.

I was being violated. My privacy, or imagined privacy, was shattered.

Janice paraded past my window more often than necessary to conduct the business of her life. It seemed that whenever I got one of my favorite infusions and climbed into my bubble, she appeared on the screen, a bad B-flick that I couldn't turn off.

We never actually made eye contact, but she was always there, like a peacock, strutting her stuff before me. She wasn't watching me. She was allowing me to watch her.

I asked Tommy to do some checking for me and he responded, as always, glad to be my main man.

The first couple of weeks Janice shopped for her new apartment. Money was no object. She opened new bank accounts and requested credit cards, listing me as a reference. Tommy loved that one.

She went faithfully to her sessions with some new therapist and worked out twice a week at a pseudo-spiritual holistic health center. She jogged along the East River every morning, her Walkman dutifully shutting out the noise of the traffic.

She got a job as a caseworker in a city-sponsored home for abused children. That was too outrageous even for Tommy, and he'd seen some fairly outrageous stuff in his time.

She was starting over, right before our eyes.

Then she purchased a puppy, a male golden retriever about three months old. It was yet another excuse to stroll by my window twice a day.

That did it. I lost the first campaign. I gave up the window seat.

Chapter Twenty

A couple of days after Thanksgiving, she called.

"Hello, Simon." She purred like a kitten in overdrive. "This is Janice."

I didn't have a flag, so I didn't wave it. "Yes, Janice, I know. Is there something I can do for you?" I asked insincerely.

"You sound very professional on the phone. I hardly recognize your voice." I imagined by her breathing that she was brushing her hair and had hit an uncooperative snag. "Did you know we were neighbors?"

"Of course I knew. Janice, why did you do that?"

"I sent Daddy back to Ann Arbor and with him gone I couldn't bear to stay in that hotel another minute." Earlier she'd said she couldn't bear it with him there.

"I mean, why are you installed across the street from me?"

"It's a nice place and it was available." She paused as if she were think-ing. "It's close to my new job." She paused again, longer. The last part she blurted out in a rush. "And I wanted to be near you. Can you make it for dinner tomorrow night? Call it a housewarming, nothing formal. Kinda come as you are." As if we did this sort of thing all the time.

I savored a sip of mint tea, homegrown. This was no ordinary transfer-ence. This was God testing me.

"It wouldn't be very professional," I said, buying time.

"I certainly hope not." Her eyes twinkled. Shrinks know these things. "Will you come?" She reverted to her feline aphrodisiac tone.

"I'll come." It would be a neat trick explaining this one to Tommy.

"The woman is taking over my space, and little by little, my life. She's raping me before my very eyes," I said to Kate, exactly as angrily as I felt.

"Simon, you're not sounding your most rational."

"I know. I don't want to be rational. I'm pissed off. That's why I called. In another week I'll be living in the kitchen. This has got to stop."

"What does?"

"Her invasion. I'm losing."

"Exactly who is at war? You and she or you and you? Listen, she likes you. This you have known for some time. Her father is gone and she's alone and probably scared to death. Didn't her therapist tell you that she felt close to you? Well, now she *is* close to you, or at least she's near you. Maybe that's all she needs."

"You believe that? I don't want her near me or close to me. I'm telling you, Kate, the woman's trouble."

"I still think you're afraid of what she makes you feel. Now, before you go to war, check out who the enemy is."

"I can see I'm going to have to work on this until my adrenaline returns to tolerable levels."

"I hope you work it out soon."

"I will. Is tomorrow night soon enough? I'm going to dinner at her house."

"What's your plan?" she asked.

"I'm going to straighten her out, once and for all."

"Be sure to give her my best."

"You're kidding."

"Yes, I am. Simon, before you straighten her out, make sure you straighten yourself out."

Good advice. Only a fool would have ignored it. And good shrinks recognize when to throw up their hands and ask someone else what's going on. Whenever I needed straightening out on a case, I visited Olga Klein, the world's oldest Rorschach expert.

Olga was one of the reasons I chose psychiatry in the first place, along with the wholly naïve notion that psychological insight, knowing thyself, makes life better. She was only a minor player in the lives of most of the interns. If the others remembered Olga at all, it was because they thought she was a witch.

She became a major player in my life. "Psychiatry is legalized drug dealing," she said. "You won't learn the first thing about helping anyone. You'd have to study for that." She was right, and I later added a Ph.D. in clinical psychology to my résumé. I finally learned something about psychotherapy, enough to know I didn't want to practice it. And I got to play student for another three years.

When we first met, Olga was teaching psychodiagnosis and her home was her classroom. She insisted on removing us from the hospital so we wouldn't forget that there was a world out there filled with characters like herself.

Her apartment resembled a crypt, displaying urns and pots thrown thousands of years ago. She didn't use furniture, but there were rugs in abundance, Middle and Far Eastern, mixed with South American and African. She smiled to herself at the rug each of us chose, some sort of private joke. It was always dark, and she lit a stick of incense to begin the class, or the seance, whichever it was.

Olga was a purist. She took vegetarianism to its zenith, eating nothing but fruits and berries, food that had already fallen from the tree or vine. She refused to kill to eat, not even a carrot. As a result, she looked like Mahatma Gandhi. I estimated her age to be somewhere between seventy-five and one hundred and nine.

But when she focused her considerable energies, she could unearth every secret hidden in her treasured tests. She was the ultimate psychological detective. She simply wouldn't surrender to another human's mind. That's what we had in common.

I remember asking Olga to check the form in which I had recorded the undecipherable verbiage put forth by a woman I had met in an elevator. That had been the assignment. Find someone in an elevator who's willing to go through a grueling battery of tests so a tired psychiatric intern could learn to take shorthand.

The first person I asked, a lone woman who should probably have been suspicious of me, agreed to take the tests that very evening. To everyone's surprise except Olga's, often four or five people on the same elevator volunteered, and arguments ensued until the lucky winner was chosen. People were dying to reveal themselves.

We were not interpreting test results yet, only learning how not to screw up while giving the test battery. Olga checked our protocols in about a minute and a half and pronounced them either professionally done or trash. She would teach us her diagnostic tricks later.

As Olga flipped through my scrawl of the woman's Rorschach responses, she turned to me.

"Do you know this woman?" she asked.

"No, I found her in an elevator, as ordered."

"Could you find her again?"

"Yes, she lives in my building."

"I would advise you to work out the following dilemma: A woman you hardly know has told you that she is about to kill herself. She might not have intended to tell you. Or she might be calling for help, hard to tell. In any event, if somebody doesn't do something this lady's going to be dead."

I worked it out. Aware that I had no idea what to say when I reached her, I knew I had to try. I showed up at her door and was admitted by an older woman. It was her mother, alone in the apartment. Two nights earlier, her daughter had combined secobarbital, alcohol, and a very sharp razor blade to end her suffering.

Too little, too late. And so I entered psychoanalytic training.

And Olga Klein, who claimed to have worked with every member of Freud's inner circle, and under most, chose me as her apprentice.

She would call at any hour of the day or night, bark out the number of the Rorschach card, and read me a response. I was supposed to tell her what it meant.

"Card ten, blue detail. 'Those are blood-sucking leeches. They drain the cows grazing in this field.'"

"If that's all, I suspect she'll get over it. Give her three months to get used to the idea of the baby and the depression will pass."

"That's what I thought," she'd say and hang up. Never said good-bye.

Since then, whenever I had a tough one, one that really bothered me, I took the evidence to Olga. She was relentless and I was dogged. An Aquarian and a Leo, we made a great team.

I brought her Janice's Rorschach. Olga never wanted to know anything but the age and sex of the subject. I knew how she worked. I might sit there anywhere from five minutes to five hours while she checked and cross-checked, wandered, communed with the spirits, and smoked cigarettes. She was a purist about smoking, too. She did it every waking moment of her life, however long that had been. I always wondered how she found cigarettes made exclusively of leaves that had fallen from the plant, but considered it prudent not to ask. I did ask her once why she smoked so much and she said, "You've got to die of something."

She studied Janice for about an hour before she spoke. Her voice sounded like glass grinding into flesh.

"It bothers me," she said, stubbing out her last butt and lighting a fresh one. "No, it's worse than that. It scares me.

"This woman is showing us several characters. Not facets of one personality, not multiple personalities, not schizophrenia or any other illness that I know of. This woman manufactures personalities as needed. She probably has several stashed away. She should have been an actress.

"This is, of course, all defensive. She is a damaged child, scorched in the womb. Mother's an alcoholic, I'd venture. Father, too, probably, because there's no one in here," she said to the pages of protocol, "to save her.

"I would say she's sexually insatiable. She eats, sustains herself, through her vagina. I wouldn't recommend intimacy with her.

"There is an almost total absence of conscience, a lot like the profile of a rapist. You hardly ever see that in women. I don't see even a pocket of guilt." She puffed in silence for several minutes.

"What else?" she asked herself. She took out her set of cards, an original, she claims, and started turning them around, taking them in from several angles, the way Janice had done. "I would place her in the ninetieth percentile in terms of intelligence." That worried her.

"She detests her mother, wants to throw her into a meat grinder, and I wouldn't want to be her kid, either. She might want to put me through the meat grinder, too. Her husband, if she has one, is surely exhausted and possibly missing his appurtenances." She paused and cocked her head like she was searching for a particular frequency.

"Mostly, I'm worried about you. You are quite involved with her, aren't you, Simon?"

"You can tell that from the Rorschach?" I asked, continually amazed by Olga's wizardry.

"No. I can tell that from your face. You're worried about her, worried what she might do. You feel an obligation to intervene. And she's already thrown someone into that meat grinder or you wouldn't be here inhaling my secondhand smoke. When I put it together I know you're in trouble.

"You see, this woman is on a perennial search for a father, one who will be as unlike her real father as psychological space will allow. She wants a man who is effective, powerful, someone who can finally get her under some sort of control. She hates men, really, but continues to seek the one she can count on. I think you're it, or at least a good candidate. There might be others. This is not a woman who leaves herself vulnerable to one man unless she has already devoured him.

"Simon, she loves you like a father, which in her case isn't much of a compliment. She wants to dominate you, while hoping that you will be strong enough to dominate her. She wants to play with you." Olga sucked her cigarette, shutting her right eye against the smoke.

"She wants to possess you and she usually gets what she wants. And she can hurt. I don't like this at all. I'm concerned for you. Okay, now you can tell me the story. What did she do?"

I told her first of my suspicions about Ed and Margery, then what she had done to Dennis and Sean. "Do you think she could kill again?" I asked.

"Why not? She liked it. And it worked for her. It got rid of people in her way."

"Three more questions. Does she have a plan? What I'm trying to find out is whether she has some long-term script, because I need to know what part I play in it."

"I don't think she operates that way. She isn't old enough emotionally to consider a future. She's more like a disembodied mouth, insatiable because it is not connected to anything. And that's what she seeks—connection. Don't misunderstand. I didn't say relationship. She seeks a host organism that she can envelop. She thinks that will finally satisfy her, but it won't.

"She plans, all right, but short-term. She's an ambulatory appetite. She can only see as far as the next meal. And if she doesn't get it or it's not good enough, which it can never be, she gets angry. Very angry. And she's not afraid to act out. Her rage frightens me. It could easily turn on you. Be careful, Simon. You appear to be the main course." Finally, here was my ally, someone who also felt Janice's dangerousness.

"And if she does get angry with me, what can I expect?"

"An outburst or an all-out campaign." Not another campaign, I didn't think I could tolerate it. "Either way, you lose. She's meaner than you. Then, at some point, she'll move on because she's the ultimate pragmatist. I don't know. It's hard to say what she'll do, but you know that."

"One last question. Don't laugh at me, Olga. A straight answer will suffice. Would you go to her house for dinner?"

She laughed at me anyway. "Are you crazy? For dinner? Who's for dinner?" She cackled heartily, but lost out to a wrenching tobacco-induced cough. When she could speak again, she said, "I wouldn't be caught dead with her, much less alone."

A lot of people said that about Olga Klein.

"Give me her word," I said. Olga had taught me a useful mental exercise: to search for one word in the entire language that best describes a subject. She had a talent for coming up with the precise image.

"Mangled."

Chapter Twenty-one

O lga's voice reverberating in my head, I prepared for my date with Janice. Once upon a time, I would have relished the anticipation, drawing it out like extended foreplay. Now, all I could think about was the shower afterwards. I drank a glass of fresh papaya juice, an anti-inflammatory, and ate four raw carrots for keener vision.

I never seriously considered refusing Janice's invitation, a courageous attitude but not very bright. It was simply necessary. I had to give her a chance to play out her fantasy so we could all get on with the rest of our lives. It had gone on much too long already.

I selected my clothes with safety in mind: brown wide-wale corduroy pants, stiff and scratchy, ratty old black T-shirt with a yellow peace sign under a very settled Oxford cloth shirt with faint mauve stripes, brown tie done in a Windsor noose, and a Bolivian wool vest complete with grazing llamas, also raw and scratchy. The purpose of the tie, other than to make me uncomfortable, was to remind me of the consequences of getting casual. Let down your guard and you will be hung by the neck until dead. I was dressed to ward off bad vibes.

I petted Tupelo for a while and rubbed my beard in her face, borrowing some golden retriever aura. Nobody has ever been mad enough to hurt a golden retriever. "Be careful, Simon," she advised. I reassured her by taking her along for protection.

Janice wasn't warding off anything. She wore painfully tight low-slung jeans that emphasized her jutting hipbones. No perceivable belly interfered with the air space behind the zipper. Her upper half was covered by a fuzzy mohair sweater, baby blue and two sizes too small, accentuating every nuance of her expressive breasts. No bra. No panties. To the seventeen-year-old in me she looked like that damned ice cream cone begging to be licked. I admonished my seventeen-year-old to keep his tongue in his mouth. He obliged.

Janice was schoolgirl nervous and fidgety. She gave me an awkward hug, no hands, and a kiss on each cheek. Her hands were covered with a shiny green cream that would probably turn into guacamole. She was in the process of transferring the gloop from her fingers onto a paper towel. She gestured for me to come all the way inside and closed the door behind me.

The living room was done in psychological eclectic: a Castro convertible covered with obviously homemade afghans, a lacquered colonial dinette set, the kind that's on sale all year, and the huge teddy bear I had first seen on the sidewalk when Janice moved in. He was too big to sit in any of the chairs. The walls featured a Modigliani print next to Andy Warhol's soup collection next to a Madonna "Like a Virgin" poster.

The standard chrome-and-glass coffee table was set with corn chips, awaiting the guacamole. A bottle rested in a shiny pail flanked by two champagne glasses.

We sat down at opposite ends of the couch, half turned toward each other.

"How have you been?" she started.

"Janice, you know how I've been. You see me almost every day."

She cast down her eyes as if caught in a naughty act, then quickly moved on to the next conversational pitch.

"So how's Debby?"

"Why do you ask?" I said from slightly underneath my brow.

"She's your family, is all. Don't get touchy. Isn't this the part where we make small talk?"

"Look, Janice, Debby is not small talk for me. She's my daughter."

"Okay. Sorry."

"I need to ask you a couple of things, please bear with me on this. If there's any chance at all for us to have a civil relationship, I have to have straight answers. One, how did you know about Debby before you came to see me? And two, why did you go to her friend's place that night?"

There wasn't a moment's hesitation on her part. "First of all I want to say that I hope we have a chance for a lot more than just a civil relationship." Her eyes twinkled just like they had on the phone. "Now, as for your questions, that's easy. I have nothing to hide. I know lots of stuff about you 'cause I've kept up with you over the years. Don't get me wrong, I haven't spied on you or anything, but whenever you worked on a case that was covered in the papers, I made it my business to read up on it.

"As far as Debby goes, she's not exactly a secret, you know. When I was in the bin they let me use the computer in the library. I started playing on the Net to kill time. It was something to do. And one time I thought I'd see if there's a *Who's Who* of psychiatrists. Sure enough, I found a blurb on you in some file of the American Psychiatric Association. So that's how I knew." She leaned back, secure in the truth of her words.

"And my other question?"

"Oh, yeah, sorry. Okay, to be perfectly honest, I jumped at the chance to hang out with her, even if it was going out of my way. She's your only significant other. I wanted to get to know her a little. That's it.

"Listen, I just gotta finish up in the kitchen," she said, switching into her Martha Stewart imitation, "and then I'm gonna take a quick shower. I'm sorry I'm running so late. I guess I'm a little nervous. Why don't you grab yourself a drink from the bar. It's that cabinet in the corner. Look around the place. The bedroom's back there. Nothing is private from you." She scurried off to continue doing great bodily harm to an avocado.

When I accepted Janice's invitation, I'd wanted a chance to do some snooping around. Here was just the opportunity I'd been hoping for. I got myself a Coke and waited patiently till I heard her turn on the shower. Then I breezed into her bedroom.

A scented candle in rainbow colors flickered on the nightstand. I ignored the queen-size bed, attractively turned down for the night, and avoided anything that might house an underwear drawer. Instead, I went straight for the desk. I looked at the books, riffled quickly through her files, and just as I was meant to do, I perused the pictures on her bulletin board. I broke out in a full-body sweat.

With all that was yet to come, nothing she ever did could quite arouse in me the hideous fear I felt in those brief seconds that I stood before her homemade altar. Because that's what it was—no other name quite fits what I saw.

And then Janice appeared at the door, showered but wearing the same midriff-baring outfit.

"What'ya doin'?" she asked.

"Looking at your yearbooks," I said, quickly recovering. "You have quite a collection."

"Yes I do, but those are from the past. Tonight is about the present," she said. "And the future," she added as she took my hand and pulled me back to the living room.

She directed me back to the couch and sat down at my feet. She uncorked the wine, pink and bubbly, and poured it. She dipped a chip in the guacamole and held it up to my face. I turned my head and reached for the wine, which was disgustingly sweet and smarmy, and she gave up trying to feed me.

"So, Simon," she said, brushing away the hair that was constantly flopping over one eye.

As if cued, the golden retriever pranced in. I hadn't run into him on my tour. He must have been in the bathroom.

"Elvis," Janice cooed, "say hello to Simon. He's our friend. And come meet Tupelo. I think she's your type."

The two dogs sniffed each other. Tupelo sat as close to the door as she could while Elvis wagged frantically in typical puppy fashion, his entire back end involved in the uncontrolled expression of emotion. He tottered sideways and fell over twice before he righted himself again. Tupelo licked her paws, her indifference palpable, and Elvis eventually cooled his jets.

I didn't say hello to the puppy. The other Elvis, if memory served, was born in Tupelo, Mississippi.

I repossessed the agenda for the humans. "How has it been for you since your father left? Have you heard from him?"

"He's fine, settled back into his retirement routine at home. You know, bridge in the afternoon, bourbon at night, Michigan football on weekends, like that. I think he's better off there, though. He's been worn out by all my troubles.

"He's never been a strong man. Losing my mother really destroyed him. And the last few years he's been drinking much more than he should. He's never gotten over the old rumors, those fucking ugly rumors about him and Mother. They hounded him, Simon." Her eyes were moist and she clenched and unclenched her fist.

"Anyway, I wish we'd talk about something else. Let's talk about us." The moisture vanished from her eyes as suddenly as it had appeared.

Talking about us was, after all, the whole point. She was clearly finished with her father. Maybe I could interest her in her favorite subject.

"Where did you disappear to after you came by?"

She glowed a little, warmed by my interest and the opportunity to tell her story.

"First, I went traveling. I took Amtrak and saw some parts of the country I never knew about. It was very helpful after the hospital. The movement after being confined for so long was therapeutic. I had time to think. I decided I wanted to come back and live in New York, which was a big part of it. This city can make you crazy, but it's where I live. And now that Daddy's gone, I have my freedom again. He was being very protective of me, you know, not wanting me to go out or anything. It's much better now.

"So mostly I've been getting settled. I mean internally settled," she said, pleased with her profound insight. "I've been doing a lot of thinking. I started in the hospital with Dr. Katz, and my new therapist is helping me, too, but I know I have to do the work myself."

I was hoping she wouldn't tell me about it. The only thing more boring than doing therapy is hearing about someone else's.

"I see things I didn't see before." She was telling me about it. "I see how hard it was, growing up with alcoholic parents. Our family was completely dysfunctional. At the same time, I can see how impossible it was for me to accept my mother's death. See? I can say it. A while ago I couldn't." A positive step on the road to recovery.

"And I recognize my ambivalence about my father. That's why I picked Dennis. He seemed strong, not like Daddy. But he turned out to be a fake. He wasn't strong, just abusive. And I put up with the abuse 'cause I thought I didn't have any choice. Up to that point. When he went overboard it was too much for me. I see that now. I'm working it out. And I'm going to beat it." She raised a fist in premature triumph.

I didn't know whether to call in the Guarneri string quartet or the Michigan marching band. "Janice, why did you invite me here?"

"Come on, Simon, don't play dumb. It's only natural. I'm alone. You're alone, or almost alone, anyway. We're old friends. We were once very good friends. And we have something else in common. We're both widowed. It's a natural."

Hearing her connect our widowhood shocked me. I hadn't come by my status voluntarily. I wanted to slug her.

Instead, I stroked my beard.

"Besides, I like you. I've always liked you. And as I recall, we have some unfinished business." She was inviting me with her eyes.

All of a sudden the guacamole, already browning around the edges, began to look attractive.

I ate to fill time, not my stomach. If it tasted like anything, I missed it. Janice barely touched the food. I expected that the main course was still to come, although I could detect no telltale aroma. Clearly, the food wasn't the highlight of the menu.

She reached over to put on a CD, a collection of Motown hits, most of which we had danced to in high school, but not together. An odd choice of music for someone who wanted to forget the past. It started out with the Temptations' "My Girl." Janice was still at my feet and I felt glued to the couch. I hadn't moved.

She began to lip-sync the words and mime the Temptations' famous routine. "I've got sunshine on a cloudy day." She spread her arms to indicate the sun. "When it's cold outside"—she shivered—"I got the month of May." Warm and cuddly. "I guess you'll say, what can make me feel this way?" Question-mark face. "My girl, my girl, my girl, talkin' 'bout my girl." And just like the Temptations did many years before and she did less than a year ago, she rocked an imaginary baby in her arms.

She finished the whole routine and laughed with pleasure at herself. If she knew them all, I was in for a lengthy MTV evening. There were a lot of Motown years. Fortunately, she sensed that she was losing her audience and gave up the show.

"Simon, you're so uptight. Maybe you need a joint." With a flourish she extracted one from a ceramic canister, fired it up, and passed it to me, as we had done in the shed a lifetime ago. Only this time when she offered, I refused.

"Simon, I'm astonished. You're gonna get old before your time."

I already felt ancient, trapped in a surreal teenage time warp. "Got any chocolate?" I said.

She jumped up and ran to the kitchen, returning with a bag of Hershey's Kisses. She didn't realize it but she was challenging me. No self-respecting chocolate maven would ever so much as mention the H-word. It's too far below our standards. And Kisses? Really, Janice. I took one and hoped she wouldn't draw any unfounded conclusions.

"Let's dance," she said, and she hopped once again to her feet.

"I'm afraid I don't dance." I save my gyrating for closer encounters.

Undaunted, and probably relieved by the absence of a partner, Janice danced. "Ain't Too Proud to Beg" melted into "The Tears of a Clown," and Janice did a potpourri of the twist, the jerk, the frug, and several others that I recognized but couldn't name anymore. She knew how to move.

I can't watch someone else dancing alone. I feel like a voyeur at an exhibition intended for a private bedroom. It has a masturbatory quality that makes me feel lonely.

I crossed my legs and tried to look like I was enjoying it. Not that Janice noticed anything. She pumped on, oblivious, until she worked up a good sweat. She finally dropped from overdramatized fatigue, once again at my feet. My one-woman harem.

I uncrossed my legs and she draped her arm over my knee. Not satisfied, she swiveled around and rested both arms over my legs, facing me. Her hair, now a complete mess, flopped over her eye, and her breasts stood at attention.

"Simon, I can't get over how much you've changed. You used to be so much livelier. Or is it that you're sorry you came?"

"Yes, I am sorry. I don't think this is going to work."

"Let's see if we can change that."

She came to her knees and insinuated herself between my legs. She began caressing the fold in my pants.

"You do find me attractive, don't you?"

"You're an attractive woman, but—"

"I knew it. I just knew it." She moved closer, took my hand and brushed my fingertips lightly over her breast. Her nipple indicated either hyper-excitation or cold.

She crossed her arms at her waist and slowly pulled her sweater up and off. Her breasts were Playboy pert. Her skin was a warm, creamy shade of café au lait, probably the result of studied exposure at the health club tanning salon. She placed my hand on her breast again, like it belonged there.

My defenses were approaching their limit. I am only human, after all. I was watching the specter of my adolescent fantasies kneeling before me, half naked, offering me a chance to rewrite the script of my first sexual encounter. Images danced across my mental screen in quick succession, leaving me immobilized. I wondered if she would kill me if we made love. Probably not.

"Simon, *you* taught *me* all about freedom. What happened to you?" She began to massage my crotch, jolting me back to the here and now.

Tupelo belched, in case I needed a reminder.

I took Janice's hand off my penis and my hand off her breast. "Janice, stop. You didn't let me finish. I said you were an attractive woman and I meant that. It's true. The fact is, I'm not available to you. I'm a confirmed widower and I want to stay that way. It wouldn't happen anyway. Probably you should know that. I simply don't feel now the way I did then. It was too long ago." To this day I cannot account for this burst of honesty. It could only piss her off.

She was standing instantly, hands on her hips, beginning to get impatient with me.

"Damn it!" she insisted. "I know you want me! I can feel it."

She peeled off her jeans and walked into me, covering me with herself. I grabbed her by those sharp hipbones and pushed her to arm's length so I could breathe.

"It's not going to happen, Janice. Put your clothes on."

"You fucker, I could cry rape, you know. Who the hell would believe you?" Now she was pissed off.

I said nothing. Nothing seemed appropriate.

"I could hurt you, you know."

She turned on her heels in frustration and shook her bare ass out of the room. She returned before I could make it out the door, but I had a good start. She had put on a pink terry-cloth bathrobe that went from her neck to the floor.

She sat on the couch, cuddling herself, watching me at the door. "I guess it's better for both of us if we just stay good friends."

I nodded in disbelief. Nothing could move this woman into adulthood.

"I'm sorry, Simon, that was bad of me. I shouldn't have lost my temper. I guess I still have some more work to do. I'm sorry. Maybe I need some meds after all. I'll work it out," she mumbled.

"I'm sorry, too." It was true. I should have listened to Olga and skipped this whole scene.

"You'll come if I ever *really* need you, won't you?"

I was just about out the door. "I can't promise you anything."

"You don't have to promise. I know you. You'll come."

"Why do you say that?"

"Because you've always loved me. You've always wanted me and you still do. You've got some kind of mental block but you'll get over it. That's why I say that."

I walked back across the street with Tupelo, who seemed as relieved as I was to get away with all our parts intact. I felt soiled. I felt as if I'd stepped into an old flick and I desperately wanted my life back. I was glad my house was empty. Shame, even someone else's, should be borne alone and washed away in private.

Chapter Twenty-two

Af t e r a long hot shower and a soothing valerian infusion, I reclaimed my window seat. I needed to think. If confronted, I would simply claim invisibility.

Janice didn't want to play with me, she wanted to devour me. She wouldn't have killed me if we'd made love. She might have killed me for refusing.

But she didn't. What she did was one of her patented turnings of the world on its ear, a tenuous psychological compromise. She decided that we would be better off being "just friends," a way to recoup some of her losses and keep some of her face. It was rational, if farfetched, but it was an acceptable solution for the moment. It would probably relieve the tension and rage she felt. She could always try again later. Good friends have been known to become lovers.

The troublesome part was her delusion that I loved her, always had and always would. It seemed to comfort her. It failed to comfort me, leaving a slight chill in my center that even tea couldn't warm.

Olga had predicted an outburst or an all-out campaign if Janice didn't get what she wanted from me. I'd seen the outburst; she'd threatened to cry rape. She'd momentarily lost her self-control and had regrouped, but just barely. I hoped she was done.

I hoped she would calculate that it was to her benefit to let me be, no matter how much she thought I loved her, and move on to greener pastures. There was no percentage in pursuing me.

It was easy enough reflecting on Janice's behavior. But what about me? Where was I in the picture?

Had I ever loved her? Had that hurting boy felt love, or was it some derivative of lust?

It was not love. Love is warm. Love came later in my life and was ripped from me in the blink of an eye. And that's where I always got stuck. Love had played its dirtiest trick on me and I literally never got over it. Kate was right. Zora's death so overshadowed any other single event in my history that I forgot that I had lived, and even hurt, before.

Widowerhood became my apparel and I had worn it with some dignity ever since. It served me, except when it blinded me to the reality of everything that happened before she died.

I was woefully unprepared to confront Janice when she returned to my life. It was as if my youth had been blotted out by the tragedy. But now I had all the data. I could deal with the psychic debris that Kate had urged me months ago to sweep out.

Janice reappeared and I felt stirrings, which even Tupelo wouldn't let me deny. "She turns you on." Don't be ridiculous, I'd thought, this damaged, mangled creature came to me for help. I am a healer. I control my stirrings.

Tonight, when Janice had peeled off her clothes and presented her gifts to me, in those seconds of indecision before I pushed her away, I saw it all. I saw what would come down if Simon Rose failed to control an impulse.

The scene I envisioned was lustful enough but could not claim real passion. Passion requires feeling. I saw only a blow-up doll and porn-flick sex, the kind young fetuses like myself confused once upon a time with love. Had I been in a theater I would have walked out.

What touched me most in these rapid-fire images was that the Simon Rose in the movie was a child. A child living in a shed next to his parents' house, smoking dope and dreaming of manhood. I saw my old yearning and pain for Janice Donahue, who wielded the power of sexual validation like a queen's scepter in her hand.

It was simple. She had the attributes that North American males in the sixties were taught to crave. I had wanted to possess those attributes, not purely for physical reasons but also for some fantasy that her power would brush off on me as a result of our sexual union. But the sexual part forgot to be magic the one and only time it happened. And then she took off for college, leaving her options open and closing mine.

I didn't have to suffer long. I came of age when, by a political accident, for fifteen minutes planetary time, the nerds and the brains—and not the jocks—got their due. Although free love was never what it was cracked up to be, it did finally allow me entrance into the world of postpubescent sex and eventual adulthood.

Janice never made the crossing. By some fluke of nature poorly mixed with nurture, she had remained stunted. When she offered me her sexual treats now I couldn't help but think that I'd be committing statutory rape, as if violating a minor, because Janice was a minor in every way but age.

At the moment when I controlled that impulse, the stirrings were laid to rest once and for all. Janice finally came clear for what she really was, an old movie playing in my head. Only this time the ancient projector ran out of film. I could hear the clicking as the end of the celluloid slapped against the spindle until gravity brought it to a halt.

We broke up, I thought, and almost laughed out loud. "The ice cream cone fell on the floor," I muttered to myself.

"Had to happen," Tupelo said.

I nodded, recognizing the truth. I bent down and scratched Tupelo vigorously from head to the tip of her tail. I suddenly wished Debby would walk in the door. After an hour of mental housecleaning I wanted to be with someone who loved me. Debby was it and she was, as usual, absent. I could have called her at Bobbi's, but psychological hubris stayed my hand. I wished she and Bobbi would come sleep here. They could have my waterbed.

I slept like dead meat and awoke with the kind of clarity that is frightening.

I ran to Debby's room but it was untouched. I called Bobbi's but there was no answer and no answering machine. Barely suppressing panic, I realized I had no choice but to wait, calling Bobbi's every two minutes or so. I chewed some raw valerian root.

I didn't know how I could have missed such a crucial and obvious connection. If Janice was still focusing her rage on me, on my rejection of her, where would the rage be directed? At me? Not likely. I was still the object of her pursuit. My faint hope of the night before, that she would simply move on to her next host organism, had faded completely. If Janice needed her pound of flesh, it could come from only one source.

I had to get Debby away, out of the line of fire. Janice had studied her and knew entirely too much about her life. Three hours and sixty calls later an empty pint of Ben and Jerry's Super Fudge Chunk lay forgotten at my feet and Debby still hadn't shown up at either of her homes.

Finally, around noon, Bobbi's lunch hour, they arrived, laughing, jabbering, unharmed. I nearly cried.

"You look like death warmed over," Debby said. "What's the matter?"

I explained in detail my concern for her safety. I told her the truth, hoping she wouldn't fight me. Janice was angry, dangerous, and in the habit of acting out her rage. In my case, Debby was her only real competition. Janice had already sleazed a ride and a cup of tea at Bobbi's apartment. They were both all too vulnerable.

I expected opposition, double-barreled, but I got none. Janice had left her impression on both of them.

"Let's get the fuck out of here," Debby said.

"I'm off at five," Bobbi answered. "Or forget it, I'll call in sick for the afternoon. Beats calling in dead on Monday. Where should we go?"

The only safe house I could think of was my father's. Debby loved it there, out at Workman's Lake, Janice's old haunt. But Janice was in New York now. I called Gabe and he said he would love the company.

I booked them on a flight to Detroit in two hours. They decided to share Debby's clothes and skip going back to Bobbi's apartment. They were gone within the hour. I asked them to call in the evening from Gabe's so that I could breathe again.

They called around seven, safe and sound, and I inhaled a complete, unrestricted lungful of air for the first time all day.

I made myself a pot of Morning Thunder tea even though it wasn't morning. I would have much preferred Kate's company to my own and had in fact called to see if she would provide my activity for the evening, but she was attending a Bar Association function. That meant a new array of men in well-tailored suits for Kate to choose from. I wasn't exactly jealous. I just couldn't figure out why she wouldn't rather be with me, especially when I needed her. Jealousy it was not. Serious resentment is what it was.

So that left me and ESPN Thursday night college football, pitting

Nowhere State against Southeastern Somewhere. All told, it beat no football at all, so I popped up some corn, ready to feign enjoyment. There would at least be a lot of passing.

I let Tupelo out for a solitary evening constitutional, something she dealt with occasionally when I wasn't into walking. I knew I'd be holed up for three and a half hours and didn't want to make her wait. The game was everything it promised, four hundred yards passing for each team, seventy points scored and somebody won.

I had forgotten Tupelo. It wasn't until after I shut off the game that I heard the anxious whimper coming from the door. She sounded like a kitten in distress.

"I'm sorry, girl," I said to myself as I hurried to let her in. I rarely forgot Tupelo, but it had happened before, most recently during an NCAA hoop tournament game that Michigan lost.

"I'm sorry, Tupelo," I repeated when I finally opened the door. "I got into the game and just forgot. Why didn't you bark?" She usually barked if I was late, delicately for a full-grown dog, but she never whimpered.

She walked past me calmly, but quickly, without stopping for a greeting. I thought she was pissed off. She barely let me touch her head as she passed. She settled herself in the head shop on her favorite Rya rug.

But she didn't seem pissed, unusual for Tupelo who does not care to be kept waiting. She just began the meticulous job of grooming herself, licking her paw, rubbing it gently over her right ear, licking it again, continuing the process for as long as it would take till she'd covered everything that needed attention. She could keep herself occupied this way for hours.

I went to the kitchen to fetch her an egg, a small apology for my thoughtlessness. I noticed that my hand was wet, some gloop she must have picked up during her two-and-a-half-hour wait. By the time I reached the kitchen my fingers were unpleasantly sticky.

I ran back to the head shop. Tupelo was still working on her right ear. She was not upset. That was me. The gluey, viscous stuff on my hand, which I could now see clearly in the light of the head shop, resembled the substance pooling at Tupelo's side.

"Tupelo!"

I went to her and held her face in my hands. There was blood on her paw and on the side of her face.

And her right ear was gone.

"It was my fault, Simon. Don't blame yourself. I knew I shouldn't go near her. I did it anyway. I wanted to see Elvis. I'm a dog." She rested her one-eared head on her paws.

I swallowed back my tears and rage and attended to her, belatedly. I disinfected the wound, sutured and dressed it. Tupelo didn't make a sound.

When I was done, I noticed the poundings of a headache already making steel coils out of my neck muscles. I get them after emergencies. I opened the front door, hoping some cold night air would clear it away, because if it didn't I would be pulsating pain for hours.

I searched the street, looking for what, I don't know. The lights were out at Janice's place. The night was crisp, calm, and pleasant, nothing to produce the slightest hint of alarm.

Except that at my feet rested the gnarled remains of Tupelo's ear.

three

CRIMINAL JUSTICE

J a n i c e had proven me wrong. There did exist a person mad enough to hurt a golden retriever.

Sleep was out of the question. I tried to calm down with breathing exercises. When that failed, I went for chanting, but the repetition of "fuck you, fuck you, fuck you" didn't do much for me either.

I turned the anger inward. I had saved Debby but I'd simply neglected to care for another loved one. I should have been alert enough to prevent the violence. I kept looking at Tupelo, sleeping soundly, while I whipped myself for not seeing, not hearing, and not knowing enough.

At dawn, I called Kate. I was still pumping and needed to discharge some of the energy before I burst. I woke her up, which Kate never appreciated, least of all when she had had a late night.

I made no apologies. I told her about my aborted evening with Janice, my subsequent fears, and the decision to send Debby away.

Then I told her what Janice had done to Tupelo.

I expected her to accuse me again of overreacting. She thought I was underreacting.

"And what about you?" she asked, clearly upset. "You've taken care of Debby. You didn't consider Tupelo in the equation but how could anyone have known? And now you're acting like there's no one else to protect. What about you?" she repeated.

I hadn't thought of myself as a target. I'd assumed immunity because I was the person Janice wanted. On the other hand, her failed seduction might just have been humiliating enough. I had felt her shame; she must have, too.

"I wish I had listened to you sooner," Kate said when I didn't respond. "This is getting way out of hand. There are legal measures that can be taken and I think it's time. Crazy or not, the woman is dangerous. And probably most dangerous to you."

"I don't know if she's crazy," I said. "Maybe she's just plain mad."

"I don't care what she is. I want you to put on your pants and get your butt over here now. Come for breakfast. Just get the hell out of there, please."

"I got something to do first."

"Don't do anything, Simon. Come here and we'll—" Somehow my index finger, acting completely on its own, squeezed the button on the phone and disconnected us.

I took Kate's first piece of advice. I put my pants on. Then I set myself in the window seat, no calming infusions for my soul, and I waited for Janice to walk Elvis, her two-eared golden retriever. I didn't have to wait long.

I closed the door on Tupelo and went out into the damp November cold. Janice didn't know it but we had an appointment for a follow-up evaluation.

She was clad in a blue pea jacket, mittens, and a wool hat with a pom-pom. A half-pint flask jutted from her right side pocket. She looked every bit the faded cheerleader. Dismay swept over her face when she saw me.

She made a first attempt to speak, but failed in the momentary confusion caused by a chance meeting. She was lost without a prepared script. Between the booze and the spontaneity, her usual defenses were down. She smelled of gin and orange blossoms.

My eyes masked nothing, an unusual failure of analytic training. But I did intend to keep my rage under control, if not hidden. She got the idea before I could say a word.

"I knew you'd figure it out. I lost it. I'm sorry," she said to her mittens.

I nodded, recognizing the occasional truth when I heard it.

"Look, I said I'm sorry I did that. It was bad of me. I lost my temper again. You're so frustrating!" She stomped her foot. "Anyway, what are you so upset about?" she asked, starting to turn away, "I didn't hurt her bad. I could have. I've hurt others before. This time, believe me, I controlled myself."

She stayed out of striking distance, as if I were about to pounce. I didn't.

"This isn't the way it was supposed to happen at all," she said.

"How was it supposed to happen?" I finally spoke.

She shook her head and smiled. "I never pictured it like this," she said. "Let's walk a little."

We walked east toward the river, Janice keeping Elvis on a tight leash, as if holding on for dear life.

She held out her flask. "You want a hit?" I shook my head and she took a long swig.

We got down to the river and she collapsed on a bench as if her knees had buckled beneath her.

"Let's sit here for a while. I'm too loaded to keep walking. Talk with me for a minute, if you can. Maybe you'll understand."

"You talk," I said. "I'll listen."

She let Elvis off the leash but followed him nervously with her eyes just like an overprotective mother.

"You know, a long time ago, my dreams weren't that different from anyone else's. And I felt hope, too. I had it all going for me and I didn't get any of it. The sad part is that dreams don't come true. If they had, even one of them, I don't think I would've . . ."—she groped for the right words—"gotten sick, and then none of this would have happened. It could have been different."

Regret, not remorse, permeated her words. She was real for once, allowing me a glimpse of a different Janice, a Janice who might have been.

"My favorite fantasy these last few months was to start over again, for real this time, with you. And no games. You're different from anyone else I've ever known in my life. You're not like Daddy or like Dennis.

"Simon, I want to have another baby, yours. More than anything in the world. I still can, you know. I haven't gone through the change yet. And I want one. It's the right time."

I couldn't believe what I was hearing. The cold penetrated to my core. A baby? Mine? And what would she do with it once she had it?

"But I know it's delusional. Deep down I do sense the truth, you know. You don't want me now. That was a long time ago, just like you said, in another life. You don't have to answer. I know what's real." She looked at me for a long moment. Then she shook her head, called Elvis, and fumbled with his leash and collar until he was again hooked up to her.

She found her place in the script. The pitch and timbre of her voice changed. She was on again. She brightened, getting playful. The transformation was remarkable, and scary.

"Look," she said, "I still think we can make it together. But at the moment, I think maybe we need a little distance, some time to think it all through, to keep our options open. But I have faith," she said. "Our time will come."

What was wrong with this woman? You don't seduce a guy by maiming his dog. Stunned, disbelieving, I could hardly find my voice. My words came out in a hoarse whisper. "Are you crazy?"

She opened her eyes wide, her whole face a question mark. "You're the expert."

She was wrong. I couldn't claim to be an expert in this case.

It is a truism that surgeons must not operate on members of their own family. Nor should forensic psychiatrists evaluate their high school sweethearts. When I asked Janice if she was crazy, my only intent had been to convey my outrage. But it was an intriguing question, yet to be satisfactorily answered. Belatedly, I thanked the universe for having given me sufficient wisdom to bail out of the defense team.

Janice and I agreed on one thing, though. We needed some distance. Maybe separate planets.

I went inside to recheck Tupelo's wound and found it clean and surprisingly well sutured. I noticed that it was still early. I could catch Kate. I left Tommy an urgent message telling him where to find me and to please do so. I put on a warmer jacket and called to Tupelo. If I couldn't get out of my skin, I could at least get out of my house.

Kate held on to me long and hard. Tears escaped when she hugged Tupelo and the torrent followed when she put her arms around me for the second time. She finally quieted to a sob. I had never seen her cry that way before. It made me want to cry, too.

She gripped me with one arm and motioned to me with the other to bring her the tissues. I managed to reach the tissues without tearing away. She extracted ten or so and patted her face with them. When she pulled the paper away it was splotched black.

"Shit," she said. "I've got to wash and start all over again. Or they'll just have to live with me au naturel today."

She was dressed for the courtroom in a severe charcoal gray wool suit with a soft, misty pearl-gray silk blouse.

"Have some breakfast while I straighten myself up. Then we need to talk, and fast. I have to put in an appearance at ten."

The kitchen table was set, brimming with scones and butter, eggs, hash browns, bagels and cream cheese, all ordered from the deli in the building. Only the coffee was home-brewed, scummy and miserable as usual. I couldn't imagine eating anything, but Tupelo accepted a scone and nibbled it delicately.

Kate reappeared, freshly painted.

"You almost never wear makeup."

"Depends on the case. This one requires liner." She looked at me sitting in front of an empty plate and at Tupelo eating the scone bit by bit. I thought she was going to burst into tears again.

"I'm so glad you're both here, I can't tell you."

"You told us. We know."

She rolled up to the table, doubtfully perusing its offerings. She poured herself a cup of coffee, grabbed a bagel and slathered it with cream cheese. She gazed at it in disgust. "If I don't eat I won't make it through the morning." She ate joylessly.

My rage had been replaced by a dazed, dreamy feeling, a mild case of shock which, by definition, I didn't identify at the time. I watched Kate vacantly. I gave Tupelo a bagel, for a more challenging chew, and she was mashing it into submission. Kate did the same with hers.

"Simon, I'm your best friend in the world, but for the moment I would like to talk strictly as your attorney. You have a legal problem and I think it needs addressing now, today." She wiped her mouth and poured a second cup of coffee. "I see three possible courses of action. I want you to think about them, all day if you need. We can decide tonight."

She must have noticed that I wasn't looking at her while she spoke. She reached over and turned my face toward her. "You have to listen," she said.

"I'm listening. You see two possible courses of action."

She sighed, recognizing diminished capacity when she saw it. "All right, never mind for now. We'll forget about taking any steps today. It's probably best not to act precipitously. Can you agree to that at least?"

I nodded, but I was thinking about the pool of blood, Tupelo's wound, and the torn flesh on my doorstep. I wondered why I hadn't tried to reattach the ear. If it worked for severed penises it had to work for ears. Then I remembered that I'm not a surgeon.

"Listen," Kate implored, "do us all a favor. Spend the day here. My house is your house. Use it. Get some sleep. You're so spaced out you're practically a cliché. Get your brain functioning. We'll talk tonight, earlier if I can get away. Will you do it?"

I nodded again while I watched Janice on my private screen, backing away from me in the street, telling me we could still make it together.

"Promise?" She knew she wasn't getting through.

"Promise," I said, but I had no idea what I was promising.

Chapter Twenty-four

I s h o w e r e d in the guest bathroom and fell asleep on the king-size bed, with Tupelo curled up next to me. When I awoke midafternoon I was hungry, so I filled up on cold bagels and cream cheese. The eight-hour-old eggs didn't look appealing and neither did the graying potatoes.

My head began the slow climb back to the light. I could think again.

I mistrust gut feelings. They're usually a sign of indigestion more than insight. Heart feelings are the most reliable, but for me they're a rare occurrence. I rely mostly on that which I know I can count on, my head, my most meritorious organ, the producer of rational thought. Up till now, my instincts about this case had been plagued by doubts because of Janice's dramatic role in my coming-of-age. This time, however, the panorama shone clear, perhaps because my vision was no longer clouded by memories of unrequited lust.

The question of craziness versus sociopathy was now academic. The only issue that mattered was what she had done and what she might yet do. The legal whys and wherefores had to take a back seat to her intent, her whims, her desires of the moment.

Janice was capable of gargantuan rage. She had proved that with the murder of Dennis and Sean. The physical response to her rage depended on the severity of the perceived wound. When Benito Falconi had scratched at her scar tissue, the reaction had been vicious. But her mutilation of Tupelo, while just as cruel, was unquestionably rational. She had said it herself: "This time, believe me, I controlled myself."

Rational or not, Janice had just had her second outburst. And I had to behave as if she was crazy enough to mount the whole campaign. I hoped Debby was enjoying the cold, gray Michigan winter skies. She was in for an extended vacation if I had anything to say about it.

Tommy owned a set of keys and cards to Kate's place. He found me where I had been sitting for an hour, at the kitchen table, staring off into space. He looked at Tupelo and me and then again at Tupelo, doing a Hollywood double-take as smoothly as if he'd rehearsed it. But this wasn't Tinseltown and he was dead serious.

He squatted next to her and inspected her head. "What the fuck . . . you okay, girl?"

She answered in that slow, caressing lick which in golden retriever means "Fine, thanks for asking."

He sat down opposite me. "Talk," he said.

I spoke like a computer in short, clipped sentences, only mine were missing most of the pronouns and verbs. He caught my drift.

"Stunted little bitch," he said. "I think it's time to act, not think. Are you willing to off her?"

"Jesus. I'll make like you didn't say that."

"I didn't really expect you to go for it. Why don't you and Kate come up with some nice little legal maneuver to put her away again?"

"Kate's working on that, I think. We haven't decided anything yet."

"Listen, I got a gig but it'll be over early, a christening down in Little Italy, couple hundred people, you know, just family. It's not about you being alone so I want you to stay here with Kate until nine or so, then go home. You'll know me, I'll be the one sleeping in your bedroom."

Kate got in about eight. It was dark outside and I still hadn't moved. She was frazzled. Her suit, so elegant in the morning, had drooped with the rest of her. Worry lined her eyes.

"You don't look so good," I said. "Hard day?"

"Look who's talking." She held the chrome toaster up in front of me. I saw dry, yellow cream cheese stuck to my mustache and beard, circling my mouth. I looked like I had been spoon-fed at the home and they forgot to clean me up.

"I thought I got all that," I said. I stood up, walked purposefully to the sink, and washed my face. It felt good, awakening if not invigorating.

"Let's get comfortable and talk." She poured herself a cognac in a huge snifter, looked my way, saw that I couldn't make a decision, and chose a large Perrier for me. With the drinks on a tray on her lap, she moved to the living room and I followed her. She set the tray down and started working on the kindling. She was always very precise about it and as a result, her fires normally blazed on for hours. She stripped long perfect curls of bark from the logs and placed them strategically in a mound as we spoke.

"What have you been thinking?" she asked. "It looks like sleeping didn't help much."

"This is going to sound like a broken record. I don't have any new or fancy words right now. I think what I've always thought. She's dangerous."

"And what do you want to do about it?"

"Nothing. Stay alert. Protect Debby. I don't want to take action, if that's what you mean. I don't have any wish to provoke her. She's already had two hissy fits. She could blow again. Why rile her up?"

"I was afraid you'd say something along those lines. Anything else?"

"I did my homework yesterday, before she hurt Tupelo. I should have done it months ago when you first mentioned it. You were right, of course, and I do see what she meant to me back then. I don't need anything from her but I did need to take a good look."

"I'm glad you see that. You haven't been thinking clearly about her."

"I've been thinking absolutely clearly about her. I just wouldn't trust myself."

"No, and I wasn't being exactly supportive. I didn't trust your instincts either. Yet another example of the value of separating the personal from the professional. I am sorry, Simon. Sorry I brought you in on it in the first place."

"You had your reasons. I could have said no. I had my reasons, too. Forget it. Apologies aren't the point between us."

"Oh, no, I can hear it coming. Next thing you're going to tell me that love means never having to say you're sorry."

I had to smile at that one, it dated us so. It felt good; it hadn't been a very amusing day. "Thanks, Kate."

"You're welcome."

We watched the flames for a while in comfortable silence.

"I've been thinking about it almost all day," Kate said. "She has acted out again, drastically. And in your direction. I don't know what she'll do next. She's too unpredictable. I think you have to send her a message, a clear one, of your intent. Like I said, we have three alternatives.

"The first and simplest is a temporary injunction. It could be delivered tomorrow. It forbids her to go near you or Tupelo and I could add Debby to it. It would work for the short run. Two, we could swear out a criminal complaint, but I can't accuse her of anything more serious than malicious mischief, which wouldn't accomplish much. Or we could go for outright commitment. She'll ask her father to block it, but I think we can make the case that she's dangerous and I know we can prove mental illness. We did that already. I need you to choose. You know her far better than I do."

"Which is your favorite?"

"I think you should authorize me to serve her with the injunction. I've already prepared it and had it signed. If she's done with you, then the injunction is superfluous. No harm done. If she's not, it tells her that we mean business and that we take her seriously. If you'll go along with that, then I have a second suggestion, and this one comes from me, your friend. Let's get the hell out of here after she's been served. There's no sense in waiting around for another dose of her anger."

I was amazed. "Is this really you? Is Katherine Newhouse actually suggesting flight?"

"No, I'm suggesting some time for reflection, some space. You're too close to it. I think you need some distance." That made three of us. "I've already arranged to take a week off and it can be more if we want. Let's go up to the Retreat. It's worked for you before. And I've always wanted you to know it in the winter, too. It's beautiful up there now. Will you do it? Will you go with me?"

Now that would have been hard to turn down even if it were flight. The Retreat was Kate's family home in Sandy Port, on the Maine coast. It was her favorite place on earth, her only true mental health center. It had indeed worked for me before. Kate summered there and I had joined her for at least a couple of weeks each year for the last ten. It was a magical spot that lived up to its name.

Kate was exhausted and so was I. The prospect of a week at the Retreat filled me with warmth and the hope of a better perspective. In fact, it sounded like heaven.

"Okay, let's do it. But isn't it cold up there this time of year?"

"It's bitter. Bring your mittens."

I laughed outright. I was already feeling better. Just the thought of a break was healing.

"What about the injunction?" Kate said. "I think you've got to act."

"I'll let you know in the morning, Counselor, before we hit the road. I want to sleep on it. Order us some goodies for the trip that I can eat, too, will you? When I arrived at the Retreat last year all you had in the fridge was a pound of sliced liverwurst."

"Not true. I had pickles, too."

I hugged her and put on my jacket.

"Where do you think you're going?"

"I've got to go home and get packed for the trip. I need my mittens."

"Go with Tommy."

"He's meeting me there."

She frowned at me. "Why don't you both spend the night? I'll feel much better if you're here where I can see you and not there, where she can."

"It's only a few hours. Don't worry."

"Simon, I'm worried. She's angry and dangerous. And she's totally obsessed with you."

Chapter Twenty-five

Kate's phone rang early the next morning just as we were leaving. Tupelo snorted her disappointment when we stopped halfway out the door.

We were off to Maine. The K-mobile was loaded with clothes, music, and enough groceries to feed greater Portland for a month. Kate wasn't taking any chances. She didn't care for unsatisfied appetites.

We had just discussed the injunction one more time. I told her I thought it was useless, like health insurance. The fact that you invest exorbitant amounts year in and year out does not insure that you will stay healthy. I pointed out that the timely delivery of an injunction doesn't necessarily ensure that the unwanted intruder will stay away from you. Kate disagreed but accepted my decision with an irritated "Suit yourself."

She was in the hallway right behind me, but by the second ring we both knew she was going back. I stopped her. "Don't answer it, Kate."

Something in my voice connected and she said, "Okay, I'll just turn on the sound."

The answering machine kicked in on the fifth ring and I listened impatiently to its staccato rhythm.

"Uh, hello . . . ?" Hesitant, adolescent, definitely not in her usual kitten-in-heat mode.

"This is Jan? I'm, uh . . . I really need to get in touch with Simon? And I thought you might know where he is. Is he . . . is he there? Simon? Are you there?"

My scalp bristled.

"Simon? I need you. I'm feeling really bad? It's . . . I'm losing myself. Listen, I gotta talk to you. I'm in trouble . . . " Her breath caught in her throat. "You're the only person that I can trust. Please. Come to me? I need you. Come."

A long pause, hanging on.

Then, quietly, "I need your help," and the final click, like the sound of an empty handgun.

Kate took the wheel first. I was too wired to drive but even had I been at my most transcendent, balanced self, I wouldn't have taken on the Saturday traffic in Manhattan. City driving had always been a formidable mystery to me. Not so to Kate. She threaded effortlessly through the Triboro Bridge maze and we were soon cruising on Interstate 95.

I had kept quiet for almost an hour, only partially due to my awe of Kate's driving skill. The plaintive sound of Janice's voice had sent chills through my system and I had yet to recover my body heat completely. I kept fiddling with the controls of the car heater, but to no avail.

"What's going on with you, Simon? You getting sick or something? You've been playing with that thing the whole time. I already told you, it's automatic."

"I can't get comfortable."

"It's the call, not the temperature."

"I guess."

"You were right, I shouldn't have answered it."

"Too late now."

"Okay, I'll make you a deal. When we got in the car I said we weren't going to discuss Janice on this trip, but I'm willing to do so if you'll agree to one condition—that we quit when we hit the Massachusetts state line. I mean it, though. Even if you're midway into the most brilliant interpretation of your career, you'll have to shut up. From Massachusetts on you get on Retreat rhythm with me whether you like it or not. You'll just have to surrender."

"It's a deal."

"So what's bothering you about her call?"

"Well, I think it needs responding to. Did you hear the desperation in her voice? She almost sobbed when she said she's in trouble. And that adolescent lilt, the way all her statements end like questions. She's regressed. Debby and her friends used to talk like that, but even they've outgrown it by now."

I stopped to gather my thoughts. I wasn't sure what I was going for.

"Ever since she got out of the hospital I've been advocating caution because I saw her as dangerous. And it's not that I think I was wrong. I just see her in a different light, now that I don't need anything from her. She's dangerous, yes. Tupelo can testify to that. But it's because she's sick, confused. She looks at the world through the eyes of a paranoid teenager. That's where I think she got stuck, at about sixteen, when her mother died. She really does need treatment. I feel an urgency to do something, I just don't think I'm the man for the job."

"Don't do anything yet. Don't even decide anything yet," Kate said. "I want to have my say, uninterrupted, and then you can have yours." She glanced at me for assent and I nodded, but she didn't speak right away. I saw her swallow a couple of times, struggling with her thoughts. Several minutes went by before she finally spoke.

"Obviously I'm having a hard time with this, you'll see why in a minute. When I was working on Janice's case I had certain impressions, what you would have called gut feelings. Now don't laugh, I'm serious.

"Every once in a while Janice would say or do something that simply jarred me inside. Something was off, I felt it instinctively but I rationalized it, to be honest, and told myself I was overreacting to the woman's peculiar brand of mental illness. But now, in light of what she did to Tupe, I've forced myself to look at the data with different eyes, and I mean *all* the data, from day one."

There was an edge to her voice that quickened my pulse. I watched her profile intently as she continued.

"Anyway, I've suffered enough with my doubts. I've looked dispassionately at the case and at my role in it and here's the hard part. I've been totally wrong. I was taken in by her and there's nothing I hate worse than to be made a fool of in my own eyes.

"I remember you lent me a tough book a couple of years ago, the one by that psychiatrist about the people of the lie. It shook me up then and it's been on my mind since yesterday morning. Not to put too fine a point on the matter, I've come to the conclusion that Janice is not crazy, maybe she never was. Simon, I think she's evil."

Kate turned my way for a split second and looked me in the eye so I'd

feel the full impact of her words. My body temperature took another profound dip, but I controlled the impulse to touch the dashboard. I said
nothing.

"I want to start at the beginning. If I tell it all to you I'll understand it
better myself. Let's go back to the week after she was arrested. You remember my notes were pretty sketchy from those first interviews. That's
because I always make it a top priority to keep my feelings out of the case
histories. I take my work seriously—this is not news to you—and my
work was to defend her. So I built a case. Objectively.

"I'll start with the murders. She showed no remorse for what she'd
done. She was glad they were dead, *both* of them. There was no sign of
grief, only rage and resentment. I could handle what she said about her
husband. I've heard lots worse. But the child, Simon. Now I think she
knew exactly what she was doing. I think she killed them because she
didn't want to bother with them anymore."

I rolled down the window for a blast of Connecticut November. It was
just as cold as New York but with a lot less carbon monoxide.

"In hindsight I'm even having my doubts about the voices. I witnessed
several bizarre conversations. Oh, she made sure of that. And there's no
doubt she talked to her mother, or at least she pretended to. But looking
back on it now, I wouldn't really call it conversation. More like a steady
monologue. Janice never listened. It sounded strange to me and I should
have heeded my instincts. It was like the only voice in her head was her
own. The rest, if it existed, could be turned on and off at will. I'm not a
shrink and I know next to nothing about auditory hallucinations, but it
doesn't seem right. Does this make any sense, Simon?"

A rhetorical question, no response required.

"And she hated her mother. She bitched about her constantly. Once,
she mentioned that her mother was a drunk, that she bonked her head on
a lamp and died, and she laughed. The comment left me hollow and cold,
and I didn't give it the attention I should have. But the more I've thought
about it, the more the whole thing seems wrong.

"Hey, you ready to drive yet?" She was already slowing down. "There's
a rest area coming up. Let's switch." She parked and waited for me to get
out of the car.

While Kate made herself comfortable in the passenger seat I walked
around to the driver's side and got in. I turned off the manual controls
and we were rolling again in no time. Kate picked up where she left off.

"And then there was Falconi. Now I'm pretty sure Janice orchestrated the whole scene. She even knew how the trial would turn out."

"What do you mean? Get specific."

"Well, she wasn't the least bit frightened. I've worked with defendants, guilty and innocent, from every race and social stratum, and they all have one thing in common. They're all scared. Remember O.J.'s face the day his trial began? Even O.J. showed it. Some suffer a little more, some a little less, but they're all afraid of what could happen to them no matter how strong a case the attorneys have prepared. It's human nature. But Janice wasn't fazed. She felt no doubt and no fear. She had it all figured out. Poor Falconi. Janice's sacrificial lamb." My hand rose of its own accord to rub my eye.

Kate went on. "I hate to admit it but you were on track all along and I was way off. When you reacted as you did to her shenanigans I tried to convince you she was harmless, a victim of her illness. But Simon, you were absolutely right. The whole seduction thing, the calls, her visit, taking that apartment, those are not the acts of a person who's out of control. I know what out of control is, I lived with it for eighteen years in its alcoholic variety. When Janice whaled on Tupelo she'd already had time. That wasn't a heated reaction. It required a cool, precise energy that could only have been calculated. She was pissed off. At you, it's obvious why. She was acting out and she loved it."

Tupelo's tail thumped emphatically. Kate glanced back at her. "Thanks, Tupe. See? She understands. You offended Janice when you turned her down and she wanted to hurt you for it. And she got you by going for a loved one. It's pure psychopathy if you ask me.

"Now check this out." She rummaged around in her voluminous shoulder bag and extracted an audiotape. She ejected the vintage Rickie Lee Jones we'd been listening to and inserted the other cassette, but her finger froze on the play button.

"The day after your ill-fated evening with Janice, sometime before she hurt Tupelo, she called me to ask if she could come over. I wasn't feeling up to it so I said no, but I stayed on the phone with her for quite a while. She was in a talkative mood. In fact, she sounded normal, if you can use that word anywhere in her vicinity. You know I always tape business calls. Well, I taped this one, too. We can skip the ritual greetings. I'm going to fast-forward it, give me a sec."

The tape wheezed and clicked a few times and I caught snatches of the conversational preliminaries. When Kate finally found the play button, Janice was in the middle of a sentence, voice calm, rational, even thoughtful.

" . . . haven't exactly had an easy time of it. You might not think so because I come off so bubbly and all that, but it was a bitch growing up in my family. It was a madhouse. Sometimes I don't know how I got out alive."

There was a brief silence followed by Kate's voice, the small voice, intimate, connecting.

"I know what you mean. In my family it was only my father who drank, but it's six of one, half dozen of the other. My mother was totally involved in his alcoholism and that was before they invented co-dependency."

"Yeah, both of my role models were fucked up, too. You met my father, a weak little man, always was. Found it easier to be married to the bottle than to my mother. You can't blame him. She kicked him around like an old junkyard dog 'til there was nothing left of him. He's a victim, really, of both of us. He isn't much of a man but I love him.

"And my mother was a fourteen-carat bitch first and a drunk second. She'd have been a mean drunk if she'd never even touched the stuff. She was evil and I came from her flesh, God knows why. I had to survive in that zoo with something of me left intact, and I did it.

"You know, I only had one good year in my entire life and Simon witnessed it. It was the year after my mother died. It was an enormous relief, really. With her gone, Daddy and I could have a life. But she didn't leave us alone. She had more power dead than alive. I don't think I ever really had a chance."

Kate stopped the tape. "Okay, here's what really gets me. Obviously, this was before she acted out, but still, that's not the voice of a disturbed person. Simon, I got sucked in. I discussed my family with her. I haven't done that in years with anyone but you. There's something about sharing insights with another survivor. I want to kick myself for letting down my guard with her that way. But that's not the point. The point is that within a couple of hours of this call she cut up Tupelo."

Except for Tupelo's gentle snoring behind us, we rode in silence for a while. Kate had finished her story but I could tell she wasn't done. She emitted that intensely concentrated aura which meant she was about to pronounce a major decision.

I focused on the road and the scenery. We were moving north on I-395 and had just passed the Norwich exits, so there was plenty of time. I was feeling calm for the first time in days because I knew what I had to do. It was obvious. I had to communicate with Janice's new shrink. All I needed was a quick call to Justin Katz to find out the name of the lucky fellow. He was the man for the job.

"Here's what I want to do, Simon. Let's call Dr. Masters."

"Who's Dr. Masters?"

"Janice's follow-up therapist. I thought you knew. She went regularly after she finished the transition program but I don't know if she still does. Good shrink, top reputation, at least in legal circles."

Scratch that call to Justin Katz. "Tell me more about him," I said.

"Who?"

"Her therapist, what's he like?"

"She."

"Huh?"

"She. What's she like. Dr. Amanda Masters. She's in her mid-thirties, very competent, stellar credentials. I've heard her testify a few times and she's extremely poised, knows her stuff, even under the duress of my scathing cross."

So *she* was the man for the job. "What do you need her for?" I asked.

"I want Janice put away. Now in my gut, I know the woman isn't crazy. But I'm going to go for civil commitment. And for that, I need evidence."

"Hey, you need evidence, just visit her apartment."

"What do you mean?"

"Actually, I don't think it would hold up in court, but I was impressed by the level of obsession I saw. No, impressed is the wrong word. I was aghast.

"First of all, she's got this shrine in her bedroom. You should see it. You know how these New Age veggie restaurants put up Buddhist altars at the back of their dining room—with a statue and pictures and flowers and incense? Well, except for the statue it's all there. And instead of portraits of the Buddha, she's got these beautifully framed photographs hanging in a semicircle over her desk. Pictures of us, Janice and me, in all these different settings, from high school."

"The woman needs to get a life."

"Wait a minute, it's worse than you think. It was so weird it spooked me. I took a while to figure it out. See, Janice and I never dated each other. We never went anywhere together with the notable exception of one outdoor R&B festival, and everyone there was too stoned to focus a camera."

"I don't get it."

"I didn't either until I examined her bookshelf. That's Exhibit B. Kate, the pictures are collages. Photographic fiction manufactured by way of a cut-and-paste job on the candids in our senior yearbook. I can only begin to imagine the intricate surgery required. Those framed photos are perfect. You'd need Sherlock Holmes's magnifying glass to detect the seams. I was blown away, what can I tell you."

"You're right, that is weird." Kate was suitably impressed. And she'd dealt with so many weirdos it wasn't that easy to impress her. "Is there more?"

"Yeah, the scrapbooks, a case study of an obsession. Apparently, she's kept track of me for years. The first entry was Xeroxed from an ancient volume of the *Journal of the American Psychiatric Association*. An obscure paper I read at the APA conference my last year in med school. It was the first time my work appeared in print for public consumption.

"I don't know how she did it but I'd swear she's got every clipping of every article that ever appeared in the press mentioning my name. I take that back, of course I know how she did it. She paid a clipping service. Anyway, some of it she found and clipped herself, 'cause the newsprint is all yellow and brittle and flaking. It totally gave me the creeps. Jesus, now I'm starting to sound like Debby. Totally gave me the creeps?"

Kate smiled. "Brings out the teenager in you, doesn't it?"

"Just what I don't need right now. Okay, I'd better move along, we're almost out of Connecticut. She has the complete text of the *Mother Jones* article bound in a fancy cover that must have cost plenty, with her favorite quotes highlighted in Day-Glo magenta. She even got herself a video copy of the interview with Peter Jennings, God only knows how.

"A couple of other items are worthy of note. She kept a scrapbook for a little while on Will Hardin. I told you about him, her high school sweetheart. He had a short and unremarkable pro career with the Detroit Lions and when he quit, of course, his name also quit appearing in print, so that's a mostly empty scrapbook.

"And last but not least, you've got to hear about her reference shelf. There are only two books on it. The latest *DSM* and a *PDR*. I don't have to spell out their significance for you."

"No. I am sorry to hear that."

The *Diagnostic and Statistical Manual of Mental Disorders* is another publication of the APA. There are two reasons to be the proud owner of such a handy manual. First, it is used by psychotherapists for the purpose of assigning numbers to the various pathologies that parade before them in clinical practice. The *DSM* is a cookbook of every conceivable mental disorder, soup to nuts, Paranoid Schizophrenia to Trichotillomania, my personal favorite, which is described as a "recurrent failure to resist impulses to pull out one's hair." It lists the ingredients of every psychopathology imaginable, and assigns a number to each one. Without the official number the insurance companies won't pay the therapists' exorbitant fees.

The second reason to have the *DSM* is to finesse the civil authorities in cases of involuntary commitment, or the criminal authorities when making a plea of Not Guilty by Reason of Insanity. The *DSM* is definitely not something you pick up for a good, spicy read.

Neither is the *Physicians' Desk Reference*. An encyclopedia of drugs and medication, the *PDR* comes complete with instructions for the medicine man. It is useful to designer drug producers, who like to change a molecule here and there to produce a new high. And it's useful to the physician, so what was Janice studying it for?

"That's it, Kate. What do you think?"

"None of that sounds like mental illness to me. And it doesn't to you either. I've said what my intention is. I'm going to do what I can to get her committed. I've made some mistakes in my career. Most of them weren't too serious. But that woman is a mistake that needs correcting.

"Now, about real admissible evidence. You and Tommy are going to have to do some buttwork. I want you to come up with a strategy, but more than that I want facts. History, records, run down the thing with her mother. And what about Dennis? He was a cop, for heaven's sake. There's stuff to know out there. The day we get back to the city, consider yourself hired by Newhouse and Associates to do an in-depth investigation of Ms. Jensen's background. All expenses paid."

"Okay. I think we should begin with Dr. Masters and work our way back from there. We've both got business with her. I'd like to know for example how Janice—"

"Sorry, Simon."

Massachusetts.

Chapter Twenty-six

Th e fragrance of freshly fallen snow washed over me as I stepped down from the K-mobile. Like Proust's cakes, the smell brought on a powerful wave of nostalgia. I stood beside the car for several minutes lost in memories of childhood, of wild exhilaration, of stepping out all bundled up into that first crystalline morning of real winter. Tupelo, never one to waste time, was already romping around in the soft ankle-deep fluff.

We were in Sandy Port, about twenty minutes up the coast from Boothbay Harbor. I'd never seen the cottage set against a backdrop of such pure, quiet white. Kate's grandfather had been a master carpenter, and his craftsmanship spoke to us from the hand-hewn beams along the back porch and the weathered gray shingles on the walls. In its first life the Retreat had been her grandparents' home, a cozy two-bedroom house where her mother had grown up and in which Kate herself had spent a considerable part of her own childhood. The best part, she always said.

A neighbor had fired up the boiler for us, and the old-fashioned radiators, the kind that look like accordions, were contentedly hissing and clanking along. I unloaded the foodstuffs and went straight to the kitchen to start dinner. Tupelo judiciously chose to keep me company there.

Kate wanted to use the last half hour of daylight to chop wood. "I don't quite feel that I'm really here until I get the fire going," she said and disappeared down a ramp to the covered patio out back. The cottage boasted state-of-the-art adaptations for her wheelchair both indoors and out.

I puttered comfortably to the rhythm of Kate's axe, a steady whack-thud, whack-thud that reminded me how important exercise was to her. I always marveled at her strength, which she maintained with twice-a-week workouts at the gym.

Two hours later, stuffed with fried rice and cucumber-yogurt salad, we sat with the last of our jasmine tea in the living room. Tupelo slept in a perfect circle, snout invisible, exactly midway between us and the fire-place, while Kate snuggled in at the opposite end of the couch from me, her legs propped in my lap. We were sharing an intricate quilt that some great-aunt had fashioned for Kate's mother's hope chest.

"We always seem to be sitting together in front of blazing fires," she said.

"I know. I can't think of anything else I'd rather be doing. Maybe ever again. Let's give it all up and just stay in this spot for the rest of our lives."

"Sounds good to me."

But jet lag eventually caught up with us and we each went off to our bedrooms. A fragment of a Sunday school recitation floated in and out of my mind as I dropped down into sleep: "And the evening and the morning were the first day."

Day two flowed by as peacefully as a slow-moving river.

Winter life at the Retreat defined tranquillity. After breakfast we read aloud to each other, chopped mountains of firewood, took turns prepar-ing snacks, listened to Bach and Van Morrison on the CD, and conversed quietly whenever the spirit moved us. We laughed in amazement any time one of us recalled some crazy detail of our "normal" city-paced life.

At twilight time Kate made a fire and started talking about her mar-riage, something she hadn't done in at least ten years.

"At the appropriate age I was handed over to Harry. He didn't abuse me at first. He was more interested in snorting coke. He was still young, a beginner. But it didn't take him long to get aggressive. The strange thing is, see if you can digest this, I actually felt that I was well off. He was so mild in his abuse, compared to my father, that I considered myself lucky to have improved my situation so much.

"And then the accident broke the chain. I got a life, my own, and I like it. What am I missing? No, don't answer that. I know what I'm missing."

We sat quietly for a while, the silence broken periodically by the pop-ping of burning cedar.

"I've thought a lot about you and men," I said.

"And I'd be willing to bet you're now going to tell me what it all means."

"I've been puzzled by one thing. Your men are always cold, distant types, with the exception of me. I think I'm your only emotional outlet. You keep the rest at bay by choosing men who don't have any affect.

"I think you learned early to choose no emotion over irrational emotion, but you pay a price. You put your mind and body into your relationships but you keep your heart out. It never works, unless what you truly want is to be alone."

Kate's lip began to curl, proof that I was treading on tender ground.

"And somehow out of this, you get what you think you deserve. You get sterile, bloodless relationships with men in secure positions and well-tailored suits. I've seen them. Not one of them is a threat to you emotionally. They're not even a challenge. So all you get is good company."

Her lip quivered, just a touch and just on the curl.

"And show me the passion in good company. I know sex is a part of your relationships—I'm not talking about sex. I'm talking about passion. Heart."

"What about you? You're a fine one to talk."

"Leave me out of it for now. We're talking about your walls this time, not mine. You have yet to choose one man who can appreciate you, one man who can really touch you."

The quivering became more pronounced and one controlled tear fell from her eye. She kept staring at the fire.

"Someday you're going to have to take the leap. You're going to have to trust that a man can love you, even passionately, without getting violent on you. They're not all your father or Harry. There are men out there, decent men, sober men, alive men, and they're not all abusive or frozen."

"Show me one," she challenged.

I spread my arms, palms uplifted, eliciting a melodious belly laugh from Kate.

"If you're an example of the emotionally available man, I'm afraid I am in deep trouble."

"I was being facetious but don't laugh it off. It's more important than that. You have a whole category of things in your life that you used to do. Dancing, walking. I think there's another—allowing yourself to be loved. It's something you used to do. Make it something you do now."

She was silent for a long moment before she responded. "You're wrong about only one thing. I never allowed it."

"You ought to consider the possibility."

"That's too depressing. Let's consider something else."

"Okay, consider this. You and I are not that different. Sure, we came by our pain in different ways, but check out the results. You're alone in the company of men and I'm alone in the company of women. What's the difference?"

"I get laid," she said, smiling through two more designated tears. "And I get drunk, occasionally, which seems at the moment a fabulous idea. Would you stay up with me? I hate drinking alone."

Kate was true to her word. She got roaring drunk. I watched, half wishing that I could join her. Afterwards, she let me help her to bed.

It was a new experience for us, this extended, intimate companionship. In the past I had always come to the Retreat in summertime, and I'd grown accustomed to sharing Kate's attention with the myriad overnight guests up from the city and the elderly neighbors who dropped in frequently to reminisce about Kate's family.

This time we had only each other for company and our friendship was deepening in subtle ways. A profound harmony pervaded our activities and even our silences. We both felt it, and yet we were reluctant to talk about it directly.

Our fourth evening, after a championship snowball fight in the front yard, we were once again ensconced in our spots at opposite ends of the couch, talking about childhood.

"Did I ever tell you about my grandfather?" Kate said.

"I know that he took care of you for a while but I don't remember the details. Tell me again."

"It's a long story. You sure you want to hear it?"

"Of course."

"I think he's who saved me."

"Saved you?"

"Yeah, like a guardian angel."

"Are you putting me on?"

"No. Listen, I know it's very 'in' now, almost trite, to have guardian angels. People wear them in their hatbands, for heaven's sake. But I'm talking the real thing here, and it was long before California picked up the concept and made it cool.

"I called him Papa. He was already retired when I came to live with them. My grandmother still worked in town—she was a clerk at the bank. I was five, I know, because that was the year I started kindergarten. At the time the reason given for my moving in with them, the family myth, really, was that it was economics. Mother had to go to work. My father was drinking a lot and always changing jobs and I guess Mother felt she had to provide some stability. But looking back on it now, I think it was the fights." Kate stared into the fire and moisture gathered at the corner of her eye.

"There were constant fights, the worst of them on weekends when he was at his most belligerent. But at least those were predictable. The unexpected explosions were much more frightening. You know how it is with alcoholics. My father could be quite docile one minute and the next he would erupt into one of his rages. He was completely irrational and polymorphously abusive. I learned to run and hide when he blew. Sometimes I got away. My mother never got away.

"Anyway, I don't want to go into that, it's just bad history. My mother must have sensed the damage it was doing to me, so she used the excuse of her new job to move me over here to my grandparents'. No big deal, it was only a mile from our house—I didn't even have to change schools."

The beverage was hot cocoa that night and at this point we both leaned over for our mugs, took a sip, and settled back into our corners.

"So for the first time in my short life I discovered what it was to feel safe. Consistently, divinely safe. Papa was a gentle man. Since he didn't have his shop anymore, he was the one who was always here for me. I remember clearly the first week I was actually living here, walking to school with him, stretching my arm up to hold his hand—he was very tall, even by adult standards. He felt he should walk me until I got used to the new route. Later I went by myself. When I got home, he'd always have lunch ready. Then he'd read to me or we'd go out back to putter in the shed or to chop firewood. That's when I learned how, you know, with a small hatchet he made for me.

"Simon, I felt like I was in a bubble. Papa's presence enveloped me and I knew that so long as he was around, no harm would come to me. Of course I couldn't have put it into words then, but had I had the words I would have called it utter peace. Something like now."

I took both her hands in mine. I didn't want to speak. No way would I interrupt Kate's process. I was just glad to be there.

"Well, the real blessing was that I got to live with him for two whole years, until we moved to the city. So for two years, with the exception of a few weekends and my mother's vacation, I lived in peace.

"When Papa died the year after we moved, I felt like I'd been left alone on the planet. But at least we had those two years. They were essential for me. I learned that there was another reality, that there was another kind of man, steady, reliable, and kind, who would not hurt me. But I've kept that bit of learning buried in my soul for all these years.

"Simon, today . . . this time we've had together, it's different from your other visits. It's the second time in my life that I feel so completely safe."

She fell silent and looked intensely into my eyes. Into my self. And I looked back, just as focused, into her. We were at a crossroads and we knew it. Time stopped.

I held my breath. In the stillness, the fire reflected the charged energy between us.

I moved slowly, coming to my knees on the couch, and leaned over Kate. We never broke eye contact. I saw clearly, as if a mist were lifting in my heart, that all previous crossroads, all the detours, all the joys and sorrows of my life were mere mileposts leading me to this moment.

I gently kissed Kate's upper lip.

And I sat back. "I've been wanting to do that ever since I've known you."

She smiled, not a trace of a curl. "Do you realize that in all these years we've never made love?"

"I did notice that, yes."

She pulled me close to her and hugged me long and tight, pressing her face into my neck. I did my fair share of hugging back. For years she'd occupied such a huge emotional space in my life that I was surprised to feel how small she was physically. Petite, compact, round and supple in all the right places.

"You smell just right," she said.

"I do?"

"Yes. Scent is very important you know."

"Your place or mine?"

"Let's stay right here."

"Is there anything I ought to know before . . . I mean about your specialness, any limitations?"

"There are no limitations, unless you have a terrible need for me to be orgasmic. That hasn't been possible since the accident. But there are compensations. For one thing, I've learned that giving pleasure is far more joyful than concentrating on what I'm getting. It was a huge lesson. As far as my ability to respond goes, there's no problem. On the contrary."

"What do you mean?"

"You know how blind people have more acute perception with their other senses? It's like that. I don't have to worry about 'getting there' so my sensitivity is much greater in all other respects. Folks who can come often overlook the profound pleasures of kissing, and that's just one example. Anyway, don't worry about me. Let's undress each other. It'll be so much more vivid than talking about it."

And so we began. Our first kiss had been light, a greeting. Now I tasted her lips, her tongue, I immersed myself in the heat and moisture of her mouth. Our breaths mixed, a sensation so intimate and sweet that tears came to my eyes. I didn't hold them back. I didn't hold anything back.

I removed her clothes slowly, piece by piece, kissing her skin as more and more of it was exposed. I lost myself in her warmth. She undressed me in turn with equal concentration. By the time we were both naked an eternity had passed.

The fire was nearly out and we decided I should stoke it up again. I must have been quite a sight bending over bare-assed, my erection pointing meaningfully at the flames. Kate's only comment, like the knowing appraisal of an expert, was "Cute butt."

I slid back under the quilt with her, took her in my arms and pressed myself full length to her body. I felt huge next to her, my chin just over the top of her hair. She didn't seem to mind.

"So how do I know where you're sensitive and where you're not?"

"Well, I have these hot spots."

"Oh, yeah? And how do I find them?"

"You look. Very carefully."

Our hands and mouths seemed to have a life of their own. We caressed each other, cautiously at first, then more freely, and soon with uninhibited passion. True to her word, Kate responded to my touch with exquisite sensitivity. She trembled, she sighed, she laughed and wept, vibrating like a finely tuned violin in the artist's hands.

"May I touch you here?"

"Why do you keep asking me that?"

"I'm a proponent of the Antioch rules. Don't assume. Ask before you proceed."

"It's too silly. We're not college kids."

"It's not silly. May I?"

"Yes, yes. I wish you would already."

So I did.

"And here?"

"Yes. Oh, God."

"No one's ever called me that before."

Joyful laughter rippled through us, waking Tupelo, who strode over, sniffed us head to toe and with a nod of approval resumed her position near the fire.

"I love laughing this way with you," I said. "It's something new for me. Lovemaking has always been such a solemn endeavor."

"I know. This is fun."

"Mistress of the understatement."

I had never seen Kate so beautiful, so radiant. The firelight glistened on her wet skin. Heat came off both of us in waves. I pulled the quilt back up and we started moving in the perfectly synchronized, rhythmic dance of the ages. Our combined energy, strong and pure as the ocean, took over. We rocked, rising and falling and rising again. My heart was beating down in my lower belly. We rocked a little faster.

"I can't bear it any longer, Simon. I want to feel you inside me. No more waiting. Now. Now."

I slipped in easily and we rose and fell, rose and fell, and then we were only rising and rising and rising once more until I became one with her, in her, of her, reaching higher, ever higher until finally, finally, I reached everything everywhere, released, fulfilled, blessed.

We were hugging and laughing, crying and holding on, then descending from the peak, rocking down, lilting down, drifting, coming to rest, at home. At peace.

I think we slept. Or maybe we just slid into another dimension of consciousness. Then, "Hey, I was wrong about something," she whispered.

"My scanner detects no errors whatsoever."

"No, really, I'm not joking. I was wrong about the Antioch rules. They aren't silly. Actually, it's wonderful to be asked."

"Yes."

"The fire's out."

"I haven't been paying too much attention to it frankly."

"Should we do something about it?"

"No, let's just lie here and keep holding each other awhile longer."

"How 'bout all night?"

"That sounds right."

"Kate, this, uh . . . about last night. I'm blown away."

"Shhh. I'm still sleeping."

"No, you're not. Listen. So many years of loving friendship, of living practically side by side, and it took us this long to . . . I don't know."

"Neither of us was ready. Until now. Let's not ruin it with too much analysis. I don't want to scare myself back into hiding. Let's just live the joy."

"No, don't worry, I don't want to analyze it either. But there is something I want to say, need to say, right now, before we go any further. I want you to hear me out. It's just this: I am making a commitment to you. That's what blows my mind. See, when Zora died I told myself NEVER AGAIN. I swore I'd never let myself care like that for anyone, ever, because I couldn't bear the possibility of another loss. You've always known this about me even if I haven't said it in so many words, because you've seen how I run every time a desirable woman appears on the horizon.

"But Kate, now it's you. I need you to hear that I am open. To whatever happens next. I'm open to you, to us, and it's something I haven't dared to let myself feel for over twenty years. I'm profoundly glad. That's it."

An hour must have passed while we lay there, embracing each other as the morning light gradually filled the room. Then Kate started squirming next to me.

"Hey, my back's getting sore. We've been on this couch for how many hours now? What do you say we do something about breakfast? I'll be responsible for liquids, you for solids. And then we'll . . . ." She was interrupted by a knock on the door.

I bundled her in the quilt and put on my jeans and sweatshirt. Kate's neighbor stood outside, stomping the snow off his boots and sending a gust of icy New England air into the room. He received a call for us because we'd disconnected the phone. The old gent had used a scrap of newsprint to take down the message. It was from Kate's assistant and he'd been looking for me.

I didn't recognize the phone number but I did know the area code, real well.

Ann Arbor.

Be v Reilly, my quiet, redheaded high school friend, my date at the Sweetheart Dance, got her football hero in the end. She was Bev Hardin now, had married Will at the end of their junior year in college; I'd read all about it in the alumni newsletter. The last time I'd seen her was at our ten-year reunion and she still held a special place in my heart.

She answered the phone, seriously upset. Janice was in Ann Arbor. Apparently, she had shifted gears. She was pursuing Will now, and not casually. She was going after him with the determination of a libidinous teenager. "Like a kid with hot pants," in Bev's words. In a few short days she'd been practically assaulting the Hardin household with persistent phone calls, drop-in visits, and deliveries of extravagant, inappropriate gifts. Will had already gone to see her at her hotel.

"Something's very wrong," Bev said. Her voice was agitated, the tone of a person desperately wringing her hands. "Simon, you were here for the reunion, you saw us. Our marriage has been blessed, we've grown so much together. Will loves me, I know it. But he's slipping away and I don't understand why. She's got some kind of hold on him."

"What can I do, Bev? Why did you call me?"

"I'm not sure. It's just a feeling. The way Janice talks about you, I think you might be able to influence her. And it isn't just that. It's also for Will. Maybe you can figure out what's going on with him, what the hook is."

"Okay, I need to go down to New York today and tomorrow I'll get the first flight out. But Bev, I'm curious. How did you know where to find me?"

"Oh, that was easy. I called your father out at the lake and got your daughter. She was really helpful and understanding. You've got a great friend there. She gave me two numbers, yours and Katherine New-house's. I only got the machine at your house so I called Ms. Newhouse's office. Simon, am I crazy or is this really happening?"

"You're not crazy. I'll be out tomorrow. We'll talk more then. Do one thing. When you hear from Janice tell her I'm on my way. It'll cool her jets."

I repeated Bev's half of the conversation for Kate's benefit. Her frown indicated that she'd switched back to professional mode. But the pronounced tilt of her upper lip spoke disappointment and anger for the disruption of our time together.

"So much for the Massachusetts state line rule. This woman can't seem to leave us alone. Literally and figuratively. I'm done being jacked around by her, I mean it." The severe lines between her brows confirmed her words. "You said on the way up that you wanted to consult first with Janice's therapist. Forget that for now. Talk to Tommy and get on with the history. Let's get her committed and let's do it fast. While you're in Ann Arbor to help out your friend, get me supporting data. You'll be right at her old stomping grounds."

I couldn't face breakfast so Kate wisely left me alone with my tea. I kept seeing that bedroom shrine in Janice's apartment and I was dead certain about one thing. Janice was *not* after Will. The tear-jerking call to Kate's house hadn't worked, so she'd been forced to get creative. She'd conned Bev into summoning me. But I knew Janice was staging a diversion. As far as I could tell, Debby was the only real attraction in Ann Arbor. We were seeing Plan B, a grand manipulation that was already working, if you judged by my anxiety level.

I gulped the tepid tea and moved into adrenaline-powered action. The first step was to call my father. It had been five days since I'd checked on Debby. Too long, with Janice acting out in the next town.

Gabe picked up the phone and reassured me that Debby was fine, visiting over at the neighbors'. No, they had not heard from Janice. We exchanged a few belated words about his friendship with Ed Donahue. But he refused to get specific, claiming client confidentiality. I hung up, disappointed but aware of the ethics behind his reticence. At least I was temporarily satisfied that Debby was okay.

Next, I called my friend Gideon Dove in New York to let him know what was up. I wanted him on the alert for one thing, but I also needed information from him. We made an appointment for that night.

I was almost ready to hit the road.

Kate and I talked briefly. She understood my urgency and agreed that I had to go. Her part of the work would come later, after my investigation, so she decided to take the rest of the week off as planned, stay at the Retreat, and then meet me in the city to start the legal ball rolling for Janice's civil commitment.

The conversation took a personal turn. Kate was feeling very protective of me, and we batted around the idea of going together to Michigan. Reluctantly, she accepted the fact that with my father's connections from a lifetime law practice, I would have all the muscle and legal backup I could possibly need if Janice should get out of hand.

There was still the matter of my concern for her well-being. She readily agreed for my sake to keep the phone connected. But I wasn't completely comfortable with her staying on alone at the Retreat, with icy walks, daunting weather, and the nearest neighbor a half mile down the road. I knew how independent she was and how she'd always resisted any attempt on my part to take care of her. I suggested that we ask Tommy to come up, expecting a heated argument. But something had changed in Kate. She thanked me. She said she would indeed feel better driving back to New York with him. But the demands of the moment dictated that Tommy accompany me to Michigan. Eventually, she convinced me that she'd be all right and I acquiesced.

I reached Tommy at home. He listened while I filled him in on Janice's latest doings.

"Jesus," he said.

"I'm going," I told him.

"Of course you are, and I'm going with you. The broad's on fire. We gotta put her out." Tommy watched too many Dirty Harry flicks.

I packed quickly, hugged Kate slowly, and let her drive me and Tupelo to the Greyhound stop in Rockland.

There was one member of the Jensen-Donahue cast whom I had neglected.

Janice and Ed I had experienced firsthand more than once in my life. And although I never had the pleasure of making Margery's acquaintance directly, all reports confirmed that she had been quite a charmer. Dennis Jensen, on the other hand, remained a pale caricature to me, an impersonal aggregate of cop stereotypes, abusive, slobbering, womanizing, brutish. Pretty much the image Janice had described. The only photograph I'd ever seen of the man who'd married her did not feature a human head as we know it.

At a quarter to nine that evening, mind alert, body a wreck from the road, I sat across from Gideon Dove at New York City police headquarters.

"Simon, you're like a son to me."

"Gideon, you would've been a ten-year-old father and leave my mother out of this. It wouldn't have happened. You're black."

"Well, now, that would explain why white people are afraid of me, wouldn't it?" Every syllable perfect, a song. The man could teach enunciation at Yale. But Gideon inspired fear in whites not because he was black but because he could do everything they could. And most of it better.

He was part preacher, part social worker, and all cop. His voice caressed. His stocky, powerful body asserted itself. His ebony skin, searching eyes, and overall beauty stunned the beholder.

He was a presence in Homicide, perhaps a legend in the making. For years he'd been clearing cases that other, clumsier cops had screwed up. My life and Gideon's had been intertwined personally and professionally for a long time. Sometimes I thought it had been forever. But what had cemented our kinship was that I'd helped out his kid.

I had bumped into his oldest son when he had bumped into some of life's issues that aren't easily discussed with a father, especially if that father is a police officer. Gideon had asked me to see Joshua. Usually such parent-initiated therapies don't work out. The kid knows who's paying the bill and assumes that anything he says will be reflected back to his parents one way or another. That's why they arranged the consultation to begin with.

Something else happened between Joshua and me. We became friends. Gideon never asked for so much as a word about our talks. He had asked only that I meet his son. The rest was up to us. He knew I liked Joshua and that pleased him. Josh was off at college now but he never failed to get in touch when he came home. We kept up with each other.

And I trusted Gideon completely. Whenever I needed him, he was there.

By the time I arrived he had called up the relevant files and thoroughly searched his memory. He had an uncanny knowledge of NYPD personnel. He referred to them as his flock.

"What do you need?"

I gave him the abridged but unsanitized version of my involvement with the Donahue-Jensen zoo. "But I'm missing a piece. I don't know anything about Dennis. What can you tell me?"

"Here, read this." He handed me a computer printout of Dennis Jensen's personnel file. I looked at the picture first. He was just as I had imagined him, only smaller—square-jawed, steel-gazed, a downscaled version of Will Hardin.

"His wife described him as a bad act," I said, "physically abusive. Is there any record of family troubles?"

"Simon, you know how I feel about family violence. Anyone who watches the evening news knows how I feel about it. Have you heard the latest? Our proposal for a preventive program in the projects is finally gaining some support. Oh, sorry, you're not here for a progress report on my obsessions.

"In answer to your question, no, Jensen was definitely not an abuser; he was more like a battered husband. I knew it and so did the rest of the department. We sent him for assertiveness training. I know, don't smirk at me, it was all we had then. Anyway, Jensen eventually landed in Public Relations because he couldn't handle the street. He got a nice soft desk to man."

"I gather the assertiveness training didn't take."

"It didn't have a chance. I saw them once at a cocktail party for the brass. Dennis felt like two left feet and he wanted to leave. His wife was having herself a time and wouldn't go. She was hungry. She flirted with everything in a uniform. When she had had enough, she let him take her home. The man was completely whipped.

"About ten years ago we were just beginning to openly address the abuse issue and the department came out with a policy to start the work 'at home,' as the PR people put it. So we hired a human relations consulting firm to determine the incidence of domestic violence among our own staff. Then we ran a campaign to raise consciousness and train the couples in communication skills.

"But the point here is that the social workers who did the study interviewed the families of a random sample of our officers and Jensen's name came up in the sample. Look in that file under 1987—there's a summary of the interview with the missus. If you want, I can get you a full transcript."

I flipped to the page in question and skimmed the report. And saw that she had lied to us about that, too. Dennis didn't abuse her. Nobody did. In fact, it appeared that Janice had married a replica of her ineffectual father.

"Any help?" Gideon asked.

"If you like it when nothing makes sense, yes." But what didn't make sense? A lot of women marry replicas of their fathers. Why was I surprised? Because Janice had lied about her husband? Truth was not her strong suit.

"And what, I fear to ask, is your plan?"

"Katherine hired me to work up the history for a commitment. I'm going to Ann Arbor. Will you vouch for me if necessary?" It always helps, when the shit hits the fan, to have a New York Homicide star swear to my legitimacy.

"What are you going to do when you get there?"

"I don't know, sniff around. You'll hear from me."

He offered to set up communication with the Ann Arbor police department. "You know there's not much else I can do. She's out of my jurisdiction. Not to mention that she's been out a couple of months already and hasn't broken any laws yet."

"The operative word is 'yet.' Hold on, you never know."

"Take Tommy with you." He always wanted me to take Tommy with me. Gideon thought of me as the brain and Tommy as my skull. "You'll need him to look up folks for you who knew her when. He can find anyone. Did he ever tell you about Montana?"

"No."

"Ask him."

Tommy was already in my kitchen, chowing down on rice and beans.

"Tell me about Montana."

"How's Gideon?"

"Fine. He told me to ask you about Montana."

"He's always liked that one. It's that I found a guy I was looking for once and the only address I had was Montana."

"How'd you do it?"

He munched steadily and swallowed. "I went to Montana and asked around."

"That's it, the whole story? Montana's a big state."

"But it don't have many people. I didn't say it was fast. It took me three days. I found him in Butte."

"Why were you looking so hard?"

"He owed me money."

"Did you get it?"

"You have to ask?"

Chapter Twenty-eight

Ne w cars filled the living room, which was too cavernous for intimacy in any case. Multicolored banners screamed out their messages from every wall.

The space had been self-consciously arranged into small conversational enclaves including leatherette couches and plastic tables, each set focused on a brand-new, dust-free Chrysler or Plymouth. I was seated at one such oasis with a Le Baron for company.

I hate the smell of new cars and don't much care for the effluvium of old ones. I recognize no new models on the road and I lust after no cam-shafts. In short, I am an American anomaly, a man oblivious to automobiles.

I did own one car in my life, a Valiant with a slant-six engine I was supposed to adore, but to this day I don't know why. It was old and decrepit and I couldn't teach it to hop to alternate sides of the street, so I sold it.

And I remain ignorant. This condition, while not fatal, has on occasion hindered my professional performance, but not enough to make me learn anything. Gideon once asked me to describe a vehicle I had seen leaving the scene of a felony.

"It was a big blue car," I said.

"A sedan?" he asked.

"No, a car," I answered.

But I wasn't in Kinder's Chrysler Plymouth in Ann Arbor, Michigan, to buy. I was there to learn, if Will Hardin would teach me. I'd bet myself a double papaya shake that he had heard from Janice long before this sudden onslaught of her affection.

Tommy and I had flown to Detroit Metro together while Tupelo suffered the indignity of traveling in a box somewhere below us. Tommy's assignment was to nose around at Workman's Lake, the little burg that had been the Donahues' home before they moved to Ann Arbor. Tommy was the real private eye of the family, and if there was anything about Janice in Workman's Lake that we needed to know, he would find out.

Tupelo's responsibilities included moral support and impromptu counseling.

Janice's psyche was all mine. My job was to reconstruct her early history.

And that's why I had returned to Ann Arbor, a place so laden with painful memories that I avoided it whenever possible. It had become impossible.

Will "the Passing Machine" Hardin rushed into the showroom, jamming his ample pecs into a sport coat with leather patches on the elbows. Under it he was wearing a skintight sweaty T-shirt that said CAT. A purry feline creature wrapped itself around the letters. If you judged by the build, Will must have been pumping Plymouths for the last twenty years. The only sign of the passage of time was a harvested spot on the back of his cornsilk-covered head. He and Janice had something in common. They didn't age.

Will had gone on to a smashing college career at Michigan, hometown boy quarterbacking the team for three years, two Big Ten championships, two Rose Bowl losses. Since he threw only about three passes a game in Michigan's vaunted three-yards-and-a-cloud-of-dust offense, he didn't go high in the draft and was converted by the Detroit Lions into a wide receiver because of his good hands. He played four undistinguished years for the Lions before a rotator cuff injury put him on the shelf. Had he been a star in the pros, like Mel Farr, he would have had his own dealership in Detroit. But as a local college hero, he got to work for someone else, telling stories to the old Michigan faithful who came by to brush up against faded glory and, occasionally, to buy a Chrysler.

His eyes darted around the showroom, checking for customers or browsers. I was the only person there and he began his approach. I watched his face. Out of the dim past a spark lit, smoldered, and finally flared into recognition. Bev apparently hadn't warned him of my visit.

"Simon Rose!" he bellowed, much too loud. "It's a miracle!"

"Nice to see you too, Will." "Miracle" struck me as hyperbolic for the occasion. Then I noticed the legend under the smiling cat on his T-shirt: Christian Athletes of Tomorrow.

I held out my hand. He pumped it.

"Were you sent?" he asked, eyes slightly inclined toward the heavens.

"No, I came on my own."

"No, I meant . . . no matter, I already know. You were sent."

"I was?"

"I have prayed to the Good Lord for guidance and I'm sure you're it. Come into my office. We can talk old times." He was still holding my hand.

He checked out the showroom with a backward glance as he hustled me into a semi-private cubicle with his name on it. Something was making him nervous and I didn't think it was me.

Will sat behind his desk, feet up, and motioned me to my seat, a Naugahyde monstrosity. "I hope you'll excuse the getup here. I don't usually work the floor in these clothes. I was practicing with the team." He indicated the Cats. "We're in the playoffs, you know, inner-city kids." Healthy hoops for the pre-steroids set. Way to keep them off the streets and off crack.

"How 'bout some coffee or a drink? I don't drink anymore myself but I never impose my values on others."

"Herb tea would be nice."

He punched a button on his telephone console and asked somebody named Beatrice to run down to the 7-Eleven for some tea, decaffeinated. He said, "God bless you," and hung up.

"You're not here to buy a car, are you?" he asked sheepishly.

"No."

"I didn't think so, but I thought I should ask." He wiped his face with a handkerchief, thoroughly. "Then you're here about Janice." Brand-new sweat beads appeared on his upper lip.

I nodded. "I've been hired by a law firm to do a psychological workup on her. Your impressions, your experiences can be very useful."

"I can't talk about her here." He wiped his upper lip, to no avail. The moisture reappeared. "I'm not sure I can talk about her anywhere."

Will rearranged some papers on his desk as if they needed it. Muscle groups I hadn't seen outside of anatomy class twitched on his chest. He grabbed the phone again, perhaps a nervous habit, punched out some numbers, and told Bev that he had a surprise for dinner.

"I want Bev there when I tell it," Will explained.

"Okay with me. Can I bring my daughter?" Debby was at loose ends since Bobbi had returned to New York.

"Sure. Bev always makes enough for a crowd."

The Hardins' dining room was a middle-American masterwork. China, crockery, pewter, needlepoint samplers, reminders of what is good and right. Jesus is love. America the Beautiful. Remember a kind word.

Bev greeted me with a huge smile. We looked each other over at arm's length. She had matured into a handsome woman, large-chested without being large-breasted. Substantial hips and a good-sized butt, not a heavy woman, but full. Her face was Norman Rockwell–pretty with too many freckles. Her hair was wild, a hurricane of red, unhindered by clips or pins.

She was the first to speak. "You look exactly like I thought you would, an old hippie. I don't mean it as an insult either, you know."

"I never take that as an insult. It's a compliment."

Will laughed.

"Even your hair is right," she added. "Good to see you, Simon." And she hugged me.

"You seem to have gotten your hair act together since I last saw you." I brushed at the curly wisps tickling my face.

"Ain't it beautiful? Ain't it a trip?" She turned her head, displaying the red storm.

"That it is. Congratulations."

I introduced Debby and there were more hugs all around. Bev hugged like an earth mother; Will, like a brick with a lower-back problem.

Bev disappeared into a bedroom and emerged with a chubby baby boy, about nine months old. His name was Brian and he was obviously happy and well-loved.

Debby was hooked. She followed Bev and Brian into the kitchen, and Will and I sat down at the dinner table. It was already set, awaiting only the evening's fare. There would be no cocktail chatter.

Bev served hearty food—cream of tomato soup, chicken pot pie, cole-slaw. Butterscotch pudding stood ready on the sideboard for dessert.

"It's all homemade, nothing from a box," Will commented, genuinely proud. "When we have company Bev makes it all from scratch."

"It's very good," I said, and it was. I was pushing the chicken pieces inconspicuously off to one side after separating them from the carrots and potatoes. I ate hungrily of everything else.

"The pudding isn't from scratch," Bev said. "I can't make pudding. Must be a trick." She pushed her wiry hair out of her field of vision. She balanced Brian on her lap while she ate. When he fussed, she gave him a breast and he wised up.

"We waited so long for Brian. We wanted to start a family early, but we couldn't. We tried so hard, it took all the fun out of it. When we finally gave up trying and accepted God's will that we were not to have children, I got pregnant. We're very thankful."

"Amen," Will said.

We helped Bev clear the table and moved into the colonial living room, complete with knobby little protrusions poking up all over the couch and armchairs like stubby erections. Bev gave Brian dessert, the other breast. He finally leaned back, sated after his double meal.

"Can I hold him?" Debby asked.

"Sure," Bev agreed eagerly, not one to monopolize her baby. Brian gurgled a little during the handoff but settled down easily in the crook of Debby's arm. Bev registered that Debby had had experience with little ones.

"Would you like to put him to bed?" she asked Debby.

"I'd love to. Can I read to him?"

"He loves it. Puts him right out." She explained where Debby would find the things she'd need, and Debby pattered off contentedly with the baby.

Story time for us, too. Will settled in, Bev at his side with her hand on his knee for support.

"I'm a happily married man, Simon, as you can see. Bev here, the boy. I'm a Christian man, which makes this even harder." He looked to Bev for approval. She nodded, encouraging him.

"Those days things were different. I did things I'm not proud of and the worst of them I did with Janice Donahue. I left it all behind me, until her letter came a few months back." I knew it. One double papaya shake and a point for the Rose. "I hadn't heard from her in years and would just as soon have left if that way. I couldn't imagine what she wanted from me." Oh, yes, he could. Will was doing a delicate balancing act with the truth.

He tossed a letter on the coffee table but I didn't pick it up. His face was a circus of emotions and I didn't want to miss any. We already had shame, guilt, excitement, and fear, with the promise of much more.

"The letter." He trudged on like his mouth was filled with mud. "The letter was about the fix she was in. She said you helped her out at the trial. Then she asked for my help. Nothing special, something like, 'I hope you'll be there if I need you.' I didn't even know what she was talking about. I couldn't imagine anything I could do for her." He glanced at Bev again.

I let the statement dangle and picked up the letter. It was almost identical to the ones she'd written to me and Kate. It asked, "Do you remember?" which she had also asked me. It was signed, "Your lifelong friend, Jan."

"What did she mean, 'Do you remember?' What was she referring to?" I asked.

"I dunno. It could have been anything." He paused, not wanting to begin.

Bev said, "Go on, Will, tell him. I already know the stories and I love you." She meant it.

He confessed to his pre-Christian ways. He had drunk excessively, hurt people on the football field, committed unclean acts with most of the desirable girls in our high school. Nothing I hadn't already imagined and nothing the best high school quarterback in the county wouldn't have been proud of. But Will wasn't bragging about his litany of sin. He was ashamed and reluctant to continue.

"And Janice?" The two-word question.

"I don't know how this is going to help," he said, head bowed.

"The truth always helps," I said, aiming my pitch at the target group.

They stole together, regular sprees through Kresge's, boosting anything Janice wanted, lipstick, nail polish, costume jewelry. A game. They did booze runs through the package goods store, shoving pints into their underwear. And she stole from her girlfriends, which Will found harder to take. Tommy had had trouble with that, too.

"It didn't matter to her that she hurt people."

Janice sold some of the booze to kids too young to be drinking, for an admirable profit. Most of it she shared with Will on their Saturday-night-after-the-game make-out marathons. They had sex in cars, locker rooms, bathrooms, classrooms, and even in her parents' bed, recently left vacant by the death of her mother.

"She was weird when it came to sex. She even asked me to hit her once while we were doing it, but I couldn't." He stopped dead.

"I'd rather not be saying any of this. I know it's not going to do her any good and I don't want to do her any harm. And besides, you get the picture. You probably remember, anyway. You were next. It's just more of the same."

Nobody believed him. Reluctantly, he went on.

After he found out that Janice was balling his fullback, his wide receiver, and one offensive end, he accepted Jesus and left his old life behind. He and Bev got together in college and eventually he married her. "The best decision I ever made."

He stopped. Prematurely, it seemed.

"Will, one part I never understood. Who ended the relationship, you or Janice? How did it happen?"

He rubbed his chin pensively. "It wasn't like that. We didn't really break up. School was over and we just went our separate ways. It was no big deal. I moved on to Jesus, no fun for her. She moved on to you. That's it."

And I had been a momentary distraction in her countdown to college. Or maybe I had been the launching pad. At any rate, the story didn't wash. It was entirely too adult a passage for them. Where were the inevitable fireworks?

"Well, that's not exactly all of it. She was already moving on to you before she left me. She always talked about you—how smart and clever you were, things you said in student council meetings. She didn't really have much respect for my mind. She put me down a lot and most of the time she did it by comparing me to you. I was the muscle. You were the brains. But she could hurt. She was good at it."

We had more in common than I thought. Janice had teased me mercilessly about being unathletic, comparing Will and me physically, attribute for attribute. She indeed could hurt.

"Remember Ellie Lomax?" Will asked.

I nodded. She was the brightest kid in our class, miles ahead of her nearest rival until Janice moved to town. As I recalled, Janice had nudged her out of the valedictorian spot by a few tenths of a point.

"Do you know what happened to her senior year during finals?"

"No, I don't."

"Ellie screwed up. She slipped to second place. Janice was number one."

I did remember, vaguely.

"Well, she wasn't sick," he went on. "She was drugged. Janice put a Mickey Finn in her Coke at lunch."

"How do you know? Did she tell you?"

"No, but I knew. We did 'em all the time. Chloral hydrate capsules, they were just like 'ludes. She used to take them from her mother's stash, and there was a ton left when she died. How 'bout Linda Brownstein, you remember her?"

"She was a cheerleader," I said.

"She was the head cheerleader until she got hurt in gym class."

"She was?" I didn't follow the cheerleading corps. I only followed Janice.

"She got her knee all messed up playing field hockey and gimped around the whole year. Janice got to be top gun and guess who accidentally smashed Linda's knee?"

I sensed that no answer was required. It occurred to me that at the time, Tonya Harding would have been a yet-to-be-united sperm and egg.

"Yeah, she could hurt, especially if you got in her way." He paused again, considering whether to tell me another story. He must have decided against it because he handed the ball off to me. "Anything else you want to know, ask. I'll tell you. I just wish I could help her."

I wondered why he'd want to help her, among other things. I started with the other things.

"When did you last see her?" I asked.

He shuffled his feet and ground his fists into his thighs, trying hard to recall an event that was not so difficult to recall.

"She popped in a couple of times over the years. Her father still lives here, or at least he did until she was arrested. I guess the last time I saw her was—"

"Tell him, hon," Bev interrupted. "Simon's a psychiatrist. He probably knows anyway. You didn't do anything wrong." Bev intercepted his lie.

I knew he was lying. But even if Bev hadn't called I would have known by the dryness of his mouth and the wetness of his face. And there was Janice's visitors' card on the Rolodex at the hospital. Her only visitor other than her father had been Will.

"Okay, I went to see her. She called a few days after I got the letter. She was in the psychiatric hospital. She said she was hurting and needed to see me. Bev and I talked about it." Bev nodded. "We're Christians, Simon. We can't ignore a call for help. It was the least I could do, offer her Jesus, Our Savior. So I went."

It made more sense to me that if Janice called, Will would run away, but I guess I'm a pagan. On the other hand, I hadn't run away either.

"What did she want?" It certainly wasn't Jesus.

"Nothing really. I was there for an hour. She talked about getting out and starting over. She talked about you, said you were gonna be her therapist. I think she wanted to know if I would help her out, too. I left her some reading, you know, inspirational stuff. Maybe she read it. I don't know. That's it. I swear." Hand to heart.

He made it sound simple enough. A friend in need calls, a Christian responds. Except that he looked terrible, a man carrying a mighty heavy burden. He was afraid of her.

"Will, do you think she's sick, mentally, I mean?"

He shrugged. "I'm no shrink."

"No, but you've known her for years. Do you think she's crazy?"

"No, she's not sick like in sick. I mean she's just like she always was, crazy as hell. I mean she's definitely crazy, always has been. She does crazy things, always did. She's nuts, no question about it, but could you call her crazy or is she just very different, that I couldn't tell you. She's not bonkers. She's not like *crazy* crazy. She's just crazy, like you and me, only a lot crazier. But I don't think she's sick. You know what I mean?"

Unfortunately, I couldn't have said it better myself.

Will slumped back on the couch exhausted by his odyssey through the past. There was more, but if I pushed too hard I would lose him. So I only pushed a little.

"What are you afraid of, Will?"

Both Will and Bev glanced back toward Brian's bedroom, and all three of us remembered one of the crazy things Janice had done.

"Let's pray for her," Will said definitively. It was an order. This session was over.

If confession is good for the soul, he wasn't reaping the benefits. There was more, but Will was through for now, seeking solace in prayer.

"Will, it doesn't take a shrink to notice how agonizing this is for you. Let me come back tomorrow and we'll talk again. We all know there's more."

"Okay, we can make it earlier. There's no practice tomorrow." We held hands again, this time the three of us. We could hear Debby and Brian giggling at each other. Bev and Will bowed their heads and while they praised God I contemplated the pink skin of his bald spot.

Chapter Twenty-nine

Janice had been the author of one birth, two deaths, and one rebirth. A busy lady. And Will's beaded lip promised more. The premature call to prayer effectively terminated his confession, but his squirming, sweating, and heightened pink coloring betrayed him.

The Hardins were pillars of their particular society and subculture, the Christian Midwest. They were the best of the breed, because underneath they tried to be decent people. They'd bought the American Dream and it had been good to them. Bev was the epitome of the stand-by-your-man woman, and what she brought to it was honesty. She was beside him not because that was her place but because that was the place she wanted to be. Will was a lucky man.

But not a man at peace. His past had returned to haunt him. His faith, usually strong, was under fire and in retreat. He still projected an imposing physical presence, but the piss and vinegar had been drained from his soul. He had a problem he couldn't bull his way through. He was perplexed, weary, off balance, and showing the strain.

Will was doubly frightened, God-fearing and Janice-fearing. The God part I would leave to him. The Janice part was still mine. Why was he so afraid of her? Why had he run to her when she called? Why hadn't he run for cover instead? He would tell me, in his own time, because he had to. He'd prayed for guidance and I had materialized. You don't hold out on your miracles for long. I was looking forward to the next installment.

I would gladly have stayed with Debby at Gabe's restored farmhouse, but with Tommy along that was impossible this time. We were camping out in low-grade luxury at the College Inn, the only place in Ann Arbor that was willing to host a golden retriever at no charge. Tommy and I each had a huge bed and Tupelo claimed one of the armchairs in front of the TV console.

Our lodgings had several advantages. One, our location was almost perfectly equidistant from Gabe's place on a dirt track northwest of town and the Hardins' quasi-ritzy subdivision off the Ypsilanti road heading out toward the east. Two, a friendly co-ed from the U. who worked the late shift scraping dishes in the hotel coffee shop had generously agreed to save some goodies for Tupelo. And three, there was a cocktail lounge downstairs where Tommy could indulge at least one of his vices, and where we were about to have the pleasure of Ed Donahue's company. He'd eagerly accepted my invitation for a drink at the hotel.

Tommy had just downed his second martini and was trying to catch the waitress's eye for another. Over the bar a Michael Jackson video flashed its images at us with the velocity of a hummingbird's wings. I had to turn my back on it before it fried my circuitry. I nursed my bloodless Mary and listened to Debby, whose red wine sat untouched on the smoky tinted glass surface of our table. She had just listed little Brian's charms for the third time.

"God, I loved it. You know, I haven't held a baby since Lisa died." She swallowed hard. "I was afraid it wouldn't feel right. Like I'm not supposed to touch kids. Like if I do, they die." The curse, the indelible stain of the survivor. "But I loved holding Brian. It made me miss Lisa. Actually, it confused the hell out of me, but I'm glad I went with you."

"I'm glad you came, too. It was nice to see you happy."

"I'm confused, I said, not happy." In fact, she was upset, deeply upset, by long-repressed pain.

"It will come clear," I reassured, but Debby had turned away toward the oversized screen. I left her alone.

Tommy liked to get loaded in response to his hometown memories, a process he'd begun in the airport. He was fairly sloshed by the time he got to the third olive.

"I got some surprises for you," he said, looking out from under the shelf created by his eyebrows.

"I love surprises," I said, which Tommy knew to be a lie. I'd never had a good surprise in my life.

"First, I boosted this for you. Look at it later, after I fall out, which I expect to do within eight minutes."

"Oh no you won't," Debby said. "You promised me a rematch on the Nintendo."

"No conflict there. I can take you easily with my eyes tied behind my back."

"We'll see about that. I still hold the family record."

Tommy handed me a yearbook from Workman's Lake Regional High. The year made Janice a junior, just before she moved to Ann Arbor.

"You stole a yearbook? From who?"

"Not 'who,' Shakespeare, 'whom.' And the proper question is where. I confiscated it from the Workman's Lake Regional High School library."

"Why didn't you just borrow it? Libraries do that."

"I asked. They said that yearbooks couldn't leave the room. They were wrong. You can thank me for it later. Now, you can listen. I spoke to the superintendent, Mr. Strauss."

"Who did you go as?" Tommy kept a set of business cards of various names and professions.

"Myself. No need to complicate matters. I told him I was freelancing an article about lower education in small-town America, contrasting it with big-city methodology, like Ann Arbor." Methodology came out in five pieces. "They hate Ann Arbor at the lake. They see it as snooty and pretentious, which it is. He was happy to talk about how it's done in the countryside. He's worked in the system for thirty years and proud of every accomplishment. The man loves to talk and I had to take notes." He showed me his wilted right hand.

"You'll live. Let's get to the surprise before Donahue gets here."

"The surprise is what he wouldn't talk about. A guy like this Strauss, loves to talk, would go on for hours if I let him, all of a sudden gets tight-lipped about the Donahues. He starts to sound like a recorded message. Janice was an excellent student, a good citizen, an all-'round peach, only his mouth is tightening over his teeth like he's hiding chewing gum under his upper lip. So I pursue the matter. 'Why did they leave the lake?' I ask him. He tells me that Ed took it very hard. I ask what did Ed take very hard, and he says, 'Margery's death. Ed needed to get away from his ghosts.' Must've said 'He took it very hard' three times. Meanwhile, he's fumbling with my card, a light dawns, and he gets pissed and asks me to leave. I ask why, because I can't figure out where our rapport went." He pronounced the *t* in rapport. "And the guy asks me who my father is. I tell him the truth. Why lie? Which is when he insists that I leave and here comes the real surprise. He says if I want to know any more about the Donahue 'situation,' I should ask my father."

"Why?"

"Fuck would I know? You ask him." And he pulled Debby to her feet. "Come on, you ain't drinkin' anyway. Let's leave big brother to wait for his teacher without us."

Melissa Etheridge was being projected in quadruplicate overhead. I ignored her, not an easy thing to do, and started leafing through the yearbook. It was permeated with Janice. It seemed she'd been involved in everything, but the bulk of the pictures showed her in costume. She appeared as the perfect guttersnipe in *Pygmalion*, the mousey daughter in *The Glass Menagerie*, and the ever-frazzled Ophelia in *Hamlet*. The blurb under her class picture said, "The whole world is her stage."

Along with being the school's premiere Thespian, Janice was a member of the debating club, the honor society, the student council, and the cheerleading squad. She was pictured at football, basketball, and baseball games, always in some freeze frame, flying in the air with her legs spread wide and her arms thrust upward in victory.

I searched the candids in particular for Janice at year-end events. She'd been elected queen of the junior prom and was caught by the camera beaming at the adoring throng as she accepted a kiss from an uncomfortable but equally adoring Will Hardin. She spoke at the junior-senior debate. She stood poised at the lectern, looking out confidently at the audience.

No sign of any change over the year. She seemed as bubbly and cheery in June as she had been in September. It was the year of her mother's death but the grief did not show on her face. She looked great. Of course, they were only pictures, many of them posed, but if the camera didn't lie, Janice wasn't depressed. Or she was already an accomplished actress, which is just what the yearbook suggested.

I turned over the velvet-covered tome when I saw Ed walk through the glass doors into the lounge. He'd obviously had a good start on the drinks. His steps betrayed a distinct uncertainty. I approached and offered an arm to help steady him. His tongue was too big and his words were just starting to lean toward the slushy side.

"Good evening, Simon. Thank you for inviting me out. Retirement can be a lonely business."

"Mr. Donahue . . ."

"Call me Ed," he interrupted. "I think it's time for you to call me Ed."

I led him to a larger table in order to accommodate his corpulence. He held off my questions with his left hand while he ordered himself three fingers of bourbon. He sat too rigidly while waiting for the drink to arrive. He bolted down a finger and a half before he started talking.

"I really was going to call you. I'm on my way out, I can feel it. Jan doesn't need me, or should I say I just don't make much difference to her anymore. It's time for her to get on with her life without her father looking over her shoulder."

He threw down a little more bourbon, leaving only a fingernail in the tumbler. He looked even worse than I'd thought at the door. He had on wrinkle-proof plastic slacks. A pajama top peeked from his threadbare V-necked pullover. His skin wasn't pale, it was transparent, the broken blood vessels adding the only color to the landscape. The bourbon was doing nothing for his diction, but he didn't care. He wasn't hiding his shame. He was parading it.

"And that's why I wanted to talk to you. I'm afraid for her, all alone there in the city, without me to at least listen to her. She needs a lot of care."

I heard it coming. I had plenty of time to formulate my refusal while he trudged out the request.

"Please take care of her, Simon. Jan trusts you. She feels very close to you. I think she'll even listen to you. Do this for me. Help her. Tell me you will, Simon. I need to hear it to have any peace at all."

"I can't take your place, Ed, and I can't accept the responsibility of caring for Janice. I'm afraid I can't be of much use. She needs a trained therapist," I said, "who isn't me."

"That's not what I mean. She has a therapist. I mean someone to care for her the way a friend would, that's all."

"Ed, I see no legitimate therapeutic value in my continued involvement with Janice. As for friendship, that was a long time ago. I'm afraid I can't offer anything. I've done what I can."

"I'm asking for a phone call now and then. Check in with her. How much is that to ask?"

Too much, I thought. "I suppose I could call her once in a while if that would make you feel better, but—"

"That's all I'm asking, a call. Now and then. That's all. Thank you, Simon."

Sentimental drunk talk, that's why I opted for humoring him. And he lied about wanting to call me. If I hadn't gotten in touch with him, this conversation would never have happened. He was just going to fade out. Before he did, I wanted some questions answered. If I wasn't quick about it, the bourbon would have him.

"Now I want you to do *me* a favor."

"Sure, anything," he offered halfheartedly.

"I've always been curious about your wife's death. And I have good reason. Whatever happened to her mother had a devastating effect on Janice. Tell me what happened to Margery, Ed, if you want me to help her."

This time he offered no resistance. Faced with lightweight blackmail, he surrendered instantly.

"Jan worries for me, Simon. She's afraid that the old rumors might come up again. Didn't your father tell you about this?"

"My father told me nothing."

"The rumors frightened Jan, always have. I think it's because she was afraid she'd lose me, too. Down deep she really loved me.

"There's no sense in my holding back any longer. It can't hurt me now anyway. Simon, there's a great deal I didn't tell you about Margery and what I did tell you was largely false. I didn't intend to mislead you. I lied to mislead myself."

He tossed back the last drops from his tumbler and his voice lost its fuzziness. He signaled to the waitress for a refill. "Margery wasn't a casual drinker. She was a dedicated alcoholic long before I joined the ranks and she was a mean, nasty, abusive drunk. She sprayed her abuse around quite at random, but she never failed to strike a nerve. She could be quite cruel. Look at Jan. It's been almost thirty years and Margery still has a grip on her.

"I certainly hated her enough to kill her. I often wished her dead. I even imagined it. I saw it hundreds of times in my mind before it finally happened.

"And yet my complicity in her death is at best equivocal. Clearly, I had the intent in my heart. It's just that at the moment that it happened my only intent was to fend off her blows. She was thrashing about in one of her rages and she was hitting me. For the first and only time I struck back. I think I was more shocked than she was. It happened in a fraction of a second. She lost her balance and fell. Her head hit the lamp and she never made another sound. It was uncanny how silently a human life expired. So you tell me, Simon, am I guilty?"

He put his hand out to stop my response, an unnecessary gesture because I wasn't sitting in judgment. "No, don't tell me," he went on. "I know what I am. Believe it or not, Simon, I know what I am." He drank some, pointedly avoiding eye contact. He was beat.

"How did the law handle it?"

"With surprising kindness. Your father had something to do with that. They took my sworn statement at the county sheriff's office and her death went down as accidental. I was just lucky, I guess. I had taught more than a few of the officers' kids and enjoyed a certain prestige in the community. Between that and your father's influence, the case was closed."

One fact didn't wash. "How is it that Janice found the body? Why didn't you call the police?"

"I ran away and hid, is what I did. I am not a very courageous man, Simon, never was. I couldn't handle it. I thought maybe it was a bad dream that would go away. I never meant to leave her for Jan to find. I never meant . . . "

He started weeping. I excused myself to relieve the pressure in my bladder and to rinse off the guilt molecules that emanated from his alcohol breath and stuck like glue to my face.

When I returned Ed was mumbling quietly to himself. He didn't recognize me. Rather than listen to his incoherent ramblings, I stuck some bills under my water glass and left quietly. If he noticed, he didn't show it.

It was late when I got back to the room but I dialed my father's number. I didn't worry about waking him. The more he aged, the less he slept, and besides, there was nothing he liked better than to chew over a live new case, especially since retirement had effectively ended his adversary period.

After I told him not to expect Debby that night I brought up Ed Donahue again. Gabe firmly maintained silence. When I reminded him that I'd accepted the case at least in part due to his urging, he reluctantly opened his mental archives and filled in some essential details of

Margery's death. He confirmed the suspicions I'd been silently entertaining, but he couldn't prove them.

"Would you appear at the commitment hearing and repeat that under oath?"

"If you can't do it without me, yes. Remember, the man was my friend first and client only second. But I believe my statement alone will not suffice. Hopefully, the boyfriend holds the missing piece."

"All right. It depends on Will Hardin then. I won't ask you if I don't have to."

Only one thing remained to be seen. Would Will come clean?

Chapter Thirty

I **w e n t** to the Hardins' alone this time.

It seemed as if a month had passed instead of only two days since our dinner together. Bev's freckles had faded and her hair was strung too tight. Will looked worse, a club fighter who had taken too many head shots. There was a certain looseness in the jowls that made me wonder if he was drinking. At the very least, he was recovering from an all-nighter.

If we were going to deal adequately with Janice, someone, either Bev or Will, would have to fess up. This time, no premature call to prayer. They were going to have to tell it all, not just the easy parts.

Bev greeted me with a hug that quickly deteriorated into a wrenching cry on my chest. Her hands grabbed my sweater as though she were afraid she'd drown. Will offered me a dead salmon to shake and a few empty words of welcome. His skin sagged like a poorly tailored suit. He sat biting the little blond hairs off the back of his hand.

"He's letting her ruin our lives. I'm at wit's end," Bev said and she looked it. "I know that woman, she hasn't changed one iota since high school. She won't stop until she has him. She never stops." She was crying, dandling Brian halfheartedly with one hand while she dabbed at her eyes with the other.

When she calmed down, she served me hot lemonade, coffee for herself, and nothing for Will. She changed Brian into his pajamas, put him down for a nap, and came back, frazzled and shaky. She didn't touch Will, no love squeeze this time to reassure him. She directed her comments to me.

"I must tell you, Simon, that Will wasn't aware that I asked you to come. I did it because I was frightened. My world is flying apart and I had to do something. I trust you and I need to talk with someone. None of this is a secret, not now, not today. But it's terribly upsetting. You see, our marriage has always been based on truth, it's part of our vows." She glanced over at Will long enough to assure me that he'd broken them.

Will bit off a few more hairs.

Bev continued. "Janice first showed up just a little over a week ago. She didn't call first, so I was caught a little bit off guard. I hadn't seen her since graduation. She's still really beautiful." As if by corollary, Bev still wasn't.

"And she was unbelievably nice. She told me she'd always liked me and hoped we could be friends. Said she was back in Ann Arbor to settle down and really came to chat about neighborhoods to live in and job possibilities. I might actually have enjoyed it if I hadn't had this feeling that she was checking me out, almost studying me. She insisted on looking through our wedding album and when I picked it up later I noticed some pictures were missing. It was really weird.

"But I know that she's a sick woman. So I thought maybe she's just nervous, you know, ill at ease. What do I know? I gave her a couple of leads on apartments. We had coffee. She thanked me and left. It seemed innocent enough.

"I should have known better. I told Will about it that night. He was worried, of course. She hadn't called him at work yet. He said he hadn't seen her.

"Then she showed up at our church study group. It's a free country, I figured. At least she's a Christian. I introduced her to Reverend Blaine. Janice was very gracious. She hugged Brian and gave Will a peck on the cheek. I managed to put her out of my mind for a whole day until Will told me she came in to look at a car."

Will moved on to chewing the tendons on his hand.

"Will figured she was using the car as an excuse to see him. I figured he was right. Then I start thinking that I'm being a lousy Christian. The woman hasn't done a thing wrong. She's starting over and she naturally needs some help. And I'm spending all my time being suspicious of her, and for no reason, except that I remember how she was. Maybe people change.

"I felt bad, so I called her. She thanked me for all my help with apartments and for Will's help with the car. She was cordial on the phone, but kind of cold. I think that's when Will was there with her." Another sharp glance.

He nodded but he didn't pick up the ball.

"The day before I talked to you she just happened by the showroom around lunchtime and she invited him to lunch. He went. And that's when she asked him to have sex with her. So far, he's refused.

"That night she came by here to visit again. I couldn't imagine what in the world she could want from me. And then she told me.

"She said she was in love with Will and that he was in love with her. 'Nobody intended it to happen this way. It just happened,' she said. She wanted me to know that it was nothing personal, but she was going to have him. The bitch told me she was going to steal my husband!"

Bev stopped, shocked by her language, and apologized. "Simon, you know me. I don't speak like that. I think I might be losing my mind." She rubbed her forehead in amazement. "I don't think I've ever been this anxious.

"I'm a Christian woman, Simon. I don't normally think the worst of people. It's not my nature and it's not my faith. I think people are basically good and well-meaning.

"But there are limits to turning the other cheek. I can't just stand by and let her take Will from me. For some reason, she has a kind of power over him. And until last night I didn't know why.

"All I knew was that Will wasn't being truthful with me. I was getting resentful and disappointed in him. So I prayed to our Lord Jesus and He showed me the way.

"Last night I asked Will straight out, 'Why don't you just tell her to get lost? Do you love her?'" Finally Bev was talking to Will. She'd been hurt and was telling him so.

"And that's when he told me what I had a right to know all along and what he should have told you when you first came to see us." She slumped back into her chair, her part of the telling complete.

Will mumbled something to the back of his hand. I didn't hear all of it, but the words "kill me" slipped through his fingers.

We both stared at him until he dropped his hand.

"I was there when Janice killed her mother." He looked me in the eye for the first time.

"Tell it, Will," I said. "From the beginning."

"The beginning," he sighed. "Anyway, you know a lot of it. The beginning is the easy part. I want to know when it'll end."

He'd first met Janice out at the lake. Will's family had a cabin there and Janice was in her junior year at Workman's Lake Regional High. He said it was a chance encounter, but since nothing in Janice's life happened by chance, she'd probably plotted her meeting with the most famous quarterback in the county.

"She was pretty. I had just broken up with my girlfriend and I was lonely. I liked the idea of dating someone who wasn't from Ann Arbor."

Before Will realized it they were going together, full-time. He liked her. She knew how to treat a guy. And she gave, sexually speaking.

"Look, it was cool. She was good-looking, had a great body, and she loved sex. I was seventeen. What more could I ask for? But her mother wouldn't leave it alone."

Janice had been, since she "grew up," at war with her mother. Will witnessed countless fights between the two. Margery, who was usually loaded, harped on her daughter constantly. She hated that Janice was still young and pretty and sought after. Janice's hair, her weight, her clothes, none of it was ever right for Margery Donahue. Nor was Janice's choice of boyfriends. Margery called Will "Airhead" and insulted him to his face. She particularly enjoyed a good public tongue-lashing.

Ed Donahue's role in the morass was as family minimizer. "'It's only a stage,' he would say to us, every time there was a fight. 'Teenage girls can never get along with their mothers. They can't be in the same room together, but it will pass. It's the same with boys and their fathers.'"

Will looked directly at me for the first time that night. "Simon, I don't know squat about psychology, but I do know about hurting people. I've played football. It isn't a game, it's war, and the object is to annihilate the opposition. Nothing less. Janice was at war with her mother. I saw it. Someone had to win. No ties in their league.

"I'd seen them slap each other around. It was ugly and I was always glad they didn't keep a gun in the house. Someone was gonna use it.

"Hell, Margery was such a raving witch, I would've considered it myself. She made *my* life miserable and I only saw her when I had to.

"Her damned voice could shatter glass. 'You will listen to me, bitch!'" Will screeched, giving us his version of a Margery Donahue outburst. "I called her The Screamer. Janice just called her The Voice. Somethin' was gonna come down. I just wanted to be far away when it did."

Janice was almost always officially grounded, a situation she handled by waiting until Margery drank herself into oblivion and then going out anyway, with Ed's tacit approval.

One night, Janice met Will in the parking lot down at Kroger's, the town's only supermarket. With the Laundromat and an Arby's across the road, it was the closest thing to a mall for Workman's Lake teenagers. They spent most of the evening parking, alternately inflaming and satisfying each other. Then they went out for roast beef and fries. Sex made Janice hungry.

"She was incredible," Will said. "I've never seen any woman eat like that. She could eat me under the table after sex," he said, too upset to catch his double entendre.

He drove her home well after two in the morning and as usual they rubbed up against each other at the door for a few more minutes. Janice liked it when he left with a hard-on. Then, as always, she tiptoed into the house. When she got to her bedroom safely she would wave to Will and he would depart, as quietly as his rusty muffler allowed.

This particular night Janice didn't make it upstairs. Her mother had waited for her in ambush in the living room, curled up with a copy of *Rosemary's Baby* and a bottle of Wild Turkey. Ed was out. Will could hear through the door that Margery was seriously plastered.

"It didn't sound good. I'd heard them go at it before, but not when they were both so drunk. It sounded like a cat fight.

"So I opened the door a crack to listen. Nobody at the lake bothered to lock their doors. The old-timers still don't. Those days people weren't so paranoid.

"Anyway, let me get this story over with. They'd been fighting about the junior prom for weeks. Janice hated her dress, her shoes, everything her mother had picked out. Margery was just waiting for an excuse to ground her, to take the prom away. Janice wasn't gonna sit still for that. She was going to that prom, wanted a shot at the queen's throne."

But this time Margery put her foot down. Since Janice had once again ignored her grounding and gone out with Will, Margery took the fateful step, whether she knew it or not.

"'I forbid you to go to the prom and I mean it this time. I'll tie you up if I have to, you little bitch, but you will not go to that prom! Your hunk will have to jack himself off without you.'

"Apparently, Janice believed her or she was just too drunk and enraged herself.

"'You're wrong, Mother,' she said. 'This time you are wrong.'"

Will was sweating profusely, dabbing at his face with a faded brown handkerchief. "I didn't see it, Simon, I swear to you. But I heard it. Janice grunted like she was lifting weights. Her mother said, 'What the fuck do you think . . . ,' and then she didn't say any more.

"I heard a sort of squishy thud, another grunt, this one from her mother, and the weight, or whatever it was, hit the carpeted floor. Janice shoved things around awhile, sounded like she was moving furniture. That's when I slipped out to the car.

"In a few minutes she came to the door, knowing that I'd still be waiting out there. She snuggled up next to me, practically pushed me out the driver's-side door. She smelled of sweat, nervous sweat, and she said, 'That ought to shut off The Voice.'"

They spent the rest of the night fornicating in his car, parked only a few blocks away. Will was confused, drunk, and scared. Janice was lusty and insatiable. When morning came they went out for breakfast and Janice asked Will to take her back to her house.

She was sure her father would be home. And if her calculations were correct, Margery would be on a slab at the county medical examiner's, awaiting an autopsy, by the time Janice appeared.

But her calculations were incorrect. Ed had not come home. Janice found her mother just as she had left her, head leaning on the lamp base on the floor. The rug was stained with purple jelly.

"She went crazy. Screamed and threw things. I never heard anything like it in my life. She was completely out of control. She was furious that her mother was still lying there. If she hadn't already been dead Janice would have killed her again."

Will called the police at Janice's urging. While they waited for the cops to arrive, Janice calmed down and spoke heart to heart with Will.

"'Will,' she said to me, 'nothing is going to come of this, you hear? We spent the night together and when we got home this morning we found this. And if you ever say it isn't so, I'll fix you. And I mean what I say. They won't get me. But I'll get *you*. That's a promise, and for me, promises are forever.' She actually winked and kissed me on the nose.

"As soon as the state troopers pulled up to the door, she went crazy again, sobbing, crying, flailing her arms. They had to restrain her.

"We continued on almost like nothing had happened. Mr. Donahue was considered a suspect for a while, but that was dropped. I told anyone who asked that we were parked all night. The death was ruled accidental. Janice mourned like she was supposed to, except that we went to the prom and Jan was crowned queen. Know what her only comment was about it? 'Life goes on, Mother always said.'

"Then Donahue got transferred to Ann Arbor. We stayed together another whole year. I don't know how. Janice kept reminding me of her promise. At the end of senior year she broke up with me. It was more like she let me go. I never heard from her after she went away to college, until the letter came from the hospital and I went to see her. That's it. I know I should have told you the other day. I've never told anyone, always been too scared."

"You're scared now," I observed.

"Oh, man. She'll kill me like that"—he snapped his fingers—"if I don't please her."

"Will, the law is on your side. Are you willing to tell your story to a judge? Now wait, don't answer yet. I see your fear and there's good reason for it. But if you'll help me put her away, none of us has to fear her any longer.

"We've been working on committing her based on mental illness, but I believe there's a way to prosecute her for Margery's murder. Think about it and we'll talk again after I consult with my lawyer friend in New York. Now, is there anything more? Are you holding out on anything else?"

He muttered and nodded. Bev said, "Tell him. I'll go check the boy." She left us alone.

I raised my right eyebrow about halfway, enough to ask the question.

"Yesterday she came to the showroom, late, around closing. She's still so good-looking, you know what I mean? She's just passing through. Whatever she'd told Bev about living here, she didn't say anything to me about it. She was going back east, had her ticket for a night flight. On business, she said. I haven't seen her since."

My internal alarm started clanging uncontrollably. A wave of heat overtook me, so fierce I thought for a minute I might pass out. Will was still talking.

"So we made out in the back of the Cherokee in the showroom. Just necking, you know, for old time's sake, sort of. I never thought things would get so out of hand. I've always been faithful to Bev before. I don't know what it is about that woman. I coulda said no, I just didn't. I don't get it myself."

I realized I was no longer listening. "Look, Will, I have to call my friend in Maine. Is it okay to use your phone?"

"Sure, go ahead. Why? Is something the matter?"

I started punching buttons. My hands were shaking so badly I made two mistakes before I finally got through.

"Hello, Simon," Janice purred.

"Where's Kate?"

"She's right here, being the perfectly cordial hostess."

"What have you done to her?"

"Nothing . . . yet. Well, I did have to sedate her. She's sleeping it off. And if you behave like a good boy and do what you're told, I won't touch her till you get here."

"Can I talk to her?"

"No, you'll just have to believe me. I need her alive."

My heart was racing. I suppressed my fear and rage and forced my voice to a lower register. "Okay, Janice, what do you want?"

"I left you a message asking you to come and you ignored it. I want to see you. I need to talk to you. I'll wait for you here, with her."

"All right, Janice, I'll come. Anything else?"

"Yes. No cops. I mean it, Simon. If you show up with an entourage, you'll never see Kate alive again."

I w a s supremely pissed off. Burning up. I couldn't accept that she'd duped me. I had sensed that the summons to Ann Arbor was a diversion but I'd failed, once again, to protect a loved one.

Debby kindly pointed out that I had to bring my body temperature down. "You'll be useless to Kate if you don't chill out."

I forced myself to sit down and go over it all yet one more time, to regain perspective.

Nothing in Will's story had surprised me. It was useful, of course, to hear the details, but I knew the truth before I went to see him. My father had already nullified Ed's confession.

"There is something you should know, Simon," Gabe had said on the phone. "Ed was never charged with Margery's death."

"Really. And why not, if I may ask?" I was still angry that he hadn't been open with me from the start.

"He had an alibi."

"Alibis can be arranged," I reminded my father.

"Not this one. He was playing poker with me."

Apparently, theater was a Donahue family pastime. Ed's little show in the hotel bar was a charade. He hadn't gone to all that trouble to confess to an accidental death. He did what any devoted father of a murderer would do. He did everything possible to protect her.

■

Getting away with murder is more common than getting nailed for it. Janice learned that fact early.

The matricide completed her psychological profile. With Margery's death, Janice gave birth to "The Voice" and it taught her the lesson of her life. She could act out her most destructive fantasies, get hysterical, and walk away. And the more extreme the emotional display, the better. Janice didn't hallucinate. She wrote dialogue.

But nobody kills without a reason. Sane or crazy, clear or convoluted, there is always a reason. What was Janice's? She simply refused to be thwarted. Most of us develop strategies to overcome the obstacles that stand between us and the objects of our desire. We learn diversionary tactics, avoidance, and some pretty juke moves to get around them. Janice learned murder.

She wasn't joking when she said she could have killed Tupelo. She could have, but she'd settled for a casual mutilation gesture. I supposed I owed her a thank-you, a Hallmark card for "That Special Woman Who Didn't Kill My Dog."

Janice was a veteran of three murders and she owned a get-out-of-jail-free card. Her history, carefully crafted and manipulated, guaranteed her a freebie. She had already been certified insane and exonerated for the deaths of Dennis and Sean. What jury in their right mind would ever convict her of a rational murder? As Janice saw it, she was free and clear. In fact, she believed she had a license to kill.

My task was to bring Janice in with Kate alive. Except for the live Kate part, it was exactly what Janice had in mind. If we followed her script, Katherine Newhouse, Counselor at Law, would be cast in the last role of her career. And she was a mere prop, her only purpose in the drama to die.

And what was my part? Janice had cast me as witness, an accomplice, really, because she was counting on me to faithfully observe and report her performance. She expected my testimony to ensure her six-months-and-out strategy. I was to be the silent audience for this American tragedy, a perfect expert witness.

As before, the key to the insanity defense would lie in "The Voice." It would be impossible for a jury not to view her as the victim of a system that failed to protect her from herself. Janice had no intention of spending her life in a back ward. With her "recuperative" powers she would do her six-month commitment and walk.

The entire scenario was consistent with her psychological profile. Kate's murder would remove what she perceived as the only obstacle between her and her fantasy. She was narcissistic enough to conceive it, cunning enough to force me to come, and sociopathic enough to execute it all.

I would have to alter the script, place a banana peel on the stage, and make sure she slipped on it.

I nearly panicked when I heard that all Boston and New York flights were full for the rest of the day. Debby and I mapped out a route through Canada to Maine, but when Tommy casually mentioned that it would take twenty hours of nonstop driving, we booked an early morning flight to Boston instead. We could take a rental car from there up to Sandy Port.

I stayed relatively calm by reminding myself that Kate was safe, at least until I got there. Janice needed her alive for Act One. Still, it wasn't about sleeping. I had a long night ahead and my anxiety needed a useful outlet. I would complete the task for which Kate had hired me in the first place.

I asked the nice matron in Room Service to send up a thermos of espresso, I set my laptop on the coffee table, and, with Tupelo stretched out at my feet, I went to work.

The words poured from my fingers. "Janice Donahue Jensen is a Caucasian female, appearing younger than her stated age . . ." I continued with an eloquent, if tardy, recitation of the true and unembellished psychological history of a multiple murderer. It ended with a twist, an item not often found in reports on criminal responsibility. I had gained some notoriety for it in the media. They thought I could predict criminal behavior.

I predicted what Janice would do next.

When the report was done I faxed it to Gideon, the D.A., the court, and Kate's office. I made sure I didn't go back on my word to Janice, although the temptation to notify the cops was great. I could have had half of Maine's state troopers mobilized via Gideon's office but it was just too risky. They might have had their own ideas about how to deal with the situation.

No. Janice had to have her theatrics or her frustration would rise to intolerable levels. I called no one. So I was finished. I crashed a half hour before the alarm went off.

Despite my clever defenses, I couldn't ward off the feelings forever. We were almost there, an hour south of Sandy Port, and Debby was driving, with Tommy and Tupelo sleeping soundly in the back seat. I had been anxiously droning on for miles about how to deal with Janice once we arrived. There was truly nothing more that could be planned.

We were left with our raw fear.

Debby broke down. Kate was the only important older woman in her life. Her own mother had left too early to count and Kate had been her friend and mentor for years.

"Oh, God, Simon, how will we survive if she kills Kate?"

She was crying so hard I ordered her to pull over. I grabbed her by the shoulders and got in her face. "We can't think like that," I said in my most confident tone. "I have to believe when I walk in there that I can stop Janice. You don't understand. I *can't* survive if Kate dies."

The impact of my words effectively cut off Debby's hysterical sobbing. "What are you telling me, Simon?"

"There's something you don't know, only because it's so new, I don't quite have words for it yet. I love Kate."

"Yeah, I know, you've always loved Kate."

"Yes, but there's more to it now. This week, up there at the cottage, it's big-time change, Debra. I'm in love with her."

"Oh, Simon." She threw herself across the front seat and hugged me. "Simon, I'm so glad for you." She looked at me and her eyes opened wide. "Holy shit!" She flew back just as abruptly and dried her tears. "What are we doing sitting here? We gotta move. Let's get there! You can tell me more as we go."

But I couldn't say another word. I had just said it all: "I'm in love with her." And hearing the words surface from the depths of my being, my voice vibrating with that truth for only the second time in my life, a floodgate opened inside. I could lose her.

I could lose Kate. My beloved Kate.

My chest contracted. I was seized by an ache so old, so profound, I wasn't sure how I'd take the next breath. I put both fists to my heart, and I was grinding at the pain when I passed a threshold.

I was no longer in the car.

I was in a tiny studio apartment and it was twenty years earlier. I was just walking in, returning home from an evening seminar.

We'd been married two months and I was high on hope. High on life.

The door had been left unlocked, a good thing because I'd forgotten my keys. I felt lucky.

"Zora," I called.

No answer.

She's in the bath. Woman loves the tub. Asleep as usual. She must have been in here for hours. Her hair is dry. Her lips are blue. A kiss to awaken Sleeping Beauty. Cool skin. And the smell. A slap in the face. A bottle of green sleepers on the edge of the tub. Almost empty.

Get her out of the bath. Onto the bed. Her breath reeks of chloral hydrate. Thank God there's breath.

Breathe, baby, breathe. Breathe, baby, breathe.

Cover her. On the bed. Nice warm body, not cold like I thought. Good. Dead bodies are cold. Pulse. No fucking pulse. I'm shaking too much to find it. As long as her chest moves up and down we're okay. No movement.

Prop her up. Clear the breathing passages.

Count. Keep up the count.

Breathe, Zora.

Now her chest is moving fine. As long as we breathe, she's alive.

"Ambulance!" I scream between breaths, hoping the neighbors will hear. "Ambulance!"

Kiss her. Right cheek. Left cheek.

No response.

As long as we breathe she's alive. Stay alive. We'll go to Peru.

Breathe, Zora, breathe.

No breath.

Come back, Zora. It's time to wake up.

Kiss her eyes. Come on, Zora, look at me. Don't go. Don't leave me.

Siren. Medics. Someone heard me. Thank you.

"Let's get her out of here."

Not so rough. She looks like a rag doll.

Siren. Back of the ambulance. Haven't been in one of these since . . .

"Hand me that mask, buddy."

Mask. Oxygen mask. Breath. No mask. There isn't any.

Medic pounding her chest.

Don't pound Zora's chest. You'll hurt her. Don't pound her chest. That means she's . . .

"Code blue," medic says.

Don't say that. Pound her chest but don't say that. That means D.O.A. Dead On Arrival.

When I came to I was bent over, hugging myself, crying literally like a baby, living the totality of her loss. Twenty years later, twenty long years of keeping it repressed, and for the first time I knew the meaning of agony. I felt as though a piece of my very self were being ripped from me.

I don't know how long I went on like that. I eventually calmed and became aware of my surroundings once again. I sensed the crazy movement of the car on the icy road. Debby was careening around the last curve and we came in sight of the cottage.

Chapter Thirty-two

I w o u l d have loved to down a pint of wheatgrass juice before I faced her. Lacking that, I fell back on years of meditation and it
served me well. I took three long, deep breaths and emptied my head. I
said a silent prayer, kissed Debby on both cheeks, and opened the door to
get out.

"You sure you don't want us to do this with you?" she asked for the
hundredth time.

"I'm sure. Wait for me out here. Stay warm. And when Tommy wakes
up, make him wait with you. I have to go in alone. I'll be fine."

"I don't know if I can stand waiting."

"You have to. There's no choice. She said she'd hurt Kate if I didn't
come alone." Debby couldn't argue with that.

Despite the urgency of the moment, it was impossible to ignore the
beauty that surrounded me. I took in the winter sunlight, the stark black
branches and their elongated shadows on the fresh snow. I walked up the
path to the front steps.

I tried the doorknob and it was unlocked. My heart skittered; I pushed
away the memory of that other open door. I stepped inside.

A lively fire crackled in the fireplace, its music the only perceivable
sound in the house. With all the curtains drawn, the firelight filled the
living room with a warm orange glow. The wheelchair faced the fire so
that from the doorway I saw only the dark of her back. I noted the soft
hair tucked behind her ears and wanted to touch it. When I shut the

door, she placed her open book face down on the table at her side.

I hated to break the silent spell, but I was so relieved to see her, I had to speak. "Hello, Kate." I took a step forward and she turned the chair. I froze.

Fear choked me and with an effort I swallowed it down. I flashed to that scene from *The Exorcist* when you first see the demon looking out from the little girl's eyes. Janice smiled at me from the wheelchair and stretched her arms out for a hug.

It was a studied gesture. Over the course of the trial she must have watched Kate greet me at least a dozen times and she'd done her home-work. Seeing her now dressed in Kate's robe, hair cropped to Kate's length and style, my equilibrium was shattered. But only for a moment.

Scene One had achieved the full dramatic effect.

Janice lowered her arms when it became obvious that no hug was forthcoming. She got up, throwing off the blanket that had been covering her legs. She stood in the center of the room, watching me carefully.

The robe bothered me. She could have hidden an Uzi under it. Or she was naked, possibly a more horrifying alternative.

She motioned me to a chair that would place me facing Kate's bed-room door.

How far will she take it?

I browsed the art on the walls, not quite ready to sit down. I concen-trated on edging toward the bedroom. Janice kept her body between me and the door. I turned to the kitchen, made an about-face, and headed di-rectly for the bedroom. She blocked my way, took my arm, and led me to the chair.

I had to be sure we were on the same page.

"I don't suppose you'd like a cup of coffee, would you?" Apparently, the entire Donahue family offered drinks for the Thespian hour, perhaps to warm the audience.

I shook my head. "No, Janice."

She sat on the couch. "So, how are you, Simon?"

Only Janice could make small talk at a time like this. "Janice, do you know why I came?"

"Yes. I always knew you'd come when I needed you, and this is my proverbial hour of need." She looked out from under her eyebrows for my reaction.

I showed none.

"I'm going back to the hospital, Simon. You're going to take me away from all this."

"I came to get Kate. I came to take *her* away from all this."

"Of course, I knew that. And I'll give her to you, I promise. Word of honor." She put her hand over the spot where her heart would have been, had she had one.

"I need to tell someone," she said. "I need to get it off my chest."

Not someone. Me. I nodded, signaling that I was ready.

"Where do I start?"

I shrugged. "It's your show."

"Maybe the beginning," she offered. "But which beginning?"

I shrugged again.

"How about from leaving the hospital, even though you already know some of it?"

I cocked my head slightly to the right.

"When I got out, I lived with Daddy in that awful hotel. No, skip that, you know all about that. That's when I visited you. Then I went on my Amtrak cross-country tour. Maybe that's a good place to start.

"Okay. First thing, I stopped taking my meds. I know I shouldn't have, but I was so happy to be free. I felt like I didn't need that stuff. It just clogs up my head, anyway. It doesn't really help."

Step one, remove chemical restraints.

"Actually, it was Mom's idea. She knew I'd be better off without the drugs."

Step two, put Mom on the menu.

"I think I first heard her voice again on the train. She was glad we were putting some distance between us and Daddy. She thought he was sweet, but stupid. She said she wanted some time for just the two of us, just the girls. That's how she put it, anyway."

Step three, reactivate The Voice. Another patch in the insanity quilt.

"She was real nice, supportive. She was glad I'd found you again. She told me you still loved me and all I had to do was listen to her and everything would work out.

"By Ohio we were bored with the train ride so I called Daddy. All he did was complain. Said he had no reason to stay in New York now that I was on my own again. He was going home to Michigan.

"Mother said I had to go back to New York so I did. And I moved into that place across the street from you.

"That's when I pulled that silly stuff. It was totally infantile, I know that now."

Another triumph of insight.

"It's that I felt safe with you. With Daddy gone, I thought that if I stayed near you nothing could hurt me. But I was wrong. *You* hurt me.

"That really pissed Mom off. She always sticks up for me, you know. 'We'll find a way to get back at him,' she said. 'You could always rough up that pasty-faced daughter of his.'"

So she had thought of it. At least I hadn't been completely off the wall.

"But Debby dropped out of sight. And just as we were talking about what to do, Mom saw Tupelo sniffing around in front of the house. So I took off her ear. Mom said it would serve you right.

"I felt a little better when you walked down to the river with me that day. You really listened to me. Afterwards, Mom said, 'See? I told you so. You have to show men you mean business, otherwise they walk all over you.' Anyway, that whole episode with the dog wasn't all that important."

It was if you were Tupelo. Or me.

"The important part was to help you see that we belong together. But then you left that morning with a suitcase. Mom was upset. 'Follow him. Don't let him get away,' she said. And that's how I found out the truth. About you and Ms. Katherine." Her voice took on a venomous edge when she said Kate's name.

"Mom got worse. She kept pressuring me. She said I was totally ineffectual. She called me names. She told me to fix it." Janice sat back and eyed me expectantly.

I didn't need the prompter to remind me. I was supposed to ask what she meant. But I held to my role as silent witness.

"Okay, I'll tell you anyway." I knew I could count on her. "She said that it was all a terrible mistake. 'That woman, that dishrag, that aging gimp in a motorized armchair, is living *your* life!'"

It was all I could do to refrain from strangling her.

"At first, I didn't know what Mom meant. I didn't know what she wanted me to do."

Too modest. Sure she did.

"I even went to see Bev and Will, you know, to see if maybe I couldn't make a go of it with him. He'd been so nice when he visited me at the hospital. And things went along pretty well for a while.

"That's when Mother told me I was wasting my time. If I didn't take care of Katherine, I was a total loss, an incompetent, not fit to walk the earth.”

So that's the way it was going to go. One grand delusion, ordered by the Mother of all mothers. Almost everything in place.

“‘Listen to me, bitch!’ Mother said. ‘What kind of a woman are you, leaving your man with someone else? Have you no pride, no character at all? Fix it, damn you. Fix it or your life won't be worth a shit.’

“I held out for as long as I could,” she said wearily. “I wasn't going to give in to her again. But she kept it up and I started to think maybe she was right. Still, I was hesitating, and Mother got really mad at me.”

Janice started to rock slightly. “She wouldn't stop screaming at me. ‘Listen to me, bitch. Go back. Get your ass out of here. Fix it,’ she said, ‘or you won't live one more day in peace. I'll see to that. Fix it!’”

This time Janice didn't just tell me what her mother said. She re-created The Voice. Her rendition was scary and grating and remarkably similar to Will's curdling imitation.

“So I did. I came here just like she told me. Katherine wouldn't let me in. I apologized for all the trouble I'd caused. I told her I had a long talk with you on the phone and I'd finally got my head straight. I said you were just picking up your daughter and would meet her in New York. But she wouldn't believe me. She was so fucking suspicious.”

Janice was rocking faster now.

“She kept asking me how I knew where to find her. I guess she doesn't have a very good imagination. I told her I convinced her assistant that I was in some kind of a crisis, I made like I was a long-lost friend.

“But she still wouldn't let me get past her to come into the house. I was freezing and she was blocking my way with the damn wheelchair. Then Mother saw her reach into her pocket and she yelled at me. ‘Look out, you stupid bitch! Can't you see she's going to pull a gun on you? Do something!’

“So I pushed her over. Sure enough, she had a handgun, but it fell as she went back. She put up some fight! She's so strong. But I've got legs, so I finally pinned her and knocked her out.

“I wanted to hurt her bad but Mom stopped me. She said I had to wait for you to come or I'd fuck it all up. ‘Shoot her up with that stuff you bought. That'll take care of her.’ I gave her some IV Valium and tied her hands behind her back. I didn't even have to do her feet, they're useless anyway. Then Mom made me give her some water with a dropper before

I gagged her. I didn't want to. I wanted her to suffer, but Mom was insisting, so I had to.

"And then I waited for you to call. I knew you'd figure it out."

I cried inside in anguish for Kate's suffering and humiliation. But it was almost over and I couldn't allow anything to distract me from the moment.

The quilt was almost complete. One, she quits taking medication. Two, The Voice comes back. Three, it tells her another woman's inhabiting her life, taking away her man. A simple delusion, really, easily understood by a jury.

Only one patch missing. She had covered what she had already done. She had yet to cover what she was about to do.

She glanced toward the bedroom and back at me. "Now that you're here, she says . . ." She looked bewildered. "Help me, Simon. I'm frightened."

She stared past me and blanked out for a minute, then focused again as if returning from some far-off land.

"I can't fight her alone. She always wins. Help me," she implored.

When she was done she lowered her eyes. End of Scene Two.

It was all in place.

Th e curtain rose on Janice's climactic finale.

She was mumbling under her breath. I couldn't make out the words. She swayed rhythmically to a tune I didn't hear. Her torso swung around with increasing determination and she whipped her head back and forth as if she were at a Metallica concert.

The rocking slowed and a slightly guttural moan escaped her throat.

A wicked smile crept over her face. She started laughing, not all out, not raucous, more like a macabre chuckle. Her eyes fixed on some invisible point of light.

"Janice?" Just checking.

No answer. Out to lunch.

Her eyes went as blank as an analyst's stare.

A few more rocks, moans, and mumbles and she began to enunciate clearly, projecting to the back row.

"No, Mother, I won't. You can't make me." She shook her head violently. "Oh, no," she moaned, covering her face with her hands. She sobbed, or at least her body wrenched.

She went rigid, stony. She sat ramrod straight and dropped her hands in her lap. Tears smeared her makeup.

Silence.

"Janice?" Checking in again. I would have been disappointed if she had answered. She didn't disappoint me.

She stood up like a machine, not recently lubed. She dropped Kate's robe, revealing black Danskins and a multicolored wraparound skirt. And there was no Uzi hidden underneath.

Just a brand-new gleaming fish knife.

She let out a scream as piercing as any rape whistle, which must have been intended to get me back on my heels. She was an effective screamer.

Before any perceivable amount of time had passed she was at the bedroom door, slowly turning the handle. I watched from my seat. I was, after all, the audience.

She looked at me in amazement, her eyes asking, "Why the fuck are you just sitting there? Do something."

My eyes answered that I am a psychoanalyst. I do not intrude upon life. I observe.

I did stand up, but only to get a better vantage point. Janice quickly swung the door open, with a bit too much flourish.

I heard a low, muffled groan from inside. Every cell in my body wanted to bolt forward but I still held myself.

Janice was indecisive. She had to wait for me. If I were to miss the action I would have little value as an eyewitness.

She went into a balletic pirouette, a grotesque montage revolving like a lazy Susan. I figured I had about seven seconds to prevent an execution.

She accelerated gradually and mumbled something, at first undiscernible, under her breath.

"No, Mother. No, Mother. No, Mother." She chanted louder and louder, going into a full-fledged spin. The end of the spin would surely lead to the end of Kate.

She spun into the room.

In three quick strides I was there.

Kate lay flat on her back on the floor. Mouth gagged and hands hidden under her, she was looking around groggily in the manner of the recently sedated. I silently thanked God she was conscious. Margery must not have deemed it necessary to keep up on the Valium shots.

Still repeating, "No, Mother, no, Mother," Janice completed her balletic spin and dropped to Kate's side. The fish knife hovered over Kate's breast.

My seven seconds were up.

"Listen to me, bitch!" I screeched. I was aiming for maximum volume and the highest pitch in my register. What came out sounded like an automobile alarm trying to speak.

Janice riveted her eyes on me in fury for having interrupted her death scene. The knife never lost contact with Kate's sweater. Another groan worked its way through the gag.

"Listen to *my* voice a minute," I commanded. "Your life may depend on it. You need me, Janice, and if you don't listen, I guarantee that you'll spend the rest of your life in prison."

She was unsure of her next move. She had been startled and then pissed that I used Margery's voice to get her attention. On another level, something in her soul remembered that I always told her the truth.

Her left arm trembled from the effort of supporting herself in a half crouch. Her right arm was steady and still kept the knife poised above Kate's chest. But she was all ears.

"Here's your legal situation. One," I lifted my right pinky. "You can't be retried on Dennis and Sean, double jeopardy. Two," I continued counting fingers, "your mother. It would be a cinch to make a case. No statute of limitations on Murder One. There were no eyewitnesses, just an earwitness, but he's willing to testify against you and his story is powerful." I hoped I was right.

I saw her eyes flinch at the reference to Will. Good.

"Three, Falconi. Assault with Intent to Do Great Bodily Harm is no lightweight charge. He's an intelligent, articulate witness, and the sight of his mutilated face will weigh heavily on the jury's collective heart. Four, Tupelo. It's only a Malicious Mischief, but the cumulative effect of your cruelty paves the way inexorably to establishing your status as a malingerer.

"That's diagnostic number V65.20 in the *DSM*, which you already know, but I'll refresh your memory. The category includes conditions not attributable to mental illness. In other words, it's excluded from the diagnoses admissible for the insanity defense.

"That brings us to five. Five is Kate." I had completed a full hand. "If you give Kate up, you've got a prayer. If you don't, prayer won't help you."

She considered my five points. They had a certain logic that would appeal to her intelligence. If she thought it over too long she would surely realize that although all true, she still had no reason not to harm Kate.

I provided that reason for her before she could ask.

"You have in your house an issue of *Mother Jones* that contains a piece about me. Do you remember the point of the article?"

If I could get her to engage me, to answer my question, her pseudo-psychotic spell would be broken. That would allow me to move into phase two, which I had just worked out. But she wouldn't respond.

"Tell me what the article said about me!" I boomed, like I was her teacher and this was the most important test of her life.

"Predictions," she muttered, the reluctant pupil.

"That's right." I kept my tone forceful and steady. "They called my premonitions uncanny. The author suggested the possibility that it was all blind luck, not clinical insight, but he was wrong. I proved it. And I've done it again.

"I wrote a report on you, Janice, and submitted it to all the proper authorities, the district attorney, the court, and a friend in Homicide.

"The report sets the record straight. It outlines your real history, but I already covered that, points one through four. The diagnosis is unequivocally Malingering, with a side of Antisocial Personality. But that isn't the best part.

"I added something extra to the prognosis section. I'll try to quote the pertinent passage. Quote: 'Within the realm of reasonable clinical certainty, it can be expected that the defendant'—that's you—'will attempt to do great bodily harm to Katherine Newhouse. These actions do *not* result from an existing mental illness nor did any of the previously enumerated offenses.' Unquote.

"You spill one drop of Kate's blood and you go down. I made sure of that. If you doubt me, call Lieutenant Gideon Dove, Homicide, New York Police Department. He knew Dennis and he knows you." I gave her his office and home numbers. "Call him. I'll bring you the phone."

Her face looked pinched as she thought it over.

"You really did that?" Incredulous.

"Yes." I had not lied to her yet.

"I thought you actually cared for me. Why?"

"Because it has to end, Janice. Can't you see? It has to end. This dream isn't going to come true either. Put the fish knife down and you have a chance. Hurt her and it's the end."

She seemed perplexed and disappointed. But she showed no signs of releasing the knife. She held on, tighter than ever. She shuffled anxiously on her bent knees and it was obvious that an emotional volcano was about to blow. I had to channel the eruption.

"I'm sorry I had to be the one." This time I lied. "But someone had to call your game. You're a hoax. You're not insane and never have been, although you *are* sick, profoundly sick. I'm just sorry I had to be the one."

I shook my head. "No, I won't lie to you. I'm not sorry I had to be the one. You deserve what you're going to get. Basically, you're nothing more than run-of-the-mill wicked. You'll never have another peaceful day in your life. I'll see to it. I already have. Women's prison is filled with evil trash like you."

That did it. "You son of a bitch," she hissed. Her fury was now focused. On me. She rose and circled to my right. She was so enraged that she didn't notice Kate squirming over by the bed.

She raised the knife and kept moving toward me. I was shielding my face and chest like a prizefighter. I had no idea what else to do. I was sure of only one thing. I wanted to keep her attention on me. I knew I'd willingly die before I'd face the loss of Kate.

The next part I lived in slow motion and it took a year. In reality, it happened in seconds, so fast it was all over before the pain registered.

Janice initiated her lunge. Kate was sitting up, straining with the effort to support herself on bound hands. In a gymnast's move, she swung both legs around in a wide arc that caught Janice across the ankles, making her lose her balance but not her forward momentum.

I reached down with my left hand to protect my genitals and I swiped with my right at the arm that drove the rapidly descending blade. I was partially successful.

My left hand was pinned to my leg by the fish knife, which had penetrated the fleshy, muscular part of my thigh. It looked like another one of Janice's bloodstained notes stuck to a bulletin board.

I pressed the impaled hand against my leg and with the other I yanked the blade free. Blood soaked my jeans and dripped over and around my fingers. The pain was not immediate. It was distant and dull. My knees gave way and I collapsed.

Janice recovered and headed for the door. A gun exploded. She screamed in anger and frustration. Then she crashed to the floor, clutching her foot.

I looked over at Kate in amazement. She was lying on her side. Her arms resembled a contortionist's, the handgun barely visible beside her hip.

"Where'd you get that?"

"From under the bed."

"How many of those things do you keep stashed in your dwellings?" I asked.

"Hey, you're ambulatory." And she closed her eyes.

Meanwhile, Janice was dragging herself across the living room, leaving a trail of blood on the carpet.

I lurched toward the door in an effort to stop her flight, but I stumbled, fell, and couldn't move again. She was going to get away.

"Where th' fuck you think you're going?" I heard Tommy say.

And I passed out.

Chapter Thirty-four

De b b y stopped in my doorway. Her faded green army surplus satchel hung from one shoulder, bulging with her books and papers.

"Catch you later. I have to check out some stuff in the library."

"Any plans for afterwards?" I said.

"I'm meeting Bobbi at the Bella Italia. Today's the last day Tommy plays there. Wanna come?"

From my spot in the window seat, I looked over at Kate. Steaming coffee mug in her hand, the queen of the Sunday papers sat regally in the center of the waterbed, afloat on a sea of newsprint. She didn't say a word but her upper lip spoke volumes. I was getting much better at discriminating the finer nuances of the curl.

"No, I think we'll stay in today," I said to Debby. "Tell Tommy not to be so scarce. Thanks anyway."

Debby lowered her eyelids to half mast and looked at me knowingly. Then, in her best gravelly Greta Garbo: "I see, you va-a-ant to be alo-o-ne." And she slinked out.

Kate was smiling at me. "She's really good at it. Must be all the years of research in front of the VCR."

"Garbo has always been her favorite. Hey, have you found anything on the trial?"

"Not a word. What's another NGRI to the media? On a mere Assault with Intent. It's not even back-page."

"I'm not surprised."

"Simon, I know it's absurd to even bring this up at such a late date, but just between you and me, I'm still not a hundred percent sure what Janice's motive was for wanting me dead. Was it pure venom? Her idea of vengeance for your rejection?"

"Yes, but I don't think that was all. She saw you as a monumental obstacle. She expected that once you were out of the way, I would be available. To her. The inimitable logic of a sociopath."

"I can't quite bend my mind around that one. To me it's outrageous for her to believe she could have you after offing your loved one."

"It *is* outrageous. But not in her case. Her narcissism is so pure, so completely devoid of any sense of the 'other,' that she could actually foresee a time when I would again be seduced by her irresistible charms. She can't fathom the notion that I truly do not desire her. So she attributes my rejection to your presence in my life."

"Okay, I can follow that, although I find it hard to believe. You ready for more coffee?"

"No, thanks. Two cups of your wicked brew are all I can take."

"That reminds me, there's something I've been meaning to mention. You haven't eaten anything chocolate since we got back from the Retreat. Are you feeling okay?"

"Better than ever. I even know why I lost the jones. You ever heard the theory that chocolate stimulates the same neural centers in our brains that loving does? That has always been my favorite justification for my obsession. I think we have a case here of an addiction cured. I can drop the glutton and junkie part and still enjoy the pleasure now and again. And I have a postscript. Love is better than chocolate."

"I'll say. Well, that makes sense. I never could understand why an apparently well-adjusted adult man consumed such inordinate amounts of sweets. So what did you think of the defense?"

"You've already heard what I thought of it. Too many times."

"I'll rephrase the question, Your Honor. What did you think of the choice of key witness?"

"I can't really get into applauding it too much. It was effective. Not too tough, you know, with Janice's history."

"Still, you've got to admit it was an ingenious strategy to use Falconi for the defense. I was shocked at first but then of course it made absolute sense."

"I'll admit that was the highlight of the presentation."

"Frankly, I'd have loved to prosecute this one. To get my legal teeth into her. But the system frowns on victims prosecuting their own case."

"I still think we should have gone after her for the matricide."

"Now don't start that again. It wouldn't have worked. I heard Will. He would have been worse than useless. Too nervous. Made him sound like he was lying."

"I'm afraid I must invoke the Massachusetts state line rule. I need to talk about something else. Anything else."

"Okay, let's talk about us."

"Fine, but first I'm coming over there."

I made space on the bed by gathering the four corners of the top blanket and depositing the lumpy mass on the floor, almost burying Tupelo. I stretched out alongside Kate. "I'm listening."

She slid down to fully horizontal position next to me. "Well, I've been thinking."

"Have you now?"

"Don't be smartass. Just listen like you said you would. I've been thinking it's awful expensive in these times to maintain two households, especially since we spend so much of our time together. It's just not practical. I did some figuring the other day and the numbers are significant. If we give up one apartment we could invest that money and—"

"Kate. Stop. That is the funniest proposition I have ever heard. You sound like the advice column in the *Wall Street Journal*." I put my arms around her and inhaled the familiar fragrance of her hair. "Do you want to live together? Is that what you're saying?"

"Well, yes, I'm thinking about it." She pulled back a little, enough to let me see her face, but she wouldn't lift her eyes. "With Debby's new job, she says she'll be ready to get herself a little place by next fall. You won't need all this space anymore. That might be a good time to make the change."

"Kate, look at me."

She kept her eyes lowered.

I tilted her chin gently and she met my gaze. "I read something interesting the other day," I said. "In certain Oriental cultures it is believed that if you save someone's life, you're responsible for that person forever after. You know what that means, don't you?"

There were tears in her eyes. They came more easily these days. To me, too. So much time to make up for.

"Kate. I love you, Kate. It's all working out just as it's supposed to. No fears, remember? We're together now. The time of fear is over."

Another hug, long and deep. She snuffled something inaudible into my collarbone.

"What'd you say?"

"I said I love your warmth next to me."

"May I?"

Janice held a fresh daisy in her left hand. It was late spring and they were blooming all over the grounds. As she plucked each delicate white petal she held it up briefly in the sunlight pouring in the barred window.

She was sitting on the floor in the corridor, her legs crossed in a half-lotus. The nurses liked having her close by, right across from their station, so they could call on her when they needed an errand run. For the moment, she was the only dependable patient on the ward.

She looked good. Her hair had grown out and she was pulling it back again in a stubby ponytail. She was neatly groomed, well-fed and rested, and she'd taken some care with her makeup. She exuded the fresh-scrubbed fragrance of Ivory soap.

The daisy was almost naked. She dropped the last petals one by one to the cold linoleum floor, chanting an ageless refrain.

"He loves me. He loves me not. He loves me. He loves me not. He . . ."

Acknowledgments

Immeasurable love and faith have made this dream come true. I am grateful to the Invisible in all Its forms, and particularly—

to our friend and "angelita," Phyllis Richman, for helping serendipity along,

to our agent, Rafe Sagalyn, for seeing the potential, and demonstrating superhuman patience,

to our editor, Laurie Bernstein, for loving the voice enough to take a huge gamble; we couldn't have done it without your guidance,

to our unknown friends, Mr. Joe Cocker and Mr. Neil Young, for providing musical inspiration through thousands of writing hours,

to our first readers, friends all, for persistently believing in THE BOOK while fearlessly offering suggestions to our beloved A: soul sister Felita (in all ways there when we need you), Kim Best, Mary Ellen, the Heflich-Shapiro team, Bruce (who read more than the manuscript), and soul sister Peggy for living pictures,

nuestra gratitud a la familia Casa Nahuazo: Rosa, la más hermosa, Margoth (por tantos desayunos), Graciela y Don Victor, por muchos años de amor y apoyo. Agradecemos a la familia extensa de Baños por habernos adoptado y amado, especialmente a Mariana, Jorge, Bacha y Luis Miguel,

to our children: R, you always keep on giving all; S, you picked the flowers and tiptoed conscientiously, wise beyond your years; J, Tungurahua dreamer and *everything; MGG, in absentia: we wrote our first stories for your eyes, to our companions, Max, Jackson, Quinche, and Dutch: Good dog!*

And to Arthur, in loving memory, for teaching me about truth.

Aniko Bahr
Baños, Ecuador
August 1998

About the Author

Arthur W. Bahr, former Forensic Psychologist for the state of Michigan, lived in Ecuador at the foot of an active volcano with his soul mate, Aniko, their children, and numerous dogs and chickens. Before his death at age forty-seven, he wrote two novels. Aniko is currently at work editing the second novel.